WICKED: A ROCKSTAR ROMANCE SERIES

PIPER LAWSON

I wanted to fall for a boy. Not a man. Not a *legend*...

The month I wrote my first piece of code, Jax Jamieson
launched his third platinum album.
The week I drank my first beer, he spent in jail.
The day I got under his skin, I wound up on his tour.
And the night he gave me his hoodie... I fell in love
forever.

I'm a good girl. And he's the vice I'd give it all up for.

1

HALEY

Nothing in twenty years prepares me for that man on his knees.

Naked to the waist.

Sweat gleaming on his shoulders.

The spotlight caresses the ridges of a body cut from stone as though it wants to follow him around forever.

Maybe it does.

But he's not stone. His skin would be warm, not cold.

Silhouetted hands reach for him over the edge of the stage, like something out of Dante's *Inferno*. Souls in hell grasping for their last chance at heaven. That seems misguided because the way Jax Jamieson grips a mic is straight-up sinful.

Next to the poster is a photo of four men in tuxes, gold statues in their hands.

We're attracted to gold for its sheen, its promise of something elite and revered and sacred.

My gaze drags back to the man in the poster. *Elite. Revered. Sacred.*

"I've read your resume. Now tell me why you're really qualified."

The dress pants that were a bad damn idea slip on the seat. The polyester scrapes along my skin, and I force eye contact with the woman interviewing me. "I reset at least two hundred undergrad passwords a week. And I make a lot of coffee. My roommate says I'm better than the baristas at her café."

"Excuse me?"

The printed job description sticks to my fingers. "'Technical support and other duties as appropriate.' That's what you mean, right? Rebooting computers and making coffee?"

She holds up a hand. "Miss Telfer, Wicked Records is the only private label that has survived everything from Napster to streaming. There are two hundred applications for this internship. Our interns write and produce music. Run festivals."

The woman looks as if she missed getting tickets to the Stones' Voodoo Lounge tour and has been holding a grudge ever since.

Or maybe she was the next one into the record store behind me the day I found *Dark Side of the Moon* on vinyl in Topeka.

It's probably not a fair assessment. Under that harsh

exterior, she could be genuinely kind and passionate about music.

Maybe I'm in *The Devil Wears Prada* and this woman's my Stanley Tucci.

"I run an open mic night on campus," I try. "And I'm a developer. I write code practically every day, and lot of people fork my repos on GitHub, and…" My gaze sneaks back to the poster.

"Don't get too excited," she warns. "Whoever gets this job"—her tone says it's not me—"won't work with the talent. Especially that talent."

Her final questions are nails in my coffin. Closed-ended things like if the address on my forms is right and if the transcripts I submitted are up to date.

She holds out a hand at the end, and I hold my breath.

Her skin's cold, like her heart decided not to pump blood that far.

I drop her hand as fast as I can. Then I shoulder my backpack and slink out the door.

The idea that the biggest rock star of the last ten years just saw me bomb—even if it was only his poster—is depressing.

I'm on the second bus back across Philly to campus before the full weight of disappointment hits me.

Are college juniors supposed to have run music festivals in order to pour coffee? Because I missed that memo.

I drop my backpack at our two-bedroom apartment,

change out of my weird interview pants and into torn skinny jeans and my mom's brown leather jacket, then make two coffees and walk to campus, the UPenn and Hello Kitty travel mugs in tow.

"Excuse me." A girl stops me on the way into the café, right beside the sign that says *Live Music!* "There's a cover tonight."

"I'm here every week." My smile fades when I realize she really has no clue who I am. I point to my chest. "Haley. I get the bands."

"Really?" She cocks her head. "I've never noticed you."

The table at the back is de facto mine, and I set the travel mugs down before crossing to the stage.

The guy there frowns as he plays notes on his guitar with one hand, holding the headphones attached to the soundboard. When he notices me, a grin splits his face. "Haley. You like the new board?"

"I like it if it works." I take the headphones and nod at his guitar.

The first chord he plays is like the snapping of a hypnotist's fingers. My world reduces to the vibrations and waves from Dale's guitar.

I adjust the levels on the board. "There. You should be good."

Before I can lift my head, Dale's tugging the headphones off my ears. I jerk back like I've been scalded, but he doesn't notice my jumpiness.

His earnest brown eyes are level with mine. "Perfect, Haley. Thanks, Haley." *Did he say my name twice?* "You should sing with us tonight."

I glance toward the back of the café that's starting to fill. "Ah, I don't think so. I have to..." I make a motion with my fingers, and Dale raises a brow.

"Masturbate?"

I frown. "No. Code."

"Right."

I retreat to my table. The second chair is occupied.

"He tried to touch me," I say under my breath.

My roommate Serena tosses her honey-blond hair in a move that's deceptively casual. "That asshole." I roll my eyes. "You know some people communicate affection through touch. It's even welcomed."

"In hell," I say darkly as I drop into my chair. "We have our own bodies for a reason. I don't understand how some people think it's okay to stand super close to someone. And don't get me started on whispering." I shiver, remembering the contact. "If I wanted some random person to breathe on my face or grope me? I'd ask for it. I'd stand there waving a sign saying, 'Please God, run your unfamiliar hands all over my skin'."

"If you did that on campus, there would be a pileup." She winks before turning back to the stage, where Dale's bandmates have joined him and are getting ready to start their set. "Do you think Dale knows you have a man in your life? Because he's not getting so much as a 'maybe, if I'm drunk' unless his name is Carter."

"*Professor* Carter," I remind her. "He's twenty-eight and has a PhD from MIT."

"Whatever. He's cute in glasses. But he lost my respect when he bailed on your research assistant gig."

"He didn't bail. His funding fell through. It would've been perfect since I'd have more time to work on my program, but at least he's still supervising my senior project next year."

"That's his job." She snorts. "But I think he likes you tripping over him."

The look she shoots me has me shaking my head as I glance toward the stage.

Dale's no Jax Jamieson, but his latest is pretty good. The band's super acoustic, and they have a modern sound that plays well with a college crowd.

"Come on," Serena presses. "He doesn't love having college girls undressing him with their teenage eyes in Comp Sci 101? Yeah right. The man might be young enough to have danced to Britney Spears at prom, but thanks to Mr. 'Oops, I Did it Again,' you have two days to find a job so you don't get kicked out of the co-op program."

I flip open the lid of my computer. "It's my fault, not his. I suck at interviews. I haven't had to get a job before." Serena's smile slides, and I wince. "Okay, stop giving me the 'sorry your mom's dead' look."

"It's not just 'sorry your mom's dead.' There's a side of 'I can't believe you have to pay your own college.'" Serena's parents are loaded and generous.

"If it wasn't for the requirement to be employed by an actual company, I could spend the summer working on my program and enter it in that competition."

When my mom died last year, I took a semester off, lost my scholarships, and missed the financial aid deadline. Now I have to come up with tuition myself. I know I can figure it out because a lot of people do it, but if I win the coding competition in July, that'll help big time.

"Where were you interviewing today?"

I blow out a breath. "Wicked."

She shifts forward, her eyes brightening. "Shit. Did you see him?"

I don't have to ask who she means. A low-grade hum buzzes through me that has nothing to do with the music in the background.

"Jax Jamieson doesn't hang around the studio like a potted fern," I point out. "He's on tour."

"I don't care what kind of nerd god Carter is. Jax Jamieson is way better with his hands, and his mouth. Any girl would love having that mouth whisper dirty secrets in her ear. Even you."

I shift back in my seat, propping my Converse sneakers on the opposite chair across and fingering the edge of my jacket.

"I don't need to get laid. I've been there." I take a sip of coffee, and my brain lights up even before I swallow. "The travel agent promised Hawaii. Instead it was Siberia."

"Cold, numbing, and character building?"

"Exactly."

Sex is awkward at best.

What I can deduce from my own meager experience, porn, and Serena's war stories is that guys like to be teased, squeezed, popped until they burst all over you, at which point they're basically deflated hot air balloons taking up the entire bed.

And don't you tell them what you're really fantasizing about is when it will be over and you can take a scalding-hot bath.

"My vibe has more empathy in its first two settings than the guys on campus," I go on, and Serena cackles. "In fact," I say, lifting my UPenn travel mug, "I may *never* have sex again."

"Noooo!"

Her protest has me laughing. "Plato said there are two things you should never be angry at: what you can help and what you can't."

"Yeah, well. White men who got to wear bed sheets to dinner said a lot of crazy shit." Serena's green eyes slice through me. "Besides. I'm not angry. I'm planning." I raise a brow. "To find you a guy with a tongue that'll turn you inside out."

I shudder. "That's sweet. Truly. But I didn't come to

school to get laid, Serena." Her fake shocked face has me rolling my eyes. "I want to do something that matters."

When I started college, my mom told me I was lucky to have been born now, and her daughter, because I'm free to be whatever I want. By that, she meant a famous painter or a rocket scientist, or straight or gay, an advocate for children or the environment.

It's not enough.

Serena's right. I'm obsessed with Jax Jamieson, but it's not because of his hard body or the way he moves or even his voice.

It's because Jax Jamieson *matters.*

He matters by opening his mouth, by lifting his guitar, by drawing breath. He matters by taking people's hopes, their fears, and spinning poetry with them.

Every time I sit down and listen to *Abandon* on vinyl on the floor of my bedroom, a coffee in my hands and my eyes falling closed, it's like he matters a little bit more.

If I ever meet Jax Jamieson, I'm going to ask him how he does it.

Before Serena can answer, my phone rings.

"Hello?"

"This is Wendy from Wicked Records. You got the internship."

Disbelief echoes through me. I glance over my shoulder in case I'm on camera for some reality show. "But what about the other two hundred applicants?"

"Apparently their coffee making left something to be desired. Be here tomorrow at seven thirty."

2

HALEY

I can't deal with the slippery pants two days in a row, so I borrow Serena's skirt that hobbles me at the knees.

On top of my sleeveless blouse, I stick my leather jacket.

For safety and comfort.

My backpack holds my computer and the completed paperwork HR sent me by email.

Walking through the glass doors should be easier than yesterday—hell, I got the job. But it's not, because I don't know what they expect. I want to ask, "Why did you hire me?" but the security guy checking my paperwork and processing my pass probably isn't the right person to answer.

"You're on two. Up the elevator."

The first two elevators are packed full, so I find a stairwell at the end of the hall.

When I open the door to the second level, I'm in another world.

Pristine carpet, white as snow. Paneled walls in a rich red color that should look retro but doesn't.

I peel off my leather jacket because it's warm up here and glance down the hall.

Wendy's office is supposed to be to the left. But cursing from the first door in the other direction pulls me in.

Inside, a guy who can't be much older than me surveys a computer rig I'd give my leg for. An error message lights up the screen in front of him, blinking like some doomsday prophecy.

"Can I help?" I ask. With a quick head-to-toe that ends on the pass clipped to my waist, he ushers me in.

"What the hell took so long?" the tech asks. "I called IT ten minutes ago."

It's moot to point out that I wasn't with IT ten minutes ago.

My eyes adjust to the low light as the door slips closed behind me. There are no outside windows, just the glass half panel facing the studio and a closed door that connects the two.

Someone's recording in here. The figure in the other room is facing away from the glass, bent over a guitar like he's tuning it.

I push aside the bubble of nerves. My focus is on the computer.

"Is ten minutes a long time?" I ask as I set my paperwork and my jacket on the desk. My fingers start to fly over the keyboard.

"It is when *he's* here."

I hit Enter, and the error message goes away.

It isn't until I straighten that his words start to sink in.

"When who's here?"

That's when I'm viciously assaulted.

At least it feels that way because two horrible things happen in such close succession I can barely tease them apart.

Hands clamp down on my bare arms from behind.

Hot breath fans my ear, and a voice rasps, "What the fuck is going on?"

Every hair on my body stands up, my skin puckering, and I do what any reasonable woman grabbed by a stranger in a vice grip would do.

I scream.

It's not a cry for help.

It's a bellow of rage and defiance. Like a banshee or Daenerys's dragons en route to scorch some slave traders.

Channeling strength I didn't know I had, I whirl on my heel and collide with a wall. My hands flail in front of me, lashing out at my attacker.

I'm not a puncher, I'm a shover. But when I shove, all that happens is my hands flex on a hard, muscled chest.

I trip backward, my grown-up skirt hobbling me as I fall.

I grab for the desk but only get my papers, which rain down like confetti as I land on my ass.

My heart's racing at an unhealthy speed even before I take in the white sneakers inches from my face.

"Jax. I'm really sorry," the guy behind me says. "I called Jerry ages ago."

Sneakers, as white as the carpet, are pointed straight at me. Dark-blue jeans clinging to long legs, narrow hips. A faded olive-green T-shirt stretches across his chest, like it started out too tight but gave out over dozens of wears. Muscular arms—one covered in a sleeve of tattoos—look like they lift more than guitars.

I force my gaze up even though I want to melt into the floor.

A hard jaw gives way to hair the color of dirt faded in the summer sun. It's sticking straight up in most places but falling at the front to graze his forehead. His nose is straight, his lips full and pursed.

His eyes are molten amber.

Dear *God*, he's beautiful.

I've seen hundreds of pictures of Jax Jamieson, watched hours of video, and even been to one of his concerts. But the complete effect of all of him, inches from my face, might be too much for one person to handle.

And that's before he speaks.

"I repeat. What. The *fuck*. Is going on?"

His voice is raw silk. Not overly smooth, like the

Moviefone guy. A little rough. A precious gemstone cut from rock, preserved in its natural glory.

There are things I'm supposed to say if I ever meet Jax Jamieson.

I wrote them down somewhere.

"I'm Haley Telfer," I manage finally. My throat works as I shove a hand under me, shifting onto my knees to pick up the papers. "But you know that."

His irritation blurs with confusion. "Why would I know that?"

"You're standing on my Social Security number."

One of the papers is under the toe of his sneaker. I grab the edge of it, and his gaze narrows. What is it with me and pissing off these people?

Not that pissing off Wendy comes close to pissing off Jax Jamieson.

(Whom apparently I'm going to refer to with both names until the end of time.)

"Haley Telfer?"

"Yes?" I whisper because, holy shit, Jax Jamieson refers to people with two names too.

"You have ten seconds to get out of my studio."

The tech and I stand next to each other, peering through the glass studio door into the hall. My jacket's back on, not that the guy's coming anywhere near me because he thinks I'm a lunatic.

On the other side of the door, Jax exchanges angry words with a man in a suit.

"That's Shannon Cross," I say.

The tech nods, stiff. "Correct. The CEO showing up means one or both of us is fired."

"Well... which is it?"

We watch as Jax stabs a finger toward me and stalks off.

"I'm guessing you," my companion murmurs.

The door opens, and Shannon Cross looks at me. "My office. Five minutes." He turns and leaves.

After gathering my papers, I take the tech's directions to the elevator to the third floor. A watchful assistant greets me and asks me to take a seat in one of the wing-back chairs.

Great. I've been here less than an hour, and I'm about to be fired.

Instead of spinning out, I study the picture on the wall and the caption beside it.

Wicked Records's headquarters. Founded in 1995, relocated to this new building in 2003. Employs two thousand people.

"Miss Telfer."

I turn to see Cross watching me from his doorway. He exudes strength, but in a different way than Jax. He's older, for one. Tall and lean, with hair so dark it's nearly black.

The ends curl over his collar, but I can't imagine it's because he forgot to get a haircut.

His suit is crisply cut to follow the lines of his body. He was one of the men with all the gold statues in the picture yesterday. Yet on this floor, there are no pictures of him.

Weird.

He's made millions—probably billions—in the music industry. Formed stars whose careers took off, flamed out. In the golden age of record executives, he's one of the biggest.

I follow him into his black-and-white office, a continuation of the pristine carpet outside. It should look like something from an old movie, but it doesn't. It's modern.

A fluffy gray rug on the floor under a conversation set looks as if it used to walk.

I'm struck by the urge to run my fingers through it.

The photos gracing the walls here are black-and-white, but they're not of musicians or awards receptions.

They're fields and greenspace.

Err, gray space.

"Is that Ireland?" I blurt. "It looks beautiful."

I turn to find his gaze on me. "It is. My father moved here when I was a child."

I wait to see if he'll offer me a seat, but he doesn't. Nor does he take one as he rounds the black wood desk, resting his fingertips on the blotter.

"Miss Telfer, I understand you interfered with a studio

recording session. And assaulted one of our biggest artists."

My jaw drops. "I definitely did not assault him. He started it."

I realize how childish it sounds. The memory of it has my skin shivering again, and I rub my hands over my arms. "Technically, he startled me. I was trying to defend myself. Every modern woman should have a knowledge of self-defense, don't you think?"

He doesn't nod, but he hasn't kicked me out yet, so I keep going.

"I know I shouldn't have walked in, but your tech had this 'FML' look I know from a mile away. I know the software. I use it in the campus music lab all the time. There's a compatibility issue with the most recent update, and..." I trail off as he holds up a hand. "I wanted to fix it."

Appraising eyes study me. "And did you?"

I realize Cross isn't asking me about my outburst but what I'd done before that. "Yes. Yes, I think so."

Cross' lips twitch at the corner. "Jax Jamieson is heading out on the final leg of his U.S. tour, and we're short on technical support. We could use someone with your problem-solving skills to back up our sound engineer."

"You're asking me if I want to go on a rock tour?" Disbelief reverberates through me.

"Of course not." His smile thins. "I'm reassigning you to a rock tour."

"He wants you to what?" Serena shrieks over the phone.

"Go on tour. Four weeks." From the way I'm hyperventilating in the bathroom stall, I'm surprised the force of it doesn't lift me clean off the linoleum. "Then I can choose to return to the studio and spend the rest of the summer making coffee. Or they'll sign a letter saying my co-op term was completed because I'm working around the clock."

"You have to do it."

"First, I have no idea what it means to back up a sound engineer on tour. And second, spending twenty-four hours a day with other people sounds like a special kind of hell." I yank a sheet of toilet paper from the roll and start the productive task of tearing it into tiny pieces. "I bet they all travel on a bus."

"The horror."

"It is!" I insist. "They probably sleep in a pile, and..." I hiccup, yanking at my waistband. "Dammit, this skirt is *really* tight."

My fingers find the zipper, yanking it down enough that I can breathe while Serena laughs. "When does it leave?"

"This afternoon. I'm supposed to report to this address and see the tour manager." I take a breath.

"You have to admit it's kind of poetic," she observes. "Plus, you're out of options. The point of the co-operative education program is to put your training into practice. If you don't have a job in the summer where you can practice, you'll get kicked out."

Which is the only reason I'm still here instead of halfway down the street.

"I've never had a real job before. I live behind a computer." I slap my forehead. "And I was planning on a job where I'd have time to work on my program with Professor Carter."

"Forget Carter. This is a sign. You're going to fuck Jax Jamieson."

This is the risk of being friends with Serena. She regularly makes statements that, although they may be entirely false, have the immediate effect of taking years off your life.

"Serena, it's not a sign. It's a mistake chased by a coincidence wrapped in a bad idea. Jax Jamieson isn't someone you fuck. He's someone you study and watch and learn from. He's someone you worship."

"Yeah, with your tongue." Shivers run through me. "You go to college to learn and study. A guy like Jax Jamieson is *exactly* who you fuck. He probably has to lift an eyebrow and panties drop. He could blow on a girl, and she'd come. Hell, if he so much as brushes past you in the hallway? I bet you could live off the contact high for the rest of your life."

"I interrupted his recording session."

A loud bang has me holding the phone away from my

ear. "Sorry, I dropped you. What the hell, Haley? You met a rock star and got invited on his tour. This is amazing. So… is he?"

"Is he what?" I whisper.

"So hot you'll picture him every time you buzz yourself to oblivion."

I picture his amber stare, and this time I do feel a shiver. It's surprising but pleasant. It starts in my brain, trips down my spine, tingles lower.

"No?"

"You totally said that like it was a question."

Two hours later, I spill out of a cab. The rolling bag at my side and my backpack should have everything I'll need, but I feel naked.

I round the hotel to find two busses parked in the back, plus an eighteen-wheeler truck.

A woman sporting tailored jeans, heels, a cute blazer, and a blue Katy Perry ponytail comes up to me. "I'm Nina, the tour manager. You must be Haley. Shannon said we're adding one more here."

"That's me."

She tucks her tablet under her arm, presses her hands together, and executes a mini-bow. "Namaste."

"Um. Yeah, you too."

She straightens, and she's all business again. "Did you get the paperwork emailed to you?"

"I think so."

"Good. We're running late, but I can answer any questions you have once we get rolling."

She calls everyone's attention and goes over the schedule.

"We're off to Pittsburgh. Another sold-out show. We should get in by three. Curtain's at eight. It'll be a tight setup, but you've only done it fifty times."

A few people chuckle. The words bring a shiver over me as I look around the circle.

"All right, everyone get ready to roll out. Anyone seen Jerry?" Nina asks.

"Yeah. He's meeting us in Pittsburgh," a guy says.

She sighs. "Fine."

I still don't know who Jerry is, but everyone seems to want a piece of him today.

A striking redheaded woman who looks a few years older than me meets my gaze. "You must be the fresh meat."

"I'm Haley. And you're Lita Holm." I recognize her immediately. "You're opening for Jax. I loved your *Preacher* album."

"Not the new one?" She raises a brow, and I wince. "Don't take it back now. Honesty is refreshing." She doesn't offer me a hand. I like her already. "Come on. I'll show you around."

I shield my eyes from the sun with a hand, scanning the busses. "These are big."

"This one's for the crew and our band." She points at the other bus. "That one belongs to Riot Act. But rumor has it Mace, Kyle, and Brick get the front half. The rest is Jax's."

"Rumor?"

She raises a brow. "You think any of us see the inside?"

She nods toward the closer bus, and I get on, shouldering my bag.

"It's a pretty baller tour. We stay in hotels most nights." Relief courses through me. "Occasionally we have to travel overnight, and you can sleep here."

She gestures to the bunks at the back, and I take a slow breath.

I might not be able to sleep, but as long as it's not every night, it should be manageable.

A living room-type area makes up the front, and she drops onto a couch there.

"Tour rules." Her face gets serious as she holds up fingers. "One, thou shalt shower every day. It seems obvious. Apparently it's not." She shoots a look at a guy who laughs. "Two, thou shalt not touch other people's shit."

"Three," a voice shouts from somewhere behind us, "thou shalt not beat Lita in her fantasy baseball league."

The woman in question flips him her middle finger before returning to me. "Not actually. Though I'd love to see you try. Three, thou shalt not fraternize with the crew or with the artists." I must look confused, because she says, "Fuck whoever you want as long as they're not on either of these busses. You'll get fired on the spot."

"That won't be an issue."

She shoots me a look. "You'd be surprised."

3

"I'm not interested in new opportunities. I don't give a shit how big the paycheck is."

I toss the phone, still uttering persuasive sounds, across the room and pick up my guitar instead.

My agent's nothing if not insistent. Thank God I don't pay him by the word.

My fingers pluck at the strings, and the knot in my gut lessens a degree.

Like most sicknesses, motion sickness is in your head. After ten years in the business, I can control it.

But lately, the low-grade discomfort of being on tour has grown into something bigger. Something unwieldy.

A sound like rain has me shifting on the leather couch to see Mace's head sticking through the beaded curtain. "You working on something new?"

"You learn to knock?" I ask my guitarist.

He drops onto the couch across from mine. The back

of my bus is bigger than the living room of the rent-controlled apartment I grew up in. I have nothing modern to compare it to since I've never bought myself a house.

"Wouldn't kill you to give the fans something," Mace says. "It's been a year."

He pops his gum because quitting smoking's a bitch and he won't let any of us forget it.

I play him the I-V-IV-V chord progression as I croon over the music. "I know a guy. His name is Mace. He likes to get fucked in the face…"

He bursts into laughter, the kind that shakes the bus. "Sounds like a hit."

The look in his eye when the laughter stops has my own smirk fading. "What've you been doing?"

"Nothing."

We've been friends long enough he knows not to lie to me. Alcohol's one thing, but I don't let shit on my tour. Not since the longest night of both our lives.

The night I made a contract with myself. Decided I'm responsible for everyone who works here, and I will do whatever I have to to keep them safe.

Mace shifts back on the couch. "What's happening with Jerry?"

"Nothing. He's the best goddamned sound tech in the country. He's been running shows since you were in diapers."

"Since my folks were, more like. He fucked up last

week, Jax. Maybe the audience didn't notice, but it could've been a helluva lot worse. Next time..."

I silence him with a stare.

"Fine. Jerry's golden."

I'd stopped by the studio this morning to record an alternate version of a couple verses for an EP. I planned to get in, get out, and get on with my tour.

But the kid couldn't do his job, and Jerry was AWOL.

Then things had gone from annoying to X-Files weird when some unfamiliar girl shrieked at me in my own studio like I was forcing myself on her against the wall.

I can't remember a woman complaining about me putting my hands on her before. And I'd barely touched her.

Had I overreacted by telling Cross to get rid of her?

Maybe. A thread of guilt tugs at my gut, but the brakes on the bus catch and I reach for the curtains. It's too soon to be in Pittsburgh.

I set down my guitar and follow Mace toward the front of the bus.

"Watch the Death Star," Mace warns. I skirt the half-built LEGO on the floor as I pass.

Brick looks up from the video game he's playing, and Kyle pockets his drumsticks.

Outside, I stalk toward the front of our convoy, brushing through the crew pulling off the other bus. Smoke billows from the front of the truck that holds all the equipment for the stage show.

"Pyro started early," Mace says.

Nina's already standing by the front, one hand on her hip and her brows fused together. The rest of the crew forms a half circle around the truck, standing at a safe distance.

Except one.

The girl in jeans and a leather jacket inches toward the front of the truck, craning her neck to see what the driver's doing over its open hood.

"Who's that?" Brick asks.

"They called her in to cover Jerry," Kyle says.

"Unbelievable," I mutter.

The remorse I might've felt about my role in getting her fired evaporates like sweat off hot asphalt at the realization that she's *not* fired.

It's twisted, sure. But if I gave myself shit for every twisted thought I have, I'd never find time to entertain millions of people.

Meaning no one here would have jobs.

So basically, cutting myself slack is great for the economy.

"Can we put all the equipment onto the bus?" Lita asks.

"It won't fit," Nina snaps, her gaze darting between the vehicles.

"What about your Zen shit, Neen?" Brick calls. "You always say we should live in the present."

"I'm in the present. It sucks."

Brick's laughter has her glaring.

"Looks like the fan belt," the driver says to her. "Need a replacement part."

"We don't have time. Twenty-thousand ticket holders expect to see this show in six hours."

The new girl crosses to the truck's passenger door and runs a finger over the logo there. "What if you borrow one?"

"From where? We need this bus for the crew," Nina says.

"What about the other bus?"

Every pair of eyes turns to me.

"You mean *my* bus?"

"Jax, this is Haley," Nina murmurs almost as an afterthought. "It's not the worst idea. If the parts are compatible."

The driver shrugs. "Serpentine belts come in a few lengths. Got some tools in the back. I can check it out."

"It *is* the worst idea," I interrupt. "It's right up there with asbestos and "Gangnam Style." We're not leaving my bus at the side of the road and waiting for AAA."

The crew looks between us. Few people would go toe to toe with me and even fewer that I'd stick around long enough to argue with.

Nina squares her shoulders. "Jax, we have four hours of setup in Pittsburgh."

I don't want to leave the crew stuck, and she knows it. It's my name on the tour, but it's their livelihoods.

Nina closes the distance between us, her blue eyes the same color as her hair. When she speaks, it's for my ears only. "You have two interviews before tonight's show. I know the full range of issues you have with this tour. But could you please assert yourself tomorrow?"

Nina's a pro, but I can see the panic under the edges.

I rub a hand over my neck, which is suddenly itching like a mother. I can already tell it's going to be one of those days.

"Fine," I decide. "Take what you need from under the hood, but I'm not leaving my bus."

"Thank you," Nina mouths before turning on her heel. "Mace, Kyle, Brick, on the crew bus. Haley, I have a new assignment for you. Make sure Jax gets to the venue."

She's gone before I can tell her that's not part of the deal.

Ninety minutes later, my band, my crew, and my instruments—save my favorite guitar—are pulling away down the road. My driver's tucked into the cab of the bus, reading a paper, and I pretend I wasn't just outsmarted by my three-time tour manager.

I ascend the stairs to my bus, cursing as I trip over Mace's LEGO at the top. I grab what's left of it and set it on the coffee table, including the little pieces.

No one tells you having a band's like having toddlers.

I shove the controllers off the couch, grab a seat cushion, and carry it back to the stairs.

I toss it at the surprised-looking girl standing at the bottom.

Problems come in all kinds of packages. Hers isn't the worst, which only annoys me more.

Her thick lashes are the same near-black as her hair. Her nose is small, like she'd have trouble wearing glasses. Her bottom lip's too big for the top one.

Under the leather jacket, she's got curves.

Not that I'm noticing.

"I bet you're pretty proud of yourself, huh? Let's get something straight," I say before she can respond. "I don't know why you're not fired. It's probably Cross' idea of a joke, sending you to babysit me. But until we get rescued by Navy SEALs or whoever gets dispatched to save our asses out here, you will sit right there"—I point to the shoulder—"while this inspired fucking plan of yours rolls out."

Without waiting for an answer, I shut the doors and retreat to the back of the bus.

My Emerson goes into its case. I grab some clothes from my built-in dresser and shove them in a duffel bag.

There are pictures pinned up around my bus, and I take one down and lay it inside the top of my bag.

I glance out the window. She's sitting on the dusty shoulder of the highway on her backpack, her computer open on her lap. Dust has collected on her faded jeans and Converse sneakers.

You never used to be such an asshole. The familiar female voice in my head comes out of nowhere.

Pain edges into my brain, and I glance down. My thumb's bleeding again. I rip off the piece of fingernail I've been tearing without noticing.

I suck on the spot where it stings, crossing to open the mini-fridge and grabbing two bottles of water with my other hand. I lower the window and toss one. It hits the ground next to the girl's knee, and she jumps.

I take a sip from mine, watching her through the half-open window. "Fuckturd."

She looks up, shielding her eyes from the sun. "Excuse me?"

I nod toward her computer. "The internet password."

She takes a drink of water before setting the bottle in the dust next to her. "T-U-R-D?"

"Yeah. How do they spell turd where you're from?"

I close the window without waiting for an answer and finish packing, then pull up a reality home reno program on my iPad. Nothing distracts me before a show like seeing a bunch of contractors argue over cellulose and spray foam for insulating a garage. It's blissful and mind-less, which I need because in a couple of hours—assuming we ever make it to Pittsburgh—I'll be spun.

I drain my water and grab another. Before a show, I

can drink Lake Michigan into the Sahara. I glance out the window to see if she needs one too, but she's gone.

"The fuck, babysitter..." I shoulder my guitar and my duffel and go outside to find a tow truck in front of us.

The man talking to the girl is scratching the back of his neck. When she looks at her phone, he looks at her chest.

He's old enough to be her father and then some.

It's one thing for me to give her a hard time, but she's on my tour. I want to assume responsibility for this girl about as much as I want to adopt a special needs goldfish, but I didn't get the choice.

I step between them, feeling her move back immediately. I jerk my head toward the bus. "Get it to Wells Fargo by five."

If he recognizes me, he doesn't let on. "That's going to be hard, son."

I pull out my wallet, peel off three hundreds, and stuff them in the chest pocket of his stained shirt, right behind his name tag. "I have confidence in you, Mac."

A black limo pulls up, and I turn to the girl.

"Let's go, Curious George."

I go back to my bus to grab my duffel and, with a sigh, what's left of Mace's Death Star. I shouldn't care, but I have a spare hand and he's been building the thing all week.

I cross to the car and jerk the door open with unnecessary force. It takes me a second to realize she's reaching for the front door.

"In the back."

She hesitates, and I stare out the door at her.

"You coming?"

A moment later, she complies, dropping into the seat opposite.

There's lots of room in here for her, and me, and our bags, and more. But her gaze finds the toy on the seat next to me.

"It's Mace's," I explain. "He finished the Super Star Destroyer last week. It was a bitch to ship home. Bought him the *Ghostbusters* firehouse last year, and he never opened it. Says he's a purist."

"*Star Wars* only?"

"Apparently."

I study her.

Up close, I notice the dust on her jeans—and on her knees, through the ripped denim. It sticks to the cracks of her Converse. Only her hair, shiny and dark and hanging past her shoulders, seems to have escaped unharmed.

"You didn't notice how that guy was looking at you?" I comment.

Her gaze drops to her clothes. "Probably like I've been mining blood diamonds in the jungle."

The quick reply has me taking another look at her.

She's young, like me when I started in this business.

Though now that she's not on the floor at my feet, she has control of herself.

Her face is oval. Fresh skin, as though she's never done drugs or even stayed up too late. Big brown eyes with a little green near the center. The kind of mouth PR people salivate over. If she were in this business, that mouth would spawn chatrooms and have millions of fanboys jerking off to her.

Curvy legs bump mine as she sets her backpack on the seat, and she jerks them back. Now they're tucked up comically tight in the spacious car.

"If you're worried I'm going to steal your virtue on the road to Pittsburgh," I drawl, "I don't fuck my employees." I frown. "I also don't fuck on back roads, but that's a personal choice."

She looks around for something—probably a seatbelt—then turns back to me when she comes up empty.

"I'm sorry about this morning. I shouldn't have shouted at you. Or hit you."

"Oh. You think?"

"You touched me," she goes on as if it explains anything.

"I *touched* you?" I raise my hands in the air. "You're still intact. Send word to the nuns."

Her gaze narrows. "I was startled."

"Yeah, me too."

I look out the window because at this rate, it's going to be a long fucking drive to Pittsburgh.

She pulls out her phone. If she's updating Cross already, I'm going to flip.

I lean forward and swipe it out of her hand.

The sound of protest low in her throat almost has me looking up again, but when I realize what's on the screen, I'm instantly preoccupied.

"You're editing a track?" I take a moment to read the dips and valleys, the graph that music is turned into by computers when it's dissected. "What's this app?"

"I made it." My gaze snaps to hers, and for the first time, I see confidence instead of uncertainty. "It uses research on how the human brain processes lyrics and music to adjust settings to maximize emotional resonance."

"Come again?"

She shifts so she's cross-legged, then inches closer so she can see the screen while she's talking. "Basically, it makes music that affects people. It's based on the assumption that music underscores lyrics. That we respond to both music and lyrics but the music is in service of the words. Words are the primary pathway. So I use this app to adjust musical arrangements to optimize the emotional resonance of the phrasing."

I stare at her.

She's not the first woman to do something crazy within seconds of meeting me. But she's the first to follow up with this. Whatever the hell this is.

I shake off the feeling of unease as I stretch my legs

now that I have the entire space to work with. "Your assumption is wrong. The words are nothing without the music."

Instead of backing down, her expression sharpens with interest. "What about poetry?"

I cock my head. "What about it, babysitter?"

"It exists without music, but it touches people. Evokes a response."

Shit, she's committed to this idea.

Too bad I'm going to have to beat it into the ground.

"Even poetry has a meter. Besides, if words mattered so much, some of the best-known pieces of all time wouldn't be instrumental. Van Halen's "Eruption." Miles Davis' "Right Off." And don't get me started on Rush's "YYZ." The drum solo alone could level armies." I tap it out on my thigh with my free hand, and she listens.

When I finish, her attention flicks to the phone in my other hand, and I raise a brow. "You want it?"

The indecision on her face is comic gold, as if the idea of getting within a foot of me is horrifying.

Finally she leans forward, carefully plucking it from my hand and tucking it into the dusty backpack on the seat next to her.

I reach into my bag and pull out a chocolate bar.

"What is that?" she asks, her eyes widening as I unwrap it.

"Snickers. You're one of those health freaks too? Perfect."

"No. I have a peanut allergy. I almost died when I was four."

"So if I eat this thing in here..."

"You'll have to carry me out."

We stare at one another for a minute.

Two.

Finally, I buzz down the window and toss out the candy bar. She heaves a sigh of relief.

I grab a bottle of water from the bar. A piss-poor substitute for Snickers.

"Is this usually how you get to know your new employees?" she asks.

"Yes. It's part of a five-step process. Now tell me your dreams and fears. I'll take notes."

Her eyes glint. "My dreams? I want to do something that matters to the world. And I'm afraid of dying of anaphylactic shock in a limo with a rock star."

I reach for Mace's toy sphere. It's done enough to have shape, but some of the decorations are missing. I lift it, turning it in my hands as I look at her through the gaps. "Death scares you. That's healthy."

"Not dying exactly. More like making twenty thousand Pittsburgh music fans curse my immortal soul."

Normally my first impressions are spot on. But maybe —just maybe—I was a little off on this girl.

You can't blame me. Thousands of bright-eyed kids want to be me, to get close to me.

Now that we're flying down the highway in the back of a limo and not in a studio, she's not awed at all.

I set the sphere in my lap. "So, what? You're going to tell computers what to do for the rest of your life?"

"I'm pretty good at it. It's a solid career path."

I'm shaking my head before she finishes.

"Going with the flow is insidious. You'll be an animal, driven by whatever master exerts himself on you."

"But people *are* animals," she responds easily. "We live. We die. Somewhere in between, we procreate."

"Not if the nuns have their say," I say drily.

She levels me with a look. "Come on. Nuns are secretly fans of procreation. Even if they don't practice it. Otherwise there'd never be any new nuns." I swallow the laugh, but she keeps going. "Do you like animals?"

I lift two LEGO Jedi from the spots they're plugged into, turning them in my hands so their lightsabers clash.

"Not like Kyle. I see the kid on one more SPCA commercial, I'm going to shoot myself in the head. But Shark Week's still a classic."

Her eyes light up. "Have you seen the documentary *Planet Earth*?"

"Nope."

"It's insane. They use a combination of cameramen plus all of this technology to shoot footage of animals in remote areas no humans would be able to get to. In one episode about jungles, there's this jaguar that stalks the rivers and eats—"

"Whoa." I raise a hand. "Didn't anybody tell you tour rules?"

She straightens. "I got three."

"Rule twelve: no spoilers on tour."

"It's nature. You can't spoil nature." Then she pauses. "How many rules are there?"

"A lot."

"Does the fact that you don't want me to spoil it mean you're going to watch it?"

I shoot her a smirk. "I'm Jax Jamieson, babysitter. I don't have time to watch documentaries."

I plug the Jedi back onto their spots and set the toy next to me. Then I close my eyes, tapping a finger along the armrest.

Tap-tap, tap-tap, tap-tap.

Eventually, I pry open one eyelid to see her still watching me.

"Netflix or Hulu?"

4

HALEY

They say don't meet your heroes.

For a moment this afternoon, I'd thought mine was going to leave me to die by the side of the road.

So, we didn't get off to the best start. But when I caught him looking at the track on my phone, it was like the judgement fell away and a light went on. He studied the dips and valleys, the frequencies that together made the sounds.

When Jax's eyes closed, I tried to write an email to let Professor Carter know about my internship. We only have a few weeks left to finalize my Spark competition submission, and we'll have to do it by email.

I couldn't focus, and it wasn't the motion of the spacious car cruising down the interstate or the growling of my stomach after realizing I hadn't had lunch today.

It was because I was being a girl.

Sneaking looks at Jax.

How a guy pulls off looking manly while holding a LEGO set, I'll never know.

Serena would've winked if she'd been in the car.

When Jax and I roll into Pittsburgh, he's swept away for interviews by a determined Nina, leaving me to find the elusive Jerry.

The empty arena is a cavernous testament to technology and scale and the demands of mankind to be entertained.

The sound booth is at the back and midway up the rows of seats. It has a killer view of the stage. Even with twenty thousand people, it will. That thought sends chills running through me.

I stand behind the board. It's a mix of old and new. Mechanical and digital. A wall of computer screens interfaces with the switches and dials.

I feel even more out of my element than before.

"Billy Joel."

I jump at the raspy voice behind me. Its owner's hunched shoulders make him look even older, and shorter, than he really is. The man is stocky, wearing a faded black T-shirt and black jeans. His face is faded too and lined. But the blue eyes set between the creases are clear.

"The first concert I did here. Billy Joel."

"It must have been incredible. I'm Haley. You must be Jerry."

His nod is more like a bob. His hands look like crumpled paper. Rough on the surface, fragile underneath.

"You're my new assistant." He says it with a dry chuckle. I wait for him to strip me down, tell me I'm not needed or wanted, but all he does is scratch a patch of silver hair on his head. "You ever used a board like this?"

"No. I mostly use a DAW. Started on Logic, moved to Ableton."

He makes a face. "Digital. This handles more than a hundred tracks. Twelve for drums alone."

My gaze runs over the board. For the first time since this morning, I feel something flirting with my consciousness.

Comprehension. Just out of reach but nearer than it's been during this crazy day.

"No backup tracks?"

"Everything is live. Every drum beat, every guitar riff comes from that stage and through here." He reaches out to tap the board, his red plaid shirt following the movement.

He tells me a series of numbers for the guitars, mic, bass, which I commit to memory.

"What about the opening act?" I ask.

"What about them?"

"I met five musicians on the bus. We have Lita"—I point at the board—"her guitarist, bassist, drums. Where're her keys?"

Jerry shifts over to make room, then talks me through

the specs sheet of the equipment we're using. Frequency response, SPL output, dispersion.

I know all the terms, but I've never seen the equal of this equipment. I try to absorb all of it, my brain firing on every cylinder.

Part of me wonders if I should make notes, but I'm more of a visual person, so I try to soak up every piece of the desk that looks like it could fly the Enterprise.

Not the Kirk version. Definitely the Picard one.

Maybe even Archer.

"Help me with those cords, will you?"

I reach over to where he's pointing and start removing zip ties from the equipment. "So how do you know how to get the right sound in a venue? Is it based solely on the specs, or do you talk to other sound engineers?"

I pull up a window on my phone to look for venue info, but he holds up a hand. "I've mixed thirty shows in Wells Fargo."

I lower the phone, slow.

Jerry shifts back against the low wall that separates the booth from the surrounding seats, his arms folding over his thick chest. For a second I wonder if he's forgotten about me. But he says, "I have an idea. Watch tonight from up there." He points at the stage.

"Backstage?"

"To know what's working, you need to see the audience. That's your job tonight—to watch."

Shit. I think I might be having a cardiac arrest.

I'm too young to die of a heart attack. But then, it's too much to ask me to internalize the excitement of watching a Jax Jamieson show from backstage.

On stage, the roadies are setting up, along with the lighting techs and the guitar and keyboard techs. It's orchestrated chaos. Some of it will be for the opening act, but most of it's for the main event.

The next hour flies by in last-minute fixes before I'm pushed backstage as the fans fill the space.

All of it transfixes me. The setup is completed with a jerky efficiency, but it might as well be the finest ballet.

Lita's band plays first, and I'm hypnotized. She's really damn good. I watch her get her final applause and unplug her guitar.

Once the curtain falls, the crew takes over. Unplugging and plugging cords. Rearranging equipment.

"You lost, babysitter?"

The one-in-a-million voice has me turning to find Jax behind me for the second time today.

This time, I should be prepared.

You're so not.

He's dressed in black from head to toe. His body is hard and lean and sculpted, and I wish I could pull a Dr. Strange just to freeze time and check out every muscle one by one.

His hair's got some kind of product in it, and I'm pretty sure he has stage makeup on.

Those amber eyes are the same.

I always thought Jax Jamieson gutted people with his voice. I'm starting to think he could do it with that stare alone.

"Jerry said I could watch from up here," I say.

"Did he?"

I'm getting better at not melting into a pile of stuttering goop when he challenges me. It's something I'll have to practice if I'm going to be here for a month.

On stage, the crew is finishing up. Kyle takes his spot behind the drums, doing a visual check. Brick sets up behind his bass on the far side of the stage. Mace leaves his guitar unplugged as his fingers warm up over the strings. He's muttering to himself.

"He okay?" I ask.

"He'll survive. But apparently Emperor Palpatine's throne broke off and went AWOL in transit today."

I remember the Death Star that'd ridden along with us. "Crap. And he blames it on you."

"Nah. I told him it was your fault."

My jaw drops. "Why would you do that?"

"Man doesn't get his Snickers, he's bound to do some crazy shit." Jax strides past me, shaking his head as he takes the stage.

Was that a joke? I remember from a media interview that he's supposed to have a dry sense of humor, but right now I'm not sure.

Still, I can't take my eyes off him as he lifts his guitar

from its rack, shifting it over his head with the easy grace of someone who does it as effortlessly as walking.

My skin's tingling everywhere. Not in a bad way, a good one.

The crowd can't even see him yet, and they're going crazy in the darkness.

He's in his own world. Walking a slow circle, his eyes closed, he stops in front of the mic, dropping his head back.

He could be a Western gunslinger or a gladiator. The confidence. The competence.

Then the curtain rises.

The venue explodes, the roar filling my ears.

Jax looks immune, but when he lifts his head, opens his eyes, the roar gets louder.

The sea of people is marked by grins and bouncing and excitement.

But like yesterday in the interview room, my attention drags back to the man on the stage.

Jax's profile is in sharp relief, his strong nose and chin outlined against the powerful stage lights.

There's no music, no talking, just screaming that takes a moment to fade.

When it does, the arena is quiet.

Jax shifts imperceptibly closer to the mic stand. His gaze drops to the big, square mic as though he can see inside it. As though he knows every inch of it well enough to recreate it in his mind.

It's a million degrees next to the stage, but my arms are pebbled with goose bumps.

His lips part, his chest rising. He's the only one breathing in the entire venue.

And then...

A single note, low and raw, splits the silence.

The tension shatters. The quiet too, as twenty thousand people recognize the hit song and erupt into cheers.

My lips fall open, but I can't hear any sound that comes out.

I'm reminded in an instant why Jax Jamieson's a damned magician.

Not because his songs are perfect. Because they're *real.*

The program I'm building can't explain the kind of genius this man brings when he writes a song.

But every line, every verse, every chord touches me like nothing else does. The vibration fills me, owns me, in a way no person ever has.

It takes a moment to realize Nina's next to me, looking relaxed for the first time since the truck broke down.

"It's not always easy," she comments, the beatific smile making her look more like a Dove commercial than a tour manager. "But in these moments? It's worth it."

5

HALEY

Dear Professor Carter,

I wanted to let you know that I've accepted a position with a music recording company for the summer. I'm sorry we aren't able to work together, as that would have been amazing, but I hope I can continue to count on your advice as I prepare my program for the Spark competition. Thanks again for agreeing to serve as a sponsor for my application.

Sincerely,

Haley

My phone rings and I reach across the bed for it. "Hey."

"Bitch. You didn't call me last night."

"I was working."

"Chain smoking too?"

I crack a grin and shift upright to stare at the clock. Seven thirty.

"You're up early," Serena says.

"You too. I'm emailing Professor Carter. What sounds more personal: sincerely or yours truly?"

"How about 'I get off to you every night'?"

I make a face, hit Send, and shut my laptop as I slide out of bed.

"I didn't call to hear about Carter. How was it last night?"

"I got to bed at two."

"Partying like a rock star."

"Not partying. Going over the settings and cues with a guy who could be my grandfather." After the show, Jerry had wanted to see what I'd noticed, so I'd gone back to the sound booth and spent an hour with him, talking and taking notes.

I go through my bag for clean socks in the bottom.

My fingers close on…

"You snuck condoms in my bag?" I hold one up, my voice incredulous.

"Better safe than sorry," she chirps.

I drop the box back in the bag, shaking my head. "I did sleep in a hotel last night. Alone."

Besides Lita and Nina, I'm the only woman on tour, which apparently means I get my own room.

"Lucky. Need a roommate on the road?"

I yawn and stretch. "I don't think any pets are allowed. And Scrunchie is an especially tough sell." I shift out of bed, peering out the curtains to see the sunlight.

"Something came in the mail today. I think it's the ancestry test."

My spine straightens. "Open it."

I hear her rustling in the background and wait, dragging my sock-covered toe against the baseboard.

"Well?"

"No relatives found." I drop the curtain, my stomach flip-flopping. "I'm sorry, Haley."

"It's okay. I knew there wasn't a good chance. But it's actually not that bad. Maybe it's not meant to be. I never felt like I was missing out by not knowing who my father is. Maybe he doesn't even know about me. That would be one hell of a surprise. Or he could be in jail for all I know."

"Your mom doesn't strike me as the type."

"I don't know what her type was. I never really saw her with a man." I wander into the bathroom, inspecting the little toiletries there. I guess even nice hotels have crappy shampoo, and I'm glad I brought my own. "I know it shouldn't change anything, adding a face and a name to my family tree. Even if it's more like a family shrub."

There's a little pot for coffee, and I wrinkle my nose as

I follow the instructions, pouring water into the reservoir and hitting the button.

"I want to find out who I am. But maybe that's what this month is about. Maybe I can find myself here."

I glance in the mirror opposite the bed.

"Knowing your parents isn't all its cracked up to be. My dad asked me whether companies record video chats."

"What? Why?"

"Because he's doing shit I don't want to know about with some yoga instructor."

"Oh, gross. I don't want to hear about your dad's sex life."

"Me either. Let's talk about mine. Did I mention Declan from my finance class asked me out?"

The water boils, sending up a plume of steam from the plastic coffee maker.

"That was last week."

"No, that was Nolan from my media class."

I drop onto the bed with my black coffee cupped in my hands and listen to my friend on speakerphone. She tells me about all the guys she has wound around her finger, which makes me feel more at home and miss it at once.

Even if I'm never going to have the kind of confidence with guys that she does, will never crave physical contact the same way? I like hearing about it.

Eventually, we hang up.

Surprisingly—or maybe not—no one else is in the hall after I shower and get dressed in comfy jeans, a soft bra and a white cotton T-shirt that skims my boobs and hips. My leather jacket goes overtop.

I don't know what the breakfast situation is, if we can charge it to our room or what, so I stick to coffee from the continental breakfast laid out in the hallway.

I work on my program, thinking about what Jax said about music and lyrics.

Maybe when I'm done preparing for Spark, I can run some alternative models with instrumental songs. See if I can hack those too.

Lita comes downstairs after ten in skinny jeans, a long-sleeved T-shirt and sandals. Her hair's piled up on her head, and she looks like a sleepy ballerina. "New girl. Come with me."

I pack up my laptop. "Where is everyone?"

"Half of them are already at the venue, and the other half are still in bed."

Lita doesn't seem to have the same concerns about ordering breakfast. A waiter delivers two eggs and three pieces of bacon to the table in front of her.

Over breakfast, she explains what to expect. "When we're doing back-to-back shows in a town, the setup's not too bad. Most of the day's filled up with media. Then sound check. Rehearsal if there's time."

"Do you have time to communicate with the outside world?"

"Unless the outside world has a ticket to that night's show? Not usually."

I turn that over in my mind. "It must be hard. What about people's boyfriends? Girlfriends?"

"They understand. Or they don't." She smirks. "I'm unattached. I like it that way. My band is too."

"What about Riot Act?"

"Mace only cares about music. Kyle loves all women. Brick? You'll hear soon enough."

"And Jax?" I try for casual.

I don't succeed.

Lita grins, a sparkle in her eye. "Don't go there, new girl. Trust me."

We ride over to the venue together with a couple of her bandmates. Nina and Jax have apparently been in interviews for hours already.

On the way over, she pulls out her phone and starts cursing.

"What's wrong?" I ask.

Lita's bassist grins. "We're thirty days into baseball season, and her second baseman's already on the DL."

I hide the smile. "What do you like about fantasy sports? Is it the competition?"

Lita lifts her gaze from the screen. "It's no competition, new girl. If I wasn't already employed as a musician, I'd make the best owner in baseball."

When I get to the sound booth, I see the familiar setup from last night.

What I don't see is Jerry.

I use the time to go over the desk, the program. I try to

match up the settings with what I saw backstage. I go over the specs for this stop, start on the ones for our next stop. My running list of questions gets inputted to my phone.

Still no Jerry.

I sneak an hour working on my program while I wait.

Eventually I look up to find him shuffling down the aisle toward the booth. Today's plaid shirt is green.

He grunts when he sees me. "What are you doing here?"

"Um. You told me to meet you here at one." I check my watch. It's nearly three.

Instead of explaining, he scoffs. "You're keeping tabs on me."

"I'm your assistant."

"If you were my assistant, you'd do what I say." His voice sharpens. "Now don't touch that and leave me to do my damned job."

He shoves past me.

I stare after him as he hunches over the desk in front of the computer.

I'm used to people being protective of their work, but this is something else.

How am I supposed to assist Jerry if he won't let me in the sound booth? I sense there's something bigger going on here but have no idea what it is.

What is obvious is that everyone else at the venue is occupied with their own work. Nina's nowhere in sight. Security's busy.

I go backstage to try to figure out what I should do.

Nina's voice comes from the open door at the end of the hall. "We'll find it later."

"No. We'll find it *now*." The growl echoes off the walls.

My spine stiffens as I stop in front of the doorway. It looks like a tornado hit. The room is full of scattered costumes, equipment, and food.

Jax grabs an amp off the floor and hurls it across the room. I jump as it hits the wall.

Finally he stops spinning, his eyes wild as our gazes lock. I look from him to Nina, who's talking into her phone, and back.

"Where is it?" he demands.

"What?"

I look around because why is he suddenly talking only to me?

"My *phone*, babysitter," he says it as though I'm purposely keeping it from him.

"I… when did you lose it?"

"If I knew that, I'd have it right now," he grinds out.

Nina's running down their itinerary from earlier, calling every studio they interviewed at.

I can't remember seeing the phone in the limo or during any of our time together. "Did you leave it on your bus?"

"Not possible," he mutters, stalking past me.

I follow him into the hall. Jax rubs a hand over his head, sending the muscles under his tight T-shirt leaping.

Yesterday he was irritated, but I'd figured it was just edginess before the show.

Now, he's not edgy. He's volatile.

"We'll find it after the show." Nina's calm voice cuts in from behind us.

"No, Nina, we will *not* find it after the show. There will not *be* a fucking show."

Kyle sticks his head out the door. Of Jax's band members, he seems the most approachable, looking as if he could be a grad student.

"He has a password on it, right?" I ask.

"It's not about privacy. He needs to make a call tonight."

I stare. "Can't he borrow a phone? All phones reach all other phones. That's how phones work."

"It's a long story."

The feeling stirring up inside me should be annoyance. But as I watch Jax rub a hand over his neck, eyes wild, the only thing I feel is concern.

I check the clock. The opening act goes on in an hour.

You need to get back to the sound booth, a voice reminds me. *Figure out how to do the job you were given.*

Instead, I reach for my phone and slip out the door.

"It's me, Haley. I called about the bus."

The man at the auto shop, Mac, looks the same as yesterday. "You want on it."

"Yes." I flash him my ID. I remember Jax's comment, and a ripple of uncertainty runs through me. Maybe this wasn't a good idea.

"Wicked Records, right? It's not ready. Work order says it'll be done tomorrow morning."

"I need to get onto it now."

For a moment, he blinks. Then he looks past me toward the door, like he's wondering if someone else is with me.

Of course, I'm alone.

Which I'm starting to think was a dumb idea.

His gaze drops down my body, then back up. He sneers. "What'll you do for me?"

I can hear Serena's voice telling me to kick him in the balls or something.

"What I'll do is tell management at Wicked Records how cooperative you were." I force myself to stand my ground. "Now can I get on the bus?"

The front of the bus is leather and glass. Couches on both sides, a chandelier on the ceiling. Gaming controllers are scattered across the couch cushions. It smells faintly of cigarettes, as if someone used to smoke here.

When I brush through a beaded curtain, I'm in Jax's world.

Everything is dark red. The walls are covered in

photos of a woman with a sweet face. A kid. In some pictures, they're with Jax, his arm around them. He's grinning like he's won the lottery.

Is he married? A father?

None of that has ever been reported in the media.

That's not why you're here, I remind myself, though it feels like the world's been turned inside out in the last few seconds.

It takes me a couple of minutes to find what I'm looking for because it's tucked under the edge of the couch.

"Holy shit. Is this it?" I hold up the flip phone.

Creaking behind me has me stumbling upright. Ty's coming on the bus.

"You find what you need?" he asks, leering. He moves toward me, and an alarm sounds in the back of my mind.

He doesn't look like he wants to touch me in that benevolent, annoying way society seems to permit.

He looks as if he wants to do a whole lot more than that.

"Mac," I whisper. "Please don't touch me."

"Someone going to have a problem with that?"

I hold my breath because no.

No one's going to have a problem with it.

No one knows I'm here.

He reaches for me, and my heart kicks in my chest.

I twist away.

He catches hold of my jacket, and I use the chance to wriggle free.

I duck under his arm. The phone and charger in tow, I race out of the bus.

My jacket! part of me protests.

But I run and keep running.

The car I took over here picks me up, and somewhere on the drive back to the arena, I hit the power button.

The phone has messages from someone named Annie. The woman in the photos?

Where are you?

When I get back to the backstage door, the guards have changed and they stare me down.

"I work here, I swear." I reach for my ID, but I can't find it. I hope to hell I didn't leave it at the garage...

"Nina! Jax!" The words are hollered at the top of my lungs.

The security guy goes for me, and I back up.

Through the crack in the door, I see Jax burst through the door partway down the hall, but before I can say anything, the door shuts in my face.

Shit.

A moment later the door opens. A breath whooshes

out of my lungs as I brush past the security guard and toward Jax.

He notices the phone in my hand, and his shoulders relax. "Where did you find this?"

"Your bus." I hand Jax the phone and dig the charger out of my bag. "I figured no one else would be able to charge... whatever that is."

Jax studies me as if he's trying to decide what I'm made of on a cellular level.

"Thanks, babysitter," he says finally.

He turns and starts toward the stage door.

"My name is Haley," I call after him. Jax pauses, hesitation only noticeable because I'm watching him so closely, then keeps walking.

The last hour catches up to me, the fact that I hauled my ass across town to bargain with some guy who clearly likes his girls younger than half his age plus seven.

I lost my jacket, all for some ten-year-old piece-of-shit handset that doesn't even matter. I squeeze my hands into fists.

Maybe Serena's right.

Not just about the sex part, but that Jax Jamieson's not someone I can learn from. He shouldn't be on a pedestal.

He's talented, but he's also self-centered.

He goes through life with people throwing themselves at his feet.

People like that lose touch with what it's like to be human. They don't remember what it's like to need other people. They can act however they want and do whatever they want because the world caters to them.

I take a minute to rub my hands over my face, then start toward the backstage door.

When I pass through the doorway, my eyes adjusting to the dark beyond, I pull up.

Jax is on the phone, his face transformed from earlier. I can't hear what he's saying, but the way he says it is caring. Like the man in the photos.

He's leaning forward, and his mouth curves at the corner. When he rubs a hand over his neck, the tattoos on his biceps leap.

There's none of the cockiness that's part of his persona onstage. He's just a guy.

Jax isn't acting for the fans or the paparazzi or anyone. He's basically alone, or as close as you can get backstage at a rock concert.

And he's lit up like a Christmas tree.

My chest squeezes because it's beautiful to watch. I move closer in the dark.

I don't realize I'm blocking the way until one of the crew brushes past me.

I inch closer to the stage with a muttered apology that won't be heard over the sound of Lita and her band less than twenty yards away.

When I glance back up, Jax is pocketing the phone.

"If that rings while you're out there..." Nina warns.

I brace for an explosion, but Jax is a different person.

He ruffles her hair, and she ducks away with a reluctant grin.

I don't realize I'm staring until Jax's gaze levels on me.

Shit.

I'm definitely in the wrong here. Not because I shouldn't be backstage because, hello, I work here.

More because I feel like I witnessed a moment that wasn't mine to see.

I start to turn, but Jax is walking toward me. It's too late.

"Do me a favor," he says when he pulls up.

His body's bigger than I remember, his hard chest inches from my face.

I force myself to breathe as if he's not close enough to encircle me with his arms.

My hips are yanked forward as if by an invisible cord, and it takes a second to realize it's his finger in my belt loop.

Holy shit.

"Hang onto this for me. *Haley*." His voice rumbles over the applause on the other side of the curtain.

My mouth falls open on a gasp as the phone slides inside the front pocket of my jeans, wedging in the narrow opening and creating friction everywhere it touches.

I'm not used to shaking hands with strangers, but right now, I feel his touch somewhere I never expected a rock star's *anything* to get near in my lifetime.

Ripples of sensation shoot down my spine, between my thighs.

Jax's grin is long gone, and as his amber stare bores into me, I swear he knows exactly what he's doing.

My skin burns like the phone is hot. Part of me wants to yank the thing out and toss it across the floor.

Instead, as I watch him take the stage, I press my palm over my pocket so the outline digs into my hip.

6

HALEY

"You ever going to play a cover?" Lita calls over the muffled shuffling of feet on the hotel's carpeted lobby floor as we wait for elevators. The overhead lights cast a harsh glow on artists and crew alike, all holding the same energy of excitement and exhaustion. "They loved our Cranberries song."

"Not going to happen," Jax says. "I don't do other people's shit."

"What about 'Inside'? That's *your* shit. From another lifetime." Mace says it like a joke as we pile onto two elevators.

I'm swept into the one with Lita, Nina, Jax, Mace, and their drummer Kyle, plus a couple of the techs whose names I'm still learning.

"Would it kill you to play it for your fans?" Nina glances up from her phone, looking as alert as she did at noon even though it's after midnight.

"It might."

The doors start to close, then hesitate.

"I'll get the next one." I start to step out, but Lita sticks her arm in front of me.

"Don't be dumb. If you haven't figured it out, personal space doesn't exist here."

Tour rule number twenty-three: no one is content to live in their own bubble; they need to bust uninvited into yours as well.

Disliking being touched by strangers should largely go unnoticed in life, but you'd be surprised how many times it comes up.

Everywhere from café lines to house parties to movie theatres.

By far the worst offender is elevators.

"Kyle, you have to stop giving shout-outs to random charities." This is Nina's voice.

"We're lucky to be famous, Neen," the drummer replies easily. "We should use that making the world a better place."

"We need to scope them before we tell your fans to give their money to the *Coalition for Panda Feelings*. That is not a real organization."

As the doors close again, my feet inch back until I'm pressed against a hard chest.

I know without looking who it is. I feel the sweat through his shirt, smell the salt.

"I'm going to start a charity," Brick drawls. "The *Free*

Blowjob Society." Everyone groans. "You tell me that's not making the world a better place, you're full of shit."

I try to move, but there's nowhere to go. I turn my head, and my ponytail bumps something. Probably Jax's face, I realize as Brick stifles a laugh.

"Sorry." I face forward again.

"How did you like the show, Haley?" Mace asks.

"It was, ah"—Jax's chest rubs my back as he shifts—"loud. I mean... good."

After Jax slipped me the phone, I'd found my way back to the sound booth.

Jerry had acted as if he'd never tried to get rid of me earlier, even berating me for being late.

I couldn't get a handle on it.

I can't get a handle on a lot of things.

"Good?" Mace glances in amusement between me and the man behind me. "I think that's the first 'good' we ever got, Jax."

I'm counting the floors in this tiny box rising through the air.

Being in a confined space with lots of sensory stimulation makes me want to crawl out of my skin. Now, there's the buzz of chatter, the faint scent of sweat and makeup. A breath at my ear cuts through the rest, sending shivers down my spine.

The elevator dings, and I burst out first.

The hallway feels as open as the Grand Canyon, and I suck in fresh air.

"I thought we had the entire floor?" I ask Lita, nodding toward the open door at the end of the hall. Loud music and female laughter pour out of it.

"We do."

"Incoming!" Kyle hollers as he and Mace bound toward the room.

A woman sticks her head out, grinning and holding up a bottle of tequila. "About time!"

It clicks for me even before Nina warns, "Get a good night's sleep. The busses will be ready to roll out at ten."

Brick darts past Nina, turning to salute her with a mocking grin. Jax trails a few paces behind.

The band and crew disperse down the hall to their rooms, like pool balls after the break.

But I'm focused on one particular back.

"Do they do this every night?" I ask, staring after the band.

Lita doesn't respond, and I turn back to find her sympathetic gaze on me.

"Rule number thirty: don't."

"Don't what?"

"Don't ask. Don't wonder. Don't think about going down there. After having twenty thousand fans scream their names, they're all kinds of spun." With a wink, she vanishes into her room.

They're all kinds of spun.

The image of Jax talking to Annie on the phone flashes across my mind.

I read my room number off the card and pad down the hall to the second door opposite the elevator. I drop my duffel and swipe the key over the pad, making the light go green.

"What's your deal?" My head jerks up to see Jax standing outside the door at the end of the hall. "You practically sprinted off the elevator. You holding something against me?"

I blow out a breath. "Touching strangers weirds me out."

I didn't mean for it to be a conversation starter, but he strolls closer, the lights on the walls casting a bronze glow on his face.

He changed T-shirts after the show, and I wish he'd put on more because my gaze is drawn to the ink on his muscled arm.

"My mom tried to send me to daycare when I was three," I go on, looking for something to say that's not about his biceps. "Apparently I kicked an open bottle of finger paint at the woman who ran it when she tried to put an apron on me. After that, she put me in my own corner. Not great for social skills."

He pulls up right in front of me. "Some days it feels like all I do is have strangers touch me."

I wrap my arms around myself, shivering. "Sounds like my hell."

A ghost of a smile crosses his face, but it's gone so fast I might be wrong. "You get used to it. Or maybe you don't."

He shrugs, though the look in his eye is anything but casual. “Anyone gives you a hard time, come to me.”

The protectiveness in his voice is unexpected. “I can take care of myself.”

“Never said you couldn’t. But you’re on my tour. Your job is to look out for me. Least I can do is look out for you.”

I never thought of it that way. “Okay. Thanks.”

His gaze drops down my body. When it drags back up, I realize Lita’s right—he does look spun. “I need something from you.”

Jax nods to my jeans, and I think my airway closes. It takes a long second for my brain to click into gear. “Oh!”

I dig in my pocket for the phone and hold it out.

He takes it from me, careful not to let our fingers brush, and I’m sure it’s on purpose.

“Why do you have a flip phone,” I blurt as he tucks the device in his pocket.

“To remember where I come from.”

“2007?”

My comment earns me a slow grin that sends tingles all the way to my toes.

The smile freezes on my face when I hear a door open down the hall. One of Lita’s band members emerges, ice bucket in hand. He waves in greeting, then continues past us toward the ice room, which, judging by the sign, is at the end of the hall.

I’m suddenly aware it’s just two of us in this hallway.

I shove my hands in my back pockets. “Well, I should get to sleep, or I’m not going to retain the ten million things Jerry told me.”

“Wait.” Jax’s voice has me stilling, and for a second I wonder if he doesn’t want to leave either. “Who was better than me.”

He’s talking about the show. He has to be.

Though now that he’s so close, his amber eyes glinting with challenge, I want to say, “No one’s better,” because how could they be? At anything?

He’s intense and beautiful and unlike even the prettiest of the pretty boys Serena brings through our house. Jax is different.

He’s not a boy. He’s a man.

He’s a legend.

“Leonard Cohen,” I whisper. “Radio City Music Hall. He was eighty.”

His frown softens into confusion. “I’m competing with an eighty-year-old man?”

“He was forced to tour when his money was mismanaged and ran out. He started out with Canadian dates but ended up selling out all over the world, and... never mind.”

The guy from Lita’s band makes his return journey down the hall, and I step back on instinct because I’m pretty sure the space between us is short of professional.

“Haley,” Jax murmurs when the door down the hall

closes. His lips are parted. His hair is still sweaty from the show. He needs a shower.

Judging from the tingling at the base of my spine, I might too.

"I know who Leonard fucking Cohen is." Jax's words drag me back. "I saw him at the Orpheum in Memphis."

I blink. The smile's faded, but there's still amusement in his eyes. "Oh my God. I've always wanted to see a show at the Orpheum. Was it incredible?"

Laughter sounds from down the hall, but I don't turn until the woman's voice shrieks, "Jax!"

I jump a mile, and both Jax's head and mine jerk toward the party room at the end.

A blond woman in a tube top and the smallest shorts I've ever seen spills out of the door.

And also the tube top.

"Get your hot ass down here!" Her voice is full of intention and attention, and there's no question what she wants to do with his hot ass.

That's when I realize there's a hand on my hip.

Jax's hand.

I glance down at it, and he does too.

He drops me.

For a second, I resent the fact that Jax Jamieson is beloved the world over, because it means everyone wants a piece of him.

And there's only one of him to go around.

Jax turns back to me, and I imagine there's indecision in his gaze.

I'm willing to bet the woman down the hall doesn't want to talk about the Orpheum. Or probably talk at all.

"I bet there's a Snickers waiting for you down the hall," I offer. "She'd probably even unwrap it for you."

He rubs a hand over his neck, and I swallow at the way the ink moves across his arm as he flexes. "No doubt." Jax tosses his hair out of his face. "Sleep well, babysitter," he murmurs.

Then turns and walks back down the hall toward the Den of Sin.

7

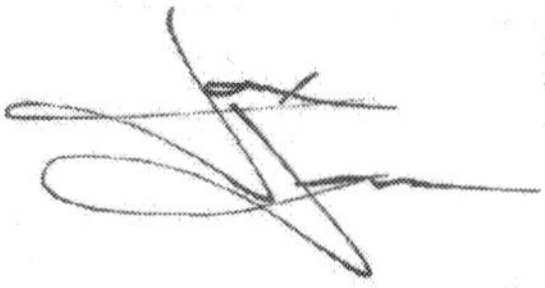

People who haven't been on tour think it's basically like living in *The Hangover*.

Booze. Drugs. Strippers.

Tigers.

Zach Galifianakis wandering through the background in his underwear.

It's not true.

The scene around me tonight, though, is pretty cliché.

"Jax, baby, come on." The blonde shifts onto my lap, wiggling to get there. Her mouth pouts with whatever gloss she slicked on while she was thinking about me, or Brick, or Kyle, or Mace. Most of them don't care which.

Right now, I'm a hard pass.

It's been a long time since I screwed around on tour, and almost as long since I've wanted to.

I shift out from underneath her and reach into my

pocket for the device I'm suddenly more protective of. I bang out a text.

Need 2 take my mnd off thgs

I glance at Mace, who's making out with a brunette. I'd never hear the end of it if he knew what I was doing.

At the bar across the room, I fix myself a bourbon because I like the way it makes my throat curl inward after a long night of spilling my guts into the mic.

Kyle and two redheads who look like twins are dueling on *Guitar Hero* in the next room.

Brick is plugged into a console in the corner playing *Fortnite.*

The only woman he even looks at is Nina, and I'd know if something happened there. Even if one of them wasn't too proud to admit it, neither of them would break the rules.

I can imagine it's a shitty place to be. When the person you want's the one person you can't have.

The drink's gone, and still my phone's silent. I send another message.

Where r u?

I slip out of the band's room and into my suite at the end of the hall. My bags are there, still zipped up.

The first week of tour, some assistant's assistant tried to unpack for me. It didn't end well.

On top is a stack of paper, different sizes, held together with a clip.

I could try to write—a phrase, a verse, a bridge—but I haven't turned out a good song in years. I'm not just losing my edge—I've lost it.

I pull my phone from my pocket and drop it on the bed. I strip the shirt over my head, wincing as I do. The mirror reveals a bruise near my rib, and I don't know how I got it.

I strip off my jeans, dropping them and my shirt in a pile in the corner of the room. My shorts go next.

The shower's hot and welcoming as I soap off the sweat, the grime, the makeup.

I let my mind go blank. For all of Neen's obsession with Buddhist monks or whatever, there's something to be said for living in the moment. It gives you relief from your thoughts.

One thought drifts through my mind and refuses to let go.

Leonard fucking Cohen.

The girl knows music, I'll give her that.

I'm tempted to ask Nina where Haley came from, but knowing the background of every tech on my tour is definitely below my paygrade.

I'm curious. That's all.

Maybe because she's the opposite of everyone else around here. The women who want to strip naked and do anything I ask.

I don't judge them. It's part of the aura, the sheen.

I have a halo around my head that's as fake as the rest of this circus.

But I get it. They don't really want me. They want the circus.

Haley on the other hand...

Being close to me physically seems to sicken her.

Though when I'd grabbed her hip—a reflex when she jumped at the sudden noise down the hall—she hadn't screamed.

Or hit me.

Or run away.

I reach for the tap. Instead of turning it off, I turn it cold. The water has my abs clenching, my thighs hard.

What threw me was the way she'd looked at me when I told her I saw the Memphis show. Those eyes—I still can't decide if they're brown or green, and it's starting to bug me—widened, and she'd sucked in an excited breath so big she was practically vibrating with it.

But if there's one thing I don't do on tour, it's hang out with interns.

At 2 a.m.

Alone.

By the time I step out and pull on track pants and favorite hoodie, there's a response to my message.

Lobby bar

I slip out the door and take the elevator. No one's in the lounge save the bartender and two figures in chairs hunched over a table.

But Jerry's not waiting for me because he's already playing with someone.

Haley's curled up in the opposite chair wearing purple pajama pants under a white hotel robe.

Plus slippers.

I can't remember the last time I saw a woman in slippers.

"If you do that," Jerry says, "then I'll go like this." He swipes a piece off the board, and she watches intently. He starts to reverse it, but she stops him.

"No. Take it off."

I wonder if she knows she's learning from the master. Of chess and sound engineering.

A group of people older than me come into the bar, and I flip the hood of my sweatshirt up.

Jerry's as much a legend as I am, but she doesn't pump him for information or suck up.

"I heard you got the boss's phone back."

She shrugs a shoulder without lifting her gaze from the board. "Yeah. I had to give something up to get it back, though."

I'm bristling before Jerry asks what.

"My jacket. I mean, I can get another one, but it was my mom's. She gave it to me before she died."

My hands ball into fists, but Jerry *hmms* over the chess board.

They play in silence for a few moves. Then he says, "If I worried you earlier, I didn't mean to."

"It's okay. I thought I did something wrong."

He makes a dismissive noise. "Being on tour is the best thing and the worst thing for a human being. It's a lonely business. There's a lot of time to spin in your head, which means we all have our...moods."

She smiles. "I get it. My roommate Serena says I have my moods too. Usually two days a month. And during midterms."

Two moves later, he has her in a checkmate.

"Thank you. For teaching me." Haley rises, and her robe slips open before she refastens the tie. "I'm going to go work on a program, but can we do this again sometime?"

"Sure. Goodnight, Miss Telfer."

"Night, Jerry."

I watch her round the corner toward the elevator before I drop into the chair she vacated.

"'Miss Telfer.' You trying to score a spot on her dance card?" I prod as I reset the chess pieces on my side.

"I'm too old for her. So are you," he jabs with a toothy smile.

I ignore him.

Jerry wins the white pieces, and he opens with a pawn.

I match him.

"You had an appointment before we left Philly." He moves another pawn. "What'd the doctor say, Jerry?"

"I'm an old man."

"That's all?" I send my bishop along the diagonal, covering his king.

His hand trembles on the pawn as he takes mine with his. "It's Alzheimer's."

A wave of nausea washes over me and I shove it down. "This is the second doctor. You could see a third."

"No more doctors, Jax. Besides, I have help. Or didn't you notice?"

I let out a half laugh I don't feel. "I'm not worried you're going to forget to plug me in one night, Jerry. I'm worried about *you*."

"Maybe you should worry less about me and more about you. I hear you've got another album to make."

I grimace. "Cross has been leaving messages daily. Sometimes I'm surprised he's letting me finish the tour before dragging me back in the studio."

But he can't. We agreed to a year's break before the last album I'll ever make.

"You written anything?"

If I can't talk to Jerry, I can't talk to anyone. The man's had my back since I was twenty. He might be the only one who has. "I'm not sure I have it in me. The first album was too personal. The next two..."

"There's less of you and more of them," he finishes.

I nod because he's right. The production studio takes over. Starts focus grouping and auto-tuning, and before you know it you're just one input in the marketing machine.

I take his pawn. "I've been at this a long time. I'm ready to go the hell home."

The group at the bar is laughing and drinking and oblivious to us.

I focus only on his king. He takes my bishop, sparing me a narrowed glance.

"I almost missed calling Annie on her birthday today because I was too distracted by all of this shit." Familiar bitterness rises in the back of my throat. "Ten more stops. Then I'm done, Jerry. I'm out."

"How many albums you sold?"

My gaze works over the board between us. "Forty-six million."

"How many shows?"

"Hundred eighty-three."

"How much have you made in the last ten years?"

"Okay, now you're being rude." I lift my attention to Jerry's lined face.

"Memory serves—and I know sometimes it don't..." His face lines as he grins. "...you're the one who signed on for this shit."

"I was eighteen. Living in a one-bedroom apartment, no food and no future. Wasn't much of a choice."

Jerry glances at my bourbon. "That Bulleit?"

"You know it."

He takes it from me, sipping and making a sound of appreciation.

At least until he coughs.

"Should you be drinking that?" I ask wryly.

"I'm too old to drink bourbon. I'm too old to walk," he replies, handing the glass back. "You ever heard of Robert Johnson?"

I shake my head.

"Bluesman from the thirties. His work was remade by Clapton. Keith Richards. Anyway. They say he was driving through Mississippi late at night when he came on a crossroads. The devil offered him the chance to turn around or take the blues in exchange for his soul. You know what he did?"

"I'm guessing he didn't turn around."

"Nope. And before he died at twenty-seven, he made some of the best damn music that's ever existed, present company included."

"What's your point?"

He grunts, his gaze never leaving the board. "You signed on the line. You chose your path, son. I'm glad you did because I wouldn't have the privilege of sitting in that box every night watching you do your work.

"Now you got another choice. You can spend your life regretting the deal you made, shutting everyone and everything out while you're at it, or"—he moves his queen down the board, and I see the checkmate too late—"you can play the blues the devil gave you."

8

HALEY

I don't bother hiding a yawn as I pull up a screen on my computer. I see how it's impossible to keep up on sleep while on tour. If I'm going to find time to work on my program without sacrificing my sleep, I need to stop playing chess and start eking out time.

"Babysitter."

Jax's voice has me glancing up from the board at the booth in the Air Canada Centre.

Today he's wearing a blue T-shirt that sets off his amber eyes and jeans over white sneakers. His hair's tucked under an Astros cap.

I don't like baseball. Or hats.

I like both on him.

"Where's Jerry?"

I nod toward the aisle. "Talking with one of the venue guys. I'm on setup."

If there's pride in my voice, it's because I am proud.

Jerry let me lead on organizing for the night ahead. Of course he'll fix all the stuff I screw up, but I get the chance to do it.

Instead of leaving, Jax moves closer, leaning his elbows on the half wall between us and running his gaze over me. I'm suddenly self-conscious in my black tank top and jeans.

"I bet you've never gotten in trouble a day in your life. At least not since the finger painting incident."

I fold my arms over my chest "Untrue. I was suspended in high school."

His eyes glint. "For what?"

"Our math teacher used to post our grades after tests. So, I started taking pictures of them. Then wrote a program correlating them with whether the students were on varsity athletic teams."

"And?"

"And—shocker—if you could kick a football, you were also a god at factoring quadratic equations." I wrinkle my nose. "But the principal seemed more concerned with my hypothesis than the findings."

"How did they find out?"

"I hacked the school's webpage and posted it there."

I dust my hands on my jeans, looking up from the board to find Jax giving me that look again. Amusement mixed with curiosity.

"You do have a little rebel in you."

Maybe he's making fun of me. Or maybe he thinks I'm cool after all.

I give myself the benefit of the doubt and a mental fist bump to boot.

"Aren't you supposed to be doing press?" I ask. "Nina will kill you if she finds you down here."

"I'm done. Media piranhas have been fed for the day, and Neen's off flirting with Brick somewhere."

I can't tell if he's joking about the last part.

"I bet they love talking about your music."

"No. They love asking if I take it up the ass." He replies so easily I'm sure I've misheard him. "Most interviewers care less about the music and more about my lifestyle." He cocks his head, a smirk on handsome face as he leans in. "In case you're curious, I told them only from my label."

I can't believe how supremely comfortable he is with *everything*. As if he could strip naked right here and walk up on that stage wearing nothing but the smirk and be completely self-possessed.

After last night, I'd promised to take Lita's advice and keep things strictly business. Because I lost a night's sleep imagining him with those women. I need to stay focused on my work.

But I didn't promise I wouldn't talk to him.

"I want to talk about music," I blurt.

He recovers from the flicker of surprise almost immediately, spreading his hands. "Ask away."

"Last night, you were going to tell me about seeing Leonard Cohen."

"So I was."

He does.

I hang on every word as he describes the concert, and the way he talks about it, I can picture myself there.

Then we go through our favorite concerts of all time, trading stories. I can't believe how many shows he's been to.

"I would've thought you'd never get to any shows."

"On tour it's hard," Jax admits. "But sometimes it's all that keeps you sane."

An alert beeps on my phone, reminding me of my task. "Shit. I need to get this finished."

With a moment's hesitation, he rounds the half wall and comes to stand next to me. He takes one look at the setup I'm doing and reaches for the board, flicking switches like he's playing an arcade game.

My jaw drops. "What are you doing?"

"Array configuration's different here than Pittsburgh." He bends over, checking a connection under the board before straightening. All of his focus is on the dials as his hands move over them. "You need to accommodate for that in the mix."

He realizes I've gone still, and mute, and stops, sighing. "The array's the speakers stacked by the stage—"

"I know what an array is," I mumble.

That's not the problem.

The problem is that Jax Jamieson knows how to do my job.

He just got fifty per cent hotter. Which is a statistical impossibility, because the man's already on par with the sun.

Stay professional. He's basically your boss.

Who's eight years older and has a sleeve of tattoos and who you have a poster of in your room like you're twelve instead of twenty.

He finishes what he was doing, then shifts a hip against the board as he turns to face me.

"So, the app you built," he says casually, cutting into my daydreams. "It tells you how to mix better songs."

Get a grip. I shake myself. "Um. In theory."

"To make money."

"Sort of. But also for science." I click into competent mode and out of "drooling on the floor" mode. "It tells us things about our brains and how we relate to music. Some people would say that's even more interesting."

"People like you."

"Well. Yeah."

"How does it decide what's 'good'?"

"It's based on a database of hit songs from the last fifty years. Including yours."

"Mine?" He cocks his head. "How many of them."

"All of them," I confess. "I couldn't decide what to

leave off. 'Redline' has this guitar hook that won't quit. 'Inside' is this acoustic exploration that guts you, then resolves right when you'd swear it won't." I swallow, feeling hot all of a sudden. Maybe it's because his stare has intensified or because it feels like I'm spilling my guts. "In case no one's told you, you're kind of a genius," I finish.

That hangs between us for a good five seconds, and I'm cursing myself for going too fangirl.

"People probably tell you that every day. I can stop."

His jaw works, but there's a glint of something in his eyes.

"Jax! You want in on sound check?" someone calls from the stage.

He stares at me a second longer before pulling something from his pocket and setting it on the board.

Then Jax jogs up to the front and plugs in his guitar. He grabs a stool and pulls it up to the mic.

He starts to play, and I glance down to realize he's left me his phone.

Again.

Like the last three shows.

What did he do with it before this?

Is it weird that I don't really care?

I lift the phone in my hand, turning it over. It's warm from his pocket. The smooth surface is marred by scratches, and I wonder how they got there.

"Strange." I turn to find Jerry at my back, setting his bag gently down on the chair.

"What's that?" I stare at the board, wondering which of my settings I've gotten wrong.

"He hasn't done sound check in weeks."

My gaze follows Jerry's toward the stage.

And now I'm thinking dirty thoughts about a rock star.

It should be innocent, but it's not. Not when I know he has a girlfriend. Not when I'm here to do a job.

The fact that I have zero chance with him doesn't matter in the slightest. It's the principle of it.

The phone burns a hole in my pocket through the final sound check. After, Jax vanishes from stage to get ready.

The rise of the curtain. The opening act. The main event.

The next hours fly by working with Jerry. He's so competent, and he always knows what to do.

Except at one point he stops, staring at the board.

"What is it?" I ask him.

"I don't..."

I've noticed that before, what's possibly the reason Cross assigned me here. Jerry has lapses. He'll remember everything about the venue, the acoustics, the tech, but he'll forget people he's supposed to meet or what time he's supposed to be on-site.

I open my notes from earlier, check, and point at the setting he'd told me about. "Is it this one?"

He nods, and we finish the show.

Eight encores.

I've never seen a band play eight encores, but Jax, Brick, Kyle, and Mace do it as if it's the last night of their lives.

At the ninth encore, my pocket buzzes.

I don't want to look at it. Don't want to be pulled out of this.

But when it buzzes again with a text from Annie, I do.

Call me back
Please
Something bad happened

Fear streaks down my spine as I lean over Jerry. "I have to go."

I cut through the halls, finding my way to backstage and flashing my pass to get through. The ninth encore is the last, and Jax comes off the stage, the building nearly falling down from the roar of the crowd. Sweat's running down his forehead as he chugs water next to the stage.

His gaze lands on me.

"It's Annie," I pant. "Something's wrong."

His body goes stiff as if he's been shot. Then he grabs the phone from my hand and stalks toward the dressing rooms.

I'm not sure if I'm supposed to follow him, but I can't not.

"Annie. What is it, baby?" I hear him say.

My chest tightens. I realize I've followed him right into his dressing room, but I can't leave. I'm rooted to the spot.

He listens, and I'm desperate to know what's happening, but I can't hear the voice on the other end.

After a moment, though, Jax's shoulders slump. "Division? Yeah, that sucks. Okay. It's late. I'll call you in the morning." I start to duck out, but he crooks a finger, telling me to stay. "We'll do all the math you want."

When Jax hangs up, he crosses to the old-fashioned wooden dressing table at the far end and reaches for a towel to wipe his face. He braces his hands on the wood, still breathing heavily from the show as he meets my gaze in the mirror. "She lives for social studies, but math is the devil. Ten-year-olds' drama."

"Ten years old?" I'm still struggling to catch up with the wry twist in his mouth.

"Annie's my niece."

I drop onto the couch, the fake leather smooth on my bare shoulders as my eyes fall closed.

"Who'd you think she was?" There's curiosity in his tone, and an odd edge.

"I don't know. You have pictures of a woman in your bus. Your arm's around her."

He hesitates barely a second. "My little sister, Grace."

I don't normally get wrapped up in other people's

lives, but I couldn't have predicted the cascade of emotions that follows. It's like dominos, shock chasing understanding chasing anticipation chasing hope, until one crashes into the next and leaves me a bundle of humming nerves.

Part of me's filled with dread and the rest wants to jump for joy.

The fact that you're alone with Jax Jamieson in his dressing room and he's single changes nothing.

He's not a sex symbol. He's an artist, a business person, a...

My rambling thought train comes to a screeching halt when I blink my eyes open. A sensory spectacle on the other side of the room accosts me in slow motion.

Jax Jamieson is stripping his shirt over his head. His back muscles ripple, and my eyes trace the tattoos over his arm, across his shoulder, to where they end midway down his back.

This is so much more than the poster. It's surround sound Dolby hotness, and as he turns, showing off equally sexy chest, all I can think about is what it would be like to trace those lines with—

"You thought I had a girlfriend. And that bothered you." He totally caught me staring.

My lips move, but nothing comes out. "Yes," I manage finally. "Because you go to that room to party. Not for any other reason."

He stares me down like he can see every dirty thought in my twisted head. "You don't need to save my soul,

Hales." The nickname sends prickles through me. "But I like that you want to."

I have a long moment to soak in the effect of his gorgeous body from under my half-lowered lashes before he reaches for a T-shirt. Then drags a black hoodie over that.

I bet you wouldn't take a bath after he touched you. The random thought invades my brain.

He crosses to the couch, and when his gaze drops to my bare arms, any trace of a smirk vanishes. "You're shivering."

"It's fine."

"Where's your jacket."

I swallow. "I lost it."

And holy shit, it must be my birthday because he's reaching for the hem of his shirt again.

Scratch that. His sweatshirt.

He strips it over his head in a way that tugs his T-shirt up a few tantalizing inches before dropping it down again.

He holds it out to me.

"You're loaning me your sweatshirt?"

"Keep it."

"Oh. I couldn't."

"You have a problem with accepting help, don't you?"

My brows pull together. "No! I mean... only if I haven't earned it. I don't like people feeling sorry for me."

Just when I'm about to reach for it, he seems to reconsider. Before I can protest, he grabs a sharpie off a table across the room and scrawls something on the fabric. I lift my hands fast enough to catch the shirt he tosses at my head. “There. Now it’s personalized. You can’t give it back.”

My fingers dig into the soft fabric.

“Thank you.” I want to tell him I love it. Instead, I hold the sweater up by the shoulders. “I can’t see what you wrote.”

“Just as well.” I’m totally imagining the teasing note in his voice as he drops onto the couch next to me.

The shirt smells like laundry soap and him, and until he smirks, I don’t realize I’m smelling it.

Shit.

I don’t know why I’m still here, or why he is, but I’m afraid to change a thing.

“Why do people feel sorry for you.”

I blow out a breath. “My mom died last year. In a car accident. She’d come home from a work trip to take me to a concert for my birthday. On the way back, it was raining. She had to hit her brakes to stop from running into a car in front of her. The eighteen wheeler behind her couldn’t stop in time.”

His nostrils flare. “Your dad?”

I shake my head. “He’s never been in my life. I don’t know who he is.”

The way his mouth twists at the corner is dark. “Hope it was a good concert.”

Death makes most people squirm. His response should make me angry, or indignant.

It's satisfying somehow because I know he's not laughing at my mom or the terrible thing that happened to her.

He's laughing at life. If there's one thing I've learned, it's that if you can't laugh at life's coincidences—the good things and the bad things and the horrible ones—you might as well be dead.

"It was," I say finally.

"Whose?"

"Yours."

I'm used to seeing shock on people's faces when they hear what happened, but Jax recovers quickly.

"Your mom died coming back from my concert and now you're on my tour. That's twisted." I half expect him to walk out but he just studies me. "Is this some kind of retribution thing?"

"No. Not even a little." I shift forward, bringing our faces close enough I can see the dark flecks in his gold eyes.

"See, I put on your music—*Inside* actually—and played it on repeat for weeks. My friend Serena says she doesn't know how I was so strong. The thing is I wasn't. You were. You were there for me, and you didn't even know it."

I take a breath because now that I've started, I can't seem to stop.

"That's what made me start building this program. It's also my biggest problem. Computers can analyze pitch and frequency and levels and what's pleasing to the human ear. Machine learning algorithms can predict hits on the basis of what's come before. But what none of it can do is tell you what kind of person creates those songs. What they're thinking, feeling, when they do.

"I want to know that," I say, breathless. "I want to know *you*."

Silence stretches between us. Except it's not really. I can hear sounds of metal on metal in the hallway. Of footsteps.

Neither of us looks toward the door.

Jax looks like he's turning something over in his mind. He smells like sandalwood and sweat. Like he came back from battle.

"I wrote 'Inside' when I thought I was going to die. When I was out of control. I don't play it, I don't even let anyone cover it, because it takes me back there."

I swallow the sudden thickness in my throat. "I heard about your parents. I never heard you had a sister."

"I don't like paparazzi harassing what family I have left. I left Dallas to make a better life for my family. But my little sister got knocked around by this guy while I was recording. She married him when I was on tour. Now they're raising Annie together. If I'd been there instead of here, this wouldn't have happened."

My chest squeezes, hard. I see why he carries so much

around with him, but there's something wrong about what he's saying.

"How do you know it wouldn't have happened if you were there?"

His jaw tightens. "I just do. It's why I count down every show in this damned tour until I can go home and make up for all of it."

Jax looks as if he's going to say something, but his intake of breath has me looking down.

"Jax, your fingers are bleeding." I frown, resisting the urge to grab his hands to take a better look. "I used to bite my nails."

He scoffs. "From playing guitar." But he holds my gaze for a beat. Two. "How'd you stop?"

"I glued peanuts on them."

His brows shoot up into his hairline. "Holy shit, really?"

"No, not really."

Laughter starts somewhere deep inside him, warm and full and incredulous.

And like that, the whole world is me and him, the dimple in his cheek I've somehow never noticed, the light in his eyes as our bodies rock.

"Well?" Jax asks finally, his gaze dropping to the sweatshirt clutched in my hands. "You gonna put it on or just cuddle?"

The fabric bunches in my fingers. I don't take my gaze

from his as I shift on the couch, tugging his sweatshirt over my head.

I didn't expect it to be warm and comforting, but more than that...

God it smells like him. It's all fabric softener and man, and if fame had a scent I know it would be this.

I shove the hood back, resisting the temptation to fix my hair.

"There," he says, a hint of satisfaction in his voice as his amber eyes darken.

"What?"

"It's like I'm touching you everywhere."

Words like "boss" and "distance" and "older" fall away because they can't compete with that.

When the biggest rock star on the planet says "I'm touching you everywhere" because you put on his hoodie, it's the biggest tease in the world.

But Jax looks completely relaxed when he shoves at the hair falling over his forehead, sliding a tattooed arm along the back of the couch. Curiosity edges into his expression. "So the whole hating it when strangers touch you thing... that's only strangers, right? It doesn't stop you from doing other stuff."

"What kind of other stuff." My ears are ringing.

He lifts a brow. "Like sex."

I stare him down but the only thing in his expression is concern. It's as if he appointed himself my personal therapist without telling me, or asking permission.

"Right," I manage. "Yeah, I have sex. But I don't like to drag it out. You know. It's better if it's fast."

Dark brows draw together on his face as if maybe I'm speaking another language. "Shit," he says finally. "That's a damned crime, Hales, because the best sex?" Jax's eyes glint as he stretches out his legs, dragging my gaze down his hard, perfect body without permission. "The best sex is *slow.*"

I think I stop breathing when he says it.

He looks as if he's not aware of the effect he's having. I think he likes having someone to talk to who's not interested in him.

If only that were true, I think as I sneak a look at him from under my lashes.

The first time I met him, I was beyond intimidated.

When he's like this, he doesn't seem older or different or scary.

Jax Jamieson is timeless.

He's perfect.

The door opens, and Mace sticks his head in. "Jax, Nina's asking if you can do an appearance tomorrow at..."

He trails off as he sees us. "Am I interrupting?"

"No." He hesitates, and for a second, I want him to say yes. Yes, you're interrupting. Please go away and come back in an hour.

Or never.

"Let's get out of here." Jax shifts out from under me and follows his bandmate out the door.

I stare after him.

Until this moment, I wasn't sure why I'm on this tour.

Jax Jamieson has saved me more times than I can count.

Maybe it's my turn to save him.

9

HALEY

Haley: I figured out what you wrote on the sweatshirt.

Jax: ??

Haley: Good luck wearing this when it's ninety degrees.

Jax: AC broke on ur bus?

Haley: No, but Lita likes to sit on top of it when she's managing her fantasy baseball team.

Haley: She says a cool ass makes for a cooler head and she makes better trades this way.

Jax: tell hr she can't have altuve

Haley: She gave you the finger. Who's Altuve?

Jax: ask her typing 2 hrd

Haley: You could always get a real phone.

Jax: blsphemy

Haley: Seriously. Save those million-dollar fingers for something worthwhile.

Haley: Like playing guitar. Or building LEGO.

Jax: no point

Jax: mace is 2 proud 2 let me hlp ;)

Haley,

Good to hear you're enjoying the summer. You're only young once.

I've uploaded some comments in the attached files. The program needs a lot of work before we can submit it to Spark, but I know you can get it there.

Talk soon,

Chris

By Kansas City, we're falling into a routine.

Five shows in and not only can I hold a flip phone, I can work the soundboard. Not quite by myself because Jerry's still the master. But I'm getting better. I like the combination of digital and analog.

I sneak out a bit of time to work on my program. Mostly at night after the shows because it helps me transition to sleeping. I've built in ideas Jax has shared with me.

Though I'm not about to admit it because his ego would blow up.

Some nights I play with Jerry. His mind's not great, but he's amazing at chess, and I've learned he's the most patient teacher.

I've also learned Jax looks after him. He drops by the sound booth before every gig, usually with the excuse to check on something. But they end up talking and joking for a few minutes, sometimes half an hour. That much time might not seem like a lot, but I'm realizing that when you're headlining a production like this one? It's a lifetime.

This morning should feel like every other morning. The surroundings are the same. But since Toronto, I've been edgy.

I spend a lot of time thinking about Jax.

We all do because it's his tour.

I'm guessing the others don't sniff his hoodie and wear it to bed.

Miss placing a coffee order because they're picturing his body. Or that smirk.

It's reasonable that I'm a little distracted since finding out that the voice in the phone I'd assumed was his girlfriend is actually in third grade.

Sue me for being happy. I'm never touching Jax and he's never touching me.

Still.

I feel better about the times my gaze lingers on him, knowing there's not someone out there who's earned the right.

Serena calls me right after lunch.

"How're you getting off?"

"Huh?"

"I said how are you getting on?"

"Oh." We've stopped at a diner where I wolfed down a sandwich. Now, I'm sneaking a few moments of privacy behind the bus. "It's weird being around people 24/7."

"I thought you had your own room?"

"I do. But even then..." I struggle to explain it. "It's like you can't forget the whole crew is sleeping a few steps away."

"Creepy." I laugh. "The tuition bill arrived."

The smile fades. "When's it due?"

"August."

I curse. "I haven't gotten a paycheck yet. That competition better work out. I have another two weeks before the deadline. If we win..."

"You're rolling in cash."

"At least I'm rolling in enough to pay for next semester."

"Please tell me you're not spending every waking moment working on that computer program."

"Carter sent me a bunch of tweaks to work on. Basically, I need different versions of the same track, so I'm going through these databases to find—"

"Whoa." I stop. "When are you going to lift your head from Carter's ass and look around?"

"I am looking around. And then I realize I'm on a rock tour, and it's insane, and I put my head down again."

I've listened to everyone I can to learn the business. Production crew members setting up. Nina rattling off orders like a Smurfette drill sergeant. To Jax, whether he's fine-tuning an arrangement with the band or giving feedback to the lighting director or reviewing the promotion schedule with Nina.

Something I've learned in between the 'actual' work is that not only does Jax look after Jerry, he looks after everyone.

He buys every meal for every crew member when we're traveling. Ensures there's a massage therapist, physiotherapist, or doctor on site the moment anyone groans, cracks, or coughs.

"The universe is change. Our life is what our thoughts make of it."

Serena's voice brings me back and I blink at the side of the bus. "Did you just quote Marcus Aurelius?"

"You think I don't remember anything from that first-year philosophy course we took together?"

"You're kind of awesome. So, how's Declan? Or Nolan?"

"Oh, I'm so past that. But there's this guy, Tristan..."

I grin as she tells me all about him.

"How's your man quest?"

"No quest. And no men." I hesitate. "But I have seen more of Jax than I expected. He...tolerates me."

"Sounds hot," she says dryly.

I chew my lip, looking around to make sure I'm alone in the parking lot. "More like we're... friendly." I realize as I say it that it's true. "He talks to me about all kinds of things, and I think he trusts me." I don't want to admit that we text each other, because that feels personal. Serena making up crazy sex ideas is one thing, but this is too close to real and I hate that she'd try to read something into this.

I glance up as the crew starts to file out of the restaurant. "I gotta go. Thanks for calling."

"What?! You can't leave."

"Serena, I have to—"

"Ugh, fine. And Haley? Don't worry about where you

came from. Think about where you are right now. Which is the Riot Act tour."

We hang up, and an hour later I'm sitting on our bus, heading to the next town. Most of the crew is playing cards in the back when Jerry drops onto the seat, and I realize there's a photo album in his hands.

"Oh, here we go," Lita comments from the opposite couch, where she's reviewing what I've learned are stats on her iPad.

"Shush," Jerry scorns.

I look between them, mystified.

"It's a rite of passage," she clarifies. "Tour rule number seventy-two: thou shalt be subjected to the History of Music According to Jerry."

But as the old man flips through the pages, it's not boring.

It's fascinating.

There are more famous faces than I can count. Moments captured on film, painstakingly tucked into sheets.

"You made all this yourself?"

"Sure did." His leathered fingers turn the pages.

We stop on a picture of Jerry drinking beer next to... God, is that Prince?

"You were badass."

"Started out as a stagehand. But I always loved sound. Took me five years before they'd let me near it."

He turns some more pages.

"That's..."

"CEO himself." Cross is way younger in the picture. "First few years after he founded Wicked. Didn't own a suit yet."

"It looks like a party." My gaze scans the other people in the picture. Rests on one.

"See? That haircut is worth blackmailing over."

"It's not the haircut. Do you know that woman?"

"No. Can't say's I do. Do you?"

I frown. "Can I grab a copy of this?"

"Don't show anyone." He winks. "He doesn't go anywhere without a suit anymore."

I lift my phone and snap a picture.

When I close out of the photo app, I see a message from Carter. I bite my cheek and reach for my laptop.

"What's that?" Jerry asks.

"Just working on an app I built for this competition."

His eyes light up. "A what?"

I get out of the terminal mode and switch into the graphics-laden interface that's more user-friendly. "So you import a track, then choose from one of these settings..."

His hand points to one of the three buttons on the screen.

"Yeah. Exactly."

The app's not perfect yet, but what strikes me is that Jerry immediately grasps how to use it.

Probably because the interface is clean and straightforward. I even modeled part of it after an analog soundboard, though it was more for whimsy than any legit reason.

Which gives me an idea.

Lita and her bassist are on the couch up front with me when I close my computer two hours later. "What are you guys working on?"

"New song. After this tour wraps, we're going out on our own. I have a friend who's set up some gigs in Nashville for us. Small venues. Different than playing arenas, but it'll be our show. Our way."

I shift back into the seat. It's my day off, and I'm determined to think about something that's not Jax for ten seconds. "So, what are you guys doing in KC?"

She fires off a message on her phone, then holds up a finger and grins at the response. "Kyle's in."

My brows shoot up. "Kyle's in on what?"

Lita explains, and I shift in my seat, playing with my phone. Serena's words echo in my head.

"Can I come with you?"

That's how five hours later, I'm no longer a college-student-turned-sound-tech-assistant. I'm watching Lita's band in a little bar in Kansas City, drinking bourbon she bought for me that she swears will change my life.

I don't know about life-changing, but it's sweet and spicy and has all my internal organs on notice.

Kyle's on drums, looking as happy as when he plays a stadium. Lita's swinging her hips as she sings, crooning into the mic.

The crowd's barely thirty people, but they're into it. It's thrilling—or maybe that's the bourbon again—until she steps off stage between songs and motions me up. "Come on. I know you can sing. I've heard you on the bus."

I stumble after her, a little slow thanks to the spirits. "I don't know your songs well enough."

We stop in front of Kyle, and she says, "What do you know well enough?"

I look around the stage. Whether it's the drinks or Serena's voice in my head, an idea takes over my mind.

I bite my lip before I say the word.

Kyle shifts back on his stool.

But Lita's beaming. "It's a song, Kyle, not a cursed monkey paw. Take the mic, Haley."

I step up to it. The chords start, and I lose myself in the song.

My favorite song.

It starts somewhere deep in me, uncurling like a flower.

The song that's always gotten me through the moments I don't feel independent, ready, or capable.

The times I wish my mom were still here.

The times I wonder who my father is.

The times I feel like something's wrong with me.

My eyes fall shut, and I sing.

I lose track of time.

I don't care about the crowd, about anything.

When my eyes open, they find one person in particular.

A guy wearing a long-sleeve black T-shirt and an Astros cap.

My heart is in my throat as he spins and stalks out the door.

10

“The National Museum of Toys and Miniatures,” Mace reads off his iPad.

“You want to spend our first day off in weeks looking at Barbies?” Kyle snorts.

“Says the asshole who shaved his head last year to support the preservation of finger monkey habitat.”

“They’re called pygmy marmosets,” Kyle tosses back.

“You coming, Jax?” Mace asks, a look of neediness on his face.

My criteria are usually where can I get time outside and where won’t I be recognized. I’m guessing the toy museum is as good a place as any to go incognito.

So I trail Mace around the museum as he pops his gum and points stuff out.

“What’s eating you? Is it Grace and Annie?” Mace asks as we stop next to a glass case of wooden Disney toys from the 1930s. The paint on Mickey’s face is curling.

He's the most perceptive person I know. Maybe that's why he struggled so much with drugs. Because he sees things, feels things. Needs to numb out the world.

I shrug. "They used to come at least three times on a tour. In between, we'd talk almost every day. Now, I've been trying to get Grace to come for three months. Nothing."

I brush past him, and we make our way through the last hall.

We go out for dinner, finding a patio to enjoy the summer weather. My ball cap is jammed down, sunglasses on, and even though our waitress looks a little too long, if she knows something, she doesn't say.

"Once this tour's done, we got another studio album to record."

I bite into my hamburger, then wash it down with beer. "I know."

"You really have nothing?"

I pull a sheet of paper from my pocket and hold it out to him.

"You need to get a phone from this century so you can write in Notes like a grownup," he mumbles, spilling ketchup in his lap.

"Says the guy who puts ketchup on his calamari."

"You can put ketchup on anything."

But I wait as he reads the notes I've been making. Some are lyrics. Some are chords, which will get translated into vibrations, sounds, in his mind as easily as they do in mine.

"What do you think?" I ask.

"I think everything you've written since 'Midnight Mass' gets a little further from who you are."

"I'm not that kid anymore."

"This"—he holds up the paper—"isn't who you are either. At least 'Midnight Mass' was the most honest shit you ever wrote."

I take back the sheet. "You ever write?"

He shrugs. "Sure. Back before you picked me up. In the dark ages." He grins.

"You ever think about whether you're writing to affect people or just get it out? And when you do, where do you start? The music or the words."

"Never thought about it."

"It used to come to me like a storm. The riff. Then when it got too much, it'd rip through me. By the time I finished, the words were there." I turn it over in my head. "Maybe that's the problem."

He studies me, a look of realization dawning. "Or the problem is you're overthinking it. This is about Haley, isn't it? I should've known there was something going on when I walked in on you. She was wearing your hoodie, man."

It's such a high school thing to say, but I don't have a good explanation except she pulled me in by being genuinely interested in my ideas. The questions she ask challenge me in a real way, unlike the ones I've been fielding for years.

"She's twenty."

"It's legal."

"It's not like that."

"She's pretty."

I swallow the laugh. "So are a lot of women."

"And I can't remember the last time you looked at any of 'em." He shifts back in his chair. "Jax. You signed up to be a musician, not a monk. You can't hold one mistake against yourself for a lifetime."

"Haley's not that kind of girl."

"Not the kind you fuck or the kind you walk away from?"

I turn it over. "Either."

For starters, Cross has rules about fraternization on tour, and they're my rules too.

Plus, she's too young for me. For anyone here. Haley's off-limits on that basis alone.

Even if she wasn't, there's no way I could tug her down the hall and into my room.

She'd barely let me touch her hand.

Not to mention pin her up against the wall with my hips to fit her slow curves to my body.

If I lowered my mouth to hers, those big brown eyes would be as big as satellites.

If I kissed her, pressed the seam of her full lips with my tongue until she opened...

She'd probably bite me.

"You okay?"

I blink up at Mace, shaking off the daydream. "Yeah."

Mace pops the last of his fried octopus into his mouth, making a noise low in his throat. "You remember that first tour?" he asks.

I push Haley from my mind. "We were fucking idiots."

He grunts his agreement, draining the rest of his beer. "Best time of my life."

I don't remind him that what followed was him falling down the rabbit hole.

I knew his using had gotten out of hand before our second tour. But that was when we had our moment, when I told him he had to get clean or I'd cut him out. He begged me to reconsider. But I held firm in the face of my best friend, needle marks in his arm and his heart rate exploding.

We spend the next hour drinking beer and reminiscing about the good times. It's dark when Mace glances at his phone, snorting. He holds it up.

"What the hell is that?" I ask.

"The bar Kyle's at."

"Wanna go see if he's chained himself to the bar in defense of single-origin rye?"

"Nah, man." He sticks the phone away. "I'm going back to the hotel."

I consider it, then I decide I'm not ready to go back just yet.

Our car drops him off first, and my eyes fall closed as my head drops back against the seat. Instead of thinking about Annie or Grace or the next seven tour stops, I think about Haley.

Maybe she is in my head.

Yeah, she's young. But she acts more mature than Mace most of the time.

When a smart woman tells you she wants to *know* you, she wants to keep your secrets and hear your problems?

It's damn hard to resist.

I know Jerry relies on her help, and she's like a sponge. Some interns have this sense of entitlement. They try to avoid the shit jobs.

Haley'll take on anything, so long as you tell her what it's about.

I respect the hell out of that. Especially since I know what her life's been like the last year.

I've been through it too.

The car pulls up at the bar, and I shake off the thoughts as I step out and start toward the open door.

The chords drifting from inside clamp down on my heart.

The closer I get to the entrance, the more my steps slow.

I can't go in, but neither can I stop. The bouncer glances at my face just long enough to see I'm of age, then he holds the door for me.

The words reach my ears as I step inside.

"All the primary colors
Burn my eyes
I'm black and white
Encased in lies
And everything blurs in between
I'm lighter fluid and gasoline
Inside"

She's there, on the stage with Lita and Kyle. Her jeans are ripped at the knees. Her tank top leaves miles of skin on display under the blue stage lights.

Not that she notices, because her eyes are closed as she sings my song in a voice as clear as a bell.

My fucking song.

As if she can feel me, her eyes open.

Long-buried hopelessness clashes with new betrayal, like waves from opposing tides.

I'm jerked back to a time when I was all helplessness, no control. I hate that she can make me feel this way.

Without a word, I spin and shove out the doors.

I need a car. But I can't wait that long to stab a number on my phone.

It's my turn to get voicemail.

"Cross. Take her back. I don't know why you sent her, but you're going to take her the fuck back."

11

HALEY

"My name is Jax Jamieson. I'm eighteen years old."

The camera jerks like he knocked it as he picks up his guitar.

I notice, but like the people responsible for the last eighty million online video views, I don't care.

I watch the boy in the dark, his fingers plucking the guitar, picking up speed. Hear his voice that begins over the top, playing between the notes of the strings. Soaking into them like rain into the hungry ground.

Which version hits me harder? The one almost my age, desperate and raw, or the one ten years later? The one who's seen everything, built the armor—and cynicism—that comes with being in the spotlight?

"Mace orders lobster at every diner. It's going to bite him in the ass one day."

I snap the laptop closed as Lita shifts into the booth

next to me. I pop out my earbuds and wrap the cord before setting them on my computer.

I glance a few booths down at where Jax, Kyle, Brick, and Mace are going over details for tonight with Nina. Kyle's half listening, simultaneously engaged in a discussion with the waitress about what looks like the plastic straws. Mace enthusiastically devours whatever's on his plate. Brick throws a french fry at Nina as if he's ten years old and learning to flirt. She turns her head, the picture of the equanimity preached in the books she reads in the stolen moments between tour stops. The potato bounces off her blue ponytail and falls into the booth.

Jax stares out the window, one arm slung over the back of the booth, as though he's contemplating the universe.

"You're in the doghouse." Lita's grin fades as she looks between Jax and me.

I snap out of it, shaking my head. "It's a misunderstanding."

Texas is the kind of hot that makes you wonder what you did to deserve it. I swipe at a chunk of hair that's fallen out of my ponytail and stuck to my forehead.

Jax hasn't texted me since he walked out of the bar. My two messages to him have gone unanswered.

He's acting as though I betrayed him by playing his song. I spent the entire night staring at the ceiling of my hotel room and feeling as though I'd violated some code.

"Well, you were great. Really. Check this out." She

pops up a video of my performance and hands me earbuds. "To be safe."

It's weird to see myself on stage, but it's pretty good. I pick at my salad as I watch and listen.

"It's okay," I say, pulling out the headphones.

"You're good, new girl. I see you working on that program. I've watched a lot of new people on tour. You're like the lifers. You keep going back for more. What're you doing after?"

"Back to Philly. Finish up my project. Then senior year starts in September."

"Until then?"

I shrug.

"We're going to Nashville. Playing honky-tonks for a few months. You should come with. We'd have fun together."

"I need to make some money."

"Can you bartend? A friend owns one of the honky-tonks. There's always a wait list to serve, but I could put in a good word. You'd get killer tips."

My eyebrows rise.

The idea's crazy, but it pulls at my mind as I shift out of the booth and start toward the counter. The coffee's actually pretty good, and—

I squeak as I collide with a wall emerging from the bathroom.

I know it's him before I look up into those eyes. "Sorry. I didn't see you."

He bends to grab his wallet. He's wearing the Astros hat again, and under that, his jaw works.

"Can I help y'all?"

We both turn toward the waitress at the counter.

"Yeah. Can I get a coffee to go?" I ask.

"And I'm going to pick up the bill," Jax mutters.

The waitress smiles. "Which bill?"

"All of them."

"No," I interrupt. "I'll pay for mine."

"I said I'll take them all," Jax says, his voice hardening.

"And I said thank you but no."

Jax drops a black card on the counter, and that, apparently, is the end of the discussion.

The waitress grabs the card and hits a few buttons on the register. "Shoot. Out of paper. One sec."

She retreats to a back room, and I'm stuck standing next to him.

It's hard to remind myself he's irrational when he's doing such a seriously decent thing. "Jax. About last night—"

"Don't." The syllable is flat against the backdrop of laughter and music in the diner. "And don't do that female thing where you make this a thing. This isn't a thing."

"Yeah, arguing in front of everyone makes it look like it's not a thing."

His exhale sounds like a punishment.

"Jax. I sang your song because I love it."

"I told you what it meant to me."

"So you don't want anyone to play it ever because it hurts you? Because you were out of control? Newsflash. We all have moments like that, Jax. Not all of them have eighty million witnesses, that's all. Maybe your pain can help someone else cope with theirs."

The waitress returns and runs Jax's card. "Wow, I thought you looked familiar. Can I get an autograph?"

"On the bill or for you?" The grin he flashes has the waitress blinking at him.

"Both, I guess."

The reversal shouldn't hurt me, but it does. His easy smile for the waitress digs into my side like a piece of glass I can't get out. It's all I can do to wait for my coffee.

Jax signs something for her then strides out the door.

"He's something else, isn't he?" she murmurs as she hands me my cup.

"Yeah. He is."

I glance at the floor. There's a scrap of paper on it, and I think it's his receipt until I unfold it.

12

When we roll into Dallas, I go straight to my hotel to clean up and get ready for interviews.

I swipe my key by the door and crank the handle. It takes me a minute to notice the man sitting in the armchair in the corner, one ankle crossed over the knee of his suit.

"What are you doing here?"

"Unlike you, I check my voicemails." Cross sounds amused.

I stalk toward the bathroom, stripping off my shirt, feeling Cross's presence behind me.

Without looking at him, I kick off my shoes. Yank off my socks. The marble shower is cold under my feet. I crank the water to cold, and it rains on my chest, making the hairs on my neck stand up.

"You know, when I found you, you were living on mac

and cheese and trying to keep your sister away from child services. Your mother was in jail. Your father dead. You couldn't keep a job. I saved you."

Cross's gaze never moves from mine as the spray rains down on my face, my chest, my thighs.

"Now apparently I'm here to save you again." He studies me. "You really hate her so much you'd call me to fix it? Is she bad at her job? Does she disrupt the rest of the crew? Because Jerry has had nothing but glowing comments both times I asked him."

Discomfort works through me because it's a resounding no to all of those. "She's just there. Asking things she shouldn't ask. Doing things she shouldn't do."

Making me feel things I have no desire to feel. Ever again.

Cross doesn't press me. "Well, I want something too. Extend the tour. Two months."

Icy cold steals my breath, making my abs flex involuntarily. "And you'll take Haley back."

"No. Two months and you'll keep her."

I turn, letting the water run down my back as I look at him. Somehow with him, I feel as though I'm eighteen again. "Why did you even send her here. To piss me off?"

I turn off the shower and step out, reaching for a towel.

"You know what it's like to learn there's someone in your life you didn't expect. Someone you can help," he says.

"You're not helping me." I wrap the towel around my waist, not bothering to dry my hair.

"I'm helping her."

Haley's face flashes in my mind, and it confuses the hell out of me why he dragged her into this. "Some college intern? An orphan, no less. Can't see why you'd bother. She's not like me—you can't make money out of her."

"She's not an orphan."

My heartbeat slows. I'm standing in the middle of the floor, dripping wet, and I can't move. He shakes his head, and the awful pieces click into place.

"Does she…?"

"She doesn't know. For a time, I didn't either. I only recently learned about her mother's death." He tugs at the collar of his shirt. The only indication he's uncomfortable. "She needed a job. What kind of father would I be to leave her out?"

My throat works, and in that moment, I hate her and feel for her at the same time.

The woman I can't get out of my head came from the man I've spent the last decade trying to leave behind.

Now I can see it in his face, in hers. The resemblance.

"Now, let's talk about how things will play out. If you care at all about her, you won't tell her and you won't ask her to leave. I will tell her in my own time."

"You want me to lie to her."

"I want time," he corrects. "You get time too. Another two months of tour stops."

The tile is cool under my feet as I pass him, crossing onto the red carpet of the living area. "And if I say no?"

"Maybe I'll decide that trust fund I've put together for Haley is better invested elsewhere."

There's his play. I should have known he'd have one. "You want me to choose between my family and yours."

"I want you to make a small concession in your life to open up a world of possibility in hers."

I can say I hate Haley. That I don't give a shit what happens to her.

But it's a lie.

I know what it's like to be where she's been, and the way she handles it, the grace, the optimism... I wish I'd been that mature at twenty.

"I won't give up everything for someone I barely know. Someone who's your responsibility, not mine."

With a half smile, Cross strides toward the door, adjusting his cuffs.

"Think it over. You have one week to decide."

13

HALEY

"Who're the passes for?" I ask Nina, glancing at the table backstage by security.

"Jax has visitors tonight."

"Annie and Grace are coming?" My heart lifts.

I wish he'd told me, but we haven't spoken since yesterday in the diner.

I should be pissed at him. He's being a baby.

But the piece of paper burns a hole in my pocket.

The words on it are evidence that he's trying. That even if he doesn't want anyone to know, he hasn't given up. He's still trying to create.

A cord wrapped around each arm, I start past the band's dressing room on my way to meet Jerry at the soundboard.

The silence is strange, and I stick my head in. Every face in the room looks at me.

Or rather they look at Nina, who passes me, her tablet in hand.

It's not unusual for Jax to be late. But someone else is missing.

"Where's Mace?" she asks.

A groan from the corner of the room answers her question. The bassist is curled up on a bean bag chair in the fetal position.

"That's what you get for ordering diner lobster every day for lunch," Kyle calls, not without sympathy.

"Let me guess. He can't go on tonight."

"The front row better have splash guards," Brick offers.

Nina holds up a hand and swivels to face the wall. I hear her counting backward from a hundred under her breath.

At ninety-six, she turns back with a sigh.

"Fuck it. We have a backup bassist. But we need another vocalist."

"What about Lita?"

The woman in question is watching me from where she's perched on the couch, a strange look on her face. "I don't know the arrangements," she says slowly.

"Then we'll have to make do without," Nina bites out.

"Haley does."

No one breathes after Lita says those words.

"Not happening."

I didn't hear Jax stalk into the room, but his response

shuts me down. The finality of it is like a fist squeezing my heart.

"She's pretty good." Kyle shoves his hands in his pockets, tossing his head and making his hair fly. "I heard her in KC."

"No."

"Can I talk to you?" My gaze cuts from Jax to the bathroom.

"Talk." Jax ignores my silent request for privacy.

I focus on his stubborn gaze. "I sang four years of choir. I'm no Aretha, but I can do it. If you guys want." I acknowledge the fact that we're having this conversation in front of the entire band.

"You want fifteen minutes of fame? Is that what this is about?"

"Jesus, Jax," Lita murmurs to him.

The hand shoved through the front of his hair is impatient.

I'm hollowed out by the angst, not frustration, I recognize in his face.

My voice softens. "I don't care about being famous. I'm doing this for you. All of you," I amend, swallowing.

"Let's vote," Kyle chirps from the back of the room. "All in favor of Haley singing backup?" Kyle raises a hand.

Brick too.

Nina watches, unmoving.

Lita moves faster than I've ever seen her. "You're not even in the band," Jax snaps.

Which doesn't dissuade her.

Motion from the corner of the room draws our attention. Mace's hand is lifted half-heartedly.

Then it's gone, covering his mouth as he rolls off the chair and lurches toward the bathroom.

Jax blows out a long breath.

"Don't fuck it up, babysitter," he murmurs.

So, we're back to that, I want to say. But he's already turned and left.

I feel as if I've won, but my heart's racing so hard from what I've committed to I'm not sure anymore.

Lita approaches. "I'll help you get ready."

I go to clear it with Jerry, making sure he has what he needs for tonight. Then I meet Lita at her dressing room.

She passes me black jeans with ripped knees. I shimmy out of my own faded denim and pull them on, wincing as I work on the zipper. "I can't breathe."

"They look good. You need a top." She holds out a leather-looking halter top that has me raising my brows.

"Um, I don't have a bra for that." Plus it looks like it'd be as comfortable as wearing a plastic bag.

Duct-taped around your torso.

Under stage lights.

She stares at my chest. "You don't need one. You have a good body. Show it off a little."

Sweat breaks out on my neck. "Fine, but I'm keeping the shoes."

Ten minutes later, I'm sitting in front of the mirror

while Lita rummages through a black bag too big to hold just makeup. After a brief showdown, I let her put curlers in my hair, and they tug on my scalp.

Soon my hair's been pulled out, brushed out, pinned up at one side, and left to fall over one shoulder.

It's been a long time since I tried to look like something other than me. Serena plays dress up but, aside from lending me outfits, doesn't try to make me her Barbie. I've never really thought about how to boost my looks. Never had a reason to.

The next time I glance in the mirror, I don't recognize myself. After using an ungodly amount of willpower to resist ripping the mascara wand and pencil from her hands, my eyes are lined and sooty, my lashes long and full. Even my brows are more defined. But it's my mouth I stare at.

"It's... red."

"You hate it."

"I love it." I hold a finger over my lips, afraid to touch it.

Her hair brushes my cheek as she leans down next to me.

After Lita leaves for her set, I walk out into the hall and find Nina on the phone. She clicks off when she sees me. "Haley. Wow."

Jax emerges from the other room. "Nina, where the fuck is..."

He trails off as his gaze lands on me. I swear his jaw

tightens. His eyes rake down my body, then back up. Linger on my face.

I feel hot all of a sudden despite the air-conditioned hallway.

"Haley!" Kyle calls from the open doorway down the hall, making me jump. "You're a babe."

"Thanks."

He and Brick go to pass us. Brick barely spares me a glance. Kyle grabs for my ass, and I duck out of reach in a well-practiced maneuver.

Then it's Jax and me.

It's the first time we've been alone since his dressing room. Since he sat next to me, laughed with me, told me his secrets.

Since I betrayed him.

At least, that's how he saw it.

The intensity of his expression has me looking away. My gaze lands on the table, the two passes that are still there.

My nerves and excitement wane. "Jax. Aren't Grace and Annie coming?"

That's when I notice the tension in his shoulders. "Not tonight." He clears his throat.

In a few minutes, thousands of people will be screaming his name.

At this moment, he looks completely alone.

Ignoring the buzzing in my head, I close the distance between us and throw my arms around his neck.

"Hales," he murmurs, surprised, and I feel the vibration along my skin.

I think he's going to push me away, but he doesn't.

His arms encircle my waist, and he pulls me hard against him.

Jax's breath warms my neck, and I breathe in his masculine scent.

I want to find Grace and shake her, to ask if she knows how much he worries about her. To ask if she knows how lucky she is to have someone who cares that much.

When I pull back, I swear some of the darkness is gone from his expression. "You look like you needed that."

He doesn't answer, but his gaze runs down my outfit again, ending at the floor. "Nice shoes."

I dig the toe of my Converse into the tile. "Thanks. I wanted something familiar."

Jax shifts toward the wall, tugging me with him as a tech moves past us with a piece of lighting equipment. His strong hand lingers on my arm for a beat longer than necessary, sending tingles up my spine.

"First time I played a stadium was Madison Square Garden. I'd opened for another group for a year. But when the first album caught? I'd seen hockey games from there, and all of a sudden, I was playing it."

I shake my head, feeling curls sway at my cheeks. "It must have been a trip."

His mouth twitches at the corner. "It was a total trip."

Jax may not have forgiven me, but I feel it again. That

realness between us that's so precious I'm afraid to reach for it in case I tear it like tissue paper.

I hear Lita's band in the background, echoes of the second song in their set list coming down the hall. My stomach lurches.

"I know you're supposed to picture the audience naked," I whisper, "but the only thing scarier than tens of thousands of drunk people is tens of thousands of naked drunk people."

Jax inclines his head, his hair falling across his face. Maybe he forgot to gel it today, but I like it better like that.

"Do me a favor, Hales." I don't know if it's his rumbling voice or the nickname that sends my pulse skittering.

"What's that?"

"Don't ever change."

14

"Jax, it's me. I'm sorry the concert didn't happen. I had to work. I'll try again. Maybe in a week?"

I delete Grace's voicemail in the car on the way back to the hotel after the show.

Straight after the last encore, I bolted. Normally I wait for my band, sometimes even the crew.

Not tonight.

Some people don't like time alone. Me, I need to process. To turn things over, to unpack them, look at them.

But it's a fine line between that and spinning out in my own shit.

Haley knew I was pissed. What she didn't know was that only half of it was her fault. The rest was Cross' ultimatum, fresh in my mind.

When I saw her walk into the hall wearing that outfit, her mouth painted the color of cherries...

It was all I could do not to drag her into my dressing room.

Then she'd hugged me.

I can't remember the last time a girl who wasn't my sister hugged me. I can't remember wanting one to.

I mean, it's a fucking hug. As innocent as it gets.

That's why there's no excuse for the fact that I let myself into my room, drop my shit by the door, and collapse on the bed.

The blood is pumping through my veins, and I'm alive with it.

I reach for my belt, snapping it open.

Then the button on my jeans. The zipper.

My hand is on my hard cock as I picture her singing my songs.

The way her tits looked in that top.

The curve of a smile on her red mouth when she started to relax.

I shouldn't be doing this, but I'm tired of telling myself no.

I stroke down my cock, and a long groan escapes.

Yes. This is exactly what I fucking need. My balls are tighter than Kyle's drum kit, and I know I'm going to come forever in about sixty seconds.

My hand plays my body, but it's my mind calling the shots as I imagine dragging her off stage at the end of the show. This time, instead of escaping back here, I pull her into the shadows and run my hands down her sides, over her ass. I swallow her gasp because we need to be quiet if no one's going to find us.

Because I'm sure as hell not stopping for anything short of an earthquake.

It's pain and pleasure at once, my hand moving easily thanks to the wetness already leaking from my tip. I grip my cock harder, putting pressure on the sensitive underside. Imagining it's Haley's hand and I'm telling her to be rough with me.

A knock on my door has my hand stilling.

"Jax, you in there? You seen Haley?"

It's Kyle's voice.

I've got half a mind to ignore it, but the question sinks in, along with the implication.

I shift off the bed, fastening my jeans, and cross to the door.

"She's missing?"

He holds up a glass. "I made her a drink."

The hairs rise on my neck. "Wait. Don't tell me she's partying with you."

"Yeah. She's part of the band tonight." He laughs as if he made a joke, but the idea of her drinking with the guys makes me livid.

I brush past him, going down to the room with music streaming from it and shoving inside.

She's not in there.

I try texting. Then calling.

Then without waiting for a response, I snatch up the room phone, dialing 0 and pressing the front desk clerk into giving me her room number. Then I storm down the hall and knock on the door.

No answer.

I find her at a high top table down at the bar, sitting with her computer.

She's changed. Now she's wearing shorts. The same sneakers as usual. But she still has stage hair. It's big and poufy and Country Music Award worthy.

She's also wearing something that affects me more than anything she wore on stage.

My hoodie.

I shove my hands in the pockets of my jeans.

Hard.

I shouldn't be here. Being this restless around this girl won't end well.

But I can't walk away tonight.

"Close this room," I tell the bartender. "Everyone out but her."

He nods, and I give him a moment to clear the room.

Haley doesn't notice me come up behind her. I peer over her shoulder, taking a moment to appreciate the profile of her face. Her small nose. Full lips. Dark lashes.

"Nice computer."

She smiles at my voice, before she even looks up, and my abs clench.

"How'd you find me?"

I can't help matching that smile. Raising her a smirk.

"I'm Jax Jamieson, baby." I clear my throat. "Kyle said you were unwinding with the band."

"I needed to unwind from the unwinding." She makes a face.

"What're you drinking."

"Water." Her lips twitch.

I order a bourbon from the bartender, and Haley watches with interest as he hands it to me. "That's what Lita likes too."

"Who d'you think got her hooked on it?" I force my gaze to the screen in front of her. "This is your school project?"

Guilt washes over her expression. "Not exactly. I should be working on that, but this is something else."

I shift into the seat next to her. My arm brushes hers, but for once she doesn't jump. She doesn't even shift away.

Interesting.

Before I can make sense of that, she hits a button that makes another window pop up.

"It looks like the program Jerry uses," I observe. "But the buttons are bigger."

"I thought this might be easier for him to see. And there are prompts based on the routines we usually run. I've been interviewing him about the different venues, adding what's in his head into the code."

Her gaze turns fierce, her mouth set in a determined line.

There's no market for sound programs for users with cognitive degeneration, but it doesn't matter because Haley's worried about him.

I take a deep breath. "I know, Hales. About his Alzheimer's."

Her eyes go round, and the emotion in them turns me inside out. "Oh." Her voice is small, and un-Haley-like. "I thought I could help him."

This *girl*.

This fucking girl...

"Why do you care?"

Her mouth twitches as if she's just come up with an inside joke she's not sure about sharing with me. "You can't ask that. You care about every person on this tour. I see how you take care of them. People talk about how brilliant you are, but they don't talk about how kind. They really should."

"That's bullshit," I say softly. "I've got enough darkness in me to swallow the world, and enough scar tissue to bury it with. You? You're bright. And shiny. And so damned new it's a crime to take you out of the box."

She tucks a piece of hair behind her ear, and I have the sudden insane urge to trace the shell with my tongue.

Get a grip, I tell myself.

A smile dances on her lips. "You know the difference

between you and me, Jax Jamieson?" I wait because I can't do anything else when she's looking at me like that.

"*Nothing,*" she says finally. "I mean, besides the obvious."

I raise a brow. "That I'm a multi-platinum recording artist and you're a college computer whisperer."

"No!" she exclaims. "That I can't come close to peanuts and you can probably devour them by the handful."

I want to crawl inside her.

But I decided before the dangerous series of events starting in KC that she's off-limits. And in that sense, nothing's changed.

She unplugs the earbuds from her computer, wrapping the cord into a tidy little ball before her gaze comes back to mine. "I thought I'd be exhausted after tonight. It's more energy than I thought. But..."

"But you can't unwind," I finish.

Haley looks past me toward the door, the smile lingering on her lips. For the first time I notice the music in the background. Something low and bluesy.

As if deciding something, she shuts the lid of her notebook and tucks it under her arm, rising and peering down at me. "Hey, Jax," she whispers.

Electricity lights up my body. My torso tightens in anticipation. "Yeah, Hales."

"Want to get out of here?"

I know I'm going to regret this before I even shoot a look toward the door. "I have an idea."

The Dolly Rock-N-Bowl is open twenty-four hours, and at midnight, it's hopping.

There's no way I won't get recognized, but I grab the fake moustache I haven't used in ages and do my best incognito.

When she comes up to me, she laughs. "You look like such a redneck."

A gray-haired couple in line behind us interrupts as we're getting our shoes.

"Aren't you the cutest," the woman says. "What're your names?"

"Leonard," Haley supplies with a grin.

"And Dolly," I say, deadpan.

"Like the name of the bowling alley?"

"One and the same."

I can tell they don't know who I am, so I let down the hood of my hoodie.

"How long y'all been dating?"

We exchange a look.

"A year," I say at the same time as she says, "Two weeks."

It feels good to be anonymous, to pretend. We used to be able to get away with it, but I gave up trying two tours ago.

Tonight I need it.

We stake out our lane, and when the server comes around, I order two beers.

"Can I see your ID?" he asks Haley sheepishly.

Haley straightens and flushes. "My birthday's next week."

For a moment, I'm afraid he's going to ask for mine, but he doesn't.

I hand one of the beers to Haley when he leaves. She glances up from where she's entered Leonard and Dolly into the electronic scoring system, and I grin.

"Can I tell you something?" she says after taking a sip of her beer.

"I wish you would."

"I go back and forth between wanting to find out who my dad is and thinking I'm better off not knowing." I ignore the pang of guilt. "I finally decided to do one of those Ancestry tests. You know, the kind that checks against the general population to find people in your family tree?"

My heart thuds dully in my back. "And?"

"Nothing came back," she says. "Maybe it was an immaculate conception."

"The nuns would approve."

She laughs as she rises from the seat to throw her first ball, taking out five pins.

Guilt works through me because I'm leaving the tour, and her, and she deserves so much better than Cross.

Part of me wants to forget I ever learned they're related. She'd be better off without him.

But if he is ready to acknowledge her, apparently that comes with a trust fund. Which she could clearly use.

"My father was out of the picture by the time I started recording," I say as I watch her take out two more on her second, "but before that, he hurt my mom. Sometimes me."

Haley turns back to me, riveted. "What about your sister?"

I shake my head. "I never let him hurt Grace. I wouldn't. It was the one thing I could control. The only thing, sometimes, until I started playing guitar and singing." I go and choose the heaviest ball I can find, letting it loose. I turn back before it hits the pins at the other end. "My mom died when I was seventeen. Grace was three years younger."

It's the most I've talked about it in... probably ever, but with Haley, it comes easier than I expect.

"When I started recording those videos," I go on, selecting another ball and adjusting my angle to take out the final two pins, "it was a way to get out of my head. I never dreamed anyone would watch them. I was trying to keep food in the fridge. I tried working at a corner store. Waiting tables. Nothing stuck. When Cross showed up at my door, I thought it was too good to be true."

I cross to where she's perched on the edge of the bench, hands clasped.

"No one comes to pluck you from obscurity," I go on. "But after ten years of this, I realize how wrong I was. So much is luck and chance and the whims of men powerful enough to make you a god by snapping their fingers."

Her face is a mask of empathy. "You regret leaving."

"I should've been there to take care of them."

I offer my hand. After a moment's hesitation, she takes it, rising, and moves past me to choose a ball.

The electricity between us is gone as quickly as it came.

She throws a decisive strike and turns on her heel. I offer her a fist bump, which she takes. "Maybe you were taking care of them here."

Her gaze is level, but I shake it off. "It's not that simple, Hales. Money doesn't fix absence."

"You hate Cross for what he did?"

"Yes," I say, though I'm sure she doesn't know what I mean. "He's used a lot of people to get where he is."

"The tour's almost over." I swear there's a note of sadness in her voice. "What're you going to do?"

"Atone." I throw again, missing entirely.

"That's not a job description."

My mouth twitches.

"Are you going to keep recording? Go on some speaking circuit?" She makes a face. "Or you could get married. Have kids."

I throw once again, this time clearing half the pins. I

turn back to her as the pins reset, peering into her flushed face. "So now you're worried about me dying alone."

She skirts me, shooting a look on the way to select a ball. "Not worrying. Just wondering."

Hairs stand up on the back of my neck. "If I want company, Hales, I'll make it happen."

Something flickers through her eyes, but it's gone as fast as it came.

Haley throws, and two pins go down. I take a seat on the bench as the song in the background switches to Elvis and yellow and pink lights swirl over the lanes.

"What about you?"

"I'll go back to school, finish my program. Professor Carter is helping me. He doesn't love music like I do, but he's a coding genius." Her voice is determined as she selects her second ball.

"Professor Carter. I'm glad you've got some old guy wrapped around your finger."

"He's the same age as you."

I don't know how if she gets a strike or misses entirely because all my attention's on her. "Wait, what?"

She comes to stand in front of me, folding her arms over her chest. "Technically, he's a year younger."

She's looking at me as if I'm crazy, but I feel as though I'm the only sane person here.

I don't know if there's a right way to respond in this moment. All I know is I'm responding the wrong way.

I don't give a shit.

"Hales. You like this guy."

She flushes. I've felt a lot of dark feelings, but the one that rises up now is more jealousy than protectiveness.

And why the hell shouldn't it be? She's off-limits to me, there's no way she's going to go back to Philly and fall into the arms of some guy who should know better.

"Too bad he can't touch you."

She brushes off her hands, giving me an arch look. "Touching someone isn't always terrible. Not when it's someone I know. And when I'm in control."

"So what. You'll blow him all night but he can't go down on you?"

I shove off the bench, eliminating the inches between us. Forcing her to lift her chin and meet my eyes.

Haley's eyes widen in surprise. I know I'm out of line, but I can't seem to stop.

"Jax?" she murmurs in a voice that has me remembering what I was doing thinking about her not even two hours ago.

"Yeah."

"You sound like you've got it bad."

Blood surges through my veins. She has no idea.

Haley points across the room. "I saw a vending machine. They probably have Snickers. You can eat it over there."

I blink.

Is she really so blind she has no idea how she affects me?

I should be grateful she's not thinking about the things we could be doing together in a hotel room right now.

"Shit, Hales. I don't need a Snickers." I let my eyes fall closed for a second, counting the breaths because I feel disoriented and it's not on account of the fake moustache.

I open my eyes, my gaze landing on her oval face, her eyes framed in extra-dark lashes leftover from the stage makeup.

"You want to know what I wrote on this sweatshirt?" I ask. "'This is me, signing your tits'."

Haley's snort cuts the tension. "You did not."

"Did too. Says so right here." Without breaking her gaze I trace the letters over her chest, my finger pressing into the swell of her breasts through what I'm suddenly regretting is the thickest sweatshirt in the history of the world.

Her eyes darken.

It could be innocent. It should be.

It's not.

I watch the awareness creep over her face, the realization that what I really want to do is touch her, and it's goddamned pornographic.

I'm daring her to back away.

She doesn't.

My fingers go dangerously low, and I catch the edge of one pebbled nipple.

Her eyes aren't brown or green now. They're black.

I wonder if her pulse is hammering like mine.

That's the only possible reason neither of us notices the whispers sooner.

But when I tear my gaze away from her, I can see we've been spotted. The group in the next lane has their phones out and is whispering and clicking away.

I grab Haley's arm—the arm of my sweatshirt, technically. "Time to go."

We take off across the bowling lanes before sprinting out the door. We find a building to hide behind and collapse, breathing heavily.

She looks down and laughs. I realize we're still wearing our bowling shoes. "Is this every day for you?" she asks.

"Usually I have enough security. And I don't spend a lot of time in public like that."

I call a car to get us, and we spend a few minutes alone in the dark.

"Sorry about the quick getaway," I murmur, careful to keep my voice low.

"Are you kidding?" She pants out a laugh. "Being on that stage tonight, sharing it with you, the crowd, your music... Tonight's the best gift anyone's ever given me."

My chest tightens.

I'm a bundle of issues, and getting closer to this girl is not what I should be doing.

Haley reaches up, and I hold my breath until I feel the tugging at my lip.

She peels the moustache off, sticking it to the arm of my T-shirt like a decoration before meeting my gaze. "Better," she decides.

"I'm not a moustache guy?"

"I like you the way you are."

When the car pulls up, I follow her inside.

The Town Car's spacious enough, but it's no limo. There're a few inches of space between us. Less than the designated middle seat because one or both of us unconsciously decided that was too big a gap.

I clear my throat. "Can I ask you something?"

"Hit me." Her voice is low and soft beside me.

"What do you do when you feel trapped? I have to make a decision. Either option is bad. Both ways hurt people I care about."

I feel her gaze work over me in the dark. She doesn't press, or judge.

She wouldn't blame me for not having her back, which only makes this harder.

"You always have a choice, Jax. Kierkegaard said when you're standing on the edge of a cliff, looking down into the abyss, you're twice afraid." Her voice is low, barely audible over the running noise of the car. "Once for the knowledge that you could fall and perish. And once for the knowledge that the choice of whether to stay or whether to jump is ultimately yours.

"He called it the dizziness of freedom. Because no

matter what we're given or what's taken from us... we're all free to choose how to live."

"Don't tell me this is another one of your professors."

She laughs. "Philosopher. Long dead."

"Good."

I want to shift over her, to take her mouth with mine and vanish into the blackness. To see if we can create the same bubble with our lips and tongues and hands we seem to be able to when we talk or smile or tease.

I've moved closer somehow, my arm brushing hers. Haley's shoulders tense, because we're closer than two people have a right to be. A little noise escapes from her throat, and that alone has desire pounding through my veins.

No one would know if I kissed her right now. Not Cross, not Nina, not anyone. Just her and me and the back of this Town Car.

I wait for her to push me away.

Instead, her fingers brush my cheek. It's light and innocent, but everything that isn't her fades away.

My mouth grazes her temple. The sharp intake of her breath sends the need inside me twisting tighter.

The other.

She smells like hairspray and sweat, but underneath I catch a hint of her tropical shampoo.

I already care too much, and the kicker is she's not mine to care for. Cross has more of a claim on her than I do.

Even if I wish it were otherwise...

I have nothing to give her.

Finding restraint I didn't know I had, I pull back to rest my forehead rests on hers. "Hales."

"Yeah." Her whisper is as quiet as mine in the dark.

We're sharing breath, and the twisted part is this is the closest I've felt to someone in years.

"I can't be what you want."

I expect her to protest or pull away.

Instead she smiles, the tiniest gesture in the blackness of the car, but I feel it in every part of me. "You already are."

And that, ladies and gentlemen, is the sound of a man who's well and truly fucked.

15

Tour exists in some surreal state, where the time either flies or drags.

The past four days have brought two shows. For once, it's not the shows I'm counting.

It's two sound checks, which I dodge.

It's four lunches I skip, throwing myself into writing that won't come.

It's eight interviews, each more frustrating than the last. Even though I know they serve a purpose, they feel like wasted time.

I want to shout that I'm retiring. That I'm grateful to my fans and I'd be even more grateful if they would accept my humble goodbye and promptly forget about me forever.

I owe Cross an answer tonight. There's no way he's forgotten.

If I tell him I'm out, he might take his secret to the grave. I can see him doing it just to spite me.

And even if Haley finds out—from me or someone else—he might simply deny her what she's owed. He has no obligation to provide for her, even if the thought leaves a metallic taste in my mouth.

Nothing's happened between me and Haley since Dallas. If I'm avoiding her, it's because that's the best possible way for this to play out.

When she leaves, I won't have the torture of resisting her.

I won't have any part of her.

"Jax, you have a visitor," Nina calls into my dressing room. "Technically two."

I turn to see the kid running at me. Red braids bounce at her shoulders, and her eyes are bright with eagerness. "Uncle Jax!"

My heart lifts even before I wrestle her into my arms, lifting and spinning her around. "Hey, squirt. Damn, you're getting heavy."

"You can't say that to girls," Grace chastises, right on Annie's heels.

"Which part, damn or heavy?" I shoot her a wink, setting Annie down and wrapping my sister in a hug.

"I'm glad you made it," I murmur against her hair, a few shades darker than mine.

"We did. Finally."

I want to escape. To take off and take Grace and Annie with me.

Until last week, that was the plan.

For the first time, something's holding me back.

I don't want to leave Haley.

Not like this.

"I'm glad you came tonight."

"Me too." Grace's smile is faint in the back seat of the Town Car after the show.

Annie's curled up and half-asleep against my shoulder.

The three of us had gone to the Olive Garden and gotten a private room there. Sometimes the most comforting things aren't limos or hotel rooms—they're breadsticks.

"You're pretty good," she says.

"I've picked up a few tricks over the years." The answer comes easily, but even I know it's not enough anymore.

I check on my niece. Annie's fast asleep between us.

"It always feels strange, seeing people cheer for you. Sometimes I want to scream at them that they don't know you at all. Like how you make the best chocolate chip cookies. How you used a nightlight until you were twelve. The way you played puppets with me when I was home alone instead of going out with your friends. That you tried to grow the world's most awful beard at sixteen and hunted down any remaining photos of it at seventeen."

I grin. "I'm glad those are the memories you have."

"I remember other things too. Us swiping food. And the games you'd play so I didn't realize we were dodging child services."

"Annie will never deal with that." It's a promise and a threat.

"Things are good. I told you."

I reach for Grace's arm and pull up the sleeve that's too long for the summer heat.

She sucks in a breath when I brush my thumb over her skin.

"Again?" I whisper hoarsely.

"Don't. Don't look at me like I'm weak. Like I'm in need of protection."

"It's getting worse."

She pulls down her sleeve. "I protected you too."

Anger burns in the back of my throat, along with regret and unfairness.

I turn her words over as the car pulls up in front of the airport, then I reach into my pocket and pull out a stack of bills. I tuck them into her hand, squeezing.

"Grace, I want you to leave. Pack a bag. Come on the tour with us. Hell, you don't need a bag, I'll buy you whatever you need. Rent you your own bus. Just don't go back there."

She blinks at me. “He’s my husband. Just because things get hard doesn’t mean you bail. He’s been there for me.”

When you haven’t. Her meaning is clear.

“I’m not letting her be raised like this. I’m not letting you go through it.”

“It’s not your choice. Whether you come home in two weeks or two years, it still won’t be.”

She tries to give the money back, but I fold her hand around it. Her shoulders cave in as she pockets it. “You might get to call the shots out here, but this is my life, big brother. Our lives.”

She brushes a hand over Annie’s hair, and the kid stirs. I sweep Annie into a fierce hug. She laughs sleepily.

“You call me every day, yeah?” I tell Annie.

She nods.

“You happy, squirt?”

Another nod, her smile in the dark. Guilt and helplessness tear through me.

“I’ll see you soon.” I don't know if the words are true.

Grace shifts out of the car, tugging Annie with her. I don’t want to let go. But I do.

16

HALEY

Haley,

I received your email about submitting the program to Spark. Upon review, I've decided it's not ready yet. Let's continue to work on it next semester and aim for next year's Spark competition.

I trust you'll understand.

Chris

It's the worst sleep I've had since being on tour.

Let's be honest—I haven't been sleeping for the better part of a week.

Since on or about the night Jax Jamieson groped me in a bowling alley.

Almost kissed me in his Town Car.

Then went back to ignoring me.

Okay, ignoring isn't quite the right word.

But the morning after he'd walked me to my room and I lay in bed all night debating whether I should walk my ass down the hall and beg him to put his mouth on me?

I didn't see him until he took the stage.

The next day was almost as bad.

Yesterday, at the lunch Jax did not partake in, I overheard from Mace that Jax's sister and niece were coming. For real this time.

And I didn't get to meet them.

Maybe he decided our friendship, if you can call it that, isn't worth tolerating the monster crush I have on him, I think.

But then, he didn't seem to hate it when he was going all braille on your boobs.

It's stupid to feel hurt. I get it intellectually. Jax is a musician, *the* musician, and I'd have to be a moron to expect anything from him.

Still, there's a tension in me I don't know how to resolve. I've tried, by throwing myself into work. Then by seeking relief late at night alone.

Any kind of relief.

This morning after getting up to Carter's delightful email, I shove my things into my bag and stab the button in the elevator.

I worked my ass off trying to finish this program, and he tossed it aside as though it didn't even matter.

Sure, I could've spent more time on it if I hadn't built the program for Jerry. Still, if Carter'd told me what more needed to be done instead of sending a dismissive email? I could've done it.

Now I'm already trying to come up with other solutions for tuition, but my mind jumps from one thing to another like cerebral Whac-A-Mole.

Part of me wants to talk to Jax. But as we pack up the bus, I realize Jax isn't the one I need to talk to.

A woman answers on the second ring. "Professor Carter's office."

I pause, tripped up by the unfamiliar voice. "Who is this?"

"Stacey. I'm Chris's research assistant. He's, ah, out this morning—" She giggles. "But he should be back this afternoon. Can I give him a message?"

"Yes. Can you tell him Haley Telfer called?"

"Haley Telfer? Sure."

"Hey, can I ask you something? How did you get this research assistant job?"

I can almost hear her shrug. "Chris just sent me an

email. Around the end of the semester. You know how these things are."

"Right. Thanks."

Betrayal tastes bitter in my throat.

Carter didn't want me as his research assistant because he had another option.

Clearly he spent enough time with Stacey that he didn't have time to spend on my program.

As I walk zombie-like to the bus, Nina calls the crew together.

Still no Jax.

"I have an important announcement. As you know, we're coming up on our final shows. But I've just gotten word that because we're selling out, the tour's being extended. Two months," Nina says.

Lita's gaze meets mine, but she doesn't look surprised.

"You all have the option of staying on after the final show or leaving," Nina continues. "But if you're leaving, I need to know now."

I don't move because every word from her mouth sounds impossible.

"Nina emailed me and my band this morning," Lita says. "It was Jax's call. And Cross's. I already told Nina we're going to Nashville tonight. She's lining up another band to open for the final two months, as well as the next two shows. You should come with us."

But I can't think about her offer because my attention's on the other bus, shining in my peripheral vision.

I go into my bag, dig out an item of clothing, and yank it over my head.

"Haley?" Lita asks. "Where are you going? We're getting ready to roll out."

"I'll be back faster than your center fielder can catch a pop fly," I mutter.

Then I stalk across the parking lot.

When I knock on the door of the other bus, Kyle's shaggy head appears. "What's up, Haley?"

Three pairs of Riot Act eyes watch me stalk toward the beaded curtain. It sings as I brush through it.

Jax looks up from his guitar. Today he's wearing a black T-shirt and jeans plus socks.

Without the stage makeup, with his hair falling over his face, he looks younger.

"Hales." His voice is wary. "You shouldn't be here."

"Yeah, well, a lot of things shouldn't happen," I inform him. "Good people shouldn't die young. Studios shouldn't reissue vinyl albums as cut from the master when they're not." I glance over my shoulder. "Kyle shouldn't answer the door wearing nothing but underwear."

He takes in my own clothing choice but doesn't comment. "The bus is leaving soon."

I ignore that. "Nina said you're extending your tour." A muscle in his jaw tics as he sets the guitar off to the side and shifts back. "So fill me in. You saw Grace and Annie last night, the people you live for, decided that was more than enough time with them and you might as well hang out on the road a little longer? That when you go back to Dallas, you'll be bored out of your skull?"

The tension in his body is a living thing as he rises from the couch and stares me down.

"I'm not explaining my choices to you. You wouldn't understand. Besides, I'll have plenty to do. I'll buy a house. The kind where the living room doesn't have wheels. And it'll have columns in the front like I'm Julius Caesar." Jax drags a finger along the door frame around the curtain, lazily following the path with his gaze. "Ten bedrooms."

His masculine scent should be a warning, but I step closer. "Why not twelve?"

He shrugs. "Sure. Fourteen."

I turn away, inspecting the photos mounted to the sides of the bus. Dozens of them. Some with the band, but more with his family.

I spin on my heel. "A pool?" I ask.

His gaze narrows. "The size of a football field."

"Do you even swim?"

"Like a fish."

The bus lurches forward, yanking me off balance. Jax grabs me by the arms to stop me from falling.

Now we're committed, because we're rolling down the road. I'm on Jax's bus and I know it's a bad idea. His expression says he does too.

"You can't be on here."

"Are you going to throw me out the window? At least

let me grab a pillow off the couch. I can take the same one as last time."

His fingers dig into my skin through the fabric of the sweatshirt.

"Why are you wearing that."

"It was a gift," I remind him, my teeth grinding together as I tug on the ends of the laces through the hood. "I thought that's how gifts worked. Once they're yours, you get to use them however you want. Unless I'm wrong about that too."

When Jax's eyes darken in confusion, I know he sees the tears stinging behind my eyes. *Great.*

"What are you talking about, Hales."

This isn't why I came here. But now that Jax is holding me—okay, not quite in his arms, but between his hands—I can't lie to him.

"Carter didn't want to work with me. He wanted some girl to fawn over him." I swallow the thick feeling in my throat. "He's older and experienced and patronizing, and apparently that's my type. Which sucks because there's no way in hell a man like that would want me. For anything."

Jax stares at me like I'm speaking another language. "That's bullshit, Hales."

It's not the warning in his eyes that does me in or the way his muscles flex under the faded T-shirt. It's not the working of his jaw or the lines around his mouth or the way he stands up for me even to myself.

It's all of them.

"Jax?"

"Yeah."

"Did I do something wrong? The other night, I mean." I hate that I'm asking the question, but I need to know.

Now that we're so close, I need to know what the hell happened.

"No." He curses, his gaze working over mine. "No, you didn't do a damn thing wrong. You couldn't if you tried."

I risk a glance at his face, and his expression has me sucking in a breath.

He doesn't look angry. He looks contrite, and something I can't quite read.

"How long has it been since you touched someone?" Jax's voice is barely audible over the running noise of the bus.

"A while."

"How about since you wanted to?" God, his voice is low. If it were a color, it would be black.

I reach up to where his hair's fallen over his forehead. I tuck it back, careful not to brush his skin when I do. "Forever."

My fingers itch, and before I can stop them, my hands stretch out to graze his abs through the thin T-shirt.

The muscles there twitch under my touch, and when he drags in a rough breath, his eyes lowering to half-mast, I know what it's like to be powerful.

That's when I realize what's in his expression.

It's longing. The kind of singular wanting that comes

from looking at something you can't ever have.

My touch drags up Jax's chest, exploring it the same way.

It's broad and hard, and I'm suddenly remembering how he looked when I caught a glimpse of him shirtless in his dressing room. I picture the lines and indentations as I touch him, and every brush of my hands on his body thrills me in a way I never expected.

"What's wrong?" I ask at his rough intake of breath. "You get touched by strangers every day."

My fingers continue their hypnotic path. The hem of my shirt tickles my back as I rise up on my toes so I can reach his shoulders.

"There's just one problem, Hales," he murmurs. His voice is every bit as dark as mine, as if maybe he's as lost in this spell as I am.

We're close enough his breath reaches my face when my gaze lifts to meet his. "What's that?"

His hands slide up my arms, his fingers threading in my hair and holding my head in a way that's strangely sweet and possessive at once, tipping my face up to his.

"You're not a stranger."

He smells like sandalwood and shampoo, and when my nose bumps his chin, I can't help the strangled little sound that escapes my throat.

Through my lashes, I see his mouth, firm and parted.

Full of possibility for a heartbeat. Two.

Then his lips crush down on mine.

Every cell in my body comes alive at once at the feel of his mouth rubbing, teasing, parting.

My hands band around his wrists to push him away. To get some space.

He's having none of it.

Jax isn't gentle. He's a hurricane, designed to wreak maximum devastation as he wakes up every nerve ending in my body.

He grabs my sweatshirt, raising his mouth long enough for me to gasp a breath as he yanks the fabric between us and over my head and back, trapping my arms in the sleeves behind me.

I'm struggling, but every move just brings me into closer contact with him. His mouth, his chest, his hands.

It's tearing me apart. I want to scream with it.

Instead of struggling, I go still. Force myself to focus on the gentle friction of his lips. His tongue.

In that moment, I find what I'm looking for.

Not the discordance, but the tension before the resolution.

We're a hook ready to split into a chorus.

A crowd moments from erupting...

I realize he's right.

We're not strangers.

I feel the moment my resistance dissolves, the second I kiss him back, my lips sliding under his. My tongue exploring his mouth.

Jax groans low in his throat, and it's the hottest sound I've ever heard in my life.

I struggle to get out of the sweatshirt, feeling like an Olympic champ when it falls away.

My hands find his jaw, his hair, needing to touch him. To remind myself this is real.

A bump in the road jars me, but it only makes him tighten his hold. Jax backs me against the side of the bus and slants his mouth at a new angle. His tongue finds mine, and damn if he isn't even more eloquent like this than he is with words.

He uses his hips to wedge mine against the side of the bus.

And holy damn, I'm lost.

Kierkegaard didn't know shit, because the feeling of looking over a cliff? It's got nothing on the feel of being kissed by Jax Jamieson. Being the center of his universe.

How long we kiss is anyone's guess.

In my head, it's a moment.

In my heart, it's forever.

When he pulls back, I can still taste him. My pulse hammers through my chest as my fingers brush across my lips.

Yup, still there.

Still tingling.

I bend down, retrieving the sweatshirt at my feet. There's definitely no need for it. I think I'm sweating.

But I hug it to my chest as I sneak a look up at Jax.

He stares at me, breathing hard, like he's trying to make sense of what just happened.

"I'm totally getting fired for that, aren't I?" I whisper.

His half smile pulls into a grin that melts me. "Come on. It was worth it."

A sound like rain at my back makes me jump.

"Are you kids going to fuck?" Kyle drawls. "Because if not, I need someone to battle on *Guitar Hero*."

Jax and I exchange a look. Then Jax rubs his hands over his face. "Put some damned pants on, and we'll talk."

17

HALEY

"Whoa. Twenty-one and you don't look a day over eighteen."

The familiar voice has me looking up from my spot in the booth during final sound check an hour from curtain in New Orleans. "Serena?!"

My friend drops her bag and runs at me, squealing.

I squeeze the air from her lungs. "What are you doing here?"

"Someone showed up at my door with a backstage pass and a plane ticket." She pouts. "I figured I could clear my schedule."

"Who would..." My gaze lands on the stage where Jax and his band are getting set up, and my heart expands.

Serena follows my gaze. "Damn. You have this tour thing down. Not only do you have Carter wrapped around your finger, but Jax Jamieson too?"

I shake it off. "First, there's no fingering of any kind.

Second, you were right about Carter. He hired someone else."

Her jaw drops. "No fucking way."

"Yeah. He also didn't submit my program for Spark."

"Guess I'd better start dancing again to pay for rent," she jokes.

I groan.

"Fine. What about that?" Her hair flips as she jerks her head toward the stage.

I glance around before lowering my voice. "He might have kissed me on his bus yesterday."

"YES!" she squeals. "Need more condoms?"

"No. But I do have the option to stay on tour for another two months."

"In that case, you should definitely keep the condoms." Serena winks and I roll my eyes. "I knew you'd crack this whole touring thing. In fact, I figured you were on to something and thought I might apply for a part-time job in PR at Wicked during the school year."

"Really?"

"I bought internet and spent the whole flight here doing research. Looking through press files. Shannon Cross is a total hottie, by the way."

"He's too old for you."

"Watch it, pot." I shake my head. "Plus, there is no such thing. I need to show you something." She holds up her phone with a picture of a dozen or so people wearing cocktail clothes. It looks like a gala of some sort. "Anyone look familiar?"

My spine stiffens. "That's my mom."

"It says the picture is from an event a decade ago."

"Why would she be in a picture taken at a party for Wicked?"

"That's a crazy coincidence."

"Yeah. Crazy."

Something tickles the back of my mind, and I reach for my phone.

I flip through the photos. The last few weeks include ones of Kyle doing a cameo at an anti-fur rally, Mace holding up his finished Death Star, and Lita posing with a cutout of one of her fantasy baseball pitchers whom she's sworn she'll marry once she retires.

I scroll back to the picture I took of the photo in Jerry's album. The woman who bore a vague resemblance to a woman I knew more than anyone.

I'd been meaning to look into it, but it had fallen down my list of priorities.

"Shit. Did she ever mention him?"

"No." My heart stops. "Can you just... stay a minute. I'll be right back."

I grab her phone and make my way up the aisle toward the stage and find Jax in the wings, bent over his guitar. "Hey."

"Hi." He looks around, then back at me. His eyes

darken, and I wonder if he's remembering yesterday's kiss too.

But we're not alone here, and now's not the time.

"Thank you," I say at last. "For the birthday present."

Jax's mouth twitches. "You're welcome. I tried to have her wrapped, but apparently it's a liability issue." I can't quite find it in me to laugh, and he picks up on that immediately. "What's wrong."

"Listen, I need to ask you something. I know you hate Cross, but you also know him better than anyone." I take a deep breath. "Do you know the woman in this picture?"

I show him the one from ten years ago, study his face as he scans the image.

"It would've been around the time you started at Wicked."

He shakes his head, slow.

"It's my mom, Jax. Apparently Cross knew her, or she knew Wicked. As far as I know, she never worked there, and I would've been ten when this was taken. But I can't help wondering if he might know who my father is."

Jax is watching me. I've never seen him so still.

As if in slow motion, he takes off his guitar, folding the neck strap as he lays it on the table next to him.

"Jax." My voice sounds tinny in my ears. "What aren't you telling me?"

He rubs a hand over his neck. "I don't know what to say."

"Try."

"Haley... he knows who your father is. He knows because he *is* your father."

The noise around me fades to nothing.

My brows pull together because nothing's making sense right now. "What? For a second I thought you said Cross is my father." I laugh, but he doesn't follow my lead.

"Oh wow. You actually think he is. Why..." I shove a hand through my hair. "Why would you think that?"

"Because he told me."

I picture the cool, calculating man in the suit who'd watched me the day I went into his office. There's no way we have a connection. Especially not one like that.

But the expression on Jax's face tells me it's true.

Jax reaches out, but I back away.

"You *knew*," I whisper. "And you didn't tell me."

Someone hollers his name from across the stage, and he curses. "We'll talk about this later."

I turn on my heel and start back to the sound booth. The seats blur into smudges as I stalk down the row.

My mind runs on logic, but it's like some tiny, desperate part of me has taken the wheel and I've jumped the tracks.

Shit, even my metaphors are chaos right now.

I can't help it. Over and over, it runs through my head.

Jax knew.

Why didn't he tell me?

And then,

Is that why I'm here?

That's why I was chosen over two hundred applicants.

Cross picked me.

When did Jax know?

Did he know when he sat across from me in that car and threw his Snickers bar out the window?

When he took me bowling and we talked in the back of the car?

He sure as hell knew when he kissed me.

The knot in my stomach grows into a darkness that seeps into every muscle. Every pore.

"Your friend Jerry said the ticket holders are getting let in soon." Through my blurry vision, Serena's face comes into focus. "Haley, what's wrong?"

It takes everything in me to keep my voice level. "I'm wrong. I was wrong about everything."

18

The first time I set foot on the stage of an arena, I was terrified.

But the same thing that scared the shit out of me then became the thing that made me invincible.

The audience. Every pair of eyes trained on you, every person invested in what you're about to do for them, create with them, makes you stronger.

Being onstage in front of twenty thousand people is like being immortal.

I don't care what you're guilty of. All of it melts away for a few hours here, under the lights.

Each night I'm Icarus, flying into the sun.

Too high to see that every move I make brings me closer to my own destruction.

At least that's how it's always been.

Tonight, I feel her eyes on me from the booth.

Though I can't see her, as the curtain rises and we break into our opening number, I pretend I can.

She's judging me.

She deserves to.

We blaze through the set list. Each song gets all of me because holding something back would be a bigger crime.

At the end, I turn to Mace and mutter in his ear.

His eyes widen. "Seriously?"

He goes to Kyle, who locks eyes with me, but I'm already turning back to my mic stand.

You're standing on the edge of a cliff, looking down into the abyss, and you're twice afraid.

Once for the knowledge that you could fall.

And once for the knowledge that the choice of whether to stay or whether to jump is yours.

The arena's silent as I wrap my hands around the mic, and for the first time in a long time, I'm exposed.

"There are moments that define us, for better and for worse. This song reminds me of the darkest time in my life. A time I wanted to leave behind. But the reason I'm playing it is a bright one." I swallow. "A hopeful one."

Cries start up, but I ignore them as I do something I haven't done in ten years.

I play "Inside."

And it's not for my band, or the fans.

It's for *her*.

I told Cross I would do the extra two months of shows because I've been dealing with the fallout from Grace and

Annie for years. I may not be able to make up for that, but for the first time, I have hope that I can.

Especially if she's here.

The crowd deafens me as we finish the number and leave the stage.

Mace calls after me, but I ignore him, winding through the backstage corridors to my dressing room.

There's a girl in there, and for a split second, I imagine she's Haley.

She can't be. She's taller with blond hair. Plus she's dressed up.

"Jax."

"Who are—"

"Serena. Haley's friend."

I notice the backstage pass swinging around her neck. "Right. Where's Haley?"

"She left."

My eyes fall closed. "Left for where?"

When she doesn't answer, I glare at her.

"You can't scare me with that look. I'm going to tell you because I think you guys should talk but not because you look like you'll kill me if I don't." She takes a breath. "She's going to Nashville. Tonight."

I spin on my heel and stalk down the hall.

19

HALEY

Two months later

"There you go, darlin'."

My fingers grab the fifty the second it hits the sticky counter. The money is soft, frayed, as if it's done this a million times before. "Thanks. I'll be right back."

"No change." The guy flashes me a grin, and I make change in the register before putting the rest in the tip jar. "Since it's windin' down in here, why don't we have a drink?"

I round the bar to put the stools on tables and collect the salt and pepper shakers, flashing the automatic smile I've learned in the last two months. "I'm a little out of my league drinking that bourbon."

He follows, and the hairs on the back of my neck stand

up. His gaze crawls up my legs under the short denim skirt that's practically a uniform here in Nashville.

I pray he's not going to do something stupid.

My manager's in the back office, talking to our bouncer.

Or possibly doing something else, which I definitely don't begrudge them doing because they got married last year and have had zero time together.

I should've closed up twenty minutes ago but got lost doing dishes.

"Sweetheart, I been in here three times this week. Ain't never seen you with a man."

I sense it before I feel him graze my back. Before I smell the booze on him. "Then your vision's 20/20."

"Maybe you like to play hard to get." He leers and reaches for me.

But before his hand grabs my ass through my jean skirt, the industrial salt shaker in my hand catches him in the junk hard enough his eyes bulge.

The beauty of the salt shaker. Small enough to be used as a defensive weapon. Sturdy enough not to break when you can a guy with it.

He writhes on the floor, adopting the fetal position like it's his job.

"Hey!" Andre's baritone hollers from the back doorway.

The guy pulls himself up and slinks out the door. I lock it behind him.

"You okay Haley?" Andre's thick brows draw together on his forehead. He's lost his cowboy hat somewhere in the thirty minutes since I saw him last, and his hair's a mess.

"Peachy." I say it with more confidence than I feel.

He studies me, hard, but decides not to press it. "I'll clean up in the back if you finish up here. And don't forget this." He fishes in the cash register where an envelope's wedged in the side and hands it to me. "Your bonus."

"Thanks."

He retreats with a salute and Lita sidles up. "Last night in Nashville."

"You guys were great," I say as I grab the last of the salt shakers and bring them behind the bar to refill. "Sorry the Dodgers lost."

"S'okay. Kershaw's killing it on the season. Which means I still have the best pitching rotation in the league."

Lita looks pointedly at my bare legs, wiggling her eyebrows. "I see you working it over there."

"Two months in this place has given me a whole new outlook on life." I lift the hem of my shirt, sniffing. "Plus clothes that'll never stop smelling like rye."

I pop open my laptop behind the bar. "I chose my classes for the fall semester. Midnight tonight"—it's after two now—"we're supposed to get our final schedule."

"You have enough for tuition?"

"Yup. Thanks to my miniskirt." She laughs.

I scroll down the page, scanning for the confirmation.

"What the..." I start. Lita peers over my shoulder. "It says I'm not enrolled."

There must be a mistake. I submitted the report on my co-op term on schedule. Early, actually.

I click through the webpage to the co-op section. There're a bunch of green checks, and at the bottom...and a red X where it says "employer verification."

"What's happening?" Lita asks.

"I have no idea."

I pull out my phone and dig up a number I've never had to use. It rings twice.

"Hi, Nina."

"Haley?"

"Sorry to call so late."

"The best time for everything is the present. In fact, it's the only time there is." Muffled scratching comes over the line.

"My letter—the one confirming my co-op term was completed—it looks like the college didn't receive it."

I hold my breath, praying she'll say something like, "Namaste, it'll be fixed by morning."

What she says instead shatters all my hopes.

"Cross hired you. It's him you need to call."

A stone settles in my stomach.

Cross is the last person I want to talk to.

Because a major record exec is my father and I haven't decided what the hell to do about it.

"Right," I murmur, realizing she's still waiting for a response. "How's the tour?"

"Insane. Riot Act announced this is their final month of concert dates. All the crazies are coming out." I heard about that announcement. Because I have a news alert on the tour. Stalkerish? Maybe.

I shove my hands in my pockets. "Nina… is the everything okay?"

A pause. "We beefed up security. Jax still has all his body parts, far as I know. We're in Atlanta tomorrow if you want to see for yourself."

"Haley, I have to run. We're getting some spec changes for the show tomorrow. Then I need to get in some meditation time so I don't accidentally kill someone. Namaste."

"Namaste," I echo as Nina hangs up. I meet Lita's clear blue gaze over the tip jar she's splitting into piles for the servers who worked tonight.

"You're thinking about something, and it's not calling Cross," Lita guesses.

Sleeping on someone's couch for two months has a way of breaking down walls between you. But I haven't been able to bring myself to tell Lita that Jax knew about Cross.

That being around Jax stirred up all these feelings I never thought I'd feel for anything that wasn't music.

That leaving hasn't brought the relief I'd hoped for. Instead, I've lain awake more nights than not, wondering if I did the right thing.

"It's nothing. It's just...Jax and I used to talk. I know this sounds insane, but I feel like I got him."

"Normally, I'd say that's completely insane," she agrees. "But Jax doesn't make time for just anyone." I turn that over in my mind as she hands me the stack of bills that's my share. "But? What does it matter. You're going to go back to Philly, and classes, and listening to vinyl or whatever you do at home."

Lita's words echo dully in my chest.

My fingers inch toward the keys of my laptop. Before I can stop myself, I'm pulling up a ticket resale site.

"Damn." Even the nosebleeds are more than my monthly groceries.

Lita drums her fingers on the bar, her mouth pursed. "I bet he'd get you a pass in a heartbeat."

"That would mean telling him."

I reach into my pocket and open the envelope from Andre. A thick stack of twenties peers up at me.

"If you're not going to talk to Jax, why go at all?"

I suck in a breath as my finger hovers over the buy button. "Closure."

Want more rock stars, brainy girls, best friends, and band mates? Keep reading to find out whether Jax and Haley find their way back to each other when the tour wraps and the lights go down in Bad Girl....

Rockstars don't chase college students.

But Jax Jamieson's never followed the rules.
I thought I knew Jax's secrets.
I was wrong.
When the fans go home and the lights fade to black, it's just me and him and the people we left behind.
I want to escape, until I realize...

We can do a lot in the dark.

BAD GIRL

WICKED PART 2

1

HALEY

For four hours on the bus to Atlanta, my earbuds plugged in and some new indie act providing a subtle soundtrack to the passing scenery, my brain's been going full-tilt. The would've waltz, the should've samba, and the could've cha-cha.

Maybe I shouldn't have run on my birthday.

Maybe Jax had a good reason for not telling me about Cross.

Maybe I should've texted him, called him, something.

I give myself until the bus pulls into the station to indulge my doubts. Then I cut it off.

Tonight's about reminding myself I did the right thing, not rehashing every decision I've made in my life like a washing machine on spin cycle.

I leave my bags in a locker at the bus depot and take my backpack with me to the venue. Find my seat near the back in the electric darkness.

Around me, people talk, drink, and gossip. Some of it's about Jax. It feels as if they're talking about a friend behind his back.

Somewhere in the midst of the opening act, I notice the buzzing. Not around me, but inside me. As though something's trying to get out.

When the changeover happens, it intensifies.

After two months bartending in Nashville, my feet are calloused from the heels, my hand-eye coordination's improved tenfold, and I'm tanned from spending my few days off outside with Lita.

I'm more exposed, but I'm tougher too.

Or so I thought.

Now, I realize I'm wrong. I shouldn't be here.

I push my way out of the row until I make it to the aisle. But before I can get to the exit door, the place comes down.

The opening line of one of Jax's classic hits splits the screaming, uttered in a voice that haunts my dreams.

I can't stop myself from turning.

The black button-down with short sleeves shows off his tattoos. Faded jeans I think I've touched worship his long, hard legs. He's a hundred feet away, but I can smell him. My fingers itch for the feeling of his body through the thin T-shirt.

If there ever was a man who looked like he was fucking a microphone on stage, it's Jax. Not because he's overtly sexual, but because Jax Jamieson is *vital.*

It's the first word that comes to mind when I see him because he's like life itself. So real it hurts.

His hair falls across his face, and I'd swear my eyes lock with his.

Of course when you're onstage, you can't see anything through the lights. But there are techniques to make it feel as though you're connecting with the audience, and Jax works them all.

If I wanted closure, there's no way in hell I'm getting it tonight.

He's on fire. This is his third-to-last show, and he's selling it, every second, as though he already misses the stage.

For that moment, I'm just a fan.

And I hate that he's leaving.

After the show, the energy dissipates, a slow leak like the crowd pouring out the venue doors.

I stay behind. My gaze finds the sound booth. The sight of the man there, stooped and gray, warms me.

Until I see him reaching for an unfamiliar piece of equipment and hefting it in his arms.

I make my way toward the booth, tripping past the last of the escaping fans in my hurry. "Jerry! Put that down."

He sets down the piece of digital equipment with a

thud and straightens. “Miss Telfer.” He smiles. “Help me with this, will you? I need to get it out to the truck.”

For a moment, I wonder if he’s even realized I haven’t been on tour.

“Why don’t you call Nina to send someone?” I look down toward the stage. The band is long gone, but the crew is packing up.

“No!” The sharpness of his tone startles me. “This is my new toy. I won’t let those animals put their hands on it. Take it to the truck for me?”

I hold in my sigh. I should be on my way back to the bus station to take the overnight home, but the look on Jerry’s face has me caving. I loop the cords over my arm and lift the box. Thanks to bartending, I’m stronger than I was.

“Where’s your new helper?” I ask as he walks toward the stage door with me.

“I told Nina I didn’t need one.”

My eyes widen. “You didn’t.”

“I had you. And now I have your program.” He says it with pride. “I’m better than new.”

Guilt creeps in as Jerry waves at the security guard to let him know that I’m with him.

The exterior door opens, and I’m deafened.

There are fans. Not dozens, but hundreds. Maybe thousands.

Security’s trying to keep it under control, but they and the barricade seem to be fighting a losing battle.

I pick my way toward the truck, trying not to trip though I can't see my feet.

I drift too close to the roped-off mob, and there's tugging on Jerry's equipment.

Dammit.

I wrestle it back.

Some girl manages to shove over one of the posts holding up the rope, and another lunges over the barricade.

It's a stampede as one after another flows through the lowered barrier.

A phone hits me. Next, a cardboard cutout of Jax scratches the side of my face. I can't block them because my hands are full, but I tilt and fall, clutching Jerry's damned toy to keep it safe.

Something sharp hits me on the head, and my mouth falls open in shock.

Numbness washes over me as if I'm on a boat being gently rocked by the waves.

Until I feel hands clamp around my arms.

Don't fucking touch me. I want to scream it, but I can't.

My stomach rolls. "Let go," I moan instead.

The grip gets tighter, and it feels like coils binding my skin. Ropes burning as I twist and try to escape.

The screaming gets louder. I'm lifted into someone's arms.

Hands are everywhere.

I fight them, or try to, until a familiar voice makes me give in.

"Shut up, Hales."

Those muttered words, too close to my ear, are the last thing I hear before the world goes black.

2

"Is she bleeding?"

"You need to splint it."

"How the hell do you know?"

"I won *Doctor Who: The Adventure Games* in like six days."

"That's a video game, asshole. And also not a real doctor."

I ignore Kyle and Brick bickering behind me.

The towel I grabbed has stage tape on one end, and I rip it off as I run the thing under cold water.

Drip marks stain the floor as I return to the dressing room, step over the coffee table, and crouch in front of the figure in the armchair.

Her chin's almost on her skinned knees, her arms looped around legs under a jean skirt I had to adjust when I set her down. The Converse sneakers haven't changed.

I brush the hair from Haley's face and press the towel to the scratch on her forehead as she hisses.

"Serves you right," I murmur. "Next time, leave crowd-surfing to the professionals."

"Never seen your firefighter routine, Jax." This from Brick, but I don't rise to the bait. "It's going to be all over the internet tomorrow."

Haley blinks, her lashes revealing brown eyes with green flecks. "Really?"

"Both of you are," Mace weighs in from where he's leaning against the wall in the corner. "What's with the cameo?"

"I heard this was the last chance to see Riot Act live." Her ankles cross in front of her as she leans back, shifting to get more comfortable as her eyes open for a moment only to drift closed again. "Had to come and get my chest signed."

Brick chuckles behind me, and Kyle sprints across the room. "I'll get a Sharpie."

I lean in to check the towel—there's hardly any blood on it, but I find a clean spot and press it back to her head.

"Already signed your chest," I murmur, low enough only she can hear.

Her shoulders twitch. The only sign she's heard me, but it's enough. My gaze lingers on the bare skin of her shoulders, and I have the random urge to cover her up.

Especially when Kyle appears at my side, bending over.

"What the hell are you doing?" I demand.

"The woman wants an autograph. Who am I to deny her?"

I turn toward him, and the look on my face has him lifting his hands in surrender. "I'll just leave this here." Kyle caps the pen and sets it on the table behind me.

"You staying away from the diner lobster, Mace?" Haley asks, looking past my shoulder.

"Try to stick to diner crab," he replies easily.

My mouth twitches, but it's not my guitarist I'm looking at. It's her.

I'm being studied by big hazel eyes framed in dark lashes, and I wish we were alone right now.

I don't know what I'd do with her. Strangle her, maybe. Kiss her, definitely.

From the look on her face, like she's overwhelmed, maybe she wants that too.

Or maybe she just hit her head.

"So Riot Act's announced their retirement," Haley says, breaking the silence. "I'm surprised no one's chained themselves to your tour bus."

"Madame Tussaud wrote to see if I could sit for my wax statue," I tell her.

She laughs, and I want to ask a million things.

How she is. If she's still pissed at me.

Whether she kept my hoodie.

It's the least appropriate thought right now, especially since I don't need a reminder of the time I yanked it off her. When I'd channeled every ounce of frustration into kissing her, swallowing her gasps as my tongue wrecked havoc with hers.

"What's that?" she asks, pointing to the braided bracelet on my wrist.

"Grace's kid made it," Mace says, dropping onto the sofa behind me.

"Annie?" Haley looks between us.

Before I can tell him to shut up, he plows on. "The night you left, she called to say her mom was missing. He flew to Dallas to find her."

Haley's expression fills with alarm. She shifts forward, wringing the towel in her hands. "What happened? Is she okay? Is Annie—"

"Grace'd checked into the hospital." The look on her face tells me she understands why. "But they're going to be fine now. They're at the hotel. They're finishing up the tour with me."

"So, she left her husband." Her voice is hollow with shock.

I nod, picturing my sister's battered body in the hospital bed. The anger and resentment that fill my gut are the kind that never really leave.

"I wish you'd told me."

It's intimate, what she says and how she says it.

Kyle catches my eye from where he's packing his bag near the door.

I scratch at my chin because I'm still in stage makeup. I

force myself not to let on how much her low voice affects me. "You were a tech on my tour for a month. We're ships passing."

If it sounds callous, it's not. It's reality.

Haley and I don't have a future.

We don't even have a past.

All we have is a stolen kiss and the kind of fragile trust that's made to be broken. By me, by her, by the world, until there's less than nothing left.

"I'm going to take this out to the bus," Mace says, shifting off the couch. I don't look to see what he's talking about.

"Kyle, you wanna come with?"

"I want to hear about Haley's summer."

I close my eyes because I'm really ready to shove my band out the door and slam it in their faces right now. At least Mace knows it.

"Kyle? I'll let you show me how to make a Patreon donation for that wildlife artist."

"For real? Let's do it."

Then they're gone and it's just the two of us.

Somehow it feels like there's more space between us rather than less.

Haley breaks the silence first. "If we're passing ships, what's with the dramatic rescue? I'm not on your tour anymore. You don't owe me anything."

"I don't like seeing you get hurt."

Her eyes darken. "Then why didn't you tell me about

Cross?"

I wonder if she's turned it over in her head as many times as I have the last two months.

I stare back at her. "I don't like seeing you get hurt," I repeat.

Since I made the deal with Cross to protect her, he's been silent.

Still... just because Haley and I won't be sleeping down the hall from one another doesn't mean I can't keep an eye on her.

She looks good despite the bump on the head that I'm pretty sure will resolve. Her sharp eyes still make me want to know what's going on behind them. The curves under her clothes are still seriously distracting. Her full lips have me wanting to see her smile or laugh or...

"School must be starting soon," I say, breaking the stillness. "You're going back to Philly?"

"Tonight." She glances up at the clock on the wall behind me. "I should probably get going." She makes no move to rise, just huffs out a little breath as she looks at me.

She's changed since she left. She's grown up. Where she would spill everything at my feet before, she's not going to now.

Endings suck no matter how you slice them. Our first was bad enough. It seems cruel to have another.

But life's cruel.

"Say something, Hales." I murmur it under my breath.

Her mouth twitches at the corner. "What kind of something."

"Anything. Let me in your head."

"Okay." Her cheeks flush, and that hint of embarrassment has me leaning in. "I had a dream you came after me. You walked in the door of the honky-tonk where I was working, and you told me you'd fucked up and you were sorry." She frowns. "And then you took the stage next to Prince and played the ukulele. That's when I should've known it was a dream."

A chuckle escapes. "You should've known it was a dream because no one just walks in the door at the Rockabilly. There's a line a mile long."

"You've been there?" Her eyes widen.

"Marty's place. She stocks some good bourbon."

"And Andre's. They got married."

"Huh." Sharing people in common makes it feel like we haven't spent the last two months apart.

It's all pretend. Because she's going back to her life and I'm—finally—going back to mine.

I don't know what to do here.

Because I don't, I stand.

She rises too.

And if that's not the perfect metaphor for how we are, I don't know what is.

This girl's my shadow. We're bound together by a thread that won't let go even though we're opposites in so many ways—she's bright, I'm dark; she's new, I'm jaded; she's curious, I'm closed off.

But from the second I noticed her, I can't unsee her.

"Haley."

We both turn to see Nina standing at the door, a knowing look on her face.

"I heard you made an impression on the crowd. Or they made one on you." Her face tightens with concern. "You okay?"

"Good as new. And I promise I'm not suing anyone."

"Good girl. Let me walk you out."

I shake my head. "I can do it."

Nina holds up her hands. "Jax? You go out there again and there's going to be an actual riot."

I wonder if that's the real reason or if Nina wants to keep us apart.

Regardless, Haley steps forward first. "Well, it was a hell of a show."

"Best ever?" I study her face.

Her expression shifts. "Yeah. Best ever." She swallows. "Goodbye, Jax."

"See you, Hales."

Before I can react, Haley closes the distance between us. Her arms wind around my neck.

Her scent washes over me, and I close my eyes. I've done two gigs in Hawaii, and I swear she smells like the air there.

I can feel Nina's gaze on us.

Fuck Nina.

I wrap my arms around Haley's waist, pulling her harder against me even though I shouldn't.

"So, you knew where I was, but you never thought about coming to check it out, huh?" she murmurs against my neck, low enough only I can hear. Her voice is a tease, stroking down my spine.

"If I'd chased your ass down"—her hair tickles my lips, and I bury my nose in her—"I wouldn't have come back."

I'm the one to step back first. When I do, I see a wry smile pulling at her mouth.

That's good.

Because it's better if we both think I'm joking.

3

HALEY

Getting into my apartment takes longer than usual. The key turns in the lock, but as I lean against the door, it won't open.

I shove, and something gives.

"Roomie!" Serena's voice sounds far away. "It's about time."

I glance at the chair that'd been blocking the way. "You barricaded yourself in here?"

"Not me. Scrunchie. He's been exercising a lot of independence lately. The door's open for even a minute, and he slips out."

My roommate, dressed in a crop top and skinny jeans that show off her naturally flat stomach, crosses to the black-and-white mop in the middle of the living room floor. "I took him to the dog park the other day, and everyone looked at me like I was nuts. I mean, he doesn't spray. Not that I would de-scent a skunk, but when the little guy came into the shelter and needed a home, I couldn't say no." She lifts Scrunchie to her face, making kissing noises.

Scrunchie maintains his trademark apathy.

He's probably the only male on campus who can in the face of Serena's affections.

"Right."

"But you're back now. For good." She sets Scrunchie down and straightens.

"Yeah. I'm back." I drop my bag and hug her.

We talked almost every day, but seeing her for the first time since she showed up at Jax's show two months ago, I realize how much I missed her.

"You look good," she says, pulling back and doing a little twirl thing with her fingers. I turn obediently. "Damn, waitressing was good for your ass."

"It was good for my bank account too."

"You mean I can stop taking gentleman callers to pay the milkman?" She bats her eyelashes.

"You haven't told me a thing about gentleman callers lately. Which means you have one and you like him," I point out.

Serena crosses to the kitchen and pulls out two glasses and something from our booze cabinet. "I like him. I haven't decided if I'll keep him."

"You decided to keep Scrunchie after one date."

"True. This guy's in a frat, and he's obsessed with his

own face. But it is a great face, and he eats me with it. So..."

I shudder.

"Haley. I swear to God oral sex is not the apocalyptic event you think is it."

"Agree to disagree."

"Have you ever tried it?"

She sounds so aghast I need to defend my position, stat. "I can't get past the part where a guy is looking at you down there, not to mention sucking on you like a damned milkshake. Call me crazy."

Serena tosses her hair, indignant. "Whoever did that to you should be shot. That's B-minus technique at best. But you find a guy who knows how to do it..." She makes a noise low in her throat I wish I could unhear "... you'll be converted."

"I'm a pretty staunch atheist."

I take one of the cups she offers and sniff it. Definitely vodka.

It's two in the afternoon, and I'm about to point that out until she speaks again.

"What if it was Jax Jamieson?"

What the hell? It's five o'clock somewhere.

I take a long drink from the cup, wincing as I swallow. "I'm probably never going to see Jax again. If there even was the beginning of anything that would conceivably lead to milkshake slurping, it's over."

"First, never say milkshake slurping again. EVER.

Second..." The laughter that starts in her belly has me wondering if she's already had a few. "It's *so* not over."

"What are you talking about?"

"Let me spell it out for you: your dad is a huge record exec who happens to own Jax Jamieson."

I roll my eyes. "Jax is retiring."

"Artists don't cut ties with a label. The contacts your father has—"

"Cross."

"Sorry. The contacts Cross has, the money, the power? You don't turn your back on that. Even if you want to. You think you'll never see Jax Jamieson again? You're deluded."

I turn that over. I'm afraid to believe her because she might be blunt, but she's a silver-lining-girl at heart. There's every possibility I won't see Jax again except on TV or YouTube. And even then, maybe he'll recede into obscurity and stop doing media altogether.

Or maybe she's right.

Maybe he'll show up when I least expect him. Looking hot as sin with that smirk that says he knows all my secrets.

Because really, he does.

That low-grade pulsing in my gut, like a bass reverb you can't quite kick, starts up again.

Seeing him in Atlanta was totally unplanned and equally thrilling. I'm glad we weren't alone because how the hell did he get hotter?

The temptation to throw myself at him was almost impossible to resist.

"Speaking of daddy dearest," she goes on, bringing me back, "when are you going to see him?"

I carry my cup-o-relief to the couch, stepping over Scrunchie, who likes to press himself up against the front like a fluffy pancake, and dropping onto the cushion. Serena follows me, perching on the arm at the other end. "I was going to say never. But now I'm thinking tomorrow."

As I explain what happened with my school enrolment, her eyes get progressively wider until she toes me with her sock foot.

"No way. You got kicked out of school?"

I hold up a hand. "Not kicked out! I'm facing a minor administrative hurdle."

But she's not fooled for a second. "They kicked your ass out of school. Haley Telfer—or is it Cross now?—you are a bad girl."

I groan and down the rest of my drink as she cackles.

"Why are you laughing?"

"Because you are so much cooler than even I knew. You're the daughter of a record executive, and the hottest guy in the world is strung out over you. And," she goes on before I can tell her how wrong she is, "I know you'll get out of this. And I can't wait to see how."

"I appreciate the vote of confidence. I think."

I shift off the couch and take my empty cup to the kitchen.

"Refill time?" Serena asks, hopeful.

"Nope, I gotta unpack." I grab my bag and start toward my room.

"Fine. But Wednesday, you should pick up music night," she calls after me. "I think Dale's going into withdrawal without you."

Getting a meeting with Cross the next day is easier than I expected. It's almost as if he's waiting for me.

Going to the meeting is harder than I expected.

Wicked is the way I remember, and not. I sit outside Cross's office, rereading the poster about the building and forcing myself not to tug at the hem of my T-shirt.

Nothing's changed. You're the same person you were yesterday. Four months ago. Twenty-one years ago.

"Mr. Cross will see you now."

I suck in a breath that fills my belly, as if the ratio of oxygen to carbon dioxide in my body can save me.

Hold it as long as I can before letting it out.

I need to get back into school, or all the plans I've made will go up in smoke. I can't bartend my whole life. Not because I don't respect the work or the people I did it with, but because I want more.

Not just want. I *need* more.

This summer only increased my conviction.

I force my feet to carry me into that black-and-white room.

"I wondered how long it would take you to come." Cross's hands are folded on the desk as if he was posing for a portrait before I interrupted.

His eyes are blue and nothing like mine. His cheeks are lean.

But his chin. Maybe the nose...

"Have a seat."

I do, my gaze falling to the floor as I shift to get comfortable, landing on that giant fur rug under the conversation set. "You shoot that yourself?"

"No. Does it bother you?"

I look up at him as my fingers curl around the cold metal of the chair armrest.

"A lot of things bother me. The attention span of undergrads when you try to tell them how to reset their passwords. The state of the Middle East. When I go to the vending machine in the computer science building and my chips get stuck in that spiral thingy. What you do or don't put on your floor doesn't bother me." There's a reason I'm here, and it's not to talk about how this man is my father or how he chooses his décor. "I need a letter to the school stating I completed my term."

His brows draw together as if he's disappointed, not guilty. "You didn't complete your term."

"What are you talking about?"

"You left without notice with two remaining shows."

I glance toward the open door and back, lowering my voice. "Because I found out you were my father."

And there it is.

The statement hangs between us. I wait for him to acknowledge it, or deny it, or start talking about my mom.

Instead, he simply folds his hands on the desk in front of him. "So?"

I pick my jaw up off the floor. "So you hired me. You put me on tour. I didn't end up there because I deserved to, because I'd earned it."

"And because you resented this assumed nepotism, you left without fulfilling the terms of said agreement. And yet you expect to be compensated for it."

When he says it like that, it does sound bad.

"I made you a deal. One month counted for four. You didn't fulfill that."

"I left because of you."

"Because of me? Or because of him?"

I know he means Jax.

I shift out of the chair because suddenly the room feels too small.

My feet are soundless on the plush carpet as I turn away, finding myself face-to-face with the painting of the field. My blood pressure declines a few points.

"I want the letter, Mr. Cross."

"You have nothing to bargain with."

Two months ago, I would've turned tail and run.

Now, I'm smart enough to know that won't work.

I turn and step up to the desk, my heart hammering.

Cross wants me here. I see it in those eyes that, now that I look into them, aren't so different from mine.

"Don't I?"

His mouth curves. It's not a smile. I bet he's handsome if he ever lets the facade go. "So, you are my daughter after all."

The word has my fingers flexing. It's been so long since someone called me that, but I'm not sure I like how it sounds.

"What do you want? Sunday dinners?" My voice is smaller than I'd like.

"I want you to pay back the time you owe. A full four months."

"One semester?" Holy shit, he's insane. "I wouldn't be back in school until next semester?"

"That's right."

My hands form fists at my sides. "How is that fair? Fathers aren't supposed to blackmail their daughters."

"Life isn't fair, Haley. Case in point: you're ready to condemn me for all I've done to help you when I'm not the one you should be judging."

Cross reaches into his drawer and produces a black flash drive. The thing lies in his hand, and I stare at it as if it's a snake.

"I don't understand."

"Women will forgive Jax anything. You're no exception. But everyone does things in their darkest moments. Things that come back to haunt them." My mind races as he says, "It's yours to do with as you see fit. Consider it a gift."

Maybe Serena was right and our story isn't over.

I don't want anything this man has to offer. But I want to know more about Jax.

The idea teases me, calls to me.

I take the drive and shove it into my pocket, ignoring the glint in Cross's eye.

I turn toward the door, but a voice brings me back.

"Well? What do you say to our new deal."

"I'll think about it."

He tilts his head, and it occurs to me what he looks like. A bird.

A raven.

"I'll throw in one more gift." He spreads his hands. "Ask me. Whatever it is that's causing you to look like that, ask me."

"No." A million thoughts circle my mind like moths swarming a flame. Choosing one seems impossible. "I'm not giving you the satisfaction of asking you why you never told me who you were. Why you never came to see me. How you could you live in the same city as me my entire life and never do anything."

His dark brows pull together. "Good. Because those are the wrong questions."

I want to tell him to go fuck himself. I'm sure that's what Jax would do.

Instead, I can't help but ask, "What's the right one?"

Cross smirks.

"When you figure that out, we'll understand one another far better."

4

HALEY

"What do you think? I wrote it about working this summer and the frustration of not being able to express yourself." Dale grins expectantly as he hits pause on the track I'm listening to.

I look past him at the familiar backdrop of the café. The tables are just starting to fill for music night.

"Yeah. It must have been really intense," I say. "Working at..."

"The library," he supplies.

"Right." I try to get excited about it, but it's harder than it used to be.

I want to see things. *Do* things.

I want to take control of my destiny.

Somewhere in between helping Jerry in the sound booth and slinging beers in a country bar, I saw a glimpse of what my life could be like.

Since meeting Cross on Monday, I've decided a few things.

I'll do what he asked and finish my work for Wicked. But I'm not waiting around for him to hand me a letter.

I got my textbooks even though I'm not in class. I'll read them all so I'm ready. And I'll knock on every door of the administration until I get readmitted.

"I'm going to make you sing with us on stage one day," Dale teases, bringing me back to the cafe. "I still remember the time you rehearsed with us."

The idea of Dale making me do anything is funny, but he's so sweet I can't resist. "What the hell. I'll sit in a set."

I pack up my computer and drop my backpack backstage before going onstage. A few people clap, and I ignore the pang of dissonance. Nothing here's changed even though I have.

Being on stage reminds me of Jax, as if I'm sharing this moment with him somehow.

I didn't expect to hear from him after his tour wrapped, but that doesn't stop me from wondering what he's doing. How he's feeling.

It's like there's a part of my body, my soul, that's gone quiet. I want to send out a signal. Make sure it's still there.

I put everything I can into the song even though I'm only half in the room.

There's a key change, and we navigate it, a little hit of dopamine in my brain as we ride the swell of it.

Then... another change.

Not in the music. In the air.

Rock stars don't chase college dropouts. It's not a story worth writing.

But my fingers tighten on the mic, and chills race down my spine, and before I open my eyes, I know.

I wonder why he's here.

I wonder what took him so long.

I wonder what he's going to do to me when I get off this stage.

Jax stands a few feet inside the door, hands in his pockets. The Astros cap is pulled low on his head, and his long-sleeved shirt hides his tattoos but not the hard lines of his body. As a result, he's drawing more than a few envious glances from around the café.

"Haley," Dale whispers, and I realize I've stopped singing.

I force myself to finish the number.

"Can we take five?" I ask the band when we're done.

I set the mic back and step off the stage before Dale can respond, my heart hammering in my ears as I cross to Jax.

Seeing him in Atlanta in his element was one thing. This time, he's in my backyard.

Somehow he owns it too, as if it's just another town, another arena.

I tilt up my chin to meet his gaze. "Do you even follow baseball, or is that just your disguise?" I ask, glancing at his hat.

"The Houston Astros are top of the AL West. Altuve is a six-time all-star. He's even shorter in person than he looks on TV."

"Right. You and Lita should go into sports broadcasting in your retirement."

"Nah. We could buy a team though."

I can't tell if he's joking. "Don't tell me you're here for the coffee, because it sucks."

"I was in town for a meeting at the label." He shoves a hand into the pocket of his jeans, retrieves a piece of black plastic that he holds up. "You know anything about this, Hales?"

That careless, intimate way he says my name makes me shaky, but I try to stay composed. "Why would you think that?"

"There's no way Cross held onto this flash drive for the better part of the decade and decided to dangle it in front of me now."

"He gave it to me. I thought you should have it, so I had his assistant send it to you."

"About what's on it—"

"I didn't look."

His eyes widen incrementally.

"Whoa." Dale's voice makes me wince. "Anyone ever tell you you look like Jax Jamieson?"

Jax doesn't flinch. "All the time."

"Huh."

"Dale, this is my friend—"

"Leonard."

The easy deadpan has me choking back a laugh. Because, dammit, even on my home turf, I can't ignore his physical presence, or the masculine scent that makes my insides warm, or the spark in Jax's eye at our private joke.

"Dale." Dale nudges his shoulder against mine, then glances toward the stage. "We should get back to it."

Jax watches him go, hands in his pockets. "Should I be worried?"

"About that flash drive? Or about Dale?"

He pockets the flash drive, and Serena's words about Jax being hung up on me come back to me.

"Haley, you want a drink?" one of the servers interrupts, and I force myself to look at her.

"Sure. Iced tea."

"What about you?" she asks Jax, her gaze lingering on his body.

"Nah, I'm good."

"You're here for music night, you have to order something," I say. "They make good iced tea."

"Fine. Make it two." She leaves, and Jax's gaze flicks back to me.

"Jax. What are you doing here?"

He studies me a moment, like he's still trying to answer that question himself.

"We finished our last show, and I packed up to go home to Dallas, and I realized something. I like knowing where you are. What you're doing. It helps stop the voices in my head."

The iced teas show up, and we reach for them. I go for my wallet, but he shakes me off, pulling out a fifty that has her raising a brow.

"You're hearing voices, you should stalk a psych major," I say when she leaves.

Jax's gaze narrows.

I thought taking control of my life would mean no more madness, no more drama. No more obsessing over rock stars.

But here we are.

It's easy to tell myself I'm deluded, that I have a harmless crush, when the object of it isn't standing in my café looking at me with amber eyes that I swear could melt the North Pole.

Right now, it doesn't matter that he's loaded or famous or inspires rational women to regress into hormone-fueled animals bearing sparkle-glitter signs with marriage proposals.

He's just a guy who makes me feel like I'm really fucking glad to be standing here. (And equally glad I brushed my hair before coming here.)

Maybe this *is* my life. Maybe I can get back into school and figure out how to deal with Cross and *still* enjoy the fact that for the first time...

Jax Jamieson came for me.

I smile as the huge weight melts off my chest.

"I'm glad you came tonight. *Leonard.*" I lift my glass in a toast and take a long sip through the straw. "Thanks for the tea."

Before he can respond, I turn on my heel and start toward the stage.

I get three steps before his voice stops me.

"Haley."

I glance over my shoulder, raising a brow.

Jax stares at me, hands in his jeans. He looks adorably out of place as he clears his throat. "What are you doing later?"

"Yes. No. Hell no. Jesus, Hales, what is this shit?" Jax leans over me, clicking through the playlist on the computer at the campus radio station.

"Those are completely defensible song choices," I protest.

"They're crap."

Before I left for the summer, I'd promised to cover some September shifts for a classmate going on exchange.

Now Jax's hat sits on the board, ditched now that we're inside and unlikely to be swarmed by fans. He looks completely at home in the tired task chair, leather reinforced with duct tape. His hair falls over his face in that way that makes my fingers itch to brush it aside. The long-sleeved overshirt's gone too, revealing a black T-shirt that clings to his chest and arms.

Now that we're not on tour, there aren't thousands of fans screaming for him, dozens of people catering to him, it's all so normal I can almost pretend we're just two friends hanging out.

At least until the warm light in the booth caresses his skin, the sleeve of tattoos, in a way that directly challenges my vow to keep things simple.

"You need an education," Jax goes on.

"That's why I'm at college."

"Not that kind of education. The kind I can give you."

Ignoring the way his rumbling voice sends heat down my spine, I get off my stool and hip-check him so he rolls across the floor. "What do you want me to play, O Supreme Curator of Musical Taste?"

He leans back in his chair, folding his hands behind his head so his shirt pulls across his muscled chest. "Something classic. The Smiths. AC/DC. Me."

The grin that pulls across his face is smug and sexy as hell.

Resisting Jax is nearly impossible. But the kicker is he's not offering me anything. All he's doing is being himself.

I'm trying to remember I'm here to play a mix of contemporary rock music for a bunch of undergrads who are probably watching Netflix, not launching myself at Jax like a human can of Silly String.

The whole 'he's just a guy' thing was working for me really well until this moment.

I turn back to the computer so I don't have to deal with the arousal stirring in my stomach. "No way."

His phone buzzes, and I glance back. "I sent Grace and Annie to Disney for the weekend," he says without looking up. "Then they have a suite at the Ritz in Dallas starting Monday."

"Mouse ears."

His gaze flicks to mine. "What?"

"Just watch. They'll bring you mouse ears."

He shakes his head, and I laugh.

"That's all it takes, huh? A few days off tour and the promise of some branded mouse ears."

His grin warms me through my toes. "Never said I was complicated." He shifts forward in his chair. "I gotta call Grace quick. I'll be back."

Jax steps out, and I add a new song to the queue. I watch him through the window as he talks to his sister, and I can't help but smile.

I don't know why he's here, but I'm glad.

It's like I'm on a different frequency with him. He excites me and challenges me, and sometimes scares me. But I also feel like I can be myself with him. He doesn't judge or criticize.

I add a few more songs to the list, including one I debate for agonizing seconds, because I'm afraid to wreck the vibe in here and I know on instinct that it will.

When the track changes, I swear I feel Jax's gaze through the glass.

I flush.

The sound of Jax's voice coming through the speakers has me shivering like always. But now it's like having surround sound, especially as he returns to the booth.

"'Redline,'" he says over the music.

Prickles run down my skin as he pulls the chair closer to the desk and drops into it.

He's on the radio and in front of me, and being faced with two gods is impossible.

I try to keep my voice easy. "Figured I could humor you and your big ego."

Something shifts, and it's not the song. It's his expression, the smile fading into the kind of deliberate intensity I doubt many guys in their twenties possess.

"Tell me something." His words skim along my skin, raising the hairs there. "Do you kiss him?"

It's such a jarring departure from our conversation that I have to replay his words in my mind.

"Who? Dale?"

Before I can respond, he snags the backs of my knees and pulls.

I land in his lap, my hands bracing on his chest for balance as my heartbeat explodes in my ears.

God, he's hot.

Not like that. I mean he's actually a human furnace under the thin T-shirt. Every ridge of his abs, his chest.

"What are you doing?" It comes out like a squeak.

Jax's hands move up my thighs, slow. His touch sears me through my jeans as he strokes up my legs, my hips.

I expected him to have a reaction to playing his song.

I didn't expect *this*.

Especially when his hands sneak under my shirt to caress my lower back.

My eyes start to drift closed, and I fight it with everything I am.

Because I'm in charge of me, even when this man threatens to wipe out all my self-control.

It's not only his touch is messing with my mind—it's the look on his face. Like a starving lion sizing up the only gazelle he's seen in weeks.

"When I pulled you out of that crowd in Atlanta," Jax murmurs, "you struggled until you realized it was me."

"So?" My voice is almost normal, and I don't know how I manage it.

"So, you like it when I touch you."

How the hell did his lips get so close?

"I like it better than being groped-slash-trampled by thousands of screaming fans, yes." I swallow, reminding myself how I said I'd keep this easy. "But I'm not on your tour anymore. I can do whatever I want. Whoever I want."

Determination crosses his face as his thumbs stroke my back, making me want to arch like a cat and taking all my willpower to resist doing exactly that.

Jax's amber eyes darken, and his scent invites me

closer. Every part of him in fact, from his hard legs to his chest, invites me closer.

But I'm not ready to give in. He's used to women throwing themselves at him. That's not happening here.

"I'm not your groupie, Jax."

"That's why I like you so much, Hales." The chorus sounds in the background, and he leans forward, his nose tracing the edge of my jaw in a way that has my fingers flexing on his abs, his T-shirt. "Tell me how many times you thought about it."

I let out a shaky breath. "What? My near-death experience when you almost unwrapped that Snickers in the limo?"

I'm amazed I have enough brain cells to bluff when every part of me's living for the places our bodies touch.

"The time I unwrapped you on my bus. You fucking *melted* for me. Don't tell me you forgot."

God, his voice is intoxicating. Jax's thumb presses against my lower lip, and my mouth opens on instinct.

A slow burn starts in my breasts, travels between my thighs.

I think I'm wet before his lips claim mine.

His tongue traces my lower lip like he's outlining the shape of it. Drawing from memory.

I'd meant to pull back. To indulge in one taste, but I underestimated the strength of that first hit.

He takes advantage, and when he nips at my lip with his teeth, Jax's kiss turns hungry on a groan I want to record. Not because that sound alone would sell a million copies, but because I want there to be one copy. And I want to listen to it every night with my hand between my thighs.

I try to stay still but my fingers itch to move up his chest. They sneak over his shoulders, into his hair.

It's still harmless. Easy.

So's lying to myself, apparently.

I might be on top, but Jax is making a play for control from the second I taste him. His hands move up my back, around to my breasts.

He cups me in his hands like he wants to memorize the shape of me, and I need to slow this thing down before it spirals off into something we can't come back from.

But part of me wants to explore, to discover. To ride out these feelings, to watch them and feel them and replay them when these few precious moments of madness are over forever.

I don't know what making out feels like for normal people because I've never been normal. It's only ever been something tolerable at best to have another person's hands on me, not to mention their mouth.

This is maddening. Torture, but the kind I escape for a breath only to launch myself back into again.

The air goes dead, and it takes a good minute for the implication to sink in.

I spin around and search for a song to put on.

Then I line up the rest of the list before I shift back against the deck.

Jax watches with hooded eyes that glow like embers.

"So. Um. This is the last song of this show. Someone will be here any second to take over."

We're so far apart compared to how we were a moment ago, but it's suddenly awkward.

How could it not be?

I blurt the first thing that comes into my head.

"Serena's seeing some frat guy. She won't be home tonight; she likes the breakfast there. They always have bacon."

Stop talking about bacon.

When Jax shifts out of the chair, grabs his cap, and crosses to the other side of the booth, I know I've done something wrong.

"We need to talk."

I tuck my hair behind my ears because somehow it got wicked messy in the last five minutes. "Wow. That's ominous."

He tugs the cap down over his head.

"Let's take a walk."

Despite the fact it's after dark, the air's warm for September, and I tug my hair up in a bun as we step outside.

Jax glances toward me as we fall into step next to one another. "What was your mom like?"

I look up at the trees. This afternoon I'd noticed them starting to turn, the leaves tinting gold. Now they're just ghostly shadows as we cross campus. Soon, students will be pouring out of their night classes.

"Protective. But not about physical things. She was freaked out for days after I went with friends to see *Gone Girl*. She didn't know what it was about until after I got home."

"Horror movies?"

I shake my head. "It wasn't the fictional boogieman she didn't want me exposed to. More like the boundary conditions of the human mind."

"See? What do I need a psych major for when I have you?"

I can't help the smile that tugs at my lips even though I know he can't see it.

We make it the rest of the way to the edge of campus in silence. We're almost another block closer to my place by the time Jax speaks again.

"Your mom wouldn't have liked me. What's on that flash drive, Hales..." Regret tinges his voice. Tension fills his shoulders, his arms. "I did a lot of shit when I was first signed."

I hitch my backpack higher on my shoulders. "You can't scare me, Jax. I've had sex. I've smoked a joint. I've watched porn."

His soft laugh fills the darkness, as if I've made myself sound more innocent instead of less. I focus on the lines in the sidewalk.

"What I mean is it doesn't matter."

"It does because it has consequences. The kind that never end."

I can't think of anything he'd have done that would change the attraction I feel for him.

Even though that label seems too superficial for the electricity still pulsing through my veins, it's completely right. He draws me in. Pulls me toward him, on every level. Physical, emotional, intellectual. There's nothing in this world that could reverse that magnetism.

Until he utters the words that change everything.

"Annie's not my niece, Haley. She's my daughter."

I stop next to a streetlight, and Jax pulls up next to me.

We're a block from my building, but we might as well be a mile. I reach up to yank his hat off because I need to see his face.

"What did you say?"

His hair is everywhere, and his eyes are wary and vulnerable.

I know I've misheard him. Except the look on his face tells me I haven't.

"She's my kid. Not Grace's. Annie doesn't know." The misery in his voice guts me.

"Who's her mother?"

"It doesn't matter. She tried to contact me but couldn't.

She dropped Annie off with Grace. I didn't find out until months later." His words are raw, as if talking about this causes him physical pain. "Cross stopped her from contacting me. Threatened her. Eventually paid for her silence. Then he kept Grace from telling me because he told her it would ruin my future."

Facts, admissions, and observations collide in my brain, pieces clicking into place one at a time. "That's why you hate him."

"It's one reason," Jax admits. "I wanted to tell you because I like telling you things. I like that you keep my secrets. And I don't want that hanging between us."

My chest aches with disbelief, understanding, anguish.

I want to tell him this changes nothing. But that's not true. Who he is is different than who he was a moment ago.

You knew he wasn't a saint. He's not like Dale or any of the boys Serena brings to the apartment.

It's all true, but I don't know what to do with it.

A breeze sweeps the hairs on the nape of my neck, and I wrap my arms around myself.

"That's my building." I nod down the block.

Jax lets out a breath. "I should get back to the hotel."

He flips open his phone, and instincts fight inside me.

I want him to leave.

I want him to stay.

Mostly, I want to rewind to five minutes ago when I felt

as though we were just two people occupying the same space and time.

"At least come in to call your car. College girls are vicious. If you got recognized out here..." I shudder. "I couldn't live with myself."

I lead the way up the walk. I'm on autopilot as he holds the door for me, as I take the stairs first.

I let us into the apartment and take off my shoes.

He hovers in the doorway, taking up most of the frame with his body.

I'm suddenly self-conscious as I notice the neutral décor, the fake hardwood, and the white appliances.

"We've lived here since second year. It's not quite a hotel, but for students, it's practically the Four Seasons."

Jax opens his phone, then curses.

"What's wrong?"

"Grace says she emailed me a picture of them at Disney. I didn't bring my tablet to Philly."

"You can check your email in a browser if you want." I pass him my phone without hesitation, swallowing as our fingers brush.

"Thanks."

I shift a hip against the wall next to him as he types away on my phone. Waits.

Then he holds up the picture of Annie.

She and Grace are wearing wide grins and mouse ears. A third set rests in Annie's raised hands.

"Mouse ears," Jax confirms, solemn.

"Mouse ears." I can't help but smile.

I don't know how I missed it. The way he talks about her. The look on his face.

My apartment suddenly feels too small, but it's filled with warmth, not emptiness.

"Listen. You've spent the last two years living in hotels. You deserve to sleep somewhere that feels like home."

He lowers the phone, looking past me like the answer to that invitation is somewhere in the living room.

Then he tosses his hair out of his face with that easy grace that says he does it a lot, kicks off his shoes, and hangs the hat by the door.

My heart thuds dully in my chest as Jax follows me into my room.

Now that the initial shock has worn off—has it?—I'm coming to grips with the other crazy reality.

Jax Jamieson is in my apartment.

In my room.

An hour ago, his tongue was tattooing mine.

After flicking on the small light by the bed, I search in my dresser drawer for an unopened toothbrush.

"That your overnight guest drawer?"

"Huh?" I flush as I get his meaning. "Oh. I don't have a lot of overnight guests."

A brow rises under his thick fall of hair.

"I mean, I have *some* guests. Really good-looking guests." Now his mouth is twitching, and I resist the urge to face-palm.

The look on his face is starting to melt my insides, a degree at a time, until...

"I'm not sleeping with you, Jax."

Jax cocks his head, a smirk on his handsome face. The muscles in his arms leap, dragging my gaze towards his tattoos when he rubs a hand over his neck. "Because I'm a dad?"

Jesus, how is he hotter after uttering those words.

"No. Yes. I'm not sure." I wish I didn't sound like such an indecisive child right now.

But Jax just shoves his hands in his pockets, shifting back on his heels to study me.

"You're not sleeping with me tonight or ever?"

Oh God. He says it so easily. As if he's thought about both options and is soliciting my opinion.

Before I can respond, he says, "Just kidding."

I let out a whoosh of breath.

"I know it takes you a while to warm up to someone," he goes on, his voice alone making me shiver. "Which is why I'm telling you this now."

He leans in, and it's all I can do not to whine when his lips brush my ear. "I'm totally going to fuck you someday, Hales. But not until you beg me to."

Toothbrush in hand, he leaves the room.

My knees give out.

For real.

I'm sitting cross-legged on the floor of my room wondering who the hell *says* that to another person.

I hear water running in the bathroom and tug my shirt over my head.

Then manage to push myself to standing as I work off my jeans.

My body tingles as I pull on sleep shorts and a tank top.

I slide into bed, my gaze trained on the door like I'm Jason Bourne and at any second I might need to make a run for it.

By the time Jax reenters, I've got hold of myself.

He sets the flash drive on the nightstand as he meets my gaze.

I wait for him to ask if he should take the couch.

He doesn't.

Of course he doesn't, because he's Jax Jamieson.

He strips off his shirt, making my throat go dry at the sight of his muscled chest, then slides in beside me.

I could ask him to move to the living room. Or grab my pillow and leave.

Instead, I roll over and force myself to feel him next to me in the dark.

And I tell myself the lie that I can sleep.

5

I'm going to kill whoever decided to make white curtains.

Not the blackout kind with a lining. The kind the sun goes straight through, burning your retinas at ungodly hours.

I pry my eyelids open because there's no pretending I'm going back to sleep now.

The vintage Betty Boop clock over the desk says it's nine o'clock.

I've never been this awake at nine o'clock.

The room is small, and her shit is everywhere. Not in a messy way. It's more like I see glimpses of her no matter which direction I turn.

I didn't get a good look at it last night, but there's a desk, a dresser. Some art prints. A turntable in the corner with a serious vinyl collection I'm definitely checking out later.

A couple of posters, including...

Hell yes.

There I am. Next to the door.

Satisfaction works through me.

I even remember the photo shoot for that one. It'd been like pulling teeth, but now? I'm glad I did it because it means two things:

One, she's totally gotten off to me. (Which makes my day even though I've only just woken up.)

Two, I will hold this over her head for fucking *ever.*

My gaze slides over to the dresser, the folded clothes lying on top.

Hold the bus. *Is that lace?* I stretch, craning my neck to get a better look.

My toes connect with the metal bed post. "*Fuck.*"

A noise behind me makes me freeze.

I roll over, careful not to take out Haley on the way.

I'm not used to sleeping with another person. I've probably woken her already.

But Haley curls into my bare chest, asleep and innocent as her breath heats my skin. Damn, she's pretty like this. Her dark lashes sweeping across her cheeks. Lips just parted.

I've never come clean to someone like I did last night.

I've turned it over in my head a dozen times, what is it about her that gets to me. Trying to find, in my feelings for her, my own weakness.

She's innocent, but she's not.

She's sweet, but she's not.

She's tough, but she's not, and...

How the hell did my arm get around her waist?

Because my thumb's stroking her side where her tank rode up, and Haley makes a little sound in her sleep that makes me want to fuck the mattress.

Or her. Obviously.

But that's not going to happen. I'm no prince, but I'm not shitty enough to think it's okay to show up unannounced, drop a ten-pound bomb—or technically, a seventy-pound one with red hair—then crash at a girl's place and expect sex.

Still...

My thumb brushes her skin again because I want to hear that sound. To memorize it in case it's the only time I hear it.

Leaving the jeans on last night was a good idea.

I can take the smell of her, the warmth.

What I can't take is when her leg drapes across mine and she snuggles closer to my bare chest.

My breath is a balloon, stretching my chest. My abs flex on instinct.

My hand slides down an inch, to the top of her hip. Shit, she's soft.

Is she that soft everywhere? It seems impossible.

But it's been so long since I actually slept with someone—in a bed, their body next to mine—I can't remember.

Haley's hips rock against mine as if I have something she knows she needs.

My biceps shake from resisting, and I can't stop the groan. "You're killing me here, Hales."

I want to haul her mouth to my mouth.

I want to give her so much pleasure she can't get off without thinking of me.

I want to tell the kid at the café with the Telecaster he doesn't have a shot in hell, whether I'm here or in Australia, because she's mine.

Before I can examine that thought too closely, something fluffy brushes against my back above the covers. "What the..."

I crane my neck, twisting in the sheets.

Then I fall out of bed on my ass. "The FUCK is that doing here?!"

"What's wrong?" Haley mumbles as I scramble to standing.

"Don't move. There's a skunk."

Her eyes fly wide and she shoots straight up. "Don't kill it!"

"I'm not going to kill it. I'm going to get it out the window."

"That's Scrunchie. It's Serena's. He doesn't spray." Haley lifts him up in front of her face. The little thing blinks at her as if the light offends it.

"I'm not sure how I feel about you now." But the smile

she flashes in my direction melts whatever grudge I'd begun to harbor.

She sets the skunk on the covers, and he wanders toward the foot of the bed.

"You want to shower before breakfast?" My gaze jerks back to hers. For a second, I fantasize Haley means together, but she shifts out of bed and hands me a towel. "I'll make coffee."

She retreats toward the living room, her ass swaying under her shorts. I call after her. "Hales."

She turns back, and I grin.

"Nice poster."

I wish to God I could take a picture of the flush on her cheeks.

As I take a shower, the normalcy of the morning gets to me.

Until I find it.

Her tropical shampoo.

I mentally catalogue the brand and kind, then because my cock's complaining about the seriously short stick he drew this morning, I weigh the pros and cons of jacking off with it.

I'm only human.

Five minutes later, I'm a human pineapple.

I dry off, pull my jeans back on, along with my T-shirt, and glance at my phone. A dozen missed calls from my agent, my business manager, and Mace. Plus a notification about my charter flight back to Dallas at noon.

"Hey, Hales, can I use your phone again?" I call as I enter the kitchen.

"If you're checking email, you can do it on my computer," Haley says. "Let me grab it." She brushes past me to go back to her room. "Oh, you remember Serena, right?"

The roommate's already at the table, wearing a sweatshirt and smudged eye makeup. She finishes the waffle she's eating and crosses her arms. "I heard you stayed over last night."

"I heard you were out with some frat boy who likes bacon," I counter.

"Because I'm sure you're the poster child for good decision-making."

"You own a skunk."

She takes her plate to the sink. "Hey, Jax Jamieson?"

"Yeah, Serena… whatever your name is?"

Her expression softens. "I told her she should fuck you, okay? Don't make me look like an asshole."

She goes into what I assume is her room, shutting the door.

Before I can make sense of what just happened, Haley's back, setting the laptop on the table in front of me.

I open my email as Haley says, "You want waffles?"

"Can I get some peanuts on top?"

She sticks her tongue out at me, and I grin as I set to work on the computer.

I confirm the charter and review my meetings for this

afternoon. I had a call this morning I need to reschedule also.

Grace and Annie will be getting back from Disney tomorrow. I need to make sure they're set up at the Ritz. And Annie will be starting school in another week, so I want to get her some back-to-school supplies.

I glance up to see Haley staring at me, a box of pancake mix in one hand.

No. *Ogling*.

I run a hand through my wet hair. "See something you like?"

She flushes, setting the box on the counter. She only half succeeds and has to make a grab for it as it tumbles off. Mix flies out the end and makes a powdery pile on the floor.

"I've never seen you use a computer."

"You want me to type slower?" My voice drops an octave. "I know what emojis are too. Eggplant means cock, and peach means ass."

It's ridiculous, but she brushes the dust off her hands and returns to the table. I'm thinking about shoving the computer off my lap and pulling her into it, until she's distracted by what's on the screen. "What's that?"

"My publicist sends me a digest of fan email once a week."

Her eyes light up as she grabs the computer and swings around, dropping onto the opposite chair.

Shit, this girl's hard on my ego. It's like I'm always second-most interesting to a black box.

Which only makes me like her more.

"Charlie in Wisconsin says your song saved his life." Haley's gaze moves back and forth over the screen. "Jennifer in Baltimore saw your show, and it was the best show she'd ever seen." Her mouth curves. "Obviously she never saw Leonard Cohen."

I kick her under the table, and she laughs.

A moment later, her eyes go round, and the smile disappears. "Whoa."

I straighten, shifting closer. "What's wrong?"

"This woman... she has very specific ideas of what she wants from you."

I frown. Usually the crazies don't get through the first filter.

"She really likes your mouth." Haley's face screws up in an expression I've never seen on her.

Not possible.

But the longer I watch, the more I realize it's true.

She's jealous.

Something in me purrs. "Really?"

Haley clears her throat. "'I dream about your mouth on my body.'"

Goodbye, smugness. Hello, desire.

Heat coils low in my gut as she continues.

"'I touch myself and imagine it's you. Thinking about it makes me so wet.'"

The words roll off her lips, and every one lights new fires throughout my body.

Phrases like "touch myself" and "wet" imprint on the back of my brain, feeding the flames stroking down my spine and making my abs flex.

"'You're the hottest thing I've ever seen, and …'"

She swallows, her brows pulling together. Her cheeks flush pink, and I should be pulling the screen back, but there's no stopping now.

I'd give every dollar I've made to hear her finish that thought.

I manage a grunted, "What?"

She doesn't disappoint.

"'When I fuck myself, I pretend it's you. Your mouth, your hands, your cock.'" Her voice catches. "'In my mind, you fuck me senseless. All night.'"

Jesus.

Every ounce of blood is now south of the 49th parallel.

Fuck waffles.

I could lower her down on this table, because God knows she's going to need something to hold onto when I strip those shorts off her hips and lose myself in her.

Haley's gaze cuts to mine, and the expression there nearly destroys me. No computer in the world can explain the way she's looking at me right now.

I know because I feel it too.

She clears her throat, but her words are still rough. "Her name is—"

“I don’t want her name, Hales.” My voice is a rasp. My cock might smell like pineapple, but it’s saluting her like a damned oak tree under the table.

I want to see if this poor excuse for foreplay has her as turned on as it has me. I want to force her to keep those pretty hazel eyes open so I can memorize the way they change color when I take her over the edge again and again.

Buzzzzz.

My gaze drags to my flip phone on the table, and I curse.

It’s a reminder of my flight.

Maybe of my sanity.

Because what was about to go down here would’ve been certifiable.

I want her. More than I’ve wanted just about anything I can remember.

But my casual remark about fucking her last night was a slip. The product of a grueling day and the way she looked when I’d kissed her.

I never meant for things to go that far.

Grace and I used to ride our bikes down this hill as kids. It started so gradual you barely noticed, but you’d pick up speed until you were flying, careening out of control toward a blind corner.

It was the best fucking feeling on Earth.

Including the time I’d nearly been hit by a truck at the bottom.

This time, I'm not worried about hurting me. I'm worried about hurting Haley.

Problem is, I don't know how I'm going to resist her either.

If I go there with her—*if*—it'll be on my terms. When I have an iron grip on my own need and nothing to prove except that I can take her higher, deeper, better than any guy who's ever thought about touching her.

"I have to go." I shove out of my chair.

Haley rises too, her mouth forming a little O that doesn't help my self-control. "What about breakfast?"

We both look at the pile on the floor at the same time.

I try to hide the smirk.

Fail.

She laughs, and damn if that isn't what I love about being around her. Haley doesn't take herself too seriously, and when I'm with her, I can't either.

"Rain check? I need to get Annie settled and back to school. I'll be back at Wicked in a few weeks for meetings. You need anything, you know where to find me."

I cross to her, because I can't leave without one more hit, and drop my lips to her temple. Her tiny sigh has my gut knotting again.

"See you, Hales."

"Bye, Jax."

I turn and start toward the door, stopping at the sight of the black-and-white mop between me and the foyer.

We stare each other down.

Then, as if he just realized his tail is on fire, he scurries off.

"Yeah, you better watch out."

6

HALEY

"That's it. She's dead." I sigh, looking up from the computer. "Why can't Wicked spend more on technology?"

Wendy's pale gaze runs over me. She hasn't softened much since the day I interviewed with her, but on this topic at least, we're allies.

"Most of the budget goes to the big revenue generators, like the tours. So, we have to keep what we have running."

I blow a piece of hair out of my face. We might be working overtime, but the air conditioning in the server room is definitely not on the plan.

In the week I've worked at Wicked, I've learned a few things. Wendy runs the tech department, which is seriously understaffed at four people plus me. Though the recording tech is state-of-the-art, everything the company runs on—servers, desktop computers, the network—is old-school.

Wendy glances at the clock, which says it's almost six. "I need to go pick up my son for the weekend. Don't forget to check your employee mailbox for your paperwork."

Wendy leaves, and I wipe my brow as I look back at the stack of computers.

If Cross wanted me to do penance, I'm doing it. I got a classmate to slip me the outlines of my would-be courses for this semester. Now between working full days here, making calls and emails to try and find a loophole that will get back into school (which so far have yielded nothing), and keeping up on "my" readings and assignments? I fall into bed exhausted at night.

Which is just as well because lying awake thinking what I've been thinking isn't healthy.

Jax Jamieson groped you at the campus radio station.

Then told you he was a dad.

(Hot dad.)

You let him sleep in your bed. Use all your body wash (wtf?). Then vanish from your kitchen only to ghost you the modern way after.

Okay, the last part's not entirely true.

I texted him Saturday afternoon to make sure his plane got in.

Sunday, he emailed me a picture of Annie on a ride, wearing both sets of mouse ears, with the text "My ears get around."

But since Tuesday...

Nothing.

I try to ignore the disappointment.

"I'm totally going to fuck you someday, Hales. But not until you beg me."

It's arrogant, but after spending the summer bartending, I've had guys tell me a lot of things.

If it were any other guy, I would've kicked him out on his ass in two seconds flat—with or without Andre's help.

With Jax, I don't want to.

I want to lock the door so the world can't get in. I want to see every inch of his perfect body. I want to feel the shivers through mine.

But it's never going to happen because the thought is completely terrifying. Compared with the guys I've been physical with, Jax is like another species. Strong and hard and confident. A meteor that's going to blow me apart, leave me picking up the pieces after.

I shove off the thoughts, grab the computer I'm working on, and tuck it under my arm.

The basement's nearly empty, and it's not until I'm on the second floor that I see even a single other employee.

On the way to the mailboxes, I pass a studio and hear my name.

I stick my head in, and my grumpiness melts away as I catch sight of the last person I'd expected.

"Jerry! What are you doing here?"

My former mentor smiles up at me from his chair.

Today he's wearing a long-sleeved tan shirt that makes him look like Yoda.

He basically is.

"Miss Telfer. Got a few months before the next tour. Figured I'd whip some kids into shape here."

I'm not at all sure he needs to be doing another tour, but I step into the studio and peer through the glass. My jaw drops more.

"Lita?"

"Haley!" She opens the door that separates the artists and the producers, grinning as she leans against the doorway.

She glances down at my accessory. "Whoa. What is that?"

"Plays Betamax," Jerry offers.

"It's a computer." I swallow my grin. "You're back recording already?"

"Yeah. Were you in a sauna?"

I wipe at the sweat on my forehead. "Close. Server room."

"Huh. You should help on this album." Lita says it like it's an easy thing, but once the idea enters my brain, I can't kick it.

"That would be awesome." Being in this office and actually doing some production has adrenaline coursing through my veins. "This is the EP you were talking about this summer?"

"Yeah. I really think this could be the difference

maker." Her eyes glow. "I'd love to run some of the tracks through your program."

My heart kicks in my chest. "Yeah. Sure."

She'd watched me tweak it this summer in Nashville, running version after version to optimize it the best way I could.

We catch up for a couple of minutes, then I start to the elevator.

"Shit," I mutter as the doors open, realizing I've forgotten my paperwork. I start to turn on my heel, but the man in the carriage calls out.

"Haley."

"I forgot something." I hitch my thumb over my shoulder, but Cross holds the door.

Eventually I step inside, shifting the shell of a computer under my arms so I don't drop it. "What's that?"

"A hard drive. A useless one. I was going to try to fix it this weekend."

The gray in his hair shines as he cocks his head. "You're taking company property off the premises."

"The premises will be more valuable without this."

I half expect him to send me back upstairs with the computer, but he doesn't. Cross just stands there, staring at the seam in the doors.

"I trust Wendy's keeping you busy."

"Actually, the state of this place is keeping me busy." I debate how much to say, then go all in because honesty's almost always better. "Wicked is ten years behind on hardware. Fifteen on software. You won't fall off a cliff, but it'll be a slow death if you don't start upgrading."

"Thank you for that perspective."

"I am doing everything I can," I say so it doesn't only sound like I'm complaining. "Over the next two months, we should be able to bring email and databases up to date."

He turns his gaze on me. "I was told this summer that project would take eight months and we'd have to delay other projects in order to do it."

I hesitate because I don't want to get Wendy in trouble. "Well, I think I can do it in two."

The door dings, and he strides out of the elevator.

I trot after him, which is ridiculous since two minutes ago I wouldn't get in the elevator with him. "Mr. Cross!"

"Shannon."

I look past him. There's no one around us, but clearly he doesn't want this to get out.

"What would it take for a chance to do something other than computer upgrades?"

His dark eyes say he's as intrigued as he is wary. "Such as?"

I bite my cheek. "Lita's new album. I want to work on it. I think I can make it better."

A slick Town Car approaches before gliding to a halt in front of us.

"No."

"No?" I nearly drop the hard drive but scramble and

manage to catch it. "But there must be a way. I can keep doing the upgrades, do this on top. Lita already said she'd be fine with it."

"You're naive." His sharp voice cuts the humidity in the air like a knife as he stares at me over the door of his car. "I had hoped when I sent you on tour this summer that you'd prove you weren't a typical college student. That, like me, you want more and will do whatever it takes to get it. But I gave you an opportunity hundreds of students would kill for, and you ran from it. Second chances don't come easily in this world, Haley."

I lift my chin. "I don't know. I'm giving you one, aren't I?"

His expression darkens, his gaze narrowing like he smells something bad.

Then Cross slides into the car, and a moment later, it glides away.

Saturday, I'm up before noon and take Scrunchie for a walk on campus to clear my head. The grounds are quiet, but even though only a handful of students are crossing the quad, I feel apart from it.

"Haley?"

That voice has me stiffening as I turn. "Professor Carter."

His button-down and T-shirt make him look like a grad student. His blond hair is styled, his smile easy.

At least until he sees Scrunchie. "What is that?"

"Exotic cat."

"Right." He shakes his head. "I haven't heard from you in ages. Or seen you in class."

Since you refused to submit my program and hired someone else?

"There was a snag with my scheduling. I'm taking a semester off."

"Huh. Well, you look fantastic." I'm not sure he even took in my yoga pants, T-shirt, flip flops, and messy bun because his grin is automatic. Less earnest than Dale's, but it comes easier than Jax's. "I was thinking about your program. I know we missed the Spark competition, but there's a bigger one this fall that was just announced. You'd need to run more trials. Which means more data to feed the beast. But if you're serious about it, we could have it ready. The prize is twenty-five thousand. The deadline is end of October."

I glance down to where Scrunchie is tugging at his leash, eager to find the perfect grub. Carter's offer brings up a host of emotions. Flattery because he thought of me for this. Excitement because getting his eyes on this would help my chances a lot. There's likely no one else I could get with the insight to help me like he can.

But he already stepped on me once this year, and I like to think I'm not stupid.

"The exposure's even better than the money," he says. "The winner gets written up on the top tech blogs."

My gaze snaps up. "I wrote some other code this summer. An interface that helps deal with memory and attention limitations. If I win, do you think I could use the platform to raise awareness for that? Maybe find other developers to work on it?"

"I suppose." He shrugs.

"Let's do it," I decide.

"Great. Oh, while I'm at it, I got some money for a research assistant position. Do you want it?"

I ignore for a moment the fact that I'm not technically enrolled because that's something I'm going to fix soon.

Do I want to work for the most brilliant guy I've ever met? The one I've been dying to work with for the last three years?

He looks so honest, but Cross's face rises up in my mind again.

Prove to me you're smart.

Prove to me you're special.

Prove to me you want it.

I'm done proving it.

"Actually, I'm pretty busy with work. And now this competition. But thanks."

I pull up the competition info on my phone as I walk away.

By the time I get home, my mind's going a mile a minute.

Serena greets me as I enter our apartment. "Hey, roomie. Aww, you took Scrunchmuffin for a walk."

"He was scrunchmuffining my shoes. You'll never guess who I saw on campus."

"Who?"

"Carter."

Her jaw drops. "What'd he say?"

"He offered to submit my program to an even bigger competition this fall, which I'm going to do. He also asked if I wanted to be his RA. Which I'm not."

"Damn. You are a *badass* with the men. Last weekend you bring home a rock star. This weekend, you shoot down the Nerd Prince of Harvard."

"MIT."

"Whatever." She slants me a look. "I can't wait to see how you're going to top this."

"There will be no topping. I'm just tired of being pushed around. By Cross. By the university. Everyone."

"Hear, hear."

"There's one problem. I agreed to the competition before I read all the specs. I need a ton more data to test my program."

Her face screws up. "You lost me."

"Basically, I need to test how my app stacks up at creating a hit track compared to the industry's best producers. Which means I need access to a lot of tracks. With different versions, which will let me test the human's choices against my algorithm. And I don't have a lot of time. I need someone who can give me approval for a lot of hit songs at once."

"Cross?"

"That was my first thought. But no." Not without leverage anyway. "There's someone else who can."

7

“You’re going to get fat.”

I look up from the paperwork at the hotel lobby restaurant and nod at the empty plate in front of me. “You don’t know what was on there.”

“Burger. Fries. Side of pickles.” Mace looms over me, his hair pulled back in a ponytail. His trademark beard has been tamed into a slick goatee.

“Tell me you’re auditioning for a hipster revival of *Pirates of Penzance*.”

He rubs a hand over his face. “I was going to apologize for being late. But I realized you wouldn’t give a shit anyway.”

“Let’s go upstairs.”

I shuffle the papers into the folder.

Our feet are soundless as we cross the lobby carpet. I stop at the concierge’s desk on the way to the elevator. “I’m expecting someone this afternoon. Buzz them up.”

"Of course, Mr. Leonard."

We ride the elevator up, and I swipe my card at my door and step inside.

Mace groans. "Nice digs."

In the final days of tour, the realtor sent me listings for three huge mansions on the outskirts of Dallas. But I didn't go to see any of them. All three felt too permanent, too big. Which led to me renting the two-bedroom penthouse of the best hotel in town.

The living room is big enough to throw a party in, with low twin couches facing one another and a dark wood table between them. Art occupies the walls. There's a TV that comes down from the ceiling at the drop of a button.

"You haven't seen the best part." I take him out to the balcony, and he whistles.

"Life is good, huh?" Mace leans over the railing.

I study the landscape, the skyline of the city. Beneath us, people bustle around.

Some days I'm not sure how Mace and I ended up playing our own songs for packed houses instead of homeless or busting our asses for minimum wage. I know what that's like because it's where I came from.

"What about your sister and Annie? Are they on this floor too?"

My mood goes to shit in two seconds. "I stopped by the house for a talk with her husband earlier this week."

His brows pull together. "You're a public figure. You'll get in a shit-ton of trouble for that."

"The asshole called Grace and said I threatened him. She left, went back to him. Annie too."

"What're you going to do?"

"I'm working on it."

That's why my lawyer's due to stop by in a couple of hours. My agent phoned around and referred me to someone local who's expensive, good, and discreet. I've spent half the week with him.

It's also why I spent this morning looking over my finances. I've got more money than I could've counted as a teenager and I'm determined not to go bankrupt like some artists. I lived enough of my life poor to know I'll never let myself end up there again.

"What do you do? Now that you're off tour."

"I see my kid. I eat food that's not from a box. I work out."

Mace grunts. "I've built the Millennium Falcon, the Y-Wing, and the snowspeeder since we got off tour. And you know what I realized?" I shake my head. "All the little yellow LEGO dudes are the same, light sabers or no." He shoves a hand through his hair.

"Maybe you need a girl."

"Fuck no. I need a *job*. I can't even remember a time before I played for a band."

I recall the dimly lit venues I'd sneak out to with friends when I could afford to. Mace was way beyond the little shows and bars—I knew it even then. That was why I asked Cross if we could bring him in when Cross made me an offer. I wanted something familiar from home.

The music, the lifestyle, seemed to be part of Mace. At the time, I hadn't realized how much.

He pulls out a pack of cigarettes, and I raise a brow. "What happened to the nicotine patches?"

"The lesser of many evils." He shoots me a nervous smile as he lights it and takes a long drag. "When're we gonna record that album?"

Prickles of warning, twined with guilt, take up residence in my gut.

"I'm not in a hurry. Been cooped up on tour for eighteen months, man."

"Give me a date. I need something to look forward to."

I could lead him on, but I owe him better. "I don't know when. When I signed the deal with Cross to do this last album, I didn't know about Annie."

His face goes pale. "So, what? You're out for good because you want to be a family man?"

"It's not just that." I snag his cigarette and take a drag before passing it back. "The first album was me on my knees. It was never supposed to catch on. The second was me figuring out what the hell was going on in a world where I wasn't scraping for enough to buy mac and cheese. The third album—"

"It was weak," Mace says. "It was you in a power struggle with Cross. And maybe the producers saved your ass, but it was the worst thing you've put out."

I nod because he's not wrong. "I'm not putting out another shit album for Cross, or the money, or the lawyers."

"Then make it a real album. The kind that leaves you bleeding on the floor."

He says the words as if it's never occurred to me. The possibility of doing exactly that's drifted through my mind dozens of times.

I love making music. There's no question.

But it's a toxic relationship, like mine with Cross. The songs I write that matter have all cost me something.

Some days, I wonder who I'd be if I hadn't cut those parts of me out.

My friend finishes his cigarette, and I hold the door for him to go inside.

We shoot the shit for an hour, talking about Kyle's new charity commercials and the fact that Brick bought a place down the street from Nina. We complain about music and TV and the price of beer before I finally walk him out.

I check my phone in the kitchen. The lawyer wants to reschedule because they didn't get some papers in time. Grace hasn't replied to the text I sent two days ago, and I'm edgy. I'm on strict instructions from the lawyer not to doing anything stupid—technically, I think he said don't do anything—but I haven't seen my kid all week and I'm agitated.

Another text from earlier this week catches my eye.

Haley.

Instead of responding, I turn off my phone and change into swim trunks and take the elevator down to the pool level.

The smell of chlorine when I pass through the doors hits me like a drug.

Coming off tour's like getting released from jail. You've got to have routines, or you'll destroy yourself.

Which is one reason I've swum thirty laps every day since returning to Dallas.

The place is empty, and I have my pick of lanes. I drop my towel on a chair and dive in.

There's something about water that's cleansing. It strips us all down, makes us equal.

I never paid attention to science in high school, but in these moments, I get that we're all just atoms. That when you look close enough, we're all part of the same stuff put together differently.

When I get to the end of my first lap, I hit the wall and flip over. Front to back. Back to front. Front to back.

Somewhere between the first laps and the last, memories drift through my mind.

They start with the swimming lessons Grace and I took at the community pool as kids.

Before long, more recent ones take over.

The night Haley and I spent a night together last weekend is still the brightest thing in my mind even though all I did was hold her.

I left last week because I wasn't ready. I needed to get control of myself.

But after everything that's happened this week, that control feels more elusive than ever. Except for these moments, when I'm punishing my muscles and all I can feel is the burn deep inside them? It feels like I'm strung tight enough to snap.

I've never been selfless in bed. The blowjobs I allowed myself on tour, the way of venting when I didn't want to lose control and have another mistake, didn't help. Letting some woman I'd never see again explore her darkest fantasies with me meant I just had to be there.

I won't let myself be that with Haley. She deserves more.

She deserves everything.

We shouldn't be friends, or anything, but now that I know she exists out there in the world, I can't forget her. Maybe it would be easier if I didn't have money and fame and influence. But dammit, I'm used to getting what I want.

The thought of her seeing that Dale guy, or her precious professor, bothers the hell out of me. But at least they don't come with the baggage I have. With the distance of a few hundred miles between us, it's easier to see how true that is.

Which means that until I get my head on straight, which I can't see happening anytime soon?

The best thing I can do is stay far, far away from her.

8

HALEY

I almost chicken out three times.

The first is on the way to the airport, when I know there's no way I can score a standby flight in my price range.

Second is when I'm in the air at thirty-five thousand feet.

But the third isn't until I'm in the elevator, realizing there's no way I'll get up to the penthouse.

Outside his door, I glance at the jean skirt and tank top I put on this morning. I traded the Converse sneakers for ballet flats and flat-ironed my hair so it falls down my back. I press my lips together, but the balm I applied on my way out this morning is gone.

I knock lightly.

Nothing.

Maybe he's not home.

Disappointment seeps through me. On its heels,

though, there's relief. Because not seeing him means I don't have to look him in the eye and ask him something he's not going to like.

Come on, Haley, suck it up.

This time I knock hard enough the wood hurts my knuckles.

Finally, I hear footsteps.

Then the door swings wide, spilling light into the plush but windowless hallway.

Dammit. I should've prepared myself better.

There's no guitar in his hands, no paparazzi lurking in the corner. Jax shouldn't look like a god sent to wreck havoc on mortals.

His jaw's a little shy of square, his lips carved and purposeful, as if someone created him knowing he'd use his mouth, his voice, to rock the world. His hair is damp and brushes his forehead on one side.

Jax's white undershirt shows off the muscles of his shoulders, the scrolling ink of his tattoos. He's also wearing sweatpants.

I never knew sweatpants could cause cardiac arrest before.

"Haley."

He's surprised, and it's not in a good way.

"Hi. Is there... are you with someone?" It had never occurred to me, but now, seeing the curl of his hair, uncertainty creeps in with misery on its heels.

"Mace left a while ago. I just got back from the pool."

Relief has my shoulders sagging. "How'd you get up here?"

"Your doorman buzzed me up. Can I come in?"

He steps back, and I follow him inside.

I had a speech prepared, but it escapes me as I take in the foyer of his penthouse. Plush carpet, cream walls. A round mahogany table with a vase spilling fresh flowers.

It's a palace.

The thing is it doesn't seem too grand for him. It seems just right.

My attention drops to the pile of glossy magazines and brochures on the table. "Whoa, what is all this?"

"From my agent."

"A soda jingle. A reality TV series." I snort, picturing the guy I know doing either of those. But it's the third that has my stomach shaking. "Japanese hairspray?"

"Got to keep the money flowing." His mouth twists, and I relax a degree. Despite the reality check of this environment—the room that probably costs more a night than my apartment does a month—I'm reminded that this is still Jax. The man I joked with on tour. The man whose hoodie I own.

Although he doesn't look the most relaxed at the moment. Considering he's finished his tour, back in the city he wanted so badly to return to, he looks like he's ready to go three rounds with the world.

"You said I could come if I needed something." My throat is suddenly dry. "Can I get a drink first?"

With a moment's hesitation, he turns, and I follow him to the kitchen.

I try to ignore the way his clothes hug the muscles of his back. His shoulders. His ass.

Jax reaches into the stainless fridge, pops the top on a soda water, and offers it to me.

My gaze pulls down the kitchen to the bar at the end. "Do you have anything stronger?"

He goes to the bar, returns with a bottle of bourbon. He pours two fingers into a glass, which I take.

"Thanks." Jax studies me as I tip the glass back, wincing as the bourbon burns down my throat.

Now or never.

"You remember the app I was working on this summer?" He nods. "I've got another chance to submit it to a competition. But this contest's even bigger. I need more data. Preferably early cuts. The more songs and the more variations, the better."

"Meaning?"

I take a breath. Then another drink. "I need permission to use your songs. Unedited, unreleased—"

"Absolutely not."

I played this moment out in my head. I pictured him looking incredulous. Sceptical even.

What I didn't picture was the lightning-quick response. The dismissive jerk of his head.

"It's for science, Jax. Sure, the program can help make songs that sell. More importantly, it can help us learn how music affects our brains, our feelings. I was doing some research on the plane, and there are all these networks of scientists looking to understand the links between music and our emotions. Even our development as kids. What's more worthy than that?"

"This is business, Hales. Not personal."

Fire starts in my gut, and it's not from the bourbon. "Your best friend is your bassist. You almost missed a show because your flip phone went missing and you couldn't call your daughter. You say I'm just a tech on your tour, then you say you're going to fuck me someday. So tell me again where personal ends and business begins."

Jax's gaze narrows. "This isn't a good time, Hales. I can't help you."

He brushes past me, and I set the glass on the counter, scrambling after him. When he reaches for the door, I slide between it and him.

We stare each other down.

I'm out of options.

Not quite.

Everyone wants something. Cross wants power. Carter wants... who the hell knows what Carter wants? I'm done guessing.

But Jax? I know what Jax wants.

"I'm going to fuck you someday. But not until you beg me for it."

Riding a wave of bravado I might regret, I reach for the hem of my shirt.

The irritation is gone, replaced by something like panic. "What are you doing?"

I have no idea, but they say doing the same thing and expecting different results is the definition of insanity.

Moving slowly, I drag my tank up and over my head, squirming a little when it gets stuck on my earring. "Ouch."

"You need help?"

"No." I flush red. Panting, I manage to get the shirt off.

It takes every ounce of courage in me to let the fabric fall from my fingertips.

I've never tried to seduce a man before. I've never wanted to, nor am I deluded enough to think I know the first thing about how to do it.

I don't have moves, or pornstar heels, or dirty talk.

All I have is me and the feedback from his expression, his body, to guide me. To tell me if I'm on to something or if this will ruin everything.

Testing, I inch closer.

His nostrils flare, but he can't scare me. Not when I see his gaze drop to my black satin bra and linger there.

That observation makes me bolder. It's a positive result that has me deeming this line of experiments worthy of further exploration.

"I need those songs, Jax."

I trace the line of his shoulder, biting my tongue at the feel of his hot skin beneath my finger, and his eyes darken.

I can smell his shower on him, and I ignore the lust that rises up.

He's used to people tripping over themselves to obey him. He's not used to being pushed.

I'm gaining confidence in my play until everything shifts.

"You want me to pay you by the minute, Hales?" His voice is a soft challenge. Or by the act?"

I swallow, thick. "What's the norm?"

He glowers down at me like an avenging angel. "None of this is the norm. And it's not you. You don't think I know I could have you right now?"

Jax's hands grab my wrists, slam them overhead.

That's when I know I was wrong. That I took this too far.

I twist in his grip, trapped between the heat of his fingers and the door.

But instead of relenting, he squeezes harder.

I'm shaking on the inside. I hope to God he doesn't see it because I don't want to be weak in front of him. Not like this.

Jax's gaze rakes down my body. His slow perusal lingers on my lips, my breasts. My skirt's twisted and bunching, and I want to fix it.

But his gaze returns to mine, fierce and determined. "You. Need. To. Leave."

He lets go of my wrists, and they drop, limp at my sides. My head falls back, hitting the door as my eyes close.

Something soft tickles my cheek.

His hair.

I turn an inch, because that's all I can do, to find his forehead pressed against the wall.

I breathe him in, inhaling the familiar scent of his...

"Jax," I whisper.

"What?" The response is barely audible as he turns his face toward mine, his eyelids at half-mast.

The corner of my mouth twitches. "Did you buy my shampoo?"

Those amber eyes open, slow. The look in them has me sucking in a breath too late.

Because he *devours* me.

Every woman should have a chance to be kissed by Jax Jamieson once, because I can't think of anything that compares when that sexy mouth slants over mine.

He tastes like smoke, or I do, and the flavor of Jax and bourbon is the best thing I've ever had on my tongue.

My fingers find his damp hair. Not because I'm ready for more, but because I need something to hold onto.

He presses me back into the door on a groan.

His hands grip my bare waist, stroke up my back, sending shimmering ripples of sensation across my skin.

My nipples are tight peaks rubbing against his chest through my bra, and the friction has me making stupid little sounds I wish I could swallow.

I don't know where this is going. Or maybe I do, and

that's even scarier. It's like we're racing toward a cliff and I can't decide whether to hit the brakes or the gas.

The fear in my stomach can linger, keep company with the doubt, but none of it stands a chance next to the promise in Jax's eyes.

It's not a promise of safety or security.

It's a promise to show me something I've never seen before. Something *incredible*.

Which is why suddenly I'm kissing him back, pressing into him, tangling my tongue with his.

My hands loosen their grip, running down his shoulders, exploring the muscles there.

Jax's hands run up under the hem of my skirt to the edge of my panties, grabbing my ass like it's his right. He drags my legs up around his hips, but his mouth continues to torment mine as he carries me across the living room.

Who knew Jax Jamieson was an epic multitasker?

He sets me on something soft, and I blink my eyes open.

The room, the four-poster bed, none of it can compete with the way Jax is looking down at me.

A smile ghosts across his handsome, wicked face as he tugs down the cup of my bra, his rough palm squeezing my breast. I always thought moaning during sex was something porn stars did to sell it. Now the joke's on me because I can't stop the noises coming from my throat.

"I wanted to take this slow, Hales. Make it good for you."

Before I can ask what he means, his dark head drops, and he sucks my nipple into his mouth.

Oh, God, that's crazy. I mean, it's actually *stupid* how good that feels.

He chuckles, and I think I might have said it out loud.

My hands fist in his hair, pulling him closer as he licks, bites, and sucks on my body in a way I never knew I wanted and sure as hell never would've asked for.

But he's so competent, so confident, it bleeds into me. I can't be self-conscious, can't question, because he has every answer before I can think to ask.

He pulls back, releasing my breast with a pop and moving down my body with a wicked gleam in his eye.

A sting at my hip has me pulling back as he snaps my thong against my skin. "Off."

It's a little obscene that I'm almost naked and he's still fully clothed. But then, it's like winning the lottery and complaining when they give you the cash in twenties.

I'm afraid of what's happening between us, but I'm more afraid he'll stop. That he'll shake his head and realize how crazy this is and I'll never get to touch him again.

I work the fabric down my hips, kicking it off.

He reaches for the bedside table, then drops something onto the bed. Without moving, I sneak a glance at the foil packet, and my heart rate accelerates again.

I reach for it, but he pins my hand to the covers. "No. Not yet."

I want to protest but his mouth drops to my jaw, my neck. It feels like he's everywhere. Like he has four hands instead of two, two mouths instead of one. I'm surrounded by his scent, the feel of his lips and teeth. The sounds of his shallow breathing.

This isn't what I wanted. This is torture. I'm losing myself with every touch.

His fingers trail down over my thighs to my knees.

I'm too dizzy and wanting to protest when Jax pulls my thighs apart.

This time, his gaze does drop.

Dragging down my heaving chest, my shaking stomach, settling between my legs, where he makes a noise that sounds like a growl.

Oh shit. I can take him whispering in my ear. I can take him being rough with me.

This? This I can't take.

I try to bring my legs together, but he holds them wide.

"So fucking pink," he rasps. "The things I'm going to do to you."

My stomach muscles evaporate, and I fall back onto the bed.

I'm pretty sure the difference between college guys and men can be summed up in those two sentences.

Maybe Serena's right. Maybe there's something to—

"Ohmigodstop!"

My fingers grab his hair and yank him away.

Because his *tongue* is fucking *inside* me.

"Hales?" The vibration against the most sensitive parts of me makes me squirm, but he holds me tight. "You okay?"

"Yes." My voice is tiny.

"Really?"

Jax shifts over me, and I expect confusion or even irritation.

All I find when I force my gaze to his is concern.

"No," I admit. "I don't think I'm cut out for this." I grab the top of the comforter, tugging it to cover myself.

He drops onto the bed on his side, blowing out a breath as if he's channeling patience he's never tapped before. "You know why I said I want to fuck you, Hales?"

I shake my head, slow.

"Partly, it's because I can't think of anything sexier than the feeling of you on my cock." I shiver at those words. "But mostly, it's because I want to watch you lose your mind. And I want to be the one who makes you do it. What do you think about that?"

I turn it over like it's a rational question. "I think I have no idea why you would find that satisfying," I admit. "But I like that you do."

"Good. Because if you'll let me, I will do everything in my power to make that happen." His jaw tics, his brows drawing together in determination.

Oh boy. The idea of Jax putting his all into something —putting his all into *me*—is dizzying.

He nudges my bare shoulder with a finger. "That's what I wrote, you know," he goes on, that mouth I love curving at the corner. "On the sweatshirt. 'You're worth the wait.'"

I think I melt. "You did not write that the week after we met."

Jax grins. "How do you know?" He tucks a piece of hair behind my ear. "You want to get dressed?"

I bite my lip, considering, as my gaze runs down his still fully-clothed body. I feel like Alice stumbling into Wonderland, because the only thing I'm sure of is that if we go through with this? Nothing in my life will be normal again.

"No," I decide at last. "But maybe we could level the playing field."

He shifts off me, standing next to the bed. I prop myself up on my elbows, the blankets still draped over me.

Jax reaches for the edge of his shirt, yanking it over his head.

This is heaven. It actually is.

Heaven is this man's chest and abs and all that golden skin and rippling muscles inches from my face.

His sweatpants go next.

And whoa. That's not better at all.

I mean, it is, but it's also way more intimidating.

I stare at him. "Um. Jax… what's going on here?"

"Where exactly?" His solemn response has me shaking my head.

Because seriously.

Not only is he more of a man than any guy I've met?

He looks like one.

Every other you-know-what I've seen vanishes from my mind. Like hitting Empty Trash on your desktop.

"How is it possible we had a super awkward talk and you're still ready to go?"

He's thick and long and so hard it must ache. The bead of wetness at his tip has me swallowing.

"Because I'm always ready to where you're concerned, Hales." Jax's response is easy and shockingly earnest. "You have no idea how hard it was not to follow you to Nashville."

"Really?"

He nods, and I'm feeling less at a disadvantage every second. My gaze roams back down his body.

I shift on the bed, reaching for the foil packet at the corner as he watches. Somehow Jax's gaze darkens more when I lift it. Hold it out.

"You want me inside you?" he rasps.

"Yes."

"Say it."

"I want you inside me."

I reach for the covers over me and slowly push them to the side so I'm naked again. His gaze flares with heat as he takes me in.

"Shit, I want that too."

I watch, fascinated, as he rips into the package and rolls the condom on. He's efficient and confident, and I could watch him touch himself all day.

But that's not his plan, because he settles himself between my thighs.

"Wait! Just tell me one thing first," I say.

The concern is back, mixed with a little desperation some sick part of me loves. "Yeah?"

I blink up at him, all innocence as I tilt my head. "Do I get those tracks?"

He lets out a laugh that turns into a groan. "What'd I say about business and pleasure, Hales?"

"I don't think we came to a consensus," I murmur.

He brushes my entrance, and I swallow a moan.

I can't tell who's winning, but I love this banter. Almost as much as the sex.

"You win," he decides. "Let's talk numbers."

For a second, I wonder if I've gotten the upper hand. But the knowing look that crosses his face makes me instantly suspicious.

When he rubs a slow circle over my clit, I can't hold in the gasp.

"'Redline' as a single alone grossed fifteen mil."

The second time has pleasure shooting down my legs, making my toes clench.

"Plus a tenth of touring on the album."

My body spasms, arching up to him.

"I assume a tenth is reasonable given it was a ten-track album."

I nod, my throat working soundlessly.

He settles into a rhythm that's too slow and too intense at once.

It's good.

It's really fucking good.

And he knows *everything*. Everything he's ever made for Wicked. The hits, the flops, the sales, the tours, the press. He's like a damned encyclopedia of his career.

It's sexy.

It's maddening.

Combined with his touch, the addictive scent of him, I'm bowing off the bed, a storm building that's as familiar as it is impossible.

"You have good hands," I murmur.

His eyes glint. "I always thought they were too big."

Then he presses inside me.

"God, how many fingers is that?!"

"One." He grins, shifting to slide into me again. "Now it's two."

But I'm already gasping for breath.

"So, the unedited versions of three songs alone are worth eight figures. And that's with the friends and family discount." Jax looks up, a smirk on his handsome face as his damp hair falls across his forehead. "I assume you'll be wiring the amount in full."

All my twisted mind hears is *full*.

Because I want to be full. Of him.

I take it back. Wave the damned white flag on my naïve, careless vow to my roommate that I'm never having sex again.

I need Jax in me, or I'm going to stop breathing.

My heart will stop beating. Then I'll be dead. The first human being to die from lack of sexual satisfaction.

Serena will have to give my eulogy with Scrunchie on a leash next to her, and...

"Forget the songs," I beg.

"I thought we were making real progress."

"I'm going to rip your balls off and sell them on eBay," I mumble.

His chuckle dissolves into a grin as he shifts over me. "There's my girl," he murmurs, his lips rubbing mine and sending sparks everywhere.

I'm beyond ready for him when he presses against me, groaning.

The triumph in his eyes is overtaken by something more earnest when he nudges my legs wide.

He sinks into me.

Jax's jaw goes tight. His eyes glaze over, and it's like I'm watching a reflection of what's happening inside me.

And I get it.

Holy God, I get it now.

He's everywhere. In every part of me. My fingers, my toes, my lips, my breasts.

"Jax," I gasp. "You feel—"

"Fucking incredible," he finishes, his voice scraping along my nerve endings.

There's some discomfort, but I don't want him to go. It's like my body wants that too, and it's changing for him, around him.

Just when I think I've almost got a handle on this, he moves.

One arm bands around his body, needing to feel him, while the other fists the sheets.

I'm drifting in the sky and tethered to the ground at once.

Each thrust of his body's the verse of a song, the chapter of a story. It builds on the last, bringing us closer, sending me higher, taking him deeper.

Jax changes the angle, and my nails dig into the muscles of his neck, making him groan.

Then we're chasing each other and the feeling until I feel it build.

Or not really build, because it was there, waiting for me.

I murmur his name into his neck.

Again. And again.

My fingers dig into his shoulders because shit, it's really happening.

It's a detonation, starting in my core. Every organ's part of it, every muscle.

The waves radiate outward with an impact that registers on the Richter scale and a blast radius that probably reaches China.

I cry out something. Maybe it's his name.

I think I'm dying, and I don't really care because life doesn't get any better than this.

At least not until Jax goes tight everywhere, his back clenching beneath my fingers as he groans.

In twenty-one years, it's the most beautiful sound I've ever heard.

9

Two weeks. I've lived here two weeks but never noticed the pattern on the ceiling. Do all hotels have that? A big light fixture with little circles running around it?

I think I'm tripping. Every part of my body hums, from my toes to my lips. Lying on my back, my heart thudding, I catch my breath. The sheets slide under my skin as I roll onto my side.

Strands of dark hair stick to Haley's face. I can't bring myself to feel anything other than damned satisfied I made her that way. I'm pretty sure there's no way this can get better, but her eyes open and she looks at me, all dark pupils and sleepy lids.

I swear I'm immortal.

At least until Haley bursts into laughter.

I clear my throat. "Not the reaction I was going for."

But she keeps laughing. "Wow, Jax. I mean... wow."

"That I'll take." I cut off her laugh when I pull her lips to mine. I kiss her long and deep, my tongue sweeping over hers. Reminding her of what we were doing a moment ago.

What I hope we'll be doing again soon.

"You're really good at that," she murmurs when we part.

"Thanks."

I stroke her from bare shoulder all the way to her waist. I do it again—because I can—and she makes a little noise in her throat.

"I bet you've never had to talk a girl off a cliff before sex."

"I didn't have to talk you off a cliff. We just had to discuss some things."

She cocks her head, looking shy in a way that's completely adorable considering I was inside her five minutes ago. "Is that bad? Because I kind of liked the discussing part."

"It was fucking perfect." I can't help grinning.

My hand skims down her chest, tugging lightly at the comforter she's holding over her chest. She drops it, watching as I cup her breast, memorizing the shape, the feel.

Obviously there are things she's more and less comfortable with, but the noise low in her throat tells me we're definitely in green-light territory.

"You're a boob guy." But her teasing has a breathy edge.

"I've always thought of myself more as an ass man. But I could be having an epiphany."

I press my lips to the underside of her breast, nipping lightly until she gasps. Then, because I can't help it, I suck her.

Hard.

"Jax..." The catch in her voice has me half-hard again already.

First things first.

I get off the bed and stride to the en suite.

As I return to the bedroom, she's like a deer caught in the headlights. All legs and eyes and innocence as she tries to slink out of bed.

"Where do you think you're going?"

"I brought some work to do."

"You came here to work?" I ask, incredulous.

"It's four in the afternoon. We're not staying in bed."

"Um, yeah, we are."

I think she's going to say no, but I manage to convince her.

Because now that she's already naked, I can take my time with her.

So I do.

I kiss her until she's breathless.

I worship her tits—which are seriously gorgeous, by the way. Not too big, but they're round and fill my hands.

When I lick circles around their hardened tips, she makes the hottest fucking sounds.

Almost like when I press two fingers inside her.

This time I have more stamina.

This time, when I sink into her tight heat, I'm ready for it.

At least that's what I tell myself.

"Fuck, Hales," I groan against the soft skin of her throat.

Her arms go around me, tentative at first, then more determined. I change the angle, edging deeper, and her fingers dig into my back.

She can leave nail marks from my shoulders to my ass for all I care.

She's going to feel me for days. I don't mind her returning the favor.

I pull back to watch her face because I can't get enough of that look. Flushed cheeks, like she just got off a stage.

Full, parted lips that make me even harder.

I tell myself this girl's innocent, but the way her eyes cloud when she looks at me, when I'm inside her, I want to corrupt her.

I want to learn what she likes, then teach her every dirty thing I know and see where we end up.

When she gets close to the edge, which I can feel from the way she's breathing, how tight she is everywhere, and the little hiccups coming from her throat every few strokes, I decide I am corrupting her.

"OhhhmigodJax." The wonder in her voice makes it sound like I've just shown her a fourth dimension.

Hell, maybe I have.

That sound has my abs shaking as I run my mouth down her jaw, her throat. She arches into me.

"I fucking love seeing you like this, Hales. I love watching you come apart for me."

I know she's close, and hell, I am too, and I can't put this off anymore. So I reach down between us and rub the spot that had her leaping off the bed earlier.

Haley goes tighter than the first string on my guitar. "Oh. Oh fuck, I can't even breathe right now."

Her hoarse whisper in my ear might as well be the filthiest confession for what it does to me.

She comes around me as I continue to thrust until I can't take it anymore. I'm shaking and sweating, and the feel of her exploding around me shoves me off the edge.

I collapse on top of her and decide I want to add a new tattoo for every orgasm I give her.

"Well?" I ask when I can speak. "Was it a fluke?"

Her head swivels back and forth. "You're legit," she pants.

I can't stop the chuckle that rolls out of me.

Eventually we get dressed and go out into the living room.

We order pizza, and I pop up On Demand on the

massive screen. She clicks into the recently watched list. "Home reno shows?" Her voice lifts with surprise.

"Yeah. I'd like to work on my own place someday."

"You want to build a house?"

"Maybe start with a shed. I'd be all rugged, with a saw in my hand."

"I was picturing a paint roller, maybe some wallpaper."

I'm starting to think I need to remind her of my masculinity when the pizza arrives.

She peers into the box, taking a sniff. "Whoa. What the hell is that?"

"Beef and Fritos. Best there is."

"We'll see."

But she eats it, offering a deferential nod after the first bite. "Okay, you got this one."

I grin as her attention goes back to the TV. "Well, if you're going to fix your house someday, you need one to start with."

She grabs her phone and pops up a new window with real estate listings. "How about this one?"

I glance at it. "Hales, that's pocket change. If I'm going to buy a house, it better be big."

"Right. Columns and a swimming pool." She clicks away. "How about that one?"

I start to tell her no way, but my gaze locks on the picture. "It's alright."

She hits a few keys.

"What are you doing?"

"Emailing the realtor to see if he can show it tomorrow."

"Shit. Any other parts of my life you want to fix while you're here?"

"What else needs fixing?"

I start to brush her off but think better of it.

I tell her what happened with Grace, with her husband. Haley's eyes get rounder and rounder, but she doesn't interrupt.

"I've been trying to get Grace to let me see Annie," I finish. "She said no."

"Well, it has to be a change for Grace too. You've been gone—"

"And now I'm back. And I'm going to fix things."

"Maybe she doesn't think they're broken." I turn that over in my head, uncomfortable. The light on my phone, sitting on the coffee table, blinks at us, and Haley raises a brow.

"Knock yourself out." I pass it to her, and she flips it open and scans the messages.

"How about this?" She types a message and holds it up.

When would be a good time to see Annie? I can pick her up.

I shrug. "Sure. But don't get your hopes up, Hales."

Her eyes shine. "I will do whatever I want with my hopes, Jax."

The earnestness in her expression has me shaking my head. It's cute that she's so optimistic still about the world and her place in it.

"I don't get why old guys date younger women. They can't keep up." I stiffen, realizing my mistake. "And by 'date' I mean hypothetically."

"Dammit, and here I was going to invite you to meet my father." She shoots me a look that puts me in my place.

I curse. "I deserve that. I just meant that I didn't plan this, Hales. And you know I like being around you, but..."

"You're not looking to settle down with someone," Haley finishes. "I'm not either, Jax. I'm twenty-one. I'm just trying to live through graduation."

The words should relieve me.

When the show ends, she picks out a wildlife documentary. As I try to lose myself in it, my stomach turns over.

Not because the idea of dating her is so offensive.

Because it *isn't*.

I never thought of myself as the kind of person who'd want to date someone. I really don't even know what dating means.

My guess is it involves being in the same place as someone else for more than a few days, which for years is something I haven't been.

Plus, people who date have sex. It's pretty much guaranteed.

But they also have *this*.

The pizza and the Netflix.

The long looks and the secrets and the inside jokes.

Haley seems like the kind of woman who'd go on dates.

As opposed to the kind who shows up at your house and seduces you.

Although she was scary good at—

"Whoa!" I jerk upright so fast Haley grabs the couch for balance. "Is that a leopard?"

The thing jumps into the lake and eats an alligator.

"I told you," she says, triumphant.

10

"Nice ride."

"It's a Benny," Annie chirps.

I glance toward the back seat of the car I bought between my last two tours. I'm surprised Annie remembers, but it's cute.

"Actually, it's a Bentley," she corrects. "But when I was little, I couldn't *say* Bentley."

"That's fair," Haley agrees. "You like it?"

"I'd like it better in purple. Uncle Jax said they didn't come in purple."

"Maybe he'd paint it if you asked him nicely."

Her gaze meets mine in the rearview mirror, and I raise a brow.

"What's your favorite color, Haley?" my kid asks.

It's the tenth question she's asked since we picked her up, and I have no idea how she gets the energy. She's tiny and bouncy, with hair like mine and brown eyes and freckles.

"Orange."

"Uncle Jax's eyes are orange."

"Really? I hadn't noticed."

Last night, Haley and I ate pizza and binge-watched television.

Home shows. Planet Earth. Around ten, we switched to HBO.

Somehow, we fell asleep.

Not naked.

Not sweaty.

Not after I made her scream my name.

Just... asleep. I slept like the dead in a way I haven't in forever.

It was so blissfully normal I can't describe how good it felt.

I let Haley and Annie out of the car. I've been to my share of mansions. This one has a gate, a long driveway, and a dozen bedrooms.

But it's hard to focus on the specs when my attention's drawn to the way the denim shorts cling to Haley's hips and leave her long legs bare. The T-shirt knotted at her navel teases me with the occasional glimpse of skin.

Grace had responded to Haley's text and let me take Annie for the day, which had left me both surprised and pleased.

Now I'm thinking Haley and I should've taken a detour first.

"What do you think?" I murmur.

Haley screws up her face, tapping a finger on her full lips. "No columns. Annie?"

The kid makes the same face as Haley, nodding. "No columns."

I think something's wrong with my chest. It shouldn't feel this tight hearing two girls talk about architecture.

The realtor meets us at the door.

Annie goes first, her braid bobbing down her back as she lifts her chin to look around the vaulted ceilings.

Haley looks only slightly less awed. "It didn't look this big in the listing. You could renovate one room every month and never run out."

"Of things to saw."

"Or wallpaper." Haley grins.

"It's like you've made it your job to keep my ego in check."

"Someone's got to."

The master could hold a small army. The en suite is marble with a soaker tub and a glassed-in shower. While Haley inspects the bathroom, Annie wanders off down the hall.

"What do you need a bench in the shower for?" Haley drops onto it, and I step closer. Her gaze is level with the zipper of my jeans, and she raises her chin with a startled look.

"To keep my ego in check," I repeat with a grin. I'm liking this place more and more.

I can see the wheels turn in her head. "Is that what a blowjob is really about? Ego?"

I shrug. "Depends who you ask. Some people would say it's about power. I say call it what it is: a really good fucking time."

She cocks her head. "Is it? I've never done that before."

I think I bite off my tongue.

The possibility that I could be the only man to have her gorgeous lips wrapped around me had never occurred to me. Now, it's the only thing I want in this world.

My thumb brushes her lower lip before pressing at the center. The softness of her skin, the damp heat of her mouth, has my voice dropping an octave. "I'm a good teacher."

Before she can respond, a shriek makes my blood run cold.

"Annie? Honey, where are you?"

I stalk toward the hall and pull up at a door. Haley bumps into my back. Annie's in the middle of a room that's pale purple.

"This is my room," she decides, spreading her arms as if she could touch the walls. "Haley, your room's the next one." She crooks a finger, beckoning us to follow her next door.

Haley dutifully follows her in.

"I dunno if there's enough space to put all your

computer crap," I say. "But your Betty Boop clock could go right there." I nod toward one wall. "Next to your poster of me," I add with a smirk.

"Right?" Annie shoots me an exaggerated wink from the other side of the room. "Haley, what's a Betty Boob clock?"

I shake my head as Haley steps closer.

"I've been here a day, and you're asking me to move in with you?" she jokes under her breath.

"Mostly I'm angling for that blowjob."

I swear her eyes darken three shades.

"Well?" the realtor calls, breaking the spell.

"I'll take it."

Annie squeals.

"Wonderful! Let me show you the tennis courts."

I brush past him. "I don't play."

After we drop Annie off, I drive back to the hotel, my fingers tapping on the steering wheel.

Haley sighs out a breath, nestled in the passenger seat like she belongs there.

"You're the best dad, Jax Jamieson," she says as we pull up at a light.

The back of my throat burns. "Thanks, Hales."

"It sucks that she doesn't even know it. When are you going to tell her you're her father?"

I shoot her a look. "Grace and I agreed not to. But if I have to fight for her, I will."

"For what it's worth, I think the truth is always better. Even if it screws things up."

"You don't regret finding out about Cross."

She considers. "No. This summer, I found myself thinking I wish I'd known sooner because maybe I would've felt less alone. But then I realized being alone is good sometimes. Because no matter what happens, there are times in your life when all you have is you. And you've got to learn to have your own back."

How she got so smart I have no idea, but I'm reminded how far ahead of me she is. "You want kids someday?"

I'm really curious. More curious than I was to see the house today, though I can't put my finger on why.

"I'm not sure. I know my mom's gone and my dad was AWOL, but kids can surprise you. They can end up screwed up for no reason or amazing for no reason."

"Ain't that the truth of it."

A song comes on the radio. Lita's band.

I sing along, and Haley looks surprised. "What happened to 'Jax Jamieson doesn't do covers'?"

"I'm in the privacy of my own car. Besides," I grudgingly admit, "she's good."

"I know. I heard her recording the other day."

"What?" I slam on the brakes, and Haley sucks in a breath. "When were you going to tell me you were at Wicked?"

She shoots me a guilty look. “Cross didn’t submit my letter of reference because I left the tour early. He agreed to help me get back into school on the condition I spend this semester working at Wicked.”

I pull over to the side of the road, throw the car in park, and spin to face her. “No. I don’t like this, Hales. You should be in school. Not in that man’s debt.”

“I’m keeping my options open,” she corrects. “I’m going to get back into school no matter what. At least this way, if nothing else works, he’ll write me the letter and I’ll be back in next semester. In the meantime, I’m working. Saving up money. Submitting my program to this competition.

“He’s not part of my life, and he doesn’t want to be. He brought me in to assess me, and apparently he found me wanting.”

Part of me wants to reach for her. Instead I drum my fingers on the steering wheel. “Hales. You should’ve told me.”

“I was a tech on your tour. We were ships passing.”

There’s hurt in her voice, and I hate that I put it there.

There’s a difference between control and power. Control is about directing your own life. Setting up the circumstances you interact with so things work out the way you want them to.

I’ve always wanted control.

I never wanted power. Power is mindless. It has no end. It exists to tempt and corrupt and enthral.

I don't want to have the power to hurt her. Because I don't want to hurt her, and because it means she can hurt me too.

Which is why I can't throw myself over the edge with her.

I need to look after myself and my kid, and for some reason I feel the need to look after Haley.

But I can't look after her if I'm falling for her.

"I need to show you something," she says before I can respond.

She shifts and pulls a scrap of paper from her pocket. I take it, scanning the handwriting.

My handwriting. "How'd you get this?"

"I found it on the floor of a diner on tour. I should've given it back, but I couldn't bring myself to. The second I read it, I knew it was a love song. And it's beautiful."

The paper's worn, like it's been folded and unfolded a million times.

I set it on the dashboard and shove a hand through my hair. "I'm never cutting another album."

"What if you change your mind?"

"I won't."

I like how much respect she has for my work. Not because she can make money off it or because she wants to suck up.

Because she just *loves* it.

"You can keep the song. And if you really want my unedited cuts for your program? They're yours." Her jaw drops. “I keep backups on a server. I can get you a drive before you leave.”

Her eyes turn the color of melted chocolate. “Thank you. I’ll take good care of them.”

11

HALEY

Serena: You coming home at a normal time tonight?

Haley: By midnight for sure.

Serena: That's three nights in a row. Tell me you haven't given up on men and fallen in love with a computer in the basement.

Haley: Definitely not.

Serena: Good. Because the weak ass excuses you've given me since getting back aren't going to fly. I'm making popcorn tonight, and you're acting out every part of your weekend with Jax.

I got back from Dallas to an email saying half the computers at Wicked had caught a virus. I've spent every waking hour there since trying to get the systems patched and updates installed.

By Wednesday night, we're finally back up and running.

I finish up at Wicked and go home. Sure enough, Serena's parked on the couch with a notepad.

She waited up for me. And I owe her.

She slides tortoiseshell glasses onto her face as I shut the door behind me and drop my bag on the floor.

"Since when do you wear glasses?" I ask as I drop onto the couch across from her.

"Since they look super cute on me." She slides them down her nose. "First is the multiple choice. Then we'll get to the short answer and eventually the essay."

"Is this a midterm or a conversation?"

"The former. Let's get started. Did you and Jax have sex? Yes or no, please."

If I had any hope of flying under the radar, it's gone now. I see it in her eyes. She'll bludgeon me with persistence until I cave.

Which is why I answer, "Yes."

"More than once?"

"Yes."

"*Yes*." Her eyes gleam. "Okay, equipment."

"I'm not describing his dick to you."

"How big is it?" She waits. "Blink once for small, multiple times for big."

I blink. And keep blinking.

"Now the bonus round. Did he go down on you?"

"Serena—"

"This is important." Her gaze narrows, but I refuse to look away.

"He tried," I say under my breath. "I ripped his hair out of his head when I shoved him away."

Serena chokes on a laugh. "What the hell?! Was he that bad?"

"No! It just freaked me out. It's like a guy's having a conversation with the wrong end of you."

My roommate dissolves into fits, holding her stomach. "Oh my God, Haley. And he still had sex with you after that?"

"Yeah." I sigh.

She stares at me like she's trying to read the answer from my pores. "You *came*," she accuses at last. "You came so hard."

"SERENA!"

"I told you he'd be better than Carter."

"I don't know how Carter is."

And I don't want to. All I can think about is Jax.

Not only was the sex something I'd never expected to experience in my lifetime, but house hunting with him didn't help me keep my cool.

I'd always known Jax was incredible.

I never expected him to be so *real.*

It's the realness that's killing me.

I'm not sure I can ever go back to college guys. Jax is such a… well… man. Not only his body, though God, he's in terrific shape, but the way he looks at me. The way he looks at everything. Like he knows who he is and what he can do and takes responsibility for himself in the world.

"So how did you leave things?" she asks.

"It's casual," I say, though the word feels completely wrong for describing anything that's ever happened between me and Jax. "He still has to come to Philly sometimes. And he said he'd pay for my travel if I come to visit him."

"He's paying you for booty calls!?"

I hold up a hand. "I told him no way. To the paying part, not the visiting part."

As my phone buzzes, Serena leans toward it. "Is that him?"

"No. It's…" My brows pull together. "Kyle."

"Who's Kyle? Wait, is this a fourth boyfriend?"

"No. Kyle Lithgow. The drummer for Riot Act."

"Why's he texting you?"

The answer becomes obvious.

Kyle: Lita gave me your number. I wanted to talk to you about making an album.

"What the... since when are you Dr. Dre?"

Haley: Sure. On the phone?

Kyle: I'm in Philly. Can we meet? Tomorrow?

"This is weird. I mean, Kyle's cool, but it's not like we're tight or—"

"This Kyle?" Serena holds up her phone, and I squint at the search engine image results.

"Yup. Where should I meet him?"

"The café," she says so fast my brows shoot up.

I get to the café after work at Wicked, and Serena insists on coming too. Kyle, Mace, and Lita swing in the door at the same time.

I introduce them, and we get back to the subject at hand.

"We want to do another album," Kyle says, his gaze lingering a little too long on Serena. "Jax is out, but we're still in."

Lita leans forward. "You know Cross."

I frown. "He won't even let me work on your album."

Kyle shifts in his seat. "I know you guys have a... relationship. Maybe you could talk to him."

"I didn't know that was public knowledge"—I shoot Lita a look, and she winces—"but still... you guys would make a great album. I know it. But I have zero pull."

"Doesn't hurt to try, does it?"

Their pleading faces make me sigh. "The thing is marketing's downsizing and everyone's way behind. Plus, there's no money in albums, right? It's all in touring."

"The money doesn't fucking matter." Mace's explosion has us all turning toward him.

"What my colleague means to say"—Kyle claps his friend on the shoulder with a warning look—"is that our needs are more modest than Jax's. If Jax wants to stop being a rock star, that's his deal. We need a way to keep doing it."

I turn it over in my head, but it's Serena who leans in. "You could release singles. Build a story, like an album but one piece at a time."

"Thanks, Jay-Z," I say, and she rolls her eyes. "But Cross won't go for it. If I talk to him, he'll be less likely to say yes, not more."

Mace shoves out of his chair before I can take another breath.

"Just try, okay?" Kyle asks, a pleading look on his face before he trails his bandmate out the door.

12

HALEY

"Hi, Hales."

There's nothing better than answering the phone when Jax Jamieson is on the other end.

Oh, wait. There is, and it's answering a video call to find not only his gorgeous face and smirk on the other end, but damp hair curling at his ears and a tantalizing glimpse of bare shoulders and pecs.

"Why are you shirtless?"

"Just practicing for an underwear campaign."

Two emotions slam into me in quick succession. The first is lust. The second might be jealousy.

"Seriously?"

"Nah. Just got back from a swim and got out of the shower."

Now I'm picturing his hard body cutting through the water. That's way less distracting.

"What're you doing?"

"Ducked out of Wicked to work on my program." I shift on my bed, shoving my hair out of my face. "Carter gave me some feedback. Now I'm even running some of Lita's songs through the program to make suggestions. Thanks again for your data."

"Ouch. I have fifteen Billboard top tens, and all I am to you is data?"

"Not only data. But also data," I say helpfully.

His amber gaze narrows. "I think what you really want is me telling you I spent the whole call with my agent yesterday staring at the balcony and picturing what it'd be like to fuck you on it."

I nearly drop the phone.

I close the bedroom door before shifting back on my bed, pulling my knees up to my chest. Serena's outside, and if she heard that, I'm never going to see the end of it.

"That's very specific," I say.

His mouth twitches, like maybe he knows it took me every ounce of courage to respond. "I bet you're wet just thinking about it."

Jax's smooth voice gets rough, and if I wasn't before, I am now.

Sex with Jax last weekend made me realize how much I have to learn. That part wasn't a surprise.

The surprising part was how much I *want* to.

I was afraid I might regret it. I don't. But I'm thinking about this whole other world that experienced rock stars know that I've never considered. A world where you can say as much with your bodies as with your words.

"Show me," he says.

"What?"

"Show me how wet you are."

I suck in a breath.

It's as if Jax is constantly feeling out my comfort zone. He walks around it, taking it all in, like he walks around a stage before a show until he knows every corner, every boundary.

Then he shoves me out of it.

This request is less scary than some of the things we've done because I'm totally in control and he's not even here.

On the other hand… it's completely filthy.

I stretch my legs out an inch at a time, my feet sticking on the comforter. Then I slide my hands down the front of my pants, brush the slick skin between my legs, and hold up my glistening fingertips.

"Good girl." His raspy voice isn't enough reward. Not nearly. "Now spread your legs."

Something occurs to me. "Jax, is this actually why you called? Or are you just annoyed I was talking to Carter?"

Jax's grin turns wolfish. "Both. Now touch yourself. Nice and easy."

His smugness transforms into need as I shift on the bed, adjusting the phone so I can drop my other hand back down my body.

He shifts too, and the headboard appears behind him.

Now I'm wondering if he's hard.

I'm wondering if he's leaking.

I wonder when I became the kind of girl who wondered about those things.

"What about you?" I murmur as my fingers drift over my skin.

"What about me?"

But his jaw clenches and he angles the phone down. I can see his hand on his cock, protruding from the fly of his jeans. He's thick and pink and my throat dries instantly.

He strokes himself a couple of times, his big hand firm on his cock, and that makes me wetter.

It's the dirtiest dream I've ever had. Except it's real.

"Fuck yourself. Two fingers," he commands when the camera returns to his tight face.

I do as he says, my back arching as I picture his hand, not mine.

"If you were here, I'd play with that perfect pussy."

I press against my fingers, gasping as I picture exactly that.

"One day, Hales, I'm going to take that little clit in my mouth." My thumb is a slave to his words, finding that spot, rubbing a circle, and my hips jerk against the pressure. "I'm going to suck on it until you're begging to come."

And that puts me over the edge.

I whimper as my climax shakes through me. His grunts come over the phone, and the tension in his face tells me he's almost there too. The sound of his hand sliding up and down his cock faster, harder, is hot as hell. A moment later, with a guttural groan, he comes.

I watch, fascinated. And the satisfaction from watching his face is different from my own orgasm, but it's not less. In some ways, it's more.

"Don't move." He shifts in the picture, his lids lowering like he's cleaning up. "I've been picturing that all week," he says when he finishes.

The shiver that works through me is involuntary. I don't know why that's so hot that I made him messy, but it is.

Jax props a hand behind his head, revealing a deliciously tattooed arm as he grins. "I'm in town next week. Some paperwork to finish up with Wicked."

I swear my hand shoots up in the air like I'm in second grade.

"You could stay here."

Jax hesitates, and for a second, I think he's going to say no. Instead, he says, "Perfect."

Warmth tingles in my chest. Not in a sex way.

In a feelings way.

I know him staying here doesn't mean anything. I love spending time with him even though it still feels *Sixth Sense* weird that one of the biggest stars on the planet spends his private moments with me.

Add to that the *way* we spend those moments?

It's pretty freaking great.

Especially when that guy also writes incredible songs, looks out for his friends and family, and uses the most beautiful voice to say the dirtiest things.

"I better go get ready," I say finally even though I don't want to.

"Where are you going tonight?"

"Out."

"Yes, I figured. With?"

I don't want to be evasive, but I know he won't like the answer. "Cross."

Storm clouds take over his expression as I tell him about Kyle and Mace wanting to record an album.

"They never should've come to you."

"Well, they did." I shift off the bed and prop the phone on my dresser as I rummage for new clothes. I strip out of my jeans and grab a skirt.

"It's a bad idea," he says, peering downward as if he can see below the frame of the phone.

I hide my smile. "Your opinion is noted. Goodnight, Jax."

Jax sighs, his gaze returning to mine. "You're really trying to piss me off, aren't you?"

"I let you watch me masturbate. I'd call that exceedingly accommodating."

An hour later, I make my way across town to the historic district of the city as the sun sets in the background.

The only way to make an evening out with your recently discovered record exec and control freak father more awkward is knowing you just had phone sex with your non-boyfriend.

Who works for your dad and hates him.

It's just like real family.

I sit on the edge of a concrete flower bed in front of our designated meeting spot and check my phone.

"Haley."

It takes a second for me to focus on the man in a navy button-down and jeans in front of me.

"I didn't notice you with the..." I gesture at his outfit.

"I do get out of a suit every now and then."

"Right."

"I was surprised when you suggested we talk. Away from the studio."

"Well, I was surprised you suggested here." I shift off the flowerbed and glance down the street. "Jazz?"

"This concert series has been happening for years. I had a hand in it once."

I'm not sure what to read into that. But it makes me think of how there're no pictures of him or his achievements in his office. He sticks his hands in his pockets as we walk side by side through the crowd of early-evening pedestrians.

Now that I have him here, I'm not sure what to say. I

can't exactly lead with Kyle and Mace's request. Cross is way too smart for that.

"Is this what you do when you're not working?" I ask instead. "I mean, I know nothing about you."

"That's not true," he chastises.

"All right, I found out you have a brother in California." I pause. "Do you have a girlfriend?"

"No."

I go to shove my hands in my pockets, realizing my skirt has none. "What made you get into music?"

"I thought I'd play trumpet in a jazz band."

My gaze cuts to him without warning. "No way."

"Mhmm. It was all very romantic." His mouth twitches, and for a moment he looks younger.

I have to remind myself I didn't come to hear him talk about growing up. That this entire meeting is means to an end, a reason to make Kyle and Mace's request.

"So what made you decide not to play trumpet?"

"I was ten when we moved to Philadelphia from Belfast. My father had a leather goods store back in Ireland. He was a sought-after craftsman there, but when he left, he had nothing. Stateside, he worked repairing shoes. But he made sure we had enough. I always remembered what he gave up for us. I wanted to make something from his legacy."

"Which is why you started Wicked?"

He nods. "I understand what it's like to want something bigger than yourself."

It's as if he knows what's in my head. It's disconcerting as hell, but somehow it's also comforting.

I can't help asking, "What about my mom?"

Cross's mouth pulls down at the corner, but not in a frown. More like he's trying to decide how to talk about something he's not used to talking about. "We had a relationship—an affair—for a few months. I could tell you it was serious. That I loved her. But that would be doing you a disservice. What I can say is you have her hair, her mouth, and her way of figuring things out no matter what comes your way."

I swallow because I didn't expect such a real answer from him. "When did you find out about me?"

"She told me she was pregnant. That I had to decide whether I wanted to be a father or not. There was no middle ground. My focus was my company. But I said I would support you."

This is news to me. "And did you?"

He shakes his head. "She wouldn't allow it."

This is so not why I'm here, but now that we're rolling, I can't seem to stop. I'd always pictured Shannon Cross as this untouchable executive. Not a refreshingly honest man with a lifetime love of the trumpet.

A man I'm suddenly dying to know more about.

"So you never tried to see me?"

"I did. We reconnected when you were a teenager. Spent time together for a few weeks." *The picture from the party Serena found.* "I'd started Wicked, was working around the clock trying to discover big talent.

"I asked if I could see you. She wasn't sure at first but eventually agreed. I was in the car to go see you when I got a call. From a jail. In Dallas."

Understanding dawns. "Jax."

He nods. "I'd been trying to sign him all year. Since his eighteenth birthday. But that was the day he hit rock bottom. He had no one to help him get out of there. So I went to him instead of you."

My chest tightens. "Because you wanted to sign him."

Cross rubs a hand over his smooth jaw, a move that's startlingly familiar. "He was lost, Haley. Gutted. A child with nothing but feelings, and those feelings were eating him alive.

"Some people are live wires, meant to electrify the night." He nods at the lights hanging from the trees. "But they need careful management so they don't burn out, or catch fire, or destroy themselves."

"Jax doesn't need that anymore."

"You may be right," he surprises me by saying.

"I know Jax is supposed to do another album. What if he doesn't want to? I mean, could he get out of it?"

"Legally, it's next to impossible."

"What would he have to do?"

Dark eyes meet mine, and there's so much more in them than I ever gave him credit for. Pride and intelligence, yes. But other things I can't name. Things I hope someone will see in my eyes someday.

"He'd have to ask," Cross says finally.

When he pulls up, I realize we've entered a square with café sets. Chairs and tables, half of them occupied.

A band is setting up at one end. I can spot a clarinet, a saxophone, a double bass, and a trumpet.

Cross pulls out an empty chair, and I slide into it.

I watch him round the table, gracefully taking his seat on the other side.

The saxophonist starts warming up, and Cross's gaze locks onto the stage. It's as if the beauty of the square falls away. There are no more stones, no more flowers, no more trees, no more lights. In his mind, it's just the notes.

"You care, don't you?" I say. "About Jax."

"Of course I care. All my artists matter."

"But Jax matters more."

Cross doesn't turn, but I know he hears me.

He doesn't answer for a long time. When he does, he's drifted.

"It's ironic, in a way, that Jax is the person who kept you from me. And now he's the one who's brought you back."

The double bass starts its mellow notes that warm my stomach, and soon the trumpet joins in.

I turn his words over in my mind as the band plays.

13

"Wow. Where is everyone?"

"It's just us, squirt. Grace said you went swimming at school last week, and I thought you might want to do some more. Now go change into your swimsuit. I'll meet you back here."

The local wave pool feels cavernous. Not just because of the high ceilings, but because I rented it out.

The idea came to me when Haley said she was spending the evening with Cross. She's seen as much of her estranged father as I've seen of my kid lately.

That ends now.

As we get into the water, Annie looks nervous.

"Something wrong?" I ask.

"When we went for school, I didn't swim. I sat in the corner."

That catches me off guard. "Grace said you love water. You take baths all the time."

"That's different."

I turn it over in my head. "Come on."

We get out of the pool, and I gesture up to the operator who's watching from above. I slice across my neck. Then I leave Annie by the pool and go out to the main desk in the deserted lobby.

The lone person there is doing paperwork. "Yes, Mr. Leonard?"

"I'm going to need some of those things." I point at my bicep.

"I'm sorry?"

"You know." I flap my arms, irritated.

"Ah. Water wings?"

"Yeah, those."

She goes into the office and comes back. "Here's a set."

"I need one more."

She complies and returns, smiling. "It's very sweet that you did this for your daughter."

I start to say, "She's my niece," but catch myself. Calling her my daughter is the truth. And the more I turn it over in my head, the more I want it to be the truth. The more I want everyone to know it.

Including Annie.

I go back to the pool and hand a set of water wings to Annie.

She shakes her head. "I don't need those. I'm too old."

"Sure. But I need them."

I start blowing them up as she watches. "Really?"

"Yeah. I can't believe I almost forgot them."

It takes two seconds to realize there's no way they'll fit over my biceps. So I deflate them most of the way and wedge my hands inside so they're ugly orange bracelets.

"Fine, I guess I'll wear them too."

I hide the smile as we blow hers up.

We go back out into the water, and I show her how to paddle. The pool's still and empty, and it's just us in the shallow end.

"What is all that?" she asks, nodding to my arm.

I glance down at the ink. "Tattoos."

"I know that. What do they mean?"

"Who says tattoos need to mean something?"

"Why else would you paint something on your body you can't take off? My friend Jamie's mom let her dye her hair with permanent dye. But even that didn't last forever. This is like... forever forever." Her head bobs with her words, her eyes going round.

"It is forever forever," I agree. "Alright, the first one I got was here." I point to the knot on my shoulder. "I got it when I first became a musician because I felt like I was part of something." My finger moves to a heart under my tricep. "This one is for your mom. Because she's always been part of me, even when I don't see her." I move down my arm, scrolling past half a dozen and stopping on an elephant. "This one—"

"An elephant!" she exclaims. "Because an elephant never forgets and you never forget a song?"

"Sure," I say. "And because my friend Mace dared me to. By the time you have a lot of tattoos, the bar just gets lower."

"What bar?"

After another ten minutes of this, I can tell she's relaxed.

We've been in here a while, but her teeth aren't chattering, and she doesn't look worried, so I think we're good.

"My turn to ask questions. You still reading *Harry Potter*?" I ask.

"Yeah. I'm on book five."

"Which one's your favorite?"

"*Goblet of Fire*," she parrots immediately.

"Why?"

Annie blinks at me like I'm being deliberately slow. "Because… dragons."

"Right." I swallow the laugh. "The Fireball's the best."

"No way. The Horntail."

"You're just saying that because it's Harry's."

"Am not!"

I never pictured myself debating *Harry Potter* with a ten-year-old.

Or reading the books so that I could.

"You know how in *Harry Potter*," I say eventually, "there're a lot of changes and surprises?"

"Like Harry finding out he's a wizard?"

"Yeah, like that." I swallow. "Though this is more like *Star Wars*…"

"I haven't read that."

"Me either." *Fuck, could this be any more awkward?*

She looks so attentive, so hopeful.

I want to tell her. To spill everything that's building up inside me, all of the emotion and the frustration that I thought would go away once I was back here.

It's not going away.

Instead, I help her out of the pool, discarding our water wings.

"Go get dressed. I'll take you home. Maybe we can get ice cream on the way."

If her happy chatter between bites of our frozen Snickers treats is any indication, she's had a good time.

When we pull up at her house, Grace's sitting in one of the two chairs on the porch that looks as if it was built a century ago and hasn't been attended to since. As a kid, I wouldn't have noticed such things. But after living in hotels, I can't help it.

"Where's the man of the house?" I ask.

She lifts a shoulder. "Out with friends."

"Shocking."

Grace shoots me a warning look. "Annie, time to get ready for bed, honey."

"I'm not tired. We just had ice cream."

I put on my most innocent expression. But I'm her older brother and I never was much for innocent to begin with.

Grace rolls her eyes at me. "Put your bathing suit on

the washing machine and get ready for bed. I'll come say good night in a few minutes."

I hug Annie good night, then after she goes inside, I drop into the chair opposite Grace. "I almost told her." I pick at the peeling plastic on the arm of the chair.

Grace stiffens. "You have no right."

It's an old argument, but we haven't had it face-to-face in a while.

We're due.

"No? My child is being raised by a man who doesn't respect women."

She flinches. "She's not only your child. She never was."

"And that's my fault? You kept it from me."

"I took care of things. Like you took care of me."

I didn't take care of you, I want to say. *You're here, aren't you?*

She sips tea as if we're talking about movies instead of her abusive husband. "I know this isn't the life you want for her, but life doesn't always turn out how you plan."

"I want to fix that. That's all I'm trying to do."

She lifts her chin, and for a minute, I see her when she was younger, mouthing off to me. "You have any plans to get your own life, brother?"

"What are you talking about?"

"I'm talking about the fact that for ten years, you had the biggest life imaginable. And now, everything you want is about that little girl. She can't hold the burden of your dreams, Jax. It's too much for her."

I shift, remembering what I'd said to Mace about him needing to find something new.

"I understand that you want to take this slow," I say after a moment of easy silence. "But I want her in my life. I want to provide for her in every way I can. Nothing will keep me from that. Not your husband. Not the law. Not the last ten years. Annie's my daughter, and there's no changing it."

A noise inside makes us both turn.

"What are you talking about?" a small voice says from behind the screen door.

Shit.

"Annie, honey." Grace's voice is calm, but there's an edge beneath the surface. "What are you doing out here?"

"You were taking too long." Her gaze moves between Grace and me, but my heart is racing. "Uncle Jax, what's going on?"

"How much did you hear?" My voice sounds tight.

"You said that I'm your daughter. But that's not right."

Shit. Shit. Shit.

Grace kneels in front of Annie. "Honey, this isn't how I wanted to tell you."

"How is that possible?"

"In one sense, yes, Jax is your father. In another sense, your daddy and I are your parents. And all you need to know is that you are loved."

"But who was my daddy first?"

"I was," I say before Grace can interject.

Annie's face changes as she looks at me. "Then why did you give me a new daddy?"

Pain slices though me. I don't know what to say. All I can say is, "I'm sorry. Annie, I'm so sorry."

Her gaze flicks between us, then to the street. "I'm going to bed."

"Okay. You want to read something together?"

"No." Her voice is unusually sharp. "No. I'm going to read to myself."

Annie retreats, the screen door clicking behind her, and I rub both hands over my face.

It doesn't help. Because when I blink my eyes open, I've still fucked everything up.

14

HALEY

The line at the registrar's office shouldn't be this long. It's the middle of the semester. Everyone's already registered, right?

I shift because my foot's fallen asleep again. I'd rather be at Wicked right now, where I know Lita's recording. But no. I'm getting back into school, and I'm not taking no for an answer.

The number called is 473. I'm 474.

Then, it's my turn.

I get to the window. "Hi, I'm Haley Telfer. I spoke to someone about getting back into school. Here's the reference letter." I hand the woman the sealed envelope.

I haven't seen Cross since our father-daughter date earlier this week, but I found this in my mailbox with a note.

In some ways, it feels like the best gift I've ever gotten.

She opens it and scans the letter. "It says the reference is for Haley Cross."

I wince. "My name is Haley Telfer. But this is my reference."

"From a Shannon Cross. Are you related?"

"Technically he's my father. Why?"

She sets the letter on the desk. "You can't have a reference letter from a family member."

"I didn't know that man was my father until a few months ago. Not while I worked for him."

She stares at me as if I'm crazy. "Miss Telfer—Cross—whatever your name is, you are ineligible to return to this institution until you have appropriate paperwork. From a non-family member."

"You have no idea what I did to get this," I whisper.

She looks past me. "There are other people in line."

"Do you have a daughter? Does she have dreams?" I try, desperate.

"I do. And she does. Neither of which are relevant to this conversation. Next!"

As I take my letter back and trudge out of the office, the full weight of disappointment hits me.

It's a month into the fall semester, and I'm no closer to getting re-enrolled.

Which maybe is for the best since I'm behind on my readings thanks to the IT breakdowns at Wicked recently.

I need to talk to someone. I can't call Serena because she's in class. Outside, I dial Jax's number.

He answers on the third ring. "Yeah?"

I swallow, sinking onto a bench. "Jax? I didn't get back into school. Cross gave me the letter, and I still couldn't get back in." I curse. "Maybe I should just drop out."

"Maybe you should." I blink at the spot where the grass meets the cobblestone. "Hales?"

"No. It's just... I figured you'd give me a pep talk or something."

"Why?"

I'm not sure.

Jax isn't my boyfriend.

It's not his job to be there, even though he is. To comfort me, even though he does.

"Hales," he goes on, sighing out a breath, "I'm good at talking about shit that's fucked up. I'm not good at fixing it. If anything, I'm better at breaking it."

Alarm bells light up in my mind. "What happened?"

"Annie found out I'm her father. And not how I planned to tell her. Now Grace's pissed, but it's Annie who won't speak to me."

"She'll get past it."

"Did you?"

I shift. "Maybe I will."

My phone beeps, and I glance at the call waiting. "It's Lita."

Kyle's been texting all week to get an update on how my conversation with Cross went about the album.

Guilt edges in because I hadn't even gone there.

This is probably Lita's attempt. I can't avoid it forever.

"Jax, I should go. Can we talk later?"

"Yeah. Sure." But he's distant, and I don't know how to change that.

Maybe there's no way to help it.

Because he's in Dallas and I'm here, and maybe all we can ever be at a distance is people who get each other off.

On that depressing note...

I switch lines, trying to shove it from my mind. "Hi, Lita. Sorry I didn't return your calls, but—"

She makes a strangled sound. "Haley."

"What's wrong? Where are you?"

"Something happened."

Hospitals are all the same. Linoleum and bright lights. Black streaks marking the floors, like people were drag racing with gurneys.

I'm pretty sure that never happens except on TV.

Next to me, Kyle's staring at the wall. Lita paces. Brick's wandering the halls.

It's been seven hours since I arrived.

I'm not good with hospitals. Especially this hospital.

I bury myself in my phone, trying to read articles and pretending I can focus on something other than the background noises of beeping, the staccato voices, and the occasional metal on metal.

In some ways, it shouldn't be that different from being on tour.

It's completely different from being on tour.

I glance at the clock. It's the same kind as in schools. The institutional one with a big face, blunt hands that always move too slow.

Movement catches my eye as Jax rounds the corner.

We all straighten. "Well?" I ask.

The man in a white lab coat with a buzzed head appears behind him, addressing all of us. "Your friend is going to survive."

"Mace stepped off the roof of the studio," Kyle says it loudly, and I wince. "That's not something you bounce back from."

The doctor says, "He has a broken leg, wrist, and collarbone. It could have been more severe. My suggestion is that you all get a good night's sleep and return in the morning."

I stand, weary. "Wanna go?"

Jax nods, and the four of us leave the hospital together.

A few minutes later, the black Town Car rolls up.

We drop Lita off first. Then Kyle off at his hotel.

Jax stares at the seat the rest of the way back to my place. When we get inside, Serena's reading a book.

The old-fashioned kind with a spine and everything.

Her worried face peers up at us from the couch.

"Jax. When did you get here?"

"About two hours ago. Chartered a plane." His voice sounds as if he's been up all week.

"How is he? What hospital is he at?" she asks.

I tell her, and she sets the book on the table in front of her with a sigh.

"Haley..."

"It's fine," I say, shaking my head. "Thanks, Serena."

I start toward my room. Halfway there, I realize Jax isn't following me. He's still standing by the door. I take his hand and tug him along.

I shut my door after us. Jax walks around the room, studying my things.

"I don't know what makes someone decide to..." My voice echoes in the silence, and I take a breath.

He stands in front of me, his hair falling in his face. "This isn't the first time."

"What?"

His amber eyes are dull. "It's been years. I didn't know he was in this place again."

Jax and I have talked about our pasts, but this is different. I sense it from the way his shoulders slump. The defeat in his expression.

"What happened last time?"

"Touring got to him. He was partying too much. Always chasing the latest high. We were supposed to meet up on an off day. I found him lying in the gutter in NOLA. Got him to a hospital, found needle tracks up his arms. I didn't know. I mean, on some level I knew, but I didn't know it was that bad."

"Did he mean to...?"

"I don't know. Guess this time he decided he did."

My eyes sting, and I wipe at them. "He and Kyle came to me about doing an album. I told them I'd help. That I'd talk to Cross. But I didn't, Jax. I should've, and I didn't."

"It's not your fault, Hales," he murmurs. "What did Serena mean about the hospital?"

I take a shuddering breath. "It's where my mom died."

Jax closes the distance between us.

I've hugged him before, but this time, he's the one folding me into his arms. I feel myself crumble, and I'm pissed at myself because I should be the one there for him.

"Let's take a shower," he says against my hair. I nod, slow.

Jax pulls back a few inches. Just enough to strip his T-shirt over his head. Then tugs off his jeans, his shorts.

I follow suit.

When we finally step under the spray together, I can't help noticing his body despite everything that's happened.

My gaze rakes down his back, his ass, his legs as the water runs over him. Darkening his hair to chocolate. He turns to face me, and the pull is there.

I squirt body wash into my palm and wash the hard

muscles of his chest. His intake of breath is the only sign he's resisting, but he doesn't stop me.

I move around to wash his back. Every part of him is beautiful. The dark hair, soaked and curling at his neck. The breadth of his shoulders, the taper of his waist. The slim hips, the firm curve of his ass.

I turn back to the front of him, and his gaze is darker.

"Here." He takes the body wash and soaps up my shoulders, my chest, my breasts.

Jax's big hands glide down my sides, my butt. He pulls me closer, and he's half-hard. I tip my face up to his, and his mouth finds mine.

We kiss out of shared sadness. Out of desperation. Out of need to make something that's not awful.

I pull back, catching my breath. "I should've done something more. I could've helped, could've convinced Cross. I had no idea..."

"Don't blame yourself, Hales. You can get caught up in it. And once you do, you never let it go." When he speaks again, his voice is a murmur over the sound of water hitting tile. "You taught me something—there's always a choice. No matter how bad things look, you get to decide. Maybe you can't decide for the world, but you can decide how you act. How you feel."

Jax has shown his anger, his self-loathing. Never his sadness.

My hands cup the sides of his face, water running over our skin. "Promise me something. Don't ever regret me.

Don't ever feel guilty. Don't wish away a moment of this. No matter what happens." He doesn't respond, and I kiss him once, hard. "*Promise.*"

Jax nods, slow.

When he backs me into the tile, my heart's hammering because I want him so badly I ache with it.

Everywhere he touches me glows. The press of his cock against my stomach has me moaning against him.

His mouth crushes mine, and this time, there's no question of his intent.

For tonight, there are no walls. Neither of us can manage to keep them up.

He's going to take everything I have and am.

And I'm going to give it to him.

His expression flares with heat and something else. Jax lifts me, pressing me against the tile and leaving my legs useless. I hook them around him. When he sinks inside me, we gasp together.

His length fills me.

His soul fills me.

He strokes into me, and I want this, I need it, but it's too much. Tears burn the backs of my eyes, and I squeeze them shut.

Neither of us is ready to last long. He pumps into me, long, slow strokes, but the groans torn from his throat tell me he's close. I am too.

"Can't take it," he utters.

"I know." My lips brush the side of his face, the cords of his neck.

I come first, and a moment later, he shakes, pulling out as he spills all over me.

The shower washes it away.

By the time we dry off, it's late, but I'm nowhere near sleep. He's not either. He spies something on my shelf and raises a brow.

"Jerry bought me that for my birthday."

He unrolls the travel chess set, the pieces too small for his fingers.

Still, he's beating me from the first move.

"How did you get so good?" I murmur. "Did Jerry teach you?"

"No. Cross did. Before I saw him for the manipulator he is."

Some people are live wires. They need careful management so they don't burn out, or catch fire, or destroy themselves.

"You really think there's nothing good in him."

"What do you mean?"

"He didn't start Wicked to destroy young lives."

"Maybe he wanted money. Fame." Jax shrugs. "Power. Why?"

I understand what it's like to want something bigger than yourself.

"No reason." I feel Jax's gaze on me, but I focus on the board.

15

HALEY

"Come on," I mutter, hitting the run key again and wrestling my lip with my teeth.

Code flashes on the screen. As I hold my breath, the solution appears.

Ninety percent.

After the last month of hard work, my program explains nine-tenths of why a song is a hit. What's more, it makes recommendations about what to change in the levels, frequency—hell, even the effects—to make it more appealing.

I sigh, relief and pleasure washing over me as I slump in my chair. I glance at the clock in the interns' office. I'm the only intern in IT this fall, and my stuff has spread out over the other desks.

But it's late enough nearly everyone's gone for the day.

Since everything that happened with Mace, I've realized being kicked out of school isn't as huge as I thought.

It's not life or death. The rest—winning the competition or getting back into school—I'll figure it out.

If anything, I'm more determined than ever to do something that matters.

I reach into my pocket for the slip of paper with Jax's lyrics. It needs a starting point, musically speaking. Chords. A key. Maybe even a melody. If only he'd do that.

Then I could actually use my app. To take it to the next level.

Before I can get too excited, my phone rings with an incoming video call.

"Hey," I say when Jax's face appears. "You're in the house."

"Closed yesterday. I'm surrounded by boxes and takeout."

"I'm surprised you notice. It's ten thousand square feet." I shift the computer off my lap. "Did Mace arrive today?"

"In one piece and grumpy as fuck. Cast on his arm and leg. Had to get him a special bed." Jax's gaze looks past me. "Where are you?"

"Wicked."

His mouth tightens. "It's midnight."

"I'm working on my program."

"You can't do that at home?"

I shoot him a look.

He blows out a breath. "You coming for Thanksoween?"

"I thought it was Halloween."

"Nah. See, when we're on tour, we don't get much downtime for the holidays. Our October to December is basically the same as the rest of the year. So, we had to roll them all into one. 'Merry Thanksoween' involves tailgating off the bus with turkey and candy."

I can't help laughing at the visual. "Right. Presents?"

Jax grins too. "Does booze count?"

"Sure." It sounds like fun. "Then I guess if it's a tour tradition, everyone on tour should come. Lita, Kyle, Brick." He curses. "That doesn't sound like Thanksoween spirit," I tease him.

"It's been a rough month."

"True. But all the more reason, Jax." I shift in my seat. "If need be, I will *personally* get you in the mood."

He tosses the hair out of his face, glancing past the camera. "I'm in a public place, but give me two minutes..."

"I mean with snacks. Festive music," I chide. "Do you ever *not* think about sex?"

"If it's a toss-up between the "Monster Mash" and sex, I'll take sex. Every time."

I'm pretty sure I'm the luckiest girl in the world. Because the sex Jax Jamieson is talking about?

Yeah. It's with me.

In his bed. In my shower. In my bed.

He suggested we do it next to my poster of him, but I shot him down.

I think he was joking.

I hope he was.

Although now that I think about it...

I shake my head. It feels like we've only scratched the surface. I can tell from the way he looks at me that he wants so much more.

I'm not sure I can keep up.

"I lived like a saint the last few years, Hales."

"Your own fault."

"Or maybe I was waiting for you."

The offhand comment hits me in the solar plexus.

Even though the days he stayed over when Mace was in hospital were hellish, I feel like they brought us closer.

Sure, he's still in Dallas, and I'm still in Philly.

He's a rock star—okay, recovering—and I'm a student —fine, not even. But I can't give up on the tiny glimmer of hope in my chest that maybe we're something special, like Jax himself.

"Get home safe, Hales." His voice pulls me back. "Text me when you get there."

I hang up and pack up my things. Maybe I'm projecting. Looking for someone to pluck me from obscurity, to tell me I mean something to them.

Since the night at the jazz concert, I haven't seen Cross once.

I know he's the head of a company, and I rarely saw him before, but now I have the feeling he's keeping me at arm's length.

I go to pick up my mail on the way out. There's an envelope there, and it doesn't look like a paycheck.

I open it carefully, my breath catching when I get to the end.

It's an employment offer to work in the tech department next semester.

Full-time.

This has to be Cross's doing, but I have zero idea why he did it. Because they need help? Or as a favor?

Maybe he wants to see you more.

I'm not sure what to make of that, but I want to find out.

Cross probably isn't here, but I take the stairs up to the third floor just in case.

As I start down the dark hallway, I notice lights on in the recording studio. The door's open a crack.

I peer through the door, through the dark mixing booth, to the bright studio beyond.

There's a teenager in there. She doesn't look like the usual commercial type.

The girl finishes, and a familiar voice comes over the mic. "Try it from the bridge. We'll get what we can in the next few minutes. I don't want to keep people waiting."

My chest tightens as I take in the silhouette in front of the single lit computer screen.

I slide out of view, flattening my back against the wall. Is this why Cross said there was no studio time? He's recording kids?

Maybe this is how he finds them. His new recruiting strategy. The age of reality TV and YouTube stars is saturated, so he's going back to first principles—recruiting from local talent.

Maybe you should leave before you land yourself in an epic amount of trouble. From what I've seen, getting on Cross's bad side is not a good idea.

On my way out, I see three more high school students walk in the front doors. I expect security to send them packing, but the guard on duty waves them through.

I can't resist stopping one of them, a kid who can't be more than fourteen, with full lips and spiked hair.

"They're running a few minutes late," I offer. He mutters a thanks, but I continue. "Are there more of you coming? Or is this it for tonight?"

He hesitates, glancing down at the badge on my hip. The credibility seems to soothe him a little. "I think we're the last slot."

His voice sends ripples down my spine, and I know he can sing. "Your parents don't notice you coming home this late?"

He smiles. "My parents can't keep track of themselves."

"Right." I match his smile, though I don't feel it on the inside.

"Tyler!" one of the other kids calls from the elevator. "Come on."

"It was nice meeting you," I say.

"Yeah, sure." He gives me a strange look, but the smile lingers.

"Hey, Tyler!" I call as the doors are about to close. They open again, one of the kids muttering under his breath. "Did you have to audition for this?"

"No. You just sign up at school and get on the wait list." He cocks his head. "Only thing I ever signed up for, I think."

The doors close, and I'm left in the dark.

16

"Where do you put this?"

Mace looks up from his iPad as I squint at the bird on the island. The package of stuffing is next to it. "Inside."

"Inside where?"

"You know." Mace makes a circle with the fingers of one hand and plunges the other through it. "Inside."

I shoot him a dirty look.

"You never made a turkey before, Jamieson?"

"Do I look like I've made a fucking turkey before?" Every bit of attention I can muster is on the turkey lying legs-up in the big foil pan. "Why are we doing this?"

"Because you told your girlfriend about our little tailgating tradition, and she did what girlfriends do and made it less weird."

I take the stuffing and start... well... stuffing it.

"You're seriously not going to respond to that?"

"And say what? That she's not my girlfriend? Call her whatever you want." He stares at me in stunned silence. "Better yet, take a fucking picture."

A few months ago, the idea of dating someone would've seemed insane. But recently, I've realized I'm slightly obsessed with Haley.

Not just physically. Hanging out with her. Hearing about her day. Finding out what riles her up. Comparing notes about TV and new albums and everything under the sun.

We used to talk once or twice a week. Since Mace's little hospital visit, it's nearly every day.

A fact that probably hasn't escaped her and sure as hell doesn't escape me.

A tritone sounds, and I turn to glance at my phone on the counter behind me.

Haley: Just landed. On our way. I have good news and bad news.

When I turn back, Mace is watching me.

"Still can't believe you ditched the flip phone."

"It was time."

With a screen and full keyboard, I can call and text her without it taking an hour to ask a simple question.

Plus, emojis.

You can get really dirty with emojis.

But impromptu eggplants aren't enough to satisfy me.

The past few days, an idea's been forming.

Haley's been busting her ass on this app, and if it's anywhere near as good as I think it is, she has a career in front of her.

If she's not in school, there's nothing keeping her in Philly. She could work on her app anywhere.

In theory.

I go back to the turkey, and my lip curls. It feels like penance.

"Wouldn't kill you to help," I say.

His brows rise as he lifts his chin to better meet my gaze over the counter from his wheelchair. Technically, he could be on crutches, but the doctors suggested this was easier given the nature of his breaks. "It might."

I go back to the bird. "All the more reason," I mutter.

The house closed on Wednesday, and a company I hired through my agent moved my shit here. Mace came on his own.

In the couple of days since, we've binge-watched three seasons of sci-fi shows, drank a lot of beer—hard liquor is off the table given the meds he's on, which I insisted he take if he's going to stay with me—and basically acted like kids.

What we haven't done is talk about what happened.

I finish filling the bird with bread and wash my hands with extra soap, turning back to him.

"Stepping off a building is pretty fucking drastic, Ryan." I can't remember the last time I called him that, and from the expression on his face, he can't either.

He blows out a breath, shaking his head and shooting me a look of supreme disappointment. "We're going to do this now?"

"Yeah. We're going to do this now." He stares at me, but I'm not done. "You think I don't get you. That I haven't been there."

He rubs his good hand over his jaw. Or I think he does, because he's rocking a *Cast Away* beard. "You haven't."

I go to the bar, start hauling bottles out for tonight. "I saved your ass. Every time touring spun you out, I pulled you back."

I unscrew the top of the bourbon and pour one for myself. The smoky flavor burns my throat as I meet my friend's somber gaze.

"It's different for you. You're Cross's fucking boy wonder—you were from the start. Everyone wanted a piece of you."

"That's crap." I don't for a second believe this is about jealousy. He's been in this business too long, been on too many stages, cashed too many checks. "You've been part of Riot Act since the beginning. You know how this works. You're on top until someone takes a swipe at you. Until the world decides you're too big and cuts you off at the knees."

"That's the stupid part, Jax. You cut yourself off at the

knees," he mutters. "You're on top of the damn universe, and instead of riding the ride, you stepped off."

Anger rises inside me, but he's not done. Under the facial hair, his blue eyes flash.

"You're quitting because what—you want to make amends? The rest of us sit around because we can't do what you want to. If we had half the chances you have, we'd be doing every one of those things. Trust me on that."

I hate hearing him talk like this because even if the words aren't true, they're true for him. He believes them.

We've been friends as long as I've been at this. He's the closest thing I have to a brother. And what burns me is I didn't know.

He didn't tell me what was going on. I wasn't there to see him. To chew him out.

To fix him.

The doorbell rings. Or more accurately, the security bell for the front gate.

I hit the buzzer to admit the car.

"You have good Thanksgivings growing up, Ry?"

"No."

"Me either. But let's fucking pretend for one night."

We finish in the kitchen, and a few minutes later, I hear the front door open. The beeping of the disabled alarm system.

"Jamieson!"

I'd know Lita's call anywhere, and I stride through the

hallway, my socks padding on the marble as they come into view.

Lita's wearing some purple dress that makes her bright-red hair even redder as she drops the overnight bag next to her. Brick slides in after her, and Kyle too. They seem to have borne the brunt of the luggage. Serena sets a suspicious-looking carrier in front of her as she steps out of tall heels.

My gaze narrows. "Tell me you didn't bring that thing to my house."

"He can't fend for himself for a weekend."

I bend and inspect the bars, the little nose poking through. I shake my head.

"We didn't think they'd let her take him on the plane," Lita says. "But she dyed him black and convinced them he was a cat."

I glance up as one more comes through the door.

I swear the front hall gets a little brighter.

Haley's wearing a dress that stops halfway down her thighs with tights and these tiny boots. Her cheeks are flushed, her lips curved.

She drops her bag and crosses to me, glancing toward the carrier on the way. "That's the bad news. Sorry." She leans in so we're sharing breath, and I'm hypnotized by the sheen of her lip gloss as she lowers her voice. "We'll wait until she's asleep, then put him in the garage. You want to hear the good news?"

I drop my mouth to hers and feel her surprised intake

of breath as I kiss her.

The chuckles and comments in the background barely register.

Haley's body melts under my hands, and when I pull back, her lips are soft.

"You're the good news, Hales."

The smile on her face takes the edge off everything.

That's when I know it's true.

I'm totally falling for this girl.

I'd expected careening headfirst for someone would be accompanied with dread.

But now that I'm admitting it, it's not. It's like a weight has lifted off me.

Haley tilts her head, her gaze working over mine. "What is it?"

I grin. "Nothing."

As much as I'd like to stay in this bubble, we've got a Thanksoween to deliver.

I link my fingers through hers and tug her after me to find the others.

When we walk into the kitchen, Lita has her arms around Mace's neck, and he's a few shades darker than I remember.

She turns her attention toward the counter. "Ooh, I love it when men cook."

"You know that needs at least four hours, right?" Serena says.

"Was just about to put it in, Skunk Girl." I fold my

arms over my chest. "We have twenty years on international tours filling stadiums. I think we can cook a damned turkey."

"Did you take out the giblets?"

"The what?" Mace and I echo.

We spend the rest of the day drinking and cooking and talking.

Then we finally sit down to dinner. It's the only time I can see using my formal dining room, and the table I had delivered yesterday works like a charm.

"Since this is a Halloween and Thanksgiving hybrid, should we say what we're thankful for?" Serena quips over the gravy.

"Wrapping albums," Lita says.

Serena says, "Old friends. And new ones."

"Good food," Kyle says.

"Hard pass," says Mace, and I shoot him a look.

"Things working out," Haley says. "I may not be in school, but I can pay the rent and program. I submitted my app to the competition yesterday."

Pride fills my chest as everyone congratulates her, as if I had some part in it.

In a way, I did.

"What about Wicked?" Lita asks.

Haley's gaze meets mine, and I swear there's guilt in it.

"I was offered a chance to stay on in the IT department. I'm thinking through it."

That comment has me dropping the spoon back in the cranberry sauce. "I thought you owed Cross four months, then you were done with it."

"Maybe I want to stay."

Everyone turns to me.

"What about you, Jax?" Lita asks, clearly sensing the tension.

"You could start with this big-ass house," Serena says.

"Or the fact that you make music that makes girls strip naked," Kyle offers.

"Think I hear something buzzing," I mutter, rising from my seat and turning toward the kitchen. A chorus of boos follows.

"I didn't mean it!" Kyle hollers.

The rest of dinner gets monopolized by Lita recounting stories from Nashville, which Haley sometimes jumps in on, and Serena answering Kyle's questions about her skunk. Including how he escapes everything.

"That better not include his damned cage," I mutter as I'm having seconds of potatoes.

Serena's answer is to gulp more wine.

But I couldn't care less about the skunk because I'm still stuck on what Haley said.

Wicked offered her a job, and she's thinking of taking it.

Just when I thought he'd finished screwing with my life.

He can't know I'm thinking of asking her to move in with me. I know that logically.

But more than that, it bugs me that she's thinking about it. That she wants anything to do with the guy after what he's done to both of us.

After we all eat way too much dinner, we move to the massive living room overlooking the patio to drink and eat candy. The pool's heated, but no one wants to swim. Lita and Brick play the requisite game of *Guitar Hero*. Mace and Haley place bets on the outcome.

Serena's gone to take the little demon for a walk. Kyle tags along, asking something about skunk charities when their voices are cut off by the closing front door.

I'm drinking and ignoring the game.

At least until my glass is empty.

I get up and go to the kitchen to refill it.

"So what are other traditions of Thanksoween?"

Haley's low voice has me looking over my shoulder.

The tights should keep me from thinking about her legs wrapped around me, but nope. Her dress has little points of sleeves and neckline that's a modest curve, but I'm jealous of the fact that it's touching her all over and I'm not.

"After dessert and drinks, the guests blow the host."

She shifts a hip against the marble island, raising a brow. "All the guests? I'm not sure I can compete with Kyle. He has that raw enthusiasm going for him."

I shake my head, turning back to pour another

bourbon.

"How's Annie?" she asks after a moment.

"She won't talk to me."

Haley makes a face, reaching for her stomach. "I'm sorry, Jax. I know it doesn't feel like it now, but she'll come around. She'll see how much you care about her and that you only want what's best for her."

"Maybe. In the meantime, the lawyers can deal with it." Haley's questioning look makes me go on. "Annie knows who I am now. There's already a confirmation of paternity, thanks to her mother. So there's nothing stopping me filing for custody."

She looks stunned. "You're going to sue for access? Jax, she's been given some information that's turned her life upside down. She needs time."

"A month? Two? I guess that's what it took for you to forgive the man who ignored you your whole life and go to work for him."

I know I'm being an asshole about this, but I can't seem to let it go.

Haley lifts her chin, and the light catches her hair. The hair she put up in some kind of style, maybe for her, but maybe—just a little—for me. "Jax. I was going to tell you about that. It just came up," she says under her breath. "But I'm not turning my back on Wicked just because you have."

She looks like she's about to say more, but in the end, she walks out of the kitchen without another word.

17

HALEY

Jax's stubble comes in redder than the rest of his hair.

I never noticed since we've only shared a bed a handful of times. But when I wake up in the four-poster bed next to him, it catches the light.

I take a second to enjoy looking at him. Not only because he looks gorgeous lying on the king mattress, the covers drifting down around his abs in a way that's completely distracting, but because he looks peaceful.

As if, for once, he's not fighting the world.

We can forgive a child who is afraid of the dark. The tragedy is when men are afraid of the light.

The quote comes back to me. I think it's Plato, but I'm not sure.

I feel closer to Jax than I've ever felt to another person. Since Mace's hospital visit, it's as if his walls have come down even more. I feel it in the way he talks to me, the way he looks at me.

But I'm not sure what to do with what I find on the other side of those walls. Jax seems to be in a tug-of-war with the world. I feel it even when he smiles. Even when we're together.

Serena asked me on the plane yesterday if I'm falling in love with Jax.

I told her no because in some ways, I've always loved him. When I knew every word to every song he wrote, I loved him.

But that's fan love, the way you love anything that's too perfect.

He's not perfect. He's strong and flawed and beautiful and wrong. He hates me working at Wicked, and it's driving a wedge between us.

But I love the way his amber eyes glow when he's thinking dirty thoughts or laughing at me when I nerd out on him. I love his obsession with reality TV, especially the home reno shows, and the fact that he can name every kind of power tool known to man even though he's never used one. I love how responsible he feels for his family, his friends, even when it strains him.

I shift out of bed and grab one of the two robes on the back of the door.

The smaller one is so soft and fluffy I suck in a breath.

It fits me perfectly.

That's what reminds me good things take time. When he does something like that.

The huge house is quiet except for Kyle's snoring coming through an open door. I make my way downstairs, my feet sinking into the plush carpet.

My phone's in my purse, where I left it last night. There's a missed call from Cross's assistant, but the battery's nearly dead and it's a Sunday. Rather than calling her back, I move the phone to the wireless charging pad in the kitchen.

Maybe she was returning my call about the "after school program."

I tried to arrange a meeting with Cross, but she told me he was out of the office for the rest of the week.

So I pieced some of it together myself from cryptic notations on studio calendars.

The nearest I can figure is Cross makes the studio's time, his time, available as some kind of charitable act. The strange part is there's no PR, no media or public announcements.

Which means he doesn't want anyone to know.

Because he's doing something wrong, or because he doesn't want to be rewarded for doing something right?

It's confusing, and as much as I'd like to tell someone, I can't talk to Jax about this. He wouldn't believe Cross would do anything for someone other than himself.

I don't feel much like eating, thanks to the big meal

last night. But the coffee maker beckons in all its chrome glory.

It's way more advanced than what's at the café, but I figure it out in no time. I press a few of the buttons, and it starts whirring, grinding beans at a deafening volume that's sure to wake everyone in this house.

I yank the cord from the wall until the quiet resumes.

Later.

I go to the back patio and watch the sun rising over the distant hills.

I feel him behind me before his hands find my shoulders.

"You're up early." Jax's voice at my ear is a low rumble, as sexy as the first time I heard it.

My smile starts inside me, unfolding like a flower. The fact that I don't jump when I feel him close, even when he surprises me, shows how much has changed. "I heard a sound. Maybe the house spawned another bedroom overnight."

His chuckle tickles my skin. "Come back to bed."

I place a hand over his and turn toward him. He's wearing pajama pants slung low on his hips, and his chest is a delicious map of muscle and ink and beautiful skin. "Anyone else awake?"

Jax shakes his head, his hand caressing my cheek.

I can tell the moment affection slides into more.

He slips a hand inside the front of my robe as he kisses me, lightly at first. Then he pulls me back with him toward the house. Turns and presses me against it. My breath catches. He hitches my leg up around his hip, and the pajama pants do nothing to hide the growing hardness between us.

I want to resist, because it shouldn't be this easy. But on some level, I crave it.

His mouth grazes mine. Lazy and assured. His fingers brush my breast, teasing my nipple in the cold morning air until it's even harder.

"What are you doing?" I manage.

"Saying good morning."

Even if my head wanted to stop him, my body craves him.

His hand strokes lower, fighting with the tie on my robe. Winning, like he usually does.

"Mmm. Good mornings start with coffee."

"I promise this will wake you up."

He brushes between my legs. My head falls back against the side of the house, my hair catching on the brick.

He's patient and insistent, as though this is an inevitability.

Maybe it is.

Jax touches me, a few deliberate strokes as he watches my expression, then presses inside. He swallows my moan, soothes my tension with his tongue and spirals it tighter at once.

I tear my lips from his, scraping my teeth along

his jaw.

It takes a few minutes, a few strokes, until I come, moaning his name into the tendons of his neck.

After, we go inside and he turns on the coffee, oblivious to the deafening noise.

I cross to his fridge.

"Nice calendar," I call over the sound.

"I like it. I like paper. Not having everything online."

The whirring stops, and the brew cycle, mercifully, starts. My gaze scans the rows of days. "What's that?" I point at an entry.

"Car commercial."

"For real?"

He shoots me a quelling look. "Got to keep the money flowing."

I know firsthand what it's like to be worried about cash, but I can't imagine Jax having that same concern.

Maybe it never goes away.

"You ever think you'd have more fun doing something musical?"

He raises a brow.

"When was the last time you picked up a guitar? You could go on YouTube again, do more acoustic sessions. Or teach kids who are into music."

"You sound like my agent. He keeps feeding me shit about my brand." Jax pulls the coffee cup from under the machine, holding it out to me. I smell it.

"Whoa. That's good."

"I've got some skills, Hales." His gaze twinkles.

"I'm serious. But you don't have to do it for your brand. Or anyone. Do it for you."

He reaches for a water glass, fills and drains it without breaking eye contact. "I need to show you something."

He walks me through the halls, flicking on lights as we go to the garage at the side of the house.

He hits a master switch that illuminates the cavernous space.

My jaw drops.

It's filled with guitars, boxes, bagged clothes, and posters stacked ten deep.

"Jax, this is a fortune worth of equipment and memorabilia..."

"Trust me, I remember all of it." His face hardens as he points at a framed poster. "This was New Orleans. From our second tour. Mace overdosed, and I held him in the streets until the ambulance came and brought him back." He lifts a guitar. "Wicked bought me this when I refused to sign the contract. It's signed by Springsteen. When I got the guitar and picked it up for the first time, Annie's mother left her with Grace."

In the corner is a gold statue, and Jax lifts it. "This is a Grammy. For the first album I cut, about the life I left behind." He straightens, his gaze hard on mine. "I meant what I said last night. That chapter is closed."

"But it's not a chapter, Jax. It's a limb. How can you cut that part of you off?" I think of the kids I watched recording with Cross. If he was anything like them, I can understand how Cross was drawn to him. "You're so bright. You matter so much to so many people."

"I never asked to," he says softly. "Some people think fame's one-sided. It's not. It's a give and take because without fans, you have nothing. I'm grateful for them. They've given me a chance to make music. To see the world. To do things my parents would've never dreamed.

"But sometimes the pull is so strong. What they want exceeds what you can give.

"I need to get my family back together, Hales, and if I need to fight for them, I will. I'm not waiting until Annie's grown up. Until she's obsessed with makeup and boys and has the option to ignore me."

I've never heard Jax talk this way before, and I can't help but be affected.

"I get it. At least, I think I do. Though I don't know many twenty-nine-year-old guys who'd turn their backs on being famous to fight for their daughter."

He takes hold of my hips, and I dig my fingers into his forearms. "I hope you don't know many twenty-nine-year-old guys. I like having you to myself."

His eyes darken, and already I'm breathless just being near him. The sound of his voice and the feel of his hands wrapping around me like silk.

"Move in with me."

I'm having trouble hearing. And as a side effect, breathing.

"Wait, what?"

"I'm serious, Hales." A ghost of a smile flickers across his handsome face. "You're out of school. My roommate situation is temporary. I don't know what life looks like after music, but I'll figure it out."

Apparently my hearing is fine. It's my processing that's fucked up. Because I can't make sense of the words he's uttering.

"I'm happy when you're with me," he goes on, his amber gaze running over my face. "It's simple. The simplest thing I've ever known. I love how I can tell you anything and you don't judge me. You don't want anything from me. You don't care if my house has four bedrooms or forty, but it's not because you don't know my world. You've seen it firsthand. You get it. Hell, you've been on that stage, Hales. And after all of it, you want *me*."

Stringing words together coherently is impossible, so I just stare at him. His hair is falling over his face at the front, and I do the one thing I can in this moment and reach up to brush it away.

The idea of living in this house is beyond insane, but getting to be with Jax every day, touching him, waking up next to him, laughing with him? It's a damned fantasy.

Because you're so in love with him you can't think of anything else.

It's true. I realize it's true even as he says, "You're hesitating. Why?"

The easy confidence he always projects wavers for the first time.

"I feel the same way," I manage. "With the happy and the simple… And I can't believe I'm saying this, because part of me just wants to say yes and kiss you, but the biggest thing is sometimes I feel like you're humoring me."

"How so?"

"You're older, experienced. I can't even get oral sex without freaking out." I raise a brow. "Unless maybe that's the plan. You've been secretly looking for a woman you can avoid going down on for all time. In which case, you've definitely found her."

His look of shock dissolves into an admiring grin. "That's not why I like you, Hales. I like how you care about people. I like that you speak your mind. I like that you take things at face value instead of looking for darkness in the world. And as for me going down on you? I'm thinking of that as a long-term project." He leans in, his lips grazing my jaw and making me arch into his kiss. "One I will work at for as long as it takes to get the job done."

Oh, God. I'm ready to sign away my life to be hammered, nailed, and screwed by this man for all time.

I squeeze my eyes shut. A million thoughts bubble up inside me, all of them saying different things. Reasons for and against, questions, and more.

When I blink, taking in the sight of Jax Jamieson in front of me, every other thought falls away.

This is the man who makes the songs I live my life by. Who loves his daughter more than any father I know. Who I can't imagine being without.

Jax clears his throat. "I understand if you need time to—"

"No," I interrupt.

"No."

"I mean, yes," I say, and his face goes blank. "Yes, I want to."

His expression dissolves into a grin, and I don't know which one of us looks happier in this moment.

Scratch that. It has to be me. Because I can't imagine feeling any more joy than what's coursing through my body.

I shift onto my toes, grabbing him to press a kiss to his mouth. His arms band around me as he returns the kiss, groaning against my mouth in a way that has me wet again.

"Haley! Jax!"

We groan in unison. But the panicked voices don't stop calling, and we go back inside.

The kitchen is full of somber faces.

"What is it?" Jax asks.

I'm already grabbing the phone from Lita's hand.

The headline on the news article has my smile and laughter falling away.

"Pioneering Music Executive Shannon Cross Dead at Fifty-Five"

Ice fills my body. My chest, my stomach, my lungs, my legs. "No."

"Haley."

I grab my phone and return the assistant's call, putting it on speaker. "What happened?"

"Haley. He passed last night. He had brain cancer, a quick-moving kind. He learned six months ago. He didn't want to treat it."

Disbelief tints everything, turning the room fuzzy. "It's not possible. I saw him last week, and..."

"He's been struggling for some time but didn't want to let on. I want to give you time, but we also need to plan."

"Excuse me?"

"He didn't want to burden you, so arrangements have been made. But as his next of kin, you should review his plans for the funeral."

"Review his..." I can't think.

"We'll call you back," Jax interrupts, his voice cutting short any argument. "We need a minute."

"Mr. Jamieson? Of course. Please don't wait too long. The hospital—"

"We won't."

18

"We nearly done here?" I shoot a look at my agent, who looks up from his phone.

The director nods. "Just a few more takes."

I swallow my frustration, reminding myself what I'm getting paid for this photo shoot.

I tried to convince Haley to stay until the funeral, but she said she needed to go back and help. The shock of Cross's death has hit everyone hard. My agent's getting calls every day from media, and for once, it's not to talk about me.

I turn them all down.

The only person who matters is her.

I asked her to move in with me last weekend, and she said yes. But we haven't talked about it since.

Still, I'm hoping it's the change she needs after all this shit with Wicked. She can start fresh here. Build her own computer company if she wants to. If she doesn't, that's fine too.

My phone rings, and the number on the call display has my stomach hardening.

"You have some nerve, Jax Jamieson," Grace snaps in my ear.

"I told you I want her back."

"So you're suing for custody?" She's livid, and I get why. "We could work through access issues. But you don't just want to see her. You want a court to say you get her half the time."

I want her all the time, but saying that won't help. For now, I don't want to take any chance of Grace packing Annie up and taking her away from me. And I want Grace's prick of a husband to know I'm watching and I have recourse if he fucks up.

Her heavy breathing fills my ear. "When we were kids and someone picked on me at school, you told him not to fuck with us. But what you meant was don't fuck with *you*. You can't stand someone telling you you can't have what you want. Can't *do* what you want. You never got over that, did you, big brother?" She curses. "I can't believe you're doing this to her."

I think of Haley, without a father her whole life, and now that she finds him, he's gone. "I'm not doing this to her. I'm doing it *for* her."

I hit End before she can respond.

19

HALEY

There are a lot of moving parts to a funeral. But the funeral of Shannon Cross is on a whole other scale.

First, lots of people knew my father.

My father.

Two, no one knew he was sick.

Now everyone wants to talk, and since the juicy bit of info that I'm his daughter seems to have leaked? The person they want to talk to is me.

Serena's been glued to my side all week at Wicked as I make arrangements, working with Cross's assistant.

I keep it together, accepting condolences and making decisions. Though really, he had most of it figured out. Speakers. Invitations. The drinks at his visitation. Hell, even the flowers.

I didn't peg Shannon Cross as a flower guy.

That's the part I want to scream when people shoot

me looks of sympathy and pity or ask what he would have wanted.

I don't know him. And I never will.

"It's a lot of people," I say, looking out the window of the limo past Jax.

"It's the end of an era. Wicked Records has ruled for decades."

I've never seen Jax in a suit, and he's so handsome I wish I could appreciate it more. Clean-shaven with a dark suit, crisp shirt, and no tattoos in sight, he could be a record executive himself.

The only hint of rock star about him—besides the fact that he's the most gorgeous man I've ever seen—is the way his hair falls over his forehead at the front.

Jax's strong fingers thread through mine, and I stare at them. He's not usually a PDA kind of guy, and after the hellish week, the move touches me more than I could've imagined.

"Thanks for coming."

"My agent would have my hide if I didn't." He forces a smile. "But I'm not here for him. I'm here for you, Hales. And I'm not going anywhere."

A warm feeling starts in my stomach, spreads through my body.

He can't possibly appreciate what it means to hear that, but knowing Jax Jamieson has my back makes everything else a little better.

And he's mine. He asked me to move in with him and I

said yes. Even if we haven't talked about it since, I know we will.

"What will happen to Wicked?" I ask under my breath.

"What do you think?"

I hesitate. "I don't know. I've spent all week thinking about the man; there's been no time to think about the company. I guess someone else will take it over."

He shrugs. "Or it could be sold off to pay for expenses. Those artists on contract will be released. Some people will get their money out, others won't."

"You mean it could be over?"

"Yeah."

My stomach clenches. Something about that feels wrong.

More wrong than the fact that Wicked's founder, its leader, is lying in a casket a few hundred feet away.

On TV, it always rains at funerals, but today is sunny. A ton of people are gathered around the cemetery.

My eye lands on a girl my age with straight platinum-blond hair that glows against her black dress.

I spoke with Ariel on the phone once this week to let her know about the arrangements, to see if her family would come.

She's with her father, who doesn't look so different from mine. They should look alike since they're brothers.

Jax and I stand in the front row. I'm in a daze as the minister speaks. When people cover the casket in roses.

"Miss Cross? Would you like to say a few words?"

It's Telfer.

Of course, I don't say it.

I reach for the folded paper in my pocket and walk toward the front.

The people in the crowd blur together as a lump rises in my throat.

I've done speaking before. I had help preparing for today from people who knew him better than I did.

Pretty much everyone.

When my mom died, I went to see a counsellor who told me there were a lot of things I might feel. Overwhelm. Grief.

Guilt.

This is different but not easier.

I open my mouth to start the speech I wrote and rewrote, but nothing comes out.

The birds in the trees don't share my affliction, chirping in the background like it's any other day.

My gaze finds Jax in the front row. He's the last person to mourn Shannon Cross, but here he is.

Jax's dark head inclines. So slight it's nearly imperceptible.

I've never asked for a savior before, but now I can't move. I want to tell him I'm frozen.

With my eyes, I try.

In the space of a breath, he's unclasped his hands and he's at my side. His dress shoes toe the damp grass next to mine, and I feel taller and braver at once.

I wait for him to speak.

He doesn't.

We stand there in a beam of cold sunlight, wrapped in our coats and hats, as Jax Jamieson sings the first cover I've ever heard him perform.

Leonard Cohen's "Hallelujah" fills the cemetery, disappearing at the edges into the crisp winter air.

There are no walls to reflect the sound, to warm it, to capture it. There is just the crowd and the trees whose leaves have fallen and the most beautiful voice I've ever heard.

"That was something else." Lita follows the direction of my stare as we stand together inside the reception hall.

"It might be the last time he sings in public."

"That'd be a crime." She pours a drink. "Did I ever tell you I was going to be a veterinarian?"

"No. For real?"

"Yup. I had straight A's in high school. Got accepted to a good college. But I got the chance to book a tour and I never looked back. Now I have a rented apartment, no car."

"You regret it?"

"Never." She takes a long sip. "When people don't do what they're meant to do, it eats at them. You saw Mace. Being told he's not needed anymore's like telling him he's living in a cage. Even Jerry can't stop because he doesn't know any other way."

"Jax isn't like that."

"No. For Jax, it'll be worse." Her words make me straighten. "He just won't realize it until it's too late." She downs the rest of the drink.

I watch her go as a man in a suit winds his way toward me.

"Excuse me, Miss Cross."

"Telfer," I say.

I've heard the name dozens of times this week. Hundreds.

It's felt petty to correct people under the circumstances, but now I need to remind the world I'm not Haley Cross. I have an identity that has nothing to do with a man I never met until this summer.

"Miss Telfer. I was your father's lawyer. I need to talk to you about his will. With his other surviving family."

He pulls me into a room where the other family's already waiting and delivers what he has to say.

Each phrase of legal jargon streams in one ear, out the other. But when he gets to the punch line, I ask him to repeat it.

Twice.

"There you are." Serena's worried eyes leap out from below the black fascinator pinned in her hair as I emerge from the room. "I've been looking for you for ages. What was that about?"

"He left me everything." Serena's eyes widen, but I can't feel anything except numbness seeping through me. "His money. His house."

She rubs my arm. "Okay. Well, that's understandable."

I press a hand to my face. "Serena, he left me his *company*."

I hear her gasp, but I'm looking past her to where Jax is talking with someone across the room. As if sensing me, he turns, a questioning look on his handsome face.

"I own Wicked."

20

HALEY

"Any word from the lawyers?" I ask Jax as he drops into the seat across from me at the campus café.

It's quiet in the morning, with most students either still asleep or in class. The familiarity of it all—the tables, the chairs, the stage area—is much needed after the chaos of the last week and a half.

"The petition for custody's gone in. Grace's lawyer's responded that they're contesting it."

The tightness in Jax's voice reminds me he hasn't had a walk in the park lately either.

I reach across the table to weave my fingers through his.

"When are you going back to Dallas?"

"Tomorrow."

He stayed at a hotel last night because he and

Scrunchie have decided the apartment isn't big enough for two alpha males.

"Come with me, Hales." His amber eyes fill with determination. "Pack a bag and come. Serena can bring the rest of your things, or you can get them later. Hell, we don't even have to go to Dallas right away; we can take a vacation on a beach somewhere. You and me and some peanut-free island we can get lost in."

I want to scream yes because the one thing that hasn't changed is how much I care about him. Through all of this, he's been there for me. Although I'm not sure life will ever feel normal again, I want to pretend it can.

I want to order some pizza and watch home reno shows and documentaries with the rock star I'm completely in love with. I want to shut the door on the world and just pretend *forever.*

"I want to, Jax. You have no idea how much." He leans in, and there's so much satisfaction in his expression I want to purr. "But I have to tell you something. Cross left me Wicked."

The tension invading his body is a living thing, and I wonder if he even notices the way he straightens in his chair.

"*Shit.*"

"I met with the lawyers this morning. They said I could look for an investor to buy it or to sell it off for parts."

Jax's jaw works. "What are you thinking?"

I tell him what I spent the morning deciding. "I'm not doing either."

His touch is gone as he folds his arms over his chest, pulling the long-sleeved shirt across his biceps. "What do you mean?"

I remember finding the kids recording late at night. There's so much I need to know. If not about Shannon Cross, then about the work he did.

"He left me his legacy, Jax. He's built something that matters. Maybe I don't fully understand it yet, and maybe he lost himself in the building of it. But he's made it possible to create music that changes the world, and changes the people who made it. I won't turn my back on it, or take it apart. Not yet."

I need him to understand this.

Judging by the way he shifts his chair back, it's not going well.

The satisfaction is long gone from his face, replaced by wariness and accusation.

"If you pulled back any further you'd be at another table right now." I mean it as a joke, but it's an observation.

"You're keeping the company," he says at last.

"Yes."

"And you'll stay here and run it?"

I know it must sound ridiculous. "I'll leave people in charge who know what they're doing. But I want to be part of it."

"You're not coming back to Dallas."

The hurt in his voice twists my gut.

"It's not the right time." I lean forward, trying to close the space between us. "We can fly back and forth. Or you could come to Philly."

"I'm fighting for my daughter, Hales," he mutters. "I can't do that from another city."

My heart squeezes. "Jax, nothing else has to change."

"Everything's changing," he insists, his voice raw. "You don't even know him—you don't even like him. But you're choosing him."

"I'm not choosing him. I…" My throat works as I try to come up with words that will make this right. "I need to *understand* him."

If anyone knows what it's like to have a family in chaos, to want to put things right, it's Jax.

He rubs a hand over his jaw, and I'm praying he's starting to get it.

At least until he says, "I'm not living my life at Shannon Cross's whim, especially now that he's dead. If you do this, we're done."

Done.

It's such a good thing, being done. All my life I've taken pride in getting through.

Through my mom's death, through tour, through more coding all-nighters than I can count.

This kind of done grabs me like a fist.

I remember our conversation in the back of a Town

Car outside a bowling alley in Dallas on a warm summer night.

You're standing on the edge of a cliff, looking down into the abyss, and you're twice afraid.

Once for the knowledge that you could fall and perish.

And once for the knowledge that the choice of whether to stay or whether to jump is ultimately yours.

"I signed the papers this morning."

My whispered words hang between us like the ice on the trees outside.

All of it feels like years ago. The bowling alley, our kiss on his bus. The day I showed up at his hotel and he took me apart and put me back together again.

Jax's jaw works as he stares past me, unseeing, for a long moment.

I want to shake him, to tell him he's making this harder than it needs to be. That everything can be simple, even if it's not the way we'd planned.

Before I can, he rises from his chair and shifts over me, dropping a soft kiss on the top of my head. "I'll see you around, Hales," he murmurs against my hair.

But there's a finality that doesn't match the words.

When Jax walks out, I swear he takes my heart with him.

I look down at my hands tucked under the table. The drop of blood on my thumb where the nail's ripped.

I never got it before. What it means to exercise your ability to choose.

It's as if the whole world is crumbling from the outside, falling in on itself. Burying you in a landslide.

Still, under the pressure and heaviness and pain and anxiety, I feel the tiniest shred of something burning inside my chest.

Purpose.

"Are you okay?" a voice asks from somewhere above me.

I blink up at one of the employees, a girl who's stopped next to the table. "I'm going to be fine," I say.

"Oh. I meant do you want another drink," she prompts, nodding to the empty glass in front of me.

I shake my head and she returns to the counter.

I'm going to be fine, I repeat, conviction building in my gut.

Because today, and tomorrow, and the day after that? I'm going to do something that matters.

Even if the man I love hates me for it.

21

HALEY

Two years later

I'm bleeding.

It's eight forty-five, and my lip looks as if it was the final victim in a B slasher flick.

"That's what liner's for," Serena's disembodied voice chirps from the phone on the marble bathroom vanity.

"I want to look like a damn grown-up for this meeting."

"You do. *Watch where you're fucking going!* This isn't the Autobahn!"

"Stop driving and talking. It's making me nervous." I wet a tissue and dab my lip. The plum color that was supposed to say "sophisticated" leaks more.

"It's Bluetooth. I'll be at your door in five. In the meantime, use some makeup remover."

She clicks off before I can tell her I don't have makeup remover.

Concealer it is. I stab it on with a finger, then take one final look in the mirror at my pencil skirt and blouse before dashing out of the upstairs bathroom and down the creaky staircase as fast as my heels will safely carry me.

In the formal dining room off the hall, I take a quick inventory—computer bag, files, makeup kit, plus the coffee that brewed automatically—and gather everything on the custom table as Serena's Range Rover pulls up at the curb of my tree-lined street.

I walk out the door. There are birds in this older neighborhood, and mature trees just starting to blossom in the spring.

"Tell me it's not that bad," I say as I slide into the car, armload of gear in tow.

Serena inspects my face. "Do you want to start the day off with lies?"

I set two travel mugs in the console cup holders.

"I love that the owner of a record company makes me coffee."

"Part owner. And I love that you stayed with me." I mean it, and her eyes glint a little before she turns back to the road. "You ever regret it?"

"What, sticking with your nerdy ass? Never."

We cross town in less than ten minutes, and Serena pulls into the Wicked lot.

"Morning, Miss Telfer. Miss Daniels."

"Morning, Jeff." I nod to security as we cross the lobby.

We ride the elevator up to the top floor.

"Haley," Derek, who used to be the VP of production and moved into the CEO role after my father's death, greets me as I enter the boardroom.

I take a seat across from the rest of the management team, Serena on my heels.

"Serena, you're joining us?" He raises a brow.

"She is."

Wicked's head of production, Todd, runs a judgmental eye over her. "I understand she joined the PR department when you took control of Wicked, but you stopped calling the shots when you sold the company."

"I sold eighty percent of the company. I'm the only owner who works here." *Without expecting a paycheck,* I add silently.

"Work here?" he scoffs. "You run an after-school program."

Derek cuts in smoothly before I can argue. "I trust you reviewed the financials. We have little slack. The music industry is changing fast, and we're losing traction."

Moving Derek into the CEO position after my father passed away had seemed like the best move. I still don't regret it, though sometimes I think he lets me out of things in deference to my father. The fact that I kept him.

The new head of production has none of those biases.

"Our junior artists will help carry this company into a new age," I point out.

"They're children," Todd protests. "We should be dropping the program, not investing in it. Free up studio space we can lease. Not to mention the equipment. Their sweaty little hands are taking up a few hundred thousand in instruments and gear."

I straighten in my chair. "You can't be serious."

"None of them are in a position to supplement this company's income," Derek says. "It's not that they're untalented, but they're kids without proper training, media coaching. Now, we've spoken to the majority shareholders, and they're in favor of cost-cutting measures. This shouldn't come as a surprise. Wicked is a business venture for them. They don't have the... affection for it that you do."

"We're not dropping the program." The words sound raw from my dry throat. "Can we take a coffee break?"

Derek shoves his hands in his pockets, and Todd lets out an annoyed sigh. "Sure," Derek offers.

I rise from my seat and top off my coffee from the carafe in the corner. I feel Derek's presence before I see him.

"Listen," he starts under his breath. "We talked about

using the program as a PR exercise. Do features on some of the kids. Hell, maybe we can claim a tax write-off if we spin it right."

I picture the faces of the high school kids who come through the studio. Performing here gives them something structured, but more importantly, it gives them space to create.

"They're not charity cases, Derek. They're artists. My father got that when he started the program. We're not doing them a favor; they're doing us one."

I go back to the table, taking my seat. Derek follows.

Across the table, Serena raises a brow. I probably look like I'm about to murder someone.

Derek turns to the lawyer. "Let's talk about our stars. How goes the outreach regarding current contracts?"

"We've tried to reach Mr. Jamieson. Reminded his attorney he's under contract."

Jax's name makes me sit up straighter.

"Nothing?" Todd sounds exasperated. "I've worked with some divas, but this is ridiculous."

"He told us to take him to court."

"Then do that." Todd's not bothering to hide his irritation. "Or let's move the hell on, Derek. He's not a rock star anymore. He's a glorified car salesman."

Serena jumps in. "As the person who runs this label's social media and half our ad budget? Jax Jamieson is still the biggest rock star on the planet. He could turn this around by breathing on it. His fans haven't forgotten him." Her gaze flicks to me. "Even if he's forgotten them."

I swallow the lump that rises in my throat at the mention of his name. "Have you talked to him?"

"He won't answer calls or return them." Wicked's lawyer weighs in.

"I don't understand how you let him walk away in the first place," the production head mutters, looking around the table.

That's a story you would never understand.

It's been two years since I saw his handsome face, but in some ways it feels like ten.

In some ways, it feels like yesterday.

My fingers slide under the table, tapping on my thigh. I pull out my phone and glance at it. The number hasn't been used in two years.

It's my best weapon right now.

Derek clears his throat. "Haley, I'm sorry about the program. But we're going to have to cut it, effective this week."

"No. You're not." I lift my face to the circle of executives.

"Excuse me?"

"I can get him for you." My voice is level even though my stomach turns over.

The head of production scoffs, but Derek leans in.

"A new Riot Act album will get Wicked attention," I go on. "A couple of singles picked up by Hollywood for summer blockbusters. And most importantly, everyone will be calling for interviews. Which means we can get our artists—all of them—back in the spotlight."

Todd laughs. "I heard about your father's track record of finding talent, but what you're talking about isn't magic. It's voodoo. Jax Jamieson's vanished off the face of the earth."

I ignore Todd and turn to Derek. "Two conditions: One, I produce the album. Two, you don't cut my program until after the album's recorded. It goes platinum in the first month, we keep the program."

"You can't be serious," Todd says flatly, but Derek's gaze is fixed on me.

"You think you can make it happen?" he asks.

"Get a studio ready." I hold out a hand. "Do we have a deal?"

He shakes.

I finger the sheet of paper in my jacket pocket, then I nod to the lawyer. "Call Jax again. Only this time, you're going to tell him this..."

Keep reading to find out whether the label that broke Jax and Haley apart can bring them back together in Wicked Girl, the final instalment of the WICKED trilogy...

He was a legend, until he walked away.

I was nobody, until I was dragged into the light.

I was never supposed to be part of Wicked, but it was always part of me.
Now it's my turn to do something that matters...
Even if the man I love hates me for it.

WICKED GIRL

WICKED PART 3

1

"Jax." Across the table, Camille Taylor's tongue darts out to brush her lip. "We need to talk."

Everything about her reads indecisive, which undermines the professional look she's got going on. High-neck blouse. Bun like a ballerina.

If she wanted to be a ballerina once, this gig must've been a rude awakening.

"What's the problem?" I ask, impatient, shifting in the padded leather chair and eyeing her up over the desk.

"It's Anne. She's been here a year. But she doesn't seem to be settling in."

Annie's eighth grade homeroom teacher flicks her gaze toward the classroom door, like my kid can hear her from the hall.

"She's creative. Smart. But she keeps to herself. I don't think she's making many friends. Occasionally she's disruptive."

My shoulders tighten. "Disruptive how."

She hesitates before uttering a string of words I'm sure I've misheard.

"What?" I demand.

"She glued feminine hygiene products to one of her classmate's books."

Shit.

I fight the urge to rip one of my fingernails. They're all pretty much gone anyway.

"Oh, and Jax?"

"Yeah?"

"Is she channeling that creativity into other outlets? She was telling one of the boys in class about your music."

I shake my head. "She swims. She doesn't even listen to my music."

"I find that hard to believe. We don't know everything our children do."

"Annie doesn't keep secrets from me." My jaw tightens.

"Anne's a bright girl. She's got excellent language and math skills. I wish she'd connect more with the other students—use her abilities more constructively." Her gaze flicks past me, nervous, then back. "I understand from her file she's had some changes recently. That can lead to acting out."

My hands tighten on the armrests. "Tell you what. You do your job and I'll do mine."

I shove out of my chair and cross to the door.

"Annie." Outside, the red head of hair lifts from where

she's studying her phone with a pained expression. "Let's go."

We follow the sidewalk out the front of the private school. It's all brick and landscaping, and I wonder again what the money pays for that's so different from the public school I went to. More trees? The lawn gets mowed every week instead of once a month?

I glance over at my kid.

In her school uniform, she looks the same as any other eighth grader in this place. But in the past few years, she's changed.

She wears her hair differently. It used to be in braids and now it's down or in a ponytail, the kind that sticks out of the top of her head.

I hit the locks on the Bentley, and we both shift inside.

I put the car in gear and pull out of the lot. "Miss Taylor says you glued something to some kid's books."

Caramel eyes land on me for the first time all night. "They're called tampons, Jax."

Her lilting voice wraps around each word like she's underlining them.

It barely registers that she calls me by my first name anymore. I curse whatever god exists that it's my job to ask, "Why?"

"She swiped mine from gym last week. So I figured if she needed them so badly, she could have them."

"When did you get your... you know?"

"Period?" She sighs, shifting in the passenger seat to

look out the window. "A few months ago. Don't worry. Mom helped me when I saw her at Christmas."

It takes all my control not to swerve.

It's almost April.

I still haven't done anything about the "you're becoming a woman" literature my manager rustled up for me. It's in a locked drawer, next to the stack of cash I'll use for the hit on the misguided kid who asks her to prom in four years.

Four years? Jesus.

Some days I think that if I'd known the custody battle with Grace for my kid would've taken a year of our lives and dragged my sister through the mud—something she blames entirely on me when I drop my kid off for holiday visits—maybe I wouldn't have done it.

But I can't say that. I can't even let myself think it for long or I find myself reaching for a crutch. Because this is what I wanted. Everything I wanted.

If it's not enough, I don't know what I'll do.

I force myself back to the conversation. "She also said you were talking about my work. My music."

The noise sounds like a snort. "That's not your work anymore. You haven't touched a guitar all year. You used to play with Ryan."

"Uncle Ryan."

"The last time he came by was six months ago."

Christ, she notices everything. It doesn't feel like that

long since I saw Mace, but her mind's like a damn video recorder.

Outside our house, I hit the button on my visor and the gates swing open. The Bentley cruises up the long drive, past the rows of trees and flower beds someone planted a long time ago.

We live fifteen minutes from the school and she doesn't have any friends close by. For the first time, I wonder why not.

"Annie?"

"Anne."

"*Annie.*"

She grinds her teeth next to me. I want to shake her or point out she's living in a damn mansion with everything she could want. And some days, it's as if she doesn't notice.

I take a breath to steady myself as I hit the button for the garage and angle the car inside. "I've never seen you with any friends from school."

"I hang out with Cash and Drew at lunch."

"No girls."

"So?"

"Your teacher thought you might be trying to impress a boy."

She snorts. "Those two are not worth impressing."

"Good." Relief has my shoulders sagging, because if she's into boys, I can't deal with that.

"Do you want to know if I'm a lesbian?"

How I manage to throw the car into park, I'll never

know. Especially when every instinct is to hit reverse and mash on the gas pedal of life.

"You're thirteen years old."

"I'll be fourteen in the summer." She opens her door and scrambles out, leaning back in after. "If I do like boys, I wouldn't waste my time on either of them. Drew is smashing Chloe Hastings, and I'm pretty sure Cash doesn't have testicles."

The door slams before I can process those words.

I rub my fingers over the bridge of my nose. There's no way this week could get worse.

Until my phone rings.

2

HALEY

V*inyl.*

Computer hardware upgrades.

A great cup of coffee.

Seafood doesn't even make the shortlist of things I'll shell out for.

Though here in Philly, mussels are hauled off boats every day, which means they don't have to be expensive.

This place is expensive.

I reach for the front door, but an attendant dressed in black beats me to it.

The restaurant is cozy, intimate, and definitely not my choosing. A dozen tables sit under fairy lights sprinkled in the ceiling and corners.

A familiar blond man stands abruptly when he spots me across the restaurant.

"Wow. You look gorgeous," Carter says as I pull up in

front of the table, his gaze running over me. "This for me?"

I smooth a hand over my skirt. "Actually, I was at Wicked for meetings. If I'm coding, it's yoga pants and coffee stains all the way."

He looks good too. He always does. Tonight he's wearing dress pants and a crisp button-down. His blond hair curls at the collar. Carter rounds the table to drop a kiss on my mouth, and I turn my face. He catches my cheek instead.

Burn, I imagine Serena saying.

The chair is pushed in behind me—maybe by the same ghoulish attendant, because he's gone before I can turn around.

I open the menu. "Food first, then work? I'm starving."

"It's always work with you." His grin is teasing, but he complies. When the server comes, Carter orders a bottle of wine. "How do you like the restaurant?"

"Very *Midsummer Night's Dream*.'" He chuckles. "How's the tenure application going?"

Carter's brows scrunch together. "It's always hard being the youngest to do something. The administration wants to find reasons to tell you no, or not yet. Of course, I'm not going to let them get away with it."

Our wine is delivered and poured, and Carter orders lobster. I get the steak. Rare.

"You're looking for blood tonight," he observes.

"Maybe a little."

"Wicked's living up to its name, huh?"

I take a sip of my wine, feel it tingle through me as I turn the stem in my fingers. "I didn't realize how hard it would be to convince people of things. Maybe it's my age. Or inexperience. Or the fact that I have a vagina."

"For the record, I love that you have a vagina."

I swallow a laugh. "But sometimes... sometimes I think people just don't like change." Work is a safe subject with Carter, and it feels good to vent to someone other than Serena.

"That's what's perfect about computers," Carter says. "It's just you and a terminal, and you can change the world."

He talks a lot about changing the world, but I know he means solving interesting technical problems while making money.

It's not a bad thing; it's just how he is. He likes a certain lifestyle and wants to be well-known. He's brilliant at what he does, so he can afford that desire.

"Sometimes I wonder how things might have been different if I'd gotten back into school. I could be a grad student by now."

"You're one of the best coders I've met, degree or not. You take apart problems like no one I know, because you're genuinely curious about them and you believe you can solve them. And, I'm glad you're not a grad student by now."

I raise a brow.

"If you were my grad student, we couldn't do this." His eyes sparkle.

Our meal arrives. When my steak, potatoes, and carrots are set on the scratchy white tablecloth, I let out a little groan that goes unnoticed by Carter, who's looking at his lobster with both anticipation and satisfaction. We dig in, and the first few bites have me sighing.

Okay, maybe there's more to this nice restaurant thing than I thought.

I look at Carter, happily devouring his lobster, and a memory flashes across my mind. Mace hurling his guts into a bucket after ordering diner lobster. My mouth twitches despite the long day.

"What're you laughing at?" Carter prompts.

"Nothing. Just a memory."

It's shocking how many memories I have of that tour.

Shocking because it was only a month. Not shocking because the human brain records new things a disproportionate amount of the time. And nearly everything I experienced on that tour was new.

Living with musicians and roadies in hotels and on a bus.

Learning how to operate one of the best sound systems in the business.

Falling in love with a man I never should've met.

I mentally slap myself. Usually I catch my brain before it goes down that path. But tonight, whether it's the long day or the wine or the fairy lights, I don't catch it in time.

He's here. Humming along my skin.

The sound of his voice laughing in my ear.

The feel of his lips the first time he kissed me.

The look on his face the day he walked away.

My stomach squeezes, and I reach for more wine.

"Good thing we got a bottle," Carter quips. "Since your mood's already improved, I don't need to show you this. I will anyway." He sets down his fork and knife and lifts his phone. "We have an offer."

He slides his phone in front of me between the dinner plates the waitress set in front of us. I shift in my chair, uncrossing and recrossing my legs to get more comfortable.

The piece of software we've been building is actually our second project together. After we won the competition with my music program Digital Record Enhancement, or DRE (as Serena named it), we decided we made a pretty good team. We turned a version of it into an app that's available on every device to amateur and professional producers and provides a steady, if small, revenue stream.

This new program we want to sell outright to a company that will do the same.

The six-figure number on the screen imprints on my mind.

"Wow. I'm not going to lie. I know where my fifty percent is going," I say.

He raises a brow. "Fifty?"

“That’s what we agreed.”

“Fine.” He grins, and I can’t tell if he was just pushing my buttons. One of the reasons I can’t quite get a handle on him—and that I never really want to. “Celebrate with me. Come home with me tonight.”

I swallow the sigh.

We’ve done it before. Not enough that I’d call it a pattern, which is why he’s not sure of himself when he asks. Carter’s intelligent and attractive. And if he’s a flake, that’s not a crime.

When I’m bored, I can resist. It’s when I’m lonely—which takes a lot given my tolerance for being alone—that it’s hard to say no.

I never crave sex, but sometimes it feels like I’m desperate for human connection, even if the human in question isn’t the one I want to connect with.

The ring of my phone interrupts us.

The number on the screen has my spine stiffening.

I hit Ignore and take a steadying breath as I fix a smile on my face and focus on my dinner companion. “I appreciate the offer, but I have work to do tomorrow.”

“You realize how wrong that is? Between your inheritance and this money, you don’t have to work at all.” I open my mouth to argue, but he does it for me. “Of course, I know you couldn’t deal with that. It’s not in you not to try new things—to learn all the time.”

And that’s why I do this. Because even if Carter’s never

going to be a kindred spirit, he understands what it's like to do the work because you can. Because you want to. Because wasting your abilities is a crime.

The phone rings again, a different tone.

Now, it's a video call.

Of course it is.

He won't stop. I know it as surely as I know the bill will come and Carter will make another play before he puts me in my car and I go home alone.

My gaze flicks around the restaurant as if I'm looking for an escape.

Maybe I am.

No luck.

My body shivers with nerves or anticipation.

I can handle Carter blindfolded. This man, even a thousand miles away and on the phone? This is going to be harder.

I hit Accept.

I've seen Jax Jamieson on TV, but his image now, a little grainy from questionable reception, is something else. Because those eyes are on me, and though it's dark wherever he is and I can't make out their trademark amber color, the shape is the same. His sculpted mouth. The hard jaw. The hair falling over his face.

"Jax." I say his name as coolly as I can. "Can I call you back?"

"No."

I lift my gaze to Carter, apologetic. "Excuse me one moment." I shift out of my chair and duck into the hallway by the coatrack.

"Are you on a date?" His commanding tone has me bristling.

I take in the near-black backdrop. "Are you in a coffin?"

His eyes narrow. "We don't talk in two years and now you're trying to enforce my contract."

"I don't enforce contracts."

"Bullshit. One of your suits threatened me. You're seriously going to take the song I gave you and produce it without me?"

I think of the sheet of paper I've carried around for the better part of three years. "It's not a threat. It's a courtesy. We want to give you notice."

"It's my song," he grinds out. "You can't do whatever the hell you want with it."

"It was a gift," I retort, my voice rising too. "In case you've forgotten, that's how gifts work."

I brace myself for a chain reaction, one detonation leading to another, but Jax surprises me by regaining his composure. "You've changed."

"So have you. We all have, Jax." I take a deep breath, hold it for a count of five, and let it out. "You have a choice. Do the album. Or let someone else finish what you started."

I hit End without waiting for him to respond.

In the bathroom, I smooth out my appearance and pretend the shortest call in history didn't shake me to my core before returning to Carter.

"So what do you say?" He grins, all teeth and boyish charm. "Nightcap at my place?"

3

"Burger or nuggets?" I slide my sunglasses down my nose and glance toward the passenger seat.

My daughter pulls out an earbud and looks between me and the drive-through window. "I told you. I'm vegetarian."

I give up and pull out of the lane.

"Why don't you order anything?"

"Huh?"

"You used to get nuggets. You said it was the sweet and sour sauce of the gods."

I'm not telling my kid "because once you turn thirty, it's harder to keep the six-pack they're paying you for."

Which puts us back in a standoff.

The silence is getting to me. I used to be able to take long trips alone. Hell, I craved them.

But the first-class flight from Dallas to Philadelphia

and the ride from the airport in my rented Acura has been filled with a quiet tension.

For a moment though, I'm grateful she's in her own world. I soak in the place—my emotions—as I drive through the streets of downtown.

The locals are still dressed in coats and a few boots. The trees are growing leaves. They look hopeful.

That makes one of us.

In the five days since I called Haley, I have run through a dozen responses.

To tell Wicked to fuck off. To ignore them. To unleash my lawyers in that snarling furor only expensive litigators can manage.

In the end, I lay awake staring at the ceiling and remembering the song I wrote. The thought of someone else taking it, making it theirs, and possibly ruining it?

I'm not going to risk it. I need to fix this in person.

We pull up to the valet at the hotel.

"I thought we were getting a house," Annie says, peering out the window and looking up.

"I said I booked the *Rittenhouse*. We have a suite. You'll be home by the summer."

"Everything will have changed in three months. Why couldn't I stay with Mom?"

Because she'd never let me live it down.

"Because you're my kid. I said we were coming to Philly for a while, so that's what we're doing."

My voice is sharp and she blinks at me. For a second I

see her, the younger version. Before she wore shiny crap on her mouth and put her hair in strange ponytails.

I miss that version. But as quick as it appeared, it's gone, and the indifference is back.

We get out of the car and the manager greets us. I hand the keys to the valet.

"Mr. Jamieson, it's a pleasure to see you again. And who is this?"

"This is Annie."

I glance back to make sure my daughter is following. Her sullen countenance lurks at my back as Rodney shows us upstairs before handing Annie and me each a keycard.

I open the door to the two-bedroom suite with a view of the park. "You've changed something."

His brows rise. "The carpet and the drapes, Mr. Jamieson."

The joke is on the tip of my tongue, but I stop myself.

"You used to stay here?" Annie asks as he leaves.

It's the first time she's sounded interested, though she's still looking out at the park. I saunter over and stop at her side, taking in the view.

"When we recorded *Redline*. And *Abandon*."

"And now you're recording the fourth. What's it called?"

I hiss out a breath. "It doesn't have a name, because I haven't decided I'm going to do it."

"Why don't you want to?" Annie asks, her gaze sharp.

"That part of my life is over. I chose to come home. To be with you."

"Awesome," she says, like it's really not. When she turns toward me, I expect her to launch into another tirade about our sudden trip, but she says, "My first memory of you was at one of your concerts. On stage, it was like no one could touch you." Tingling runs through my body, not from the memory, but from hearing how she saw me. "You're a different person now."

I drop the curtain and cross the room, setting my phone on the table by the door. "It's on stage where I was different. Now I'm the same person I was before."

Our luggage arrives, and the staff unloads four large suitcases. I slip the guy a fifty.

Annie grabs the handle of one and starts toward the door on the far side of the living room.

"Slow your roll."

She stops and turns, her movements exaggerated. "What."

"Where do you think you're going?"

"Bedroom."

"Not the master."

"It's the least you can do for dragging me here."

I try not to laugh. "You're thirteen. I go, you follow."

She enters the master and takes a look around. She lets out a little sigh at the soaker tub.

If I spoil her, it's natural. I want to make up for everything she's been through. Ten years of living in a dump with a man she never should've called her father. Who Grace never should've called her husband. Now he's serving two years for domestic assault while my sister reclaims her life.

Grace's job as a pharma rep is paying for the house he nearly lost with his drinking and drug habits. Nearly. I had my lawyer work out how to compensate them for some of their bills.

It was the one deal I ever made with her asshole of a spouse.

"So what? You need this for all your preppy shirts?" Annie looks up from the closet.

"I don't have that many preppy shirts." A few years ago, all I owned were T-shirts and hoodies.

Now I do charity auctions. Car commercials. Classy ads. A select few opportunities screened by my agent that pay well and don't force me to play music.

Clooney and Nespresso have nothing on me.

I grab Annie's wrist and tug her toward the second bedroom, where I throw open the doors. It's got a king bed and a big closet.

"There's no ensuite." Her voice is flat.

"Adversity builds character."

Okay, maybe she's a little right. I have a lot of preppy shirts.

I stick sweaters and a few T-shirts on the shelf at the top of the closet. Most of what I used to wear is long since packed up in boxes.

The bathroom already holds the shampoo and shaving cream I like—at least some things never change, and Rodney has those on file.

I'm putting the suitcases under the bed when house phone rings. "Hello?"

"Mr. Jamieson, you have a visitor. I understand she used to tour with you."

Haley? It can't be.

"Mr. Jamieson?"

I hesitate. Annie's gone down to swim, her favorite activity that we share now. "Send her up."

I glance at the door, remembering when I'd been in the Ritz in Dallas and answered the knock to find Haley standing there looking indecisive and beautiful as fuck.

More than once since we parted, I've had a weak moment and thought of her.

Seeing her on the phone last week...

The red color on her lips it had me focusing on her mouth.

The things I did to that mouth.

The things I never got a chance to.

When Haley told me she'd move in with me two years ago, it was the best thing I'd felt since getting off tour. Maybe I'd been living in a dream, expecting everything would be simple once I stopped playing three cities a week. But it wasn't.

She was the bright spot in all of it.

Then she sided with Cross, with Wicked, and the floor fell out from under my world.

Shannon Cross screwed me from beyond the grave, a final act that would have had him laughing in delight if he'd known.

I would've fought him for her. I would've fought anyone, anything, for her.

But there was nothing to fight, because she made the choice freely. She walked away first.

The knock on the door has me taking a steadying breath before I swing it wide to reveal the last person I expected.

A tall woman wearing a denim jacket and designer jeans with aviators perched on her fire-red hair is parked in the doorway holding a bottle of bourbon.

"So the rumors are true." She flashes her teeth. "Shannon Cross's prodigal son has returned."

"Damn," I drawl, resting an elbow on the frame. "A real live rock star at my door. How'd you find me?"

"We have the same manager, remember?"

The tension in my chest eases a few degrees as she wraps her arms around me. There are a handful of people I'll take a hug from. After touring nearly a year together, Lita's one of them.

I take the bottle of bourbon, and she follows me inside. I pour two glasses before we sit on the low couch.

"Heard your last album went gold in two weeks," I say, passing her a glass. "I'm sure you got my card."

"Hmm. Must've got lost in the mail."

She looks good; Like she's gotten her share of the limelight and it suits her.

"You're selling out," I state.

Lita smirks into her glass. "Wicked has been good to me."

"I meant arenas."

"No, you didn't." She takes a sip. "What do you call what you've been doing, hmm? Giving the camera sexy eyes as you fake drive a fake car down a fake road in front of a green screen?"

"I call it keeping the bills paid."

"Bullshit. There are a lot of ways to keep the bills paid with that beautiful voice. You didn't run from music. You ran from Wicked." Her words have my spine stiffening even before she goes on. "You been back since the funeral?"

"Nope."

Haley and I haven't spoken either.

Sure, she texted me a couple of times the first winter and left a voicemail asking me to call her back.

I couldn't deal with it. The wound was too fresh.

"She's not a kid anymore," Lita says softly.

It's as if she can read my mind. I hope it's because

we've spent so much time together, not because I'm getting transparent in my advanced age.

"She never was, and that's the problem," I reply. "The first time she set foot on tour, she was her father's daughter. She wanted an empire. She got one."

"Come on. You might've been hiding out in Dallas, but you're not living under a rock. You know she sold most of her share of the company over a year ago."

I grind my teeth. "Makes you wonder why she went to the trouble of taking it over to begin with." I don't care what Haley's reasons were, but Lita's tone has something occurring to me. "Are you here for me or for Haley?"

Saying her name sends prickles through my body.

"She's had my back. You know Derek and the other guys can be every bit as fickle as Cross. She's not like them. Or like him. Haley cares about the work, Jax. But more than that, she cares about the people." Lita glances around the room as though she's debating what to say. "When are you starting?"

"Meeting Monday."

"Good luck."

I toss back the rest of the bourbon, set the glass on the table with a clink. "You can tell her that."

Lita's laugh is light, tinkling. "Damn, I wish I could see that meeting. You're going to kill each other. Or—"

"I'm not here for her."

"Never said you were." She rises. "Thanks for the drink."

"You brought it."

"I did, didn't I?" With a grin, she slips out the door.

I can't resist calling after her. "Baseball season's right around the corner. Hope you had time to do your homework in between headlining."

She flips me off as she saunters away.

What Lita says doesn't change things one bit. Haley and I aren't friends. We aren't lovers. The only thing we are is at war.

Haley Cross may have lasted two years at Wicked...

But she won't last an hour with me.

4

HALEY

One of my requirements when I gave up control of the company was that I kept my father's office. There have been changes since then, but some things—the fur rug in the conversation set, the big cherry desk, the Ireland picture on the wall—haven't moved. Changing the pieces that seemed most like him felt wrong.

"Haley."

Derek's voice has me looking up from my desk Monday morning. Derek's been around the block, and while he's not bold′, he understands this place. He knew my father better than I did, having worked at his side for nearly ten years.

He steps inside, pulling the door half-closed behind him. Where Shannon Cross was always dressed for the red carpet, Derek favors slacks and sweaters.

"Jax Jamieson's coming in today."

"And you're afraid." My mouth twitches at the corner. After two years, I feel as though I can tease him a little. He has kids of his own and a sense of humor.

"Cross used to deal with Jax personally. I figured that might run in the family." He arches an eyebrow. "Given our unique deal, we agreed that you can call the shots on production, but I need to keep Todd involved since that's his department. " He glances at the clock. "See you in fifteen."

As he disappears, I let out the breath I was holding. Sometimes I forget so few people know Jax and I go back.

Wicked's rule about staff and artists not mixing hasn't changed since Cross's tenure. Not that anyone could fire me—I'm still part owner, and I don't take a salary—but Derek wouldn't be over the moon to learn about my history with Jax.

It's moot, because Jax and I are nothing, I remind myself.

I go over my plan before I collect Serena. "You coming?"

She looks up from her desk, a gleam in her blue eyes. "Let's see. The first and only guy who's ever got you hot and bothered is back and you're going to stick it to him. Plus," she amends with an eye roll, "I think I'm doing the release plan for the album, so yeah. Be there in two."

I make my way to the conference room.

Jax will be late. Although he had a near-photographic memory for the business side of the gig, he also knew that everyone here catered to him.

I expect him to put us off as long as possible. So I set down my things before taking a minute to look out the window, using the reflection to touch up my lipstick.

For the past five days, I've been wondering if this was even going to happen. I kept expecting to hear that Jax had called to tell us to go to hell. *It wouldn't be entirely unfair*. But the fact that he's in town does more than make my heart race.

It gives me hope.

"If I'd known it be the two of us, I would've brought drinks."

The low, familiar voice drags down my spine like a caress.

I cap the lipstick and turn, careful not to wobble on my heels. They're not what Serena would call "fuck me" shoes. No. These are "eat me" shoes—almost as high and pointier at the toe.

Jax fills the doorway. His shoulders are broader than I remember. His face is tan for April, and his jaw still a square angle. His hair is shorter at the sides, but still long enough on top to bend toward his forehead. He's too many steps away for me to stare at his mouth.

Small mercies.

Jax looks good. Better than good. In a collared shirt, and... Jesus, are those chinos?

"Wasn't sure I'd see the day," I tell him, my voice surprisingly level.

"When I walked back in here? Me either."

"I meant that you'd wear a belt without studs in it."

Jax rounds the table, his amber gaze sending shivers down my spine. Never once does he break my gaze as he spans the distance between us.

He stops inches away, his attention skimming down my dress, lingering on my legs. Then it drags back up.

Jax Jamieson is still walking sex. I can't tell if he's thinking about me or music or what he had for breakfast, but his firm lips and bedroom eyes threaten to destroy every piece of armor I've put on.

He hasn't aged, either. His face is strong and unlined, his nose straight, but as he leans, there's a tiny bit of gray in his sideburns.

It shouldn't be hot.

It's totally hot.

"Nice lipstick," he says, and I have to fight the urge to press my lips together.

I've watched him in the media and can't remember a mention of him with someone. But then, Jax has always been good at keeping his private life private.

His mouth skims my cheek as he leans in to whisper, "If you wanted to fuck me, Hales, all you had to do was ask."

My swallow fills the room.

"Am I interrupting?" Serena chirps from the door.

My eyes flutter shut for an instant, grateful for the reprieve.

Jax turns. "Skunk girl."

Serena drops her folders and phone next to mine on the table. "Pretty boy."

I take a seat next to Serena.

Jax drops into the chair facing our side of the table, looking around at the empty seats. "Let's get this over with." A knock sounds at the door, and Jax's face clouds with suspicion. "What's going on?"

Derek strides in with Todd. They're followed by a guy with long red hair, a blond, and one with dark hair, twirling drum sticks.

Jax stares at them as though he's seeing a parade of ghosts.

"Didn't I tell you, Jax?" My voice is light. "We got the band back together."

The look he shoots me is a mix of disbelief and incredulity, and it almost gets me back on even ground.

They say hello, exchanging bro hugs, except for Jax and Mace, who hug properly. Mace murmurs something I can't hear, and Jax replies. They drop into seats next to him.

Derek starts. "Thank you for coming."

"You didn't give me much choice."

"Music's changing, Jax," Todd, Wicked's head of production leans in. "We don't want to let more time go on before finishing the contract we agreed to. Which is why we're cutting an LP."

Normally I don't give Todd a second look. He's narrow-minded and chauvinistic, but I can't help staring at him.

Jax beats me to it. "Full-length? Since when. I heard this would be an EP."

"It is." I shoot Todd a look, because we talked about this already.

The chance of going platinum—what I'd promised Derek—is higher with a full-length album. But I don't think I can keep Jax here long enough to get that out of him. It could take months. Years.

"We need to remind people who you are," Todd goes on. "Put you back on the map. That takes more than four tracks."

I wait for Jax to tear holes in the other man, but he shows a control that's new. "Right now we have zero," he offers.

"We have one," I interrupt.

"One track isn't an album."

"Then I suggest we get to work," Todd says smoothly.

I grit my teeth. "Derek?"

"An LP will make more of an impact," he says without looking at me.

Disbelief and betrayal compete in the back of my mind as Todd spreads his hands.

"So it's settled. Welcome back, Jax."

Todd grabs his files and stalks out, followed by Derek.

I shut my eyes. The sound of slow clapping has me opening them again.

Serena is already chatting up Kyle on the other side of the room. Mace and Brick are talking too.

I want to bury my head somewhere, but I force myself to meet Jax's cold gaze.

"This place has gotten real entertaining. You guys plan this good cop, bad cop shit?"

"It's a misunderstanding," I say as I round the table to Jax.

"Tell me something." The voice that has whispered all manner of sweet and dirty things in my ear cools more. "Who's producing this ten-track marvel? Todd? Because if that prick's in my studio—"

"The production team will be more than satisfactory. You have my word on that." No matter what's happened between me and Jax, he's an artist. I'd never ask him to do work I thought would compromise that.

His mouth turns up in a smirk. He's never been the tallest guy in a room, but he has the most presence. Some he built from being on stage, but some was always him.

I step closer, carried by bravado that's unfounded when I realize I can smell his masculine scent. I fight the shiver that works through me. "I get it, Jax. You don't want to be here. But to get this album done, we need a track list. If there's anything Wicked can do to help, let me know."

I meant it as a platitude, but Jax tilts his head. "How about some inspiration?"

His gaze drops to my mouth and I suck in a shaky breath. He's all physicality, all masculinity, and even though he's being an asshole I can't pretend to be unaffected.

"Those red lips could do a lot to inspire me, babysitter," he murmurs.

My stomach clenches.

In revulsion, because it can't be anything else.

I know he's screwing with me, because now I'm thinking of his cock. We did a lot of things together, but we didn't get to *that*.

In this moment, I feel every day of the more than two years we've been apart, because each one of them contributes to the strength I need when I respond.

"Derek's assistant will be in touch to book studio time," I say coolly. "I trust Annie was able to get into school. I took the liberty of having her books arranged. And I pulled some strings to ensure her teachers understand her situation and that they'll look out for her."

His startled expression gives me the tiniest hit of satisfaction before I walk out the door.

5

"You coming or what?"

I turn back to Mace. "Huh?"

"We're going down to Monk's for lunch and to talk about the album."

I tug on the collar of my shirt. He smirks but says nothing as we start down the hall.

Haley's talking with the woman who used to be Cross's assistant and Derek. She glances at us for the briefest moment, emotionless, before turning back.

"What'd you say to her?" Mace asks under his breath.

"Nothing worth repeating."

Hell, it wasn't worth saying the first time.

I should know better, but something came over me. I went into that meeting prepared to play it cool. To get the upper hand and keep it. But since I walked in to find her, back turned, putting that lipstick on in her reflection from the window...

That dress doing mind-numbing voodoo with my brain...

The damn shoes making her legs even longer?

The plan degraded faster than my kid's good mood when she realizes we're out of Snickers ice cream.

Haley's always been pretty. Not the flashy kind that would break your neck from a distance. The kind you had to get up close to notice.

She didn't care about turning heads. She was always so absorbed in whatever problem she was working on—sometimes that problem was me—that it would be easy to pass her by.

But now, it's impossible to overlook her. She's got this confidence you can see in her straight back. The way her eyes survey a room. The sound of her voice.

She looks exactly the same and completely different. But my thoughts aren't only about how different she looks.

I'm wondering if her new haircut—razor sharp with the edges grazing her collarbone—leaves enough length to wrap around my hand.

I shake off the haze of lust, because that's getting me nowhere fast, and we take the elevator down to the parking lot.

A Toyota Highlander sits in the lot, and Kyle rounds to the driver's door.

"What?" I drawl. "You got two golden retrievers and a house in the suburbs too?"

"Jump on in, boys," Kyle offers.

I shift into the back seat with Mace, and Brick slides in the front.

"How long have you assholes been planning this little reunion?" I ask.

"Not our plan. We just went along with it."

We drive downtown, and the atmosphere in the car is giddy. Monk's is an old favorite with mussels—a clincher for Mace—and the best beer selection in town. It's dark and wood and doesn't try to be anything it's not.

We claim a table, and Brick and Kyle go up to the bar to order.

Mace's phone beeps.

"That your girlfriend?" I ask.

"Notification from class. I'm taking art history online." I stifle the laugh, but he doesn't smile. "I'm serious. It's interesting, and I like learning between gigs."

I consider that. "You haven't been around in a while."

"You haven't been free in a while." He stares at me. "I know you have a kid. And I know that getting her was a rough year. But you're doing douchey promo shit and not playing any music." Mace folds his arms. "Annie still use my LEGO?"

"She's thirteen."

Mace cocks his head. "What're you saying?"

Brick and Kyle return, setting four frothing beers on the table.

"So this album," Kyle says, grunting as he drops into his seat. "What've we got?"

"You seriously want to do this." I look around the three faces.

"Well, yeah," Mace replies. "We're on contract, but more than that, we've got a studio and rehearsal time. Wicked's underwriting the album. One last push."

"I don't get why they're doing it," Brick says. "There's no money in albums. And the contract wasn't for a tour."

"Could just be they need a front-runner," Mace pipes in. "Someone they can hook up-and-comers' names to."

"Or they have some other cash cows. Lifestyle advertising. Product placement. Music's just a way to get in the door," Kyle adds.

"Kyle's got a blog," Brick notes. "And I've been doing voice work for Titan Games," he says with pride.

Mace snickers. "They pay you in games?"

"I get real money, asshole."

I'm still wrestling with the reason we're here.

I don't know what happened in that meeting between Haley and the production guy, but something told me she hadn't planned it.

Still, the guys are genuinely enthusiastic about this, and I have to give Haley props. Using my band against me was a smart fucking move.

Looks like she got more from Cross than his company after all.

"So what've we got, Mozart?" Mace prods. "You know. For the rest of the album."

I drop back in my seat, tipping the beer to my lips. The woodsy taste of hops finds its way down my throat. "Haven't written anything."

"Haley says there's a song we can start with." Kyle shifts forward.

I raise my brows. "Really? What else does Haley say?"

Brick narrows his gaze, and Kyle smirks. Mace licks his lips as a plate of mussels is delivered and he descends on them. Three burgers come, and I reach for ketchup to douse my fries.

God damn, french fries are good. I'm going to be swimming an extra twenty laps to make up for it, but it's this or take it out on the band.

"So you and Haley," Kyle goes on. "Now that you're back, are you picking up where you left off? You know, necking like Romeo and fucking Juliet?"

"It's not going to happen," Brick notes.

Kyle frowns. "Why not?"

Shit, they could have this whole conversation without me.

"The other man." That has me straightening. "I think his name's Carter."

I nearly choke on a fry and wash it back with beer. The stein thuds on the table. "Carter?"

He shrugs. "I heard from Neen. I don't know the guy."

The bitter taste in my mouth isn't from the beer.

The dude she was on a date with was Carter. The pretty boy computer genius who screwed her over two years ago—who used her and tossed her aside.

Perfect.

Just because we're not friends anymore doesn't mean I want her with that asshole.

If I'm going to stick around this place for more than a few days, I need to know what the hell is going on.

"You're around a lot," I say to Brick. "At Wicked."

"Yeah. I'm not much for the politics, but after Cross?" He shrugs. "Derek was always good with numbers but rumor is he doesn't have the old man's baser instincts."

Which raises another question that's been lurking in the back of my mind. "Why'd she sell?"

Brick exchanges a look with Mace. "I don't know, man."

"Find out." I force down a few bites of my hamburger, but it's wasted effort. I'm not hungry anymore. I'm torn between wanting to demonize Haley and morbid curiosity.

It doesn't matter what happened since we were together. She went her way and you went yours.

I grab my beer and shove her from my mind.

Annie's new school gets out before the one in Dallas.

Unfortunately, I don't realize it until too late.

On my way back to the hotel, I try her phone. No answer.

Inside our suite, I call her name.

I head down the elevator, and fear settles in my gut as I swoop out the doors to the main floor. "Rodney. You seen my kid?"

He nods toward the security guy, who points at the screen. I round to take a look. She's in the pool, swimming laps. I heave a sigh of relief.

"She arrived home less than an hour ago," Rodney says.

"How'd she seem?"

"Like someone who'd finished her first day of school. Overwhelmed." He hesitates. "The pool's been closed for deck renovations, but I suggested she might like to try it."

His kindness gets to me. "You have teenagers, Rodney?"

"Not anymore."

"They survived, then."

"They did." He smiles. "The groceries you ordered have been delivered."

I thank him before making my way upstairs.

On impulse, I change out of the button-down, strip off my socks and tug on a T-shirt.

I want a shower, but I don't want to miss Annie coming back, so I cook.

It's another thing I never used to do. But in the past few years, I've gotten into it.

Though we have a chef back home who prepares most of our meals on the weekend, I've learned to make some staples, including all of Annie's favorites.

When the door clicks open, I glance up to find her slinking in.

Her hair's soaking wet from the pool, and somewhere along the line she changed out of her bathing suit and into shorts and a sweatshirt. My kid's always hot and cold at the same time.

"Hi, squirt. How was your first day?"

She looks taken aback. "Bolognese?"

"With"—I check the package—"soy curds."

My girl's a sucker for Italian, and it's easier than apologizing for dragging her across state lines with five days' notice. Something I hadn't thought about until Haley's comments.

I've never had to enrol my kid in school. I don't know if it's easy or hard. I know there's a shit-ton of email and paperwork to transfer over, because after the custody battle finished, my manager and lawyer handled it all when I had my hands full with Annie.

"Plus Caesar salad." It's my trump card, and her expression says she knows it too. "You need a shower?"

She shakes her head, sending her wet hair bouncing. "I did it down there."

With a moment's hesitation, she drops her swim bag and school bag by the door and approaches the kitchen.

She pulls out cutlery and sets it on the coffee table in front of the TV.

"You have homework tonight?"

"There's a lot of reading. History and social studies mostly. I'm going to be behind."

Normally I'd tell her to get on it first thing. I didn't do enough homework as a kid, and I regret it.

"Tell you what. Why don't we hang out for a bit first?"

Her eyes brighten with interest. "Really?"

I grate parmesan on top of our dinner and carry the plates over to the coffee table. "Yeah. They can't expect you to be caught up on day one. We'll watch Netflix and chill."

She wrinkles her nose. "Don't ever say that again."

6

Being back in rehearsal is familiar and awkward at once. Like driving your favorite car with the seat in the wrong position.

We move around one another like ghosts, our gazes connecting and passing unspoken signals as we tune the track over and over.

"This doesn't suck," Mace declares Thursday as we finish running through the song I gave to Haley years ago. "I think it's there."

I lift the guitar off my neck and set it down before reaching for the full bottle of water next to the two I've emptied since lunch. "Let's do the bridge again."

"Seriously? We've been running this all week. I gotta meet Neen," Brick complains.

"I still can't believe you're tapping Nina," Kyle says.

"I can't believe it took so damned long," Mace weighs in.

"Ours is a forbidden love." Brick's grin is undercut by the wistful edge in his voice. "But seriously. Now that she's still running tours and I'm off 'em, it's all good."

I only half hear my friend's comments.

Part of me still can't believe Haley distributed the song to the band as an enticement to get them to come back. I always knew she had balls. But this is another level.

I hate it.

And admire it.

Three days here has me falling into a routine. Every morning, I wait until Annie goes to school before I head to the studio.

Every afternoon, I go back to the hotel, swim a punishing number of laps, then return to my suite and stare at the song I started as if I expect it to spontaneously multiply.

Because even though I told the guys I'm not making an album, they want to try. And though I haven't committed to anything, I find myself asking whether I even can.

More than once, I've caught myself thinking of Haley. Not what she's doing on the phone when I pass her in the hall, our gazes meeting for the briefest second. Or what she and Serena are laughing about in the kitchen when I go with Mace on a caffeine run.

I think of her with Carter.

What they do together.

Whether he knows what she likes.

When I'm not rehearsing, I talk some info out of the

staff. She doesn't take a salary from Wicked, though she spends as much time here as she does at home. She lives in the old man's big Victorian house. She never finished her degree.

The last one bugs me.

A noise at the door has us looking up.

And dammit, it's the girl—woman, actually—I can't kick out of my head.

She's wearing them again.

Heels.

I miss the Converse, and it has zero to do with nostalgia.

These shoes are the same color as her legs and make them look as if they go on forever. It's not that they're porn star heels either. They're only a couple of inches. But they're fucking fascinating because I've never seen her in them.

Instead of a skirt, she's wearing jeans. But ones that hug her hips, her legs. Her sleeveless top is black and dips in the front—fluttering fabric that skims her breasts and her waist. That has me remembering what it's like to touch each of those curves in turn, and the sounds I can coax from her when I do.

Her hair's raked back from her face and braided over one shoulder. Not in the way parents braid kids' hair. This has pieces falling out around her face, the ends spiky, as though she's already been doing something that messed with it.

No red lipstick. Her mouth is sheer and a little shiny.

I swallow the arousal.

"Howdy, Hales."

Since when does Kyle call her that? My glare goes unnoticed because mine aren't the only eyes on her.

"Guys," she says in that full voice that drags down my spine like a promise. "How's rehearsal?"

Everyone turns to me, including her. Our gazes meet, and it's the longest we've looked at one another all week. Since we came face to face in the conference room.

"What've you got?" she asks, lifting her chin.

It's Mace who clears his throat. "Jax?"

I shift the guitar over my head once more, adjust the strap around my neck, and start our intro. We play the song again, and though I avoid her stare, I'm aware she's here.

That she's never heard the song.

That I wrote it for her.

I step up to the mic—not because I need it to carry my voice—out of habit, more than anything.

Playing the song is different than the times before, because she's here and even though I hate it, I can't help that part of me wants to know what she thinks.

We finish, and Haley's gone pale. Not enough for the guys to notice, but enough that I do. "It's sounding good." Her voice sticks in her throat, as if the words aren't quite right.

"Good. Think that's our first good, huh Jax?" Mace jokes. "Wait. No, it must be our second."

I shoot him a dirty look.

Because I sure as hell remember that first night she said those words to us in the elevator, but he shouldn't.

I meet Haley's gaze and the flicker in it tells me she does too.

"Right. I need the room in"—she checks her watch—"an hour. Can you pick this up tomorrow? Or somewhere else?"

"I'm outtie," Brick says, already packing up.

I slide my guitar into its case.

The other guys leave, saying goodbye to Haley on the way.

"What game are we playing, Jax?"

I straighten at the sound of her voice. "You're the one who hauled me back here like Domino Harvey. The bounty hunter," I go on at her blank stare.

If I'm trying to get a rise out of her, it doesn't work. Haley doesn't flinch, and that pisses me off more. "You're on contract for an album. All we want is for you to honor that," she says. "If you want to get this done and get back to Dallas, you might want to be more forthcoming. We need tracks."

I close the distance between us, raising a brow. "Forthcoming? Listen to you. You even sound like him."

And there it is. The flash that, for a moment, looks like

hurt. But of course it isn't. I can't hurt her anymore and she can't hurt me.

My skin prickles when I realize it's just us in the room. The acoustics of the space are close to perfect, and every word, every breath, is fuller and rounder. More complete.

We're not complete. The thought comes at me from nowhere.

We're inches apart. I inhale a long breath, and I smell her. She's so different. I expected she'd smell different too. She doesn't.

She smells like pineapple, and that fucks with my head more than any words. Because it makes me think of how she used to be. How *we* used to be.

"Todd and I want to be ready to record in two weeks." Haley's oblivious to the internal battle that has my hands fisting.

"This the EP or the LP?"

She goes still. "EP."

"Sure about that? Last I checked, looked like some trouble in paradise."

Her lips part as if she suddenly has the urge to lick them. "Let me worry about Todd."

I smirk. "Whatever you say, boss. You want more tracks, you know the deal."

Haley's expression darkens. "I'm supposed to suck your cock in exchange for your cooperation."

Her flat tone has my shoulders knotting, even as the body part in question twitches.

Fuck, it sounds wrong. Desperate.

Nothing gives me the idea she'd wrap those perfect lips around my cock, even if I paid her a million dollars.

But damn if I don't want to see her admit it.

And that's what this is all about. I want to see the Haley I knew. The one with vulnerability. Not the new version who reminds me of a man I could never tolerate.

"I'm impressed you can say that with a straight face, Hales. You're all grown up. You kick the peanut allergy too? Burn all your Converse?"

We're inches apart, both breathing as though we've been running a race.

I've been in this room a hundred times. It's never felt like this. This tension, like a chord that won't resolve. It's her against me, and it's way more personal than our meeting in that conference room. This isn't about money, or fame, or attention.

These stakes are higher.

All it takes is the brush of her fingers over my belt to have blood flowing to my groin. "This is what you want, Jax? A cheap release to get the, ah...creative juices flowing?"

Her voice drops an octave and *shit*, I think she's teasing me right now.

I've crossed a line, but I can't back down. I manage a throaty chuckle. "If you think you've still got it."

Except *still* is the wrong word, because in the times we were together, we never did this.

Sure, I thought about it every second of the damned day. But I naively assumed we'd have a lifetime to figure this shit out. That I would have months, years, to explore her. To show her. To worship her.

The things we did were new to her, but what I never told her was they were new to me too. I've never been with someone I was head over heels for, before or since. Every touch of her lips, her fingers, every sound she made, every expression on her face, was a gift.

So how the hell did we get here?

There's no answer in her face or the silent room around us.

I'm about to tap out of this messed up game.

Until Haley does something that renders me speechless.

She drops to her knees.

She fucking *drops* to her *knees*.

My stomach drops with her as her fingers find my belt.

She slides it open and lifts hazel eyes, shining with challenge, to mine.

I can't speak, can't move, when Haley's fingers find the button of my jeans and work the zipper down, one agonizing inch at a time.

And it's hard because *I'm* hard.

I realize it the same second she does, and a little sound escapes her throat.

"You want me to stop?" I'd swear Haley's voice shakes at the end.

My answering shrug isn't the least bit casual with my hands clenched into fists at my sides. "You're driving, babysitter."

Her fingers reach into my shorts and brush the underside of my cock, sending a current up my spine.

One smooth stroke that has my head dropping back.

The fluorescent lights overhead burn my eyes, but I won't close them. Anyone with a pass could walk into the rehearsal room but I drop my chin, forcing myself to watch what's happening because I know it'll never happen again.

Hell, I'm not sure it's happening now.

I can't think of all the reasons this is wrong. I can't think of anything except how Haley's tongue presses against her lower lip when she pulls my cock out with hands that feel like silk.

I swallow the groan.

Any second, I'll wake up—or she will.

I can't breathe. I watch her watch me, each of us daring the other to back out of this.

Her lips part, and the second of hesitation, the tiny V between her brows, has my gut clenching.

Then she closes her lips around the head of my dick.

"Fucking *hell...*"

Her mouth is hot and wet and the best place I've ever been.

She sucks at my tip, adding her moisture to mine

before slicking her hand down the shaft, and it's a shot of adrenaline to a dead man.

Each stroke has me shuddering, and I know I won't last. It's all I can do to keep my knees from giving out.

Every time she sucks creates a heavy drag that tugs at my balls and down my spine. The twist of her hand at my base, the brush of her thumb just below her tongue.

I try not to turn into a complete animal, but my hips thrust against her face as my fingers find her hair—tugging, yanking it from the braid. "Harder, Hales." My voice is raw. "Yeah, like that."

I wonder what it's like for her. If she's thought of this too. Since I came back, or when we were together. I wonder if she loves feeling me hit the back of her throat, or whether it has her on the same brutal edge I'm riding.

Her gaze meets mine, and her eyes are dark with what she's doing to me.

Her fingers move lower, finding my balls. And *hell*, this woman knows my body. Even if we've never done this, she remembers everything I like when it comes to her touch on my skin.

I don't think I've ever been this turned on in my life.

Sweat clings to my back, and I'm reminded why rehearsing in a dress shirt is a dumbass idea. My foot cramps and I don't give a shit. I'll cut it off.

Just as long as she never.

Ever.

Stops.

The groan torn from my throat is obscene.

So is the sound of her sucking me off, all on the backdrop of that tropical scent that hangs in the air like a dirty dream I'm never going to stop having.

I'm close, and it's an actual miracle I lasted this long.

"Holy God, your mouth..."

But instead of speeding up, she slows down.

The pleasure's turning into agony.

Need claws through my body. Hot and desperate and demanding.

"Now..." I pant. "Now, now, fucking *NOW*."

I grip her hair, moving her head up and down on my cock.

It's too perfect to last, and there's no fighting the desire building in my groin, the tension in my arms, the shaking of my abs.

It's so wrong, but it's so fucking right.

If we were gladiators in an arena, I'd be lying on the ground bleeding out and begging her to finish me.

She doesn't.

I wait for the suck of her mouth, the answering explosion in my groin.

It never comes.

The heat of her mouth is gone, replaced by cool air.

I blink as Haley shifts back on her heels. Rises in one smooth motion, her shoes bringing us almost to equal height.

Every cell in my body roars in protest. My erection

bobs between us, a silent and painful reminder that something went very wrong here.

Haley's darkened gaze is on my face as she tugs the elastic out of her hair, runs her fingers through the mussed strands, and pulls it back into a ponytail that's too tidy for what we just did.

"What the hell was that?" I rasp.

She wipes her mouth with the back of her hand, smearing a streak of lipstick. "Inspiration."

Her throaty voice has my balls aching as my heart hammers in my ears.

"You're joking."

Her gaze rakes over me, dragging down my body. Lingering without a hint of embarrassment on my rock-hard cock before lifting once more.

"You look inspired enough to me. I want those tracks by end of day tomorrow, Jax."

She's gone before I can zip my jeans.

7

HALEY

"Thanks for meeting, Haley."

"Thank you for being willing to come here at the last minute."

The accountant sitting opposite me in my dining room —my father's dining room actually—has a few years on me, and she's a numbers genius.

"Can I get you a coffee? I make a mean Americano," I say.

"No, thank you."

I tug mine closer, wrapping my fingers around it.

I told myself I didn't want to meet in public, but in reality, I couldn't stay at Wicked another minute. Not after what happened this afternoon.

"Now." The accountant pulls out the sheets of paper. "I will say it's unlikely your after-school program will become revenue-positive. Unless you take Derek's advice and use it for PR, in which case it might have a secondary effect on other sales and deals."

"But they could," I insist. "The problem is that we need a sustained marketing budget and a continued push behind any of these artists. It's not a charity. These kids are talented."

"The problem in today's industry is that albums can generate attention, but unless you're Riot Act, they can't recoup the cost of recording. It's all in tours and deals with brands. None of which come until you've built a name for an artist."

"It's a Catch-22."

"Exactly."

Her pencil traces the lines of numbers, and I follow.

I was hoping she'd be able to help me find a way to cut costs or ramp up revenues for the program.

No luck.

"Can I ask you something?" she says after she finishes.

"Of course."

"I helped you when you wanted to sell the majority of your shares in Wicked. I remember it was a difficult time and completely understand why you'd want to step away from things." Compassion transforms her face. "But I see how frustrated you are with how it's run. Why stay involved at all?"

For the first time all day, I feel the smile tug at my lips. "Listen to this."

I pull up an audio file on my phone and hit Play. I

watch her face as the guitar riff starts. Four bars, then Tyler's voice over top.

She narrows her gaze. Not because she's critical, because she's listening. I can watch the wheels turn in her mind, and although I can't read her reaction to the lyrics or the melody, I see that she's having one.

And that's the beauty of it all.

At the end of the chorus, I stop the song.

"I've always wanted to do something that matters," I say. "The software I've built and licensed has made me money. But I'm more interested in the human side of music. The way it's created, how it affects people in ways other than opening their wallets. These kids are my chance to find the next voice that will change the world. They need time and nurturing and they'll do it, I know they will."

It's already dark when the accountant's Lexus backs out of the driveway.

On impulse I go upstairs to my room and change into leggings. I pull a hoodie off my shelf and wrap it around me. Then I go back outside and sit on the step, pulling the cuffs over my hands and sighing in the cool night air.

I've turned over a dozen explanations for why I made the decision to keep Wicked going. Guilt over not getting to know Cross when I had the chance. Revenge in the form of getting back at him for leaving—twice.

In the past two years, I've pieced together as much as I can about the man himself. From his brother and niece in

California—though they rarely saw him. From his employees and coworkers. From his house and the things inside it. From his vinyl collection, which I shouldn't have been surprised to find was more impressive than mine.

I'd expected to create a single cohesive portrait of a man. Instead, I found two.

A ruthless executive who would do anything to succeed. And a man with a passion he refused to let die.

It's impossible to know what Cross set out to do with his after-school program, but I want to prepare kids with talent for careers in music by giving them the know-how to support themselves.

A familiar shape limps up the sidewalk, interrupting my ruminating.

"Serena?"

"Nice sweater." I don't respond as my friend bends double in her fitness gear. "I was out for a run and thought I'd stop by."

I'm grateful for the fiftieth time my friend lives ten blocks away as I shift off the step and let her into the house. "No Scrunchie?"

"He can't keep up. His legs are like two inches long." She stretches in my foyer. "You ever going to sell this house?"

"At the right time. When I'm ready for a change." The place is way too big for me, but it hasn't felt like the right moment yet. I've been busy with one thing or another since the day I inherited it.

I head to the kitchen. The floors creak behind me, evidence Serena's following.

"Ran into Kyle on his way out of Wicked," she calls after me. "He said you dropped by their studio. Funny thing is, I didn't see you after." Her voice is suspicious. "You want to tell me why you took off like your ass was on fire after dropping in to see our number one recording artist in the rehearsal room?"

I turn, bracing on the counter. "Because I blew our number one recording artist in the rehearsal room."

Her eyes go round. Once in a while, it's nice to be able to shock her instead of the other way around. "Holy shit. I'm surprised they didn't hear him on the third floor," she says.

I stare up at the ceiling. "I didn't let him finish."

The laugh that bubbles out of her is inappropriate and completely needed. "I love you, Haley. You should've asked him for a tour. A yacht. A diamond-encrusted skunk charm bracelet."

"That last one is for you."

"Yup." Her grin fades. "You okay?"

I nod tightly. "Yeah. I'm good."

Except that you yanked down your ex's zipper and went all amateur-sword-swallower on him.

I don't know what possessed me except that when he was staring at me—daring me—I wanted to show him I've grown up. That I can survive without him. That I'm not deferring to his age, his experience, anymore.

For his part, Jax hadn't behaved as he was supposed to either.

I sure as hell hadn't expected the intoxicating feel of him in my hands, my mouth. The groan of arousal in his throat. The "harder, Hales" that nearly destroyed me.

It killed me to stop.

In the end, I didn't do it to punish him. I did it to save myself.

I've done a lot of things in two years, changed in more ways than I can count, but seeing him come? Watching those amber eyes I used to love turn gold with satisfaction? Feeling him fall apart under my hands?

All of it would take me over an edge I'm so not prepared for.

I chew on one of the hoodie's laces. "It's not fair. It's like he comes back and I'm *awake* again. I can't look at him without thinking twisted thoughts." Even now, I press my thighs together at the memory.

"Are you going to tell him what happened after he left?"

I swallow. "This isn't about that. I want to get the album made so I can get Derek off my back about the program. If we help these kids, they're going to be the future. Did you hear the track Tyler's working on? He's a great songwriter. And he has the most beautiful voice."

"Yes. And you have helped them. You've given them space to record. Some of them might become professional musicians. Others turned their lives around and credit this program."

"It's not enough. I want them to explode."

"You can't plan another Jax. Not for yourself, or Cross, or the world." I feel her stare on me, hard and compassionate at once. "But if you want to give these kids something that matters? You have."

I start wiping down the counters for something to keep my hands busy. "I think about how Jax saved me. When my mom died. When I didn't know where I was going or what my future held. The times I wasn't sure I had a future." I take a breath as I rinse out the sponge. "I don't want to save these kids. I want these kids to save the world. And I can't say that to Derek or any of the guys in suits that run Wicked. Because they have business degrees and look at numbers and market research all day. But that's not what this is about, not really, and I don't think that's what it was about for Cross either."

"How can you have two dead parents and still be this idealistic?" Serena groans, folding me in a hug that has me dropping the damp sponge and bristling until I force myself to relax. "Sorry, but you deserve this," she murmurs against my hair.

8

Now I'm truly fucked.

The dozen sheets of paper, laid out on the table with a care I usually reserve for instruments, tell a story I don't want to hear.

Each is the start of something. Some have chords marked on them, or guitar riffs that caught my attention long enough to be captured. A few phrases, sometimes a verse.

"Northing's good enough," I summarize.

Mace shifts forward, scanning the pages. "Try writing prompts?"

"I'm not resorting to Google."

Behind him, the hotel bar is quiet, but the occasional person trails in the front doors. Enough to keep my busy mind distracted from the problem at hand.

I knew it on some level. I painted myself into this corner by coming back here.

No, it was before that.

It was two years ago when Haley sat across from me in my Bentley, looking at me like the sun shone out of my ass, and I gave her that song. Said she could keep it.

That moment of delusion was the root of all this fucked-up-ness because I gave her the one thing I wrote that didn't suck and now she thinks there's more like it.

"You need to send over two completed songs today because of… what?"

"Long story."

If I sound strung out, it's half about the songs and half about the phantom pain in my balls that's lingered since yesterday. The shitty sleep I got last night because I couldn't think of anything except those melted chocolate eyes.

Even though Haley didn't finish what she started, I can't go back on my word.

Yeah, when a girl half-blows you in exchange for songs, it's a regular moral dilemma.

Mace goes on. "I get that it's hard. The first album was the best because you had nothing to prove. You were metaphorically bleeding on the proverbial floor."

I blink at him. "Art history, huh?"

He shrugs, shoving back his long hair and reminding me of one of Haley's philosophers. "You had nothing to lose. It was an escape. I know what that's like, to feel like you need music. That you can't live without it."

Guilt hits me. It's been a while since we've talked. "You don't feel like that anymore."

"No. Not to say it won't ever come back. Depression's a beast." Mace takes a swig from the mug in front of him. "But there are ways to cope. The times you want to shut out the world are when you need it the most."

When did Mace get more mature than me?

Because he is. He's more thoughtful and well-balanced, and I missed it.

All of it.

I wonder what else I missed, shutting myself away the last two years.

It's not like I stopped living. I renovated six rooms of my house. Built a shed the size of a barn, with the help of one of my favorite reality show home reno guys. I fought for my kid, booked a bunch of appearances, and got into what's probably the best shape of my life.

But when I turned my back on Wicked, I turned my back on music.

Mace gets up to use the bathroom, and I tug one of the sheets toward me. I need to turn this into a song. I couldn't do it on tour. Who's to say I can do it now?

My phone buzzes and I reach for it.

Brick: We rehearsing today?

Jax: Not until I finish writing

Brick: K

Brick: PS you were asking about what's going on at Wicked. I found something

Brick: Haley does some mixing but mostly she's in charge of this program for teenagers

Jax: Send me a link

Brick: There is none. It's on the DL

I stare at the text a long time.

The reason she's still there is a single program? One they don't even publicize?

It gives me more questions than answers.

"Jax?" Annie pulls out her earbuds, straightening as she approaches on her way from the elevator, dressed for school with her hair pulled up in one of those high ponytails again.

She drops into the chair across from me. I can't put the papers away fast enough. She grabs one. "What are you doing?"

"Annie, come on."

I reach for it, but she holds it away. "'*No part of you can make me feel. No substitute for being real.*'" Her gaze meets mine. "You're writing a song," she accuses.

I didn't expect to feel embarrassed in front of a thirteen-year-old.

"It's not exactly the soundtrack of my life," she goes on.

It's fucking terrible is what it is.

"But I like that it's about what's real. Too many people don't talk about that anymore. Everything's fake. Who you are, who you know—"

"You're in my chair," a gruff voice insists.

Annie squeals, her eyes getting huger than the time she met Beyoncé. "Uncle Ryan!"

She drops the paper and hops out of the seat, throwing her arms around him.

Shit, I haven't gotten a reception like that since... well, before she found out my sperm gave her those eyes. For a moment, I'm actually jealous of my best friend.

"Hey, kid." She won't let go, and he practically pries her arms off at last.

Mace drops back into his seat and Annie takes the one between us. But her attention's solely on him.

"I haven't seen you in forever. Do you hate me?" she asks.

"Never." She shifts into the chair next to the one Mace sits in. "How's school?"

"That place you have to get to," I remind her, checking the time on my phone.

Her face falls. "It's hard being in the middle of the semester." Her gaze darts to me. "Can I have a friend over this weekend? If I don't, people will think I'm weird."

I turn it over in my head, but the idea's appealing. "Yeah. Sure."

Maybe it'll be good for her. She hasn't asked to have someone over in the weeks since we got here. Or a couple months before that, come to think of it.

"Uncle Ryan, you should come for dinner. Tomorrow?"

He glances toward me. "I have a night class until nine. And then you have that thing."

"The thing?" I stare blankly at him.

"Party for Jerry."

Right. The guy's retirement is being celebrated in a ballroom at a fancy hotel down the road. He's like the father I never had, and I wouldn't miss a chance to celebrate him.

"Sunday then." Annie beams, dropping a kiss on Mace's cheek before shouldering her backpack and dashing toward the door.

I grunt. "When did you become God?"

Mace chuckles, and I go back to the half-written songs.

"It's perfection, Mr. Jamieson. If I may say so."

The tailor inclines his head an inch, and I glance back toward the mirror, straightening my lapels. It doesn't suck.

I have half a dozen suits at home appropriate for a red carpet event. But for tonight, I want more. It's Jerry's retirement, and the man deserves the best. So Rodney called his guy for me and arranged to have something flown in on short notice. Altered on even shorter notice.

On my way out of the store, the call comes in. I sling the bag of street clothes over my back, ignoring the stares I get on the street as I answer the phone.

"You on your way?" Brick asks.

"Yeah. Just have a stop to make. Forgot something."

"Mace isn't coming?"

"You know he hates these things."

I drive home from the tux alteration place and take the elevator up. I tap my fingers on the handrail.

After hours picking my guitar, a pencil stuck behind my ear as I scrawled changes over the paper, I have a grand total of nothing. The feeling of failure curls in my gut.

But I'm not going to leave Haley hanging.

The doors open, and I span the foyer in a few steps. "Annie, forgot to grab my..."

The floor tilts.

Because my kid is sitting on the couch.

With a boy.

At least I think he's a boy. He has blue hair.

There are two comfy armchairs, but he's next to her, laughing at something she said.

My hands tighten into fists. "What the hell is going on? Who are you?"

"Tyler, Mr—ah—Jamieson." His eyes widen, and he lifts his hands as if I'm about to do something illegal.

Maybe I am.

"Get the hell off my couch."

He rises, but his gaze goes to Annie.

"Jax." Her voice shakes. "Don't do this."

I ignore her, turning to the kid. "You're not talking to my daughter. You're leaving."

"Mr. Jamieson, you don't understand—"

"JAX!"

"I understand fine. Get out of my house."

With an apologetic look at Annie, he grabs his bag off the floor by the door and yanks on his shoes.

I turn back to my daughter as the door closes behind him.

"What was that?" she shouts. "You said I could have a friend over."

"I meant a girl."

"What does it matter?"

"Boys want things."

"And girls don't?" Annie's eyes flash.

"Jesus, this isn't happening." I hit a button on my phone. "I need a babysitter tonight. I know. I owe you one."

9

HALEY

"This isn't working," the small, panicked voice mutters from somewhere behind me.

I excuse myself from my conversation and move up behind him. "Need a hand?"

The kid turns, his eyes going round. "Wow. Miss Telfer, you look epic."

"Thanks, Mika. What's happening?"

He explains the issue, and I lean over the computer. The movement tugs at the cap sleeves on my dress, which was not built for typing.

I code for a few minutes then step back. "There."

The kid grins at me. "Thanks. And thank you for trusting me with this."

The way he talks about handling sound for the party, it's like it's the biggest thing he's ever done. It warms my heart.

"You'll do a great job. Hey, is Tyler coming tonight?"

"He said something came up. Do you want me to call him? We were working on a demo this week. Mixing it with DRE."

I get a kick out of it every time they use my program. "No need to call him. But I'd love to hear what you're working on. Send it over. Or better yet, why don't you come by next week? We can listen together."

He beams.

I look past him at the room full of people. The stage, where the techs are finishing setup. Soon there will be speeches. Then the musical tributes.

The party's at a fancy hotel, and Lita's playing. The invitees may not include as many executives as my father's funeral, but there are way more musicians, tour managers, and producers. Everyone who knows the industry knows Jerry, and tonight they're here, wearing everything from black tie to jeans.

I settled on a gold dress that ends partway down my thighs and black heels Serena helped me pick out for the occasion. I curled my hair, bringing it up almost to my jaw line at the front. But really, the clothes don't matter. It's the collective spirit, the power, the love that matters.

I made sure Jax got an invitation, but as I look around, I don't see him. I hide the disappointment. Not because I wanted to spend time with him. Because he sent me the world's shortest email saying he has some tracks and will get them to me soon.

We're running short of time. Todd stopped in my office

yesterday afternoon to ask what the hold-up is. I stalled him. I won't be able to stall him much longer, and the fate of the program that means everything to me hangs in the balance.

At least Todd's away this weekend. Golfing in South Carolina, I think. He's probably the only person in music who declined to change their plans to be here tonight.

When the evening program starts, Derek does introductory remarks. When he calls me, I go up to the raised platform at the front of the room and take the mic.

"Gerald Timms"—I raise my brows and people laugh—"is a special person. I'm the least qualified to be talking about his contributions to music. But I couldn't pass up the chance.

"When I was on my first job with Wicked, he was the sound manager. He taught me everything I know. Which still isn't half of what he does. More than that, he taught me what's important in this industry."

My gaze finds Jerry at the front of the crowd. He's shining. Practically beaming.

I know he's struggled the past two years, but I've done everything I can to help him. Through medication the dementia is managed, if not solved. I like to think that keeping him engaged in music, his lifetime love, is helping to slow the disease.

"He's made a lot of friends in this room. He's had a profound impact on all of us. He'd never tell you this himself, but he matters. In every artist he's touched, every venue he's graced, every album he's charmed, and every intern he's inspired. To Jerry." I raise a glass, and they all toast.

After, I introduce Lita and hug her when she comes on stage.

I leave the stage and hug Jerry.

"Nice work, Miss Telfer," he murmurs.

A smile rises up from nowhere. Something he's always been able to conjure in me.

I wind toward the back of the room, offering hellos and thank yous as I go.

When I get to the back of the room where hors d'oerves are laid out on elegant silver trays, I choose a phyllo-wrapped mushroom and pop it into my mouth.

"I'm surprised you didn't ask me to play." The familiar voice at my back has me freezing.

I turn, half expecting to find Jax in a T-shirt and jeans.

He's not.

Jax Jamieson is dressed in a tux.

A goddamned tux.

And he's beautiful.

His striking jaw is the same strong angle as always. Those amber eyes are a little too light to be real. His hair is shorter than he used to keep it.

He looks like a prince.

That's the only reason I can come up with for why I lose the ability to chew and swallow.

Pieces of pastry and mushroom stick in my throat.

Now I'm coughing, the sound masked by Lita's music.

But Jax's attention's all on me. "You okay?"

I hold up a hand, shaking my head.

Jax looks past me to the table, his gaze landing on a tray of chocolate covered nuts. Moving faster than I've ever seen him move, he grabs a passing waiter, who nearly drops his tray. "Are there peanuts in there?" he snaps.

Oh, fuck.

"I don't—"

"Call 911," he thunders. "This is an emergency."

I shake my head, coughing, and grab Jax's arm.

"Hales, I'm going to get an ambulance. Hold onto her," he says.

The waiter closes in, uncertain, and I ward him off with my hands.

Jax curses. "Right. Strangers are bad. Don't hold onto her."

Finally I lunge for a drink off another passing tray and chug it down.

My throat clears and I gasp for breath. "Jax. It's okay. It just went down wrong. We always do peanut-free catering."

The panic recedes after a long moment and Jax relaxes. "You scared the shit out of me."

"Thought you'd just as soon have me dead."

I reach for a second drink off the tray and pass him one.

His brows draw together on his forehead. "Don't ever

say that, Hales." He lifts the drink to his lips, sipping as he raises a brow. "Bulleit?"

My mouth twitches. "You know it."

When the waiter disappears, Jax shifts closer to my side, surveying the room.

"Thanks for saving me. And in a tux, no less," I say. Jax glances down at my dress. "Nothing? You're not going to tease me about the shoes? The dress?"

Jax tosses back the rest of his bourbon, setting the glass on a tray of a passing waiter. "I've made millions with words. Every time I see you, I can't think of a single one."

His careless admission slams into me, warms me like the liquor.

If he wants me to read into that, I'm doing it. Even though part of me expected him to come tonight—he's worked with Jerry as long as anyone—I could hardly have expected *this* Jax. Because it makes it harder to remember we're not friends. Or anything.

"I'm surprised you didn't bring someone tonight. Like Carter," he says, so smoothly I think I've misheard.

"Carter? Why?"

Jax lifts a shoulder under his fitted jacket, and it's totally not fair that he wears that and T-shirts equally well. "Heard you were dating."

"He's my business partner."

"That's all?" His gaze intensifies.

I feel my mouth twitch at the corner as an old memory

comes back. "I kiss who I want, Jax Jamieson." His brows draw together. "But from here on in… Carter's just business." As I say the words I realize they're true.

Apparently satisfied, Jax nods toward the front of the room. "So he's finally willing to retire."

"He'd been planning to do it sooner. He talked to my father about it and they agreed, but once Cross died, Jerry stayed to help with the transition. I ensured he was always compensated well."

"'Well' is a number guys in suits cooked up around a square table," Jax muses. "You don't pay a guy like Jerry well. He's a genius. Fucking Mozart. I can make them show up, but he's the one who makes them cry."

I hate when Jax goes all sentimental. Or his version of it—compliments doled out with the kind of certainty that preempts any objection. It reminds me how deep-down decent he is, in a way few people will ever truly appreciate.

"You love him," I murmur.

His gaze turns on me, surprised. "I'm not sure it's a good thing, being loved by me." I want to ask what he means, but before I can, he goes on. "The guy's going to have a hard time leaving this place. What I don't know is why you're still here. You sold the company. You can't move on?"

I hesitate. I hadn't wanted to involve him in this, but now that he's asking, it's hard to say no. "Cross started a program years ago. I took it, changed it. We help kids who don't have access to music get a chance to play. To record. To find their voice."

"Who's we?"

"Okay, me," I admit, taking another sip and shifting so some partygoers can pass us. The consequence is we're close, inches apart. "This one kid would blow your mind. His family situation sucks, but he's got incredible instincts for music. It's like all the shit he goes through pours out of him. I'd love for you to meet him. Tyler looks kind of crazy, has blue hair—"

"Tyler?" Jax's face darkens, and I wonder what I've said. "That little shit was on my couch this afternoon. With Annie."

My brows shoot up. "What were they doing?"

"Talking."

I wait a beat. "That's it?"

"Laughing," he amends pointedly. "Together," he says, as though I'm being deliberately obtuse.

"They go to the same school." I'd helped him get into the private school on a scholarship last year. Though most of the kids I work with are in public school, I convinced his mostly-absent parents this would be an opportunity for him. "I was hoping to introduce them, but it sounds like they already met."

Jax glares and I try to hide the smirk because damn, he's entertaining when he's protective.

"You're being a hardass," I inform him. "Trying to control things you can't control."

"I don't want her screwing up."

"Screwing up or growing up?"

Jax rubs a hand over the pressed line of his mouth.

"You know, part of growing up is being able to admit your mistakes," I murmur. "What happened in the rehearsal room… it was unprofessional. I'm sorry."

Jax moves closer. "I asked you to blow me in exchange for songs—admittedly not my finest moment—and you're apologizing to *me*?" He raises a brow.

"Yes." I feel the flush crawl up my cheeks under the intensity of his stare. "Come on, Jax. You know I wouldn't have done it if I didn't want to."

His mouth twitches. "In that case, apology accepted. You left me with the worst case of blue balls in history."

I can't resist laughing when a man says 'balls' in a five thousand dollar suit.

My nerve endings are tingling all over again, partly from his dry comment and partly from thinking about what went down between us.

"I got the sense you were more than enjoying yourself," I counter.

"I was. Until I wasn't." He shudders as if he's remembering the moment I pulled back. It would've been funny if it hadn't taken everything in me to do it.

He reaches into his pocket and holds out a flash drive. "A deal's a deal. Mace and I spent all day on the songs. But I'm not sure they're what you want."

"I can't wait to listen to them." I take the drive from him.

"They're not right, Hales."

His brows draw together under his hair in worry, not anger.

My chest constricts. Seeing him in this kind of self-doubt is agonizing. "Jax... I get that it's hard. Coming up with something new. But it's always been in you."

He jams his hands in his pants. "Oh yeah? You going to share some eternal wisdom from some dead white guy?"

"I don't need it. I always had faith in you."

Jax's jaw works but he stays silent, as if he's weighing the words in his mind.

"I was surprised to hear from you after two years," he says finally.

"It wasn't two years. I tried to get in touch with you the winter after you went back to Dallas."

"You're right." Jax looks past me at the room of people, the laughter, the partying. "I should've called you back."

I take a drink, remembering the first text in January. The second in April. The bourbon blazes a soothing trail down my throat.

"I was fighting for my kid," he continues. "At least, that's how I rationalized it. But I was nursing my ego too. You walked away from me and it took me a long time to come to terms with that."

"You were the one who stopped us," I correct, going on

before he can interrupt. "But you were right. We wouldn't have worked. I wanted to build something that was mine. You wanted to step away from it all. We were out of sync." My chest squeezes as I turn it over for the millionth time. The pain is nearly gone after two years, and what's left is just an echo. "But it's okay, Jax. We can spend our lifetimes regretting. Atoning. For the things we chose, the ones we didn't. That's not why we're here. Our job isn't to regret. Our job is to live."

"That's very mature for a woman with a Betty Boop clock." His amber gaze searches mine, serious and intense and full of an emotion I can't decipher. "What would you have said if I had called you back?"

I straighten, drawing in a breath and holding it. "You really want to know?"

"Yeah. I really do." His gaze is open and curious, and this Jax is the one I remember. The one I can't say no to.

"The first time was because I was pregnant. The second time was after I miscarried."

10

Music fills the ballroom. A third progression, my brain says. I hate that part of it goes there even as Haley murmurs an excuse, turns on her heel, and vanishes into the crowd.

Pregnant.

Miscarried.

Go after her. My body is heavy. My feet are lead, my stomach an anchor.

"What's with the monkey suit, son?" The man stepping between my target and me is the only one who could slow me down.

Jerry is a foot shorter than me, but it feels like I'm looking up to him.

Always has.

I force myself to focus on his lined face. "Heard some famous guy is retiring. You know who it is?"

He laughs.

"What're you going to do with all your time?"

"Garden." His knowing eyes search mine. "You'll be okay."

"I will if you will." But my gaze drifts back to Haley across the room, my fingers flexing. Her back is straight, her face focused on what she's hearing.

I wonder if he can read my mind. "She was a hell of a girl. Now she's a hell of a woman. She's had to take on a lot. For all his faults, Shannon wanted the best for her. He would've been bothered by how much she's been through. But proud of how she's handled it."

"How do you do it, Jerry?" My voice is low enough only he can hear.

"What's that?"

"Decide you haven't screwed everything up."

His milky gaze crinkles at the edges. "That knowledge is beyond us. All we can know is that we've done the best we can. Made some good music along the way."

I want to claw at my collar. To rip off my jacket and run outside and bellow. Because this is wrong. All of it. We shouldn't be in here, drinking expensive champagne. People shouldn't be smiling at me and prodding me for info about the new album.

I've fucked up. In a way you can't come back from.

I start toward the door but get interrupted by industry execs.

It's half an hour later when I spot her again. Surrounded by a group of suits.

I start toward her, intending to interrupt, but pull up halfway there.

She's smiling. I can't tell if it's forced or real but regardless, what am I going to say to her?

She's past it.

This is mine to live with, to wrestle with.

The car takes me home, and I ride up the elevator. I jerk the bowtie off, unbuttoning the top of my shirt.

When the door opens, I see Annie and Mace playing cards on the coffee table. Her smile falls away when she sees me, and she stalks into her bedroom, slamming the door.

"Thanks for the save," I tell him.

"No problem." He rises, brushing off his jeans as his gaze runs over my tux. "You okay?"

I strip off the jacket, hanging it on the back of a chair in the dining room. "Forgot how intense it is."

"I bet."

"You want to stick around for a drink?"

"Nah, I gotta go do some schoolwork. A paper to write on Caracci's *Hercules*."

After Mace leaves I go out onto the balcony, a crystal glass in one hand and Lita's bottle of bourbon in the other. I pour two fingers into the glass, inspecting it. It's good liquor. The kind I never had until I started on this twisted, beautiful journey.

I toss it back and pour another. The glass dangles from

my fingers as I look out over the skyline, twinkling in the night.

"The first time was because I was pregnant. The second time was after I miscarried."

I feel it. The instinct to regret, to atone. The one I'd never noticed until she pointed it out.

"We can spend our lifetimes regretting what happened. Our job isn't to regret. Our job is to live."

Jerry's retired. Haley's spent two years alone. Annie hates me.

All I ever wanted was to protect the people in my life. Where does that leave me?

Alone.

I'm alone in the dark with the feelings I can't keep inside. Nothing matters. Not the money, not the recognition.

I drink the second glass, noticing every bit of flavor.

The empty crystal clinks on the glass table.

I go to my room and pick up my guitar.

Two moments fight in my memory for the worst moment in my life.

Neither was when my mom was arrested for dealing drugs and I learned she was going to jail, though it felt like that at the time.

No.

One was when I found out about Annie, that Grace and Cross had been hiding her from me.

The other was when I realized I couldn't provide for myself and my sister. I made her go to school, where she'd bum food from friends. We tried to put on a brave face. We used to joke that the sounds from our stomachs were monsters trying to get out. I spent the days in the library, which was open until midnight, where there were private rooms with computers. This one woman let me bring in my guitar.

One night, I went home to hear my sister crying in her sleep.

I swore I'd protect her and do anything it took to stop her from being in pain.

That reality is a million miles from this hotel. The expensive carpet under my thighs. The soft lighting overhead.

But the emotion connects me to it.

My fingers move over the strings, and it might as well be my first guitar that I got from a secondhand store and learned to tune and play myself.

I croon under my breath, nonsense mostly.

The door creaks at my back but I can't stop. It's spilling out of me as though I've sprung a leak.

"Jax?"

Annie's timid voice makes me stop singing. But my fingers continue, floating from one chord to another. I look up. She hovers in the doorway. Probably trying to make sense of her father sitting on the floor, back to the wall, playing his guts out.

She looks like me, like Grace. Her hair is redder, but her eyes are the same. They lighten to caramel when she's excited or upset.

I always thought Annie was like Haley. A little serious. Way too smart.

We could've had a child by now. Haley and me.

Would he or she have grown up like Annie? Would they look like me? Like Haley? Would they call me dad, like Annie won't?

Annie's gaze drops to my guitar. "I haven't heard you play in... ever."

Instead of defending it, I tell her the truth. "I haven't needed to."

She pads inside and shifts onto the corner of the bed.

"Tyler and a couple of other guys from school play at Wicked. Like you do." She hesitates. "I know you think it's weird that I don't hang out with girls. But the girls don't like me."

My jaw tightens. "What do you mean?"

She plays with the cover. "They say things. About you." Annie looks up and misery fills her expression. "They talk a lot about famous people. Famous guys especially."

I have to stop myself from shutting my eyes. Leaning my head back against the wall. "And that's why you don't make friends with them."

She nods.

"Was it the same in Dallas?"

Another nod. "It didn't used to be this bad. Just this year."

The tentativeness in her voice makes me wonder how many thousands of thoughts go through her head every day that she never shares. How many experiences she never lets me in on.

I see her each day but it's as if she's a stranger.

My fingers switch, and I'm playing something else. There are no lyrics. It's just chords, vibrations. The kind that take hold of your heart. That shine a lantern on the path ahead and tell you where to go.

Haley might disagree with me, but when you're spilling your guts through a song, that's not healing pain. It's opening it up, exposing it to the light. Diffusing it through a crystal so you can see it and share it and decide what it means.

I don't know the words that make pain go away. If I did, I could rule the world.

"Sometimes I think I hate you." Annie's small words are uttered quietly. "But even when I think that, I still want to know you."

Her earnest face has my heart squeezing. "Because I have three Grammys and got you that signed Timothée Chalamet picture?"

"No. Because you're a good cook. You bite your nails even though you try to hide it. You think watching documentaries counts as homework. You hum when you drive." She shifts closer, bracing her elbows on her knees to bring her face level with mine. "And because you care. Some of the other kids at school... they have all this money, but it's like their parents don't even care what they do. Sometimes I wish you cared less. Then I take it back. Because I don't. Not really."

My chest expands, stretching my ribs until it hurts. If there's a way you're supposed to handle this I have no fucking clue what it is.

So I stop trying.

I brush my thumb over her chin. "Good," I say finally.

I go back to playing, and she shifts forward to lie on her stomach, a smile painting the edge of her lips as her eyes drift closed. "That's pretty."

"It's nothing."

"It's still pretty."

My song finishes, my fingers stilling.

"Are you writing it down?" she asks as the final sound waves die.

"No."

She leaps off the bed and runs out the door. A moment later, she's back, dropping on the covers again. Annie sets her phone on the floor in front of me. "Play it again."

11

HALEY

"You out for lunch?" I ask Serena when I call her on Monday afternoon.

"Yeah. You want to join?"

She gives me directions, and I meet her at the fast-healthy place. A familiar black-and-white fluff ball is in her arms.

"We had to go to the vet this morning," she informs me when I sit down.

"He looks very healthy."

"I think he's depressed. He doesn't play like he used to."

I debate how much to say. "He is..." I lower my voice as if it makes a difference, "...old."

"No way. Skunks live two to three years in the wild, but they can live up to ten in a loving home. It's proof!"

"Of what?"

She sighs. "That all you need is love." I can't help but laugh at her over-the-top gushing. "Although it also occurred to me that maybe he needs another kind of love. You know." Her gaze narrows. "Something more physical?"

Oh, God.

"I thought about putting an ad on Craigslist for someone with a female skunk who wants to—"

"Don't finish that sentence. Or that ad," I beg her.

Serena sighs, looking past me. "Fine. I've put in our order, but you need to go pick it up. They won't let Scrunchie in."

I reach over to stroke a finger over his soft head. "Sorry, handsome."

I go in and grab our food, then come back to the metal table and chairs outside.

Serena lifts her sandwich off the tray and I reach for my salad. "So Jerry's party was bomb," she says. "It's been written up on five blogs in the last forty-eight hours."

"I saw you with a guy. Scratch that. A *man*." I think of the tall, dark and confident form I'd seen her laughing with at one point.

"Jacob Prince. He's got a jewelry company."

The name scratches at my brain as I stab a forkful of lettuce and cheese. "Prince Diamonds?"

"The one and only. He's a New Yorker, happened to be in town for the weekend. We went to boarding school together."

"Really?" I chew, studying her face.

"The man's got issues, but all the good ones do. The stories our crew had... Skunk sex has nothing on boarding school, believe me." She grins and I'm almost tempted to ask. "But speaking of men too handsome for their own good, I saw Jax in a tux." She fans herself. "Tell me you were unaffected by that."

I reach for my pop. "Dead women were affected by that."

Her laugh makes Scrunchie jump. "I think I heard your vagina cry a little." Serena breaks off a piece of her sandwich and slips it to the hopeful-looking fluffball in her lap. He takes it, watching me with beady eyes as he munches.

I spear some more of my lunch, chewing and swallowing before I speak again. "I told him. About the pregnancy and the miscarriage."

"Whoa. What did he say?"

"Nothing."

"Nothing?"

I lift a shoulder. "I dropped it on him and then ran. He got to do it last time. Figured it was my turn."

"So he didn't have the decency to feel like a giant lump of shit for not getting back to you? I was ready to drag his ass back here, you know I was."

Her loyalty warms me as I set the fork down in the bowl. "I know." And he would've come back.

But I still remember the words I'd said to him in the

shower after Mace was in the hospital. The promise I'd asked him to make.

Don't regret me. Ever.

"I don't want him to say he's sorry, Serena. To do anything out of obligation. That's why I didn't go after him when I found out.

"He loves Annie, but I saw on his face when he told me about her that he never wanted another mistake. I never want to be his mistake." I take a deep breath to combat the way my gut twists.

She squeezes my hand and my smile fades.

"He did come through in one way. He gave me the songs."

"And do they sound like a platinum album?"

Disappointment wrings through me. "They're not what we need." She grimaces. "I saw what it took for Lita's album to hit gold. I know Jax can do more, his fans want more. But it has to be real. Todd's breathing down my neck. I really think he wants to watch me break."

"Clearly he doesn't know you. So what's the B plan?"

"That was the F plan." I blow out a breath. "Something told me if I got Jax back here, got his band and a studio, magic would happen. Maybe it's not that simple. Maybe I'm missing something."

"Maybe he doesn't have it anymore."

My spine stiffens as objection rises up in me. I shake my head, hard enough to send my hair hitting me in the face and have Scrunchie watching me with suspicion. "No. That's not it. The month I spent on tour, even the fall after that, I had this idea that my program would explain how Jax Jamieson does how he does.

"It got close, helped make good songs better, but even it couldn't take bad songs and make them good. Or great songs and make them mind-blowing.

"Because I realized something. Jax's magic isn't the words he writes, or the chords he plays. It's that he feels like no one else does, that he can translate it into this catharsis for the rest of us. But right now, he doesn't want to feel. He's opted out. I don't know how to change that."

Her smile is sad. "I love that you won't make it his fault. No matter what, you won't believe he's less than a god. Even after everything."

I rub my hands over my face. "You think it's stupid."

"I think it's sweet."

My phone dings and there's a new text. "What...?"

Jax: Hales. Thought you might want to check this out

Jax: We recorded it on Annie's phone.

I hit Play on the track, and sound streams out. The quality isn't great, but what I hear is.

My heart thuds. "Are you getting this?"

Serena's eyes widen. "Holy shit."

"Yeah."

I type back as fast as I can.

Haley: I love it

A few moments later, he texts back.

Jax: For real?

Haley: It's going on the album. Got any more where that came from?

Dots appear. Then he sends a sound file.

"You ever look at a guy like you're looking at that phone right now, you'd have a boyfriend by now."

I grin. "Shut up."

Haley: You wrote two songs last night?

The dots appear again.

Followed by the most beautiful words I've ever read.

Jax: I wrote four

Studios never sleep. Some of the most iconic tracks in rock, jazz, and country history were laid down at all hours of the day and night.

Still, the regular staff tend to stick to the daylight hours. It's the big artists and a handful of execs responsible for the lights after dark.

Wednesday night in my office, the door is mostly closed and it's late, but I'm listening to a track that has my entire body buzzing.

It's not one of our big artists. It's one that matters more.

"What do you think?" Tyler stares at me from across the desk. His blue eyes match his hair, and though I've witnessed it blue, green, and black, I struggle to remember if I've seen its natural color. One foot's tucked up on the chair in front of him, not because he's casual but because he's nervous.

"It's really good. You cut the reverb—"

"Yeah, I ran it through DRE and it came up with some suggestions. But I also scrapped some of the recos." He shows me, his fingers flying over my computer keyboard to adjust settings. His gaze is as jerky over the screen as his voice is smooth over the speakers.

I nod as I listen. "Yeah, okay."

"How'd you even come up with the idea for DRE? Did you always want to make music better?"

I can't help smiling, because I love how this kid's mind works. He's always curious, always wanting to know why and how. "Actually, I wanted a way to explain the music that changed my life. The part about making music better happened by accident."

I hit Play on the song again and listen to the changes he made.

Excitement bubbles through me.

And shit, this is why I do this.

Once I thought the words mattered more than the chords, the melody. I was wrong.

Nothing matters more than anything else. All of it matters, together.

Movement from the doorway has me looking up.

Any instinct to chastise falls away when I see whose face it is.

The faded blue T-shirt hugs Jax's chest and arms, skimming over his abs, none of which seem to have softened over the years.

The jeans hang low on his hips, and I force my attention to his face.

Since he sent me the songs yesterday, he's been rehearsing, and I've been busy working too.

His gaze lands on Tyler, whose hands stiffen on the chair arms. “Mr. Jamieson.”

“Tyler.”

They stare each other down.

Is this is how bullfights start? Because Tyler looks like he desperately needs something to distract the very big and very irritated form in the doorway from charging.

I clear my throat, looking pointedly toward Tyler when Jax acknowledges me.

Finally, Jax speaks. “Kid. About the other night. I might have got the wrong impression.”

Tyler nods vigorously. “You did. Annie’s my friend. She’s really cool. She knows more about music than anyone.”

“Really?” That comment seems to throw Jax for a loop.

“Uh-huh. I mean, it makes sense. She has killer taste. The playlists on her phone are all over the place and she knows the entire discography of bands I’ve never heard of.”

“She does?”

“You should get going,” I say to Tyler. “The bus stops running soon.”

“I brought my bike.”

I shoot him a look. “It’s not safe to ride that at midnight.”

His lopsided grin, as if I’m worrying too much, has my chest expanding. “I’m good.”

But he slides out of the chair and gives Jax a bit of a berth as he leaves.

Jax drops into the chair next to the one Tyler vacated. "Parents don't care where he is?"

"No."

Jax's chin drops, because he knows what that's like. "Been a while since I was here." He inspects the armrests before his attention returns to me. "The view from this seat's improved."

I flush even before his gaze drifts down my body. He stiffens.

"Hales?" The look on his face slips from curiosity to wariness.

"Yeah."

"Is that my hoodie?"

I pulled it on over my dress earlier. It looks ridiculous, but people don't usually walk in on me at midnight. "It's cozy."

"I didn't think you'd keep it."

I shake my head in disbelief. "Are you kidding?" I lean in, lowering my voice. "It's signed by Jax Jamieson."

His perfect mouth curves, and my stomach turns over.

I forgot how addictive it is to have him look at me like that.

"Um. The songs you sent are amazing. How's rehearsal?"

"That's what I wanted to talk to you about. We're nearly ready to record."

"Great. Derek will get you on the schedule."

"Who's producing?"

I suck in a breath. "I was thinking me. And Todd."

"No."

The hurt cuts me quick. "Jax, come on—"

"I don't want that asshole on my album. Just you. And Jerry. Apparently a few days into retirement and he's already restless."

My heart skips, and for a moment, everything in the world is bright. "Todd's not going to like that."

"Do I look like I care?"

The grin threatens to split my face.

No matter what we've been through, how close or how far apart, he's still the biggest rock star in the world. I'll always be in awe of him.

Jax shifts forward, the shirt pulling over his biceps and dragging my gaze to the ink on his arm.

I wonder if he's gotten any new tattoos.

I wonder if he'd let me look for myself.

"You were right," he says.

I blink. "About what?"

"Annie. She's into music. I didn't know how much."

"She can come play with other kids if she wants." The words bump into one another, and I'm pretty sure I'm blushing. It's a stupid reaction, considering the things he's done to me and said to me. "I'll email the schedule to you."

He rubs a hand over his jaw, the few days of scruff there.

I want to be that hand. Or that jaw.

He leans back in his chair. It's my office, but he looks like a king holding court.

Jax's gaze skims the surface of the desk and lands on the corner. "Need a break?"

"No," I say too fast.

His amber eyes sparkle. "It'll only take a minute, Hales."

"Oh, you think so?" The challenge on his face has me shutting the lid of my notebook computer and sliding it off to the side.

He flashes me a grin. One of those devastating smiles that shouldn't be legal.

He reaches for the chess board at the corner of the desk, careful not to disturb the pieces.

Excitement tingles through me.

"Last game was a blowout," he says.

"That was a long time ago."

He grabs two pieces, one white and one black, and puts them behind his back. I nod to one side, and he reveals the black piece.

"Go," I say.

He does.

My attention snaps from him to the board in an instant.

We play like old times. With one important difference.

"You got good," he says after a few moves.

I smile, toying with the string on the hoodie. "I still play at least twice a week."

Jax shakes his head, admiring my play. "You make any mistakes anymore?"

"Some days it feels like all I do is make mistakes."

The words are out before I can think about them.

The look in his eyes isn't judgment or sympathy. It's understanding.

He reaches up to pull on his hair, rubbing a frustrated hand over his neck and dragging my attention up from the board.

When he speaks again, his voice is low and urgent.

"Hales. I can't sleep knowing what you went through alone." I swallow, fighting the emotion that threatens to rise up. "Is that why you sold Wicked? Because you miscarried?"

I find a smile. "I sold it because I was pregnant. I have enough money. I wanted time, and space."

His face fills with anguish. "You must've thought I was such an asshole."

"No. I was upset when we broke up, I'm not going to lie. But I don't blame you, Jax. It must have been hard when I chose Wicked. I know you hated Cross."

Jax leans forward, closing the distance between us. Moody amber eyes hold mine in a grip that won't let go.

"Not as much as I loved you."

Words have the power to take your life, to shape it.

To put your heart back together when you'd swear it was broken forever.

I wonder if he can see every emotion on my face. Maybe he can, because his gaze darkens on mine, his throat working.

We're inches apart. Too far and too close at once. I'm desperate to change it, I just don't know which way.

Jax nods toward the board without breaking my gaze. "Your move, Hales."

12

HALEY

Jax is watching me.

His full mouth is pursed. Those amber eyes are glowing under his dark lashes, under the hair that falls across his forehead as if it belongs there. Under the T-shirt his shoulders are tight, his arms flexed.

It's intoxicating, the weight of his attention. Having the most beautiful man in the world watch you as though he's hanging on your next word, your next breath...

He's waiting for me to choose.

Before I'm even sure what I'm choosing from, every option fades away until there's only one thing in the world I want to do.

My hands hit the desk, braced under me as I shift over the board and crush my lips to his.

I'm home even before Jax opens under me, his mouth hot and welcoming.

Taking everything I have and giving it right back.

God, yes.

It's not a thought; it's a feeling.

He's all hunger and need and deliberateness as he rounds the desk.

Then his hands are in my hair, his body slamming mine into the wall as he kisses me.

Wild.

Desperate.

I forgot what it was like to be swept up in his storm. To be afraid to succumb to the hypnotic spell he weaves with his hands, his voice, his body almost as much as I'm desperate to.

It's *everything*.

He's everything.

Jax yanks the sweatshirt over my head..

My dress is gone nearly as fast.

The heat of his lips on my neck drives me crazy. I squirm against him, and his teeth nip my sensitive skin. Punishing me or encouraging me, I don't even know.

His shirt is next. That part's my doing because I can't stand the thought of the fabric between us. I want to touch his skin. See if he's burning up like I am.

My greedy hands roam his bare chest, and I exhale on a shudder. His muscles jump under my touch as I trace them from memory, and how is it possible this isn't close enough?

I want more.

All of him.

His arms band around my waist. It's surprisingly PG, except for the sheer force of them. And the insistent hardness pressing between my legs. I reach for him, hauling his mouth back to mine so I can taste him again. The dark flavor of his mouth combined with both of our desire.

Jax pulls back an inch and I blink my eyes open, startled to find wetness stinging my cheeks.

"Did I hurt you?" he asks.

"Yes." I swallow. "Don't stop."

"Fuck." His forehead presses to mine, the first beads of sweat forming there.

Jax's hands find my thighs under my dress. His heart hammers against mine, but he's slow as he skims up and under the hem. Amber eyes burn into mine as my eyelids threaten to drift down.

"Don't," he murmurs. "Look at me."

I do.

I'm twenty-four years old. I've buried both my parents. Worked a rock tour. Been kicked out of school. Run a record label. The kind of ups and downs that give you whiplash.

I've vowed never to let myself be at anyone's mercy ever again.

Yet when it comes to this man, I couldn't care less about all of it.

"Tell me you missed me," he rasps against my throat.

"Yes."

His touch strokes higher, over the curve of my hip. He palms my ass, his finger playing with the back of my thong, and his breath hitches. I yank my dress up as he pulls my knee around his hip. The friction of his jeans burns my bare leg.

None of it matters when his fingers brush between my thighs.

I bite my lip to keep from crying out. I'm soaked. I can feel it from my panties, from the way his fingers slide. He moves the fabric aside and I hiccup a breath.

"Hales." My eyes squeeze shut because I could come just from the way he says my name. But Jax has other ideas. "Since that day in the studio, all I can think about is doing this."

His fingers sink inside me, and my moan fills the whole office, like he fills me.

We're sharing the same breath now but not kissing, not really. My hands dig into his biceps, holding him or me steady as he drives me insane with need.

His thumb joins the party, stroking up over my clit in rhythmic passes.

I wonder if that's what playing a guitar is like.

The only noises in the room are our panting breaths and the sounds of him touching, teasing, filling me where I'm so turned on.

He builds me higher with every stroke.

I'm hanging on by a thread. To him, to consciousness.

Every stroke of his hand pulls on me, and my muscles are so tight I'm shaking with it.

"I can't wait," I murmur, my fingers digging into his arms. My head falls back against the wall, and his lips cover my jaw.

"We've waited enough." His satisfied murmur against the shell of my ear combined with his touch breaks me.

I go stiff against him, trembling with the impact. He holds me up as I gasp and pant my way through it.

I don't know how I survived without this. Without him.

When I come down, he's tugging at my dress. "I need to see you."

With wobbly limbs, I help him get it off. Or maybe I make it harder. Who the hell knows?

Jax gets the damn dress off and hitches me up on the desk. His jeans get shoved down by impatient hands, then his shorts too. My hand wraps around his cock, and Jax hisses out a breath.

He lowers me onto the desk. I can't get enough of him. The hard lines of his body are the same. The muscles of his arms, his pecs. The light trail of hair down his stomach.

I play with it, making him curse.

"It's a miracle I can even get it up after what you did to me last week," he groans.

Chess pieces dig into my back and side, but I grin anyway.

He pulls back, his expression tight with need and something else as he traces a finger down my breast, along my side.

My throat turns to desert before I hear the rip of foil against the backdrop of our panting breaths.

Anticipation grips me. He's standing over me, wanting me as much as I want him.

He's between my thighs. Brushing. Nudging.

Jax lifts off me far enough to look in my eyes.

Then he sinks into me.

All.

The.

Way.

I'm underwater. Drowning in sensation. Gasping for air.

I adjust to him as he watches. His face is a mirror of mine. Disbelief. Memory clashing with reality. Past and present.

It's like listening to him play a song. There's the familiarity of every time before, competing with wanting to experience it for the first time.

Until the past falls away and all there is is *now*.

He shows me with his hands, his body. Shallow strokes flattening out to deeper ones. Jax's hands find mine, our fingers lacing as he presses my hands overhead. My knuckles bump the cool, lacquered wood of the desk.

All I can do is thrust my hips up to meet his. The futility of it is soothed by the fire in his eyes.

I feel as if he's keeping me there. As though he's afraid I'll leave and he's using every ounce of his intention, his body, to make sure I never do. With that thought, the need takes over and has me crashing into him again as I cry out.

He shakes on top of me as his sweat-slicked body crushes mine.

13

My body feels like I just swam a hundred laps.

Then ran a marathon.

The kicker is, the second I meet her gaze, I'm ready to go again.

"I always thought this was creepy," Haley murmurs, trailing her fingers through the thick fur rug on the floor.

I manage a half laugh. "Me too."

I take in her body—flushed, naked. I could stare at her all night.

Somehow she's even more beautiful than I remember. Every inch of skin begging for my hands, my mouth. She's like a forgotten language, and I want to learn her all over again.

I swallow the impulse.

"The custodian'll have a field day if they find a condom in my garbage," Haley says under her breath.

"I don't give a shit if people talk. But you do." I realize as I say it it's true.

Haley's expression clouds as she pushes a hand through her hair. "My relationship with Derek and the other executives is complicated now that I'm not a majority owner. Finding out about our history wouldn't help."

I roll onto my side to face her. "Then they won't find out we fucked each other's brains out in your dad's old office," I decide.

Her mouth tugs up at the corner as if she thinks I'm sweet or cute or some other totally inappropriate thing given the circumstances.

I clear my throat as I cast my gaze around the office. "Speaking of. That was unexpected."

"Yeah." She wraps her arms over her chest, which only drags my eyes down. "When you said that thing, about how you loved me… I guess I got caught up."

"Me too." I rub a hand over my jaw, and Haley's gaze follows the movement. Interest stirs in my groin again because attraction's never been our issue. "It's been eating me up inside how we left things, Hales. I keep thinking how much I fucked up our ending."

The green flecks in her eyes dance. "You didn't fuck it up. I made a choice, and you made one too. I'm not broken, Jax."

"I know. You were always strong. Even when I met you on tour."

Her mouth curves. "We had some good times."

Just like that, she has me remembering those times. The bowling alley. Making out on my bus. The night she sang on stage next to me. That first day, sitting in the back of my limo. Me tossing her a bottle of water out of my bus.

My heart squeezes.

"It's in the past."

"Mostly." My fingers strokes down her arm and she lets out a little sigh.

"Mostly."

A noise in the hall has us both freezing.

"Tell me Tyler's gone for sure."

She snorts. "He is."

"Good." I stare up at the ceiling, counting the pot lights there. "Listen. I'm tired of regretting. What if we had another chance."

Her hesitation nearly kills me. "With each other?"

"At an ending." I turn toward her again, and those chocolate eyes deepen with the need to understand. Something I've always loved about her. "It's like a three-minute song. The first half's full of possibility because you're just getting started. The second half's building to the end. You know it's coming, but you don't have to dread it. You can enjoy the third chorus, the bridge, because it's all part of it."

"Okay," she says slowly.

"So maybe doing this album together is a second chance at a first ending."

"The second chance at a first ending," she repeats, and her hesitation nearly kills me. "I like that. Deal."

For two years, I've been sure the chapter of my life with music, with Wicked, was over.

Now I know that's not true.

I wrote four songs this week. With a little work, they'll be damned good.

More than that, I feel alive. Like I'm part of something again.

Whatever battle Todd wants to have, I'm all in.

Because this album is *me*. My truth, for the first time in a long time.

It's a different truth than before, because I've lived ten lives in the decade since I wrote that first album.

Not all pain or joy can be experienced by a teenager. When you're grown, it has more shades, more nuance. All of it's in those songs.

As far as I'm concerned, Haley and I have unfinished business too. Whatever time we're not working on the album, I'll use to prove to her our last ending wasn't the right one. I won't leave her that way.

What if don't want to leave her at all?

The disturbing though lingers in the corner of my mind.

I'm heading over to the studio the next day when I get the call that the principal wants to see me about Annie.

I park outside of the expensive private school and find my kid. She walks with me to the office.

"You seriously don't know what she's going to say?" I ask.

Annie shakes her head, looking nervous. "No." Annie starts to wait in the hall, but I motion her in with me. Her brows rise. "You want me to come?"

"Yeah. You might as well hear what they're saying about you."

She swallows her surprise, sticking to my side.

"Mr. Jamieson."

The principal, a sixtyish woman who looks like a poster for Newport living, welcomes us in. We take our seats across a cherry desk which I now know from my construction projects would cost a lot of textbooks.

Desks. That's what the tuition money goes to in these places.

The woman clears her throat. "Anne has put some inappropriate material in her locker."

"What kind of inappropriate material?"

She shifts. "Photos. Of men." My back straightens. "The other girls' fathers. Most of them are shirtless. I think she found them on social media feeds."

I turn to Annie, who's looking at me with big eyes.

"I don't know what kind of lifestyle you support, Mr. Jamieson," the principal goes on stiffly, "but I'm concerned this is unhealthy. We are very particular about the environment we put our children in."

My instinct is to lose my shit but some impulse has me holding it at bay. "Annie, whose father is it?"

"I forget. I put a few of them up."

She's being vague, but the expression on her face is strange. Like she knows the answer but doesn't want to say.

She's not afraid. More like…embarrassed.

This isn't adding up. "Do you…" I clear my throat. "Are you having feelings for other kids' fathers?"

Annie scrunches up her face. "Of course not. They're old. That's weird."

Now I'm more confused. "So why would you do it?"

A light bulb goes on and I swallow the groan.

"Annie," I start, shifting back in my chair, "do any of the other girls have dad photos in their lockers?"

"Yes."

"Whose dad?"

"Mine. And they remind me of it every damned day," she mutters.

"I see."

I nod to the principal, who's looking perplexed.

"Are you punishing the other girls?" I ask.

"But—that's different, Mr. Jamieson."

"How so? Just because I'm in entertainment and the other kids' dads are investment bankers makes it okay for them to tease my kid about me?"

Her mouth tightens. "We do aim to ensure positive and healthy social relationships. But we also have discretion to assign punishment for behavior that doesn't fit our school's values. As a result, Anne will do four weeks' community service filing books at the library every day after school."

Normally I'm all for teachers keeping kids in line, because I think they have too much latitude to get into trouble.

But she picked the wrong day and the wrong kid.

I shift in my seat and I swear her gaze flicks down my body. Over my T-shirt. Hell, maybe it even reaches the jeans but I'm looking at her face.

"Maybe you know how difficult it is to be a single parent, but if you don't, let me help you." I lean across the desk I probably paid for, keeping my voice deliberately measured. "It's really *fucking hard.* I've traveled to sixty countries. But nothing about selling out stadiums or managing media prepares you for the day your kid glues tampons to someone's books. Or comes home with some teenaged Smurf. Or asks you if you think she's a lesbian." I think I hear Annie snort beside me. "But you know what? We do okay.

"Now let me get this straight. You're telling me my honor is threatened and my daughter's crime was defending herself, and me, from a bunch of hormonal teenagers with a thing for thirty-year-old abs. If you try to punish her for that, I will not only put a stop on her tuition checks and take her to the second best school in the city, but I will buy her a pony, an ice cream cake, a damned locker full of tampons and dad pictures and anything else she wants along the way. Do we understand one another?"

The principal stares at me in shock for the better part of a minute before recovering. "Given the gray area of the circumstances, I think we can let this go." She turns to Annie. "But you will stay out of trouble the remainder of the semester."

Annie nods dutifully.

We walk out of the office together and get six steps down the hall before I lean back against the wall, my head hitting the plaster as I shut my eyes.

"Are you okay?" Annie asks tentatively.

My shoulders rock. "You got them back by posting picture of their dads?"

"Yeah. Some pretty nasty shirtless ones from trips to the Hamptons. They haven't talked about you all week. But I guess they tattled on me." She swipes at her eyes. "You were amazing in there."

My chest tightens until it's hard to breathe. It's the best moment I can remember, and it doesn't have to do with money or lawyers or regret or our past. It's just...

Now.

She glances down at her phone.

"Who's that?"

"Tyler."

Which reminds me. “Haley said you could go to Wicked and play with other kids.”

Her eyes light up. “Really?”

“Yeah. No pressure—”

“I’m so there.”

14

HALEY

I'm pretty sure heaven is a recording studio rigged up with the best sound mixing software money can buy, plus a little help from DRE when we get stuck.

Oh yeah. And Riot Act, including the one and only Jax Jamieson, on the other side of the glass.

I could live a thousand lifetimes and never get the kind of satisfaction I get from being part of this process. Because now that Jax is in it, he's all in.

It's incredible to watch. The way he writes and rewrites, how his mind turns things over.

I see why Cross didn't want to record without Jax, because he's the spark, the catalyst. He sticks together Kyle's crazy ideas, Brick's bass line, Mace's long quiet periods punctuated with moments of excitement when he jumps on a new idea, spins it out, makes it bigger than before.

I tried to replicate this chemistry in computer programs. Now I see why I can't.

Computers can unpack our logic and build it up better than we ever could. They can beat us at chess, at investing, at planning.

But they can't out-create us. They can't out-feel us.

No one can out-feel Jax when he's like this.

"Come out with me," Jax says at the end of the day Friday on our way to the meeting with Todd. "Annie'll be there too. She killed a test this week, so she gets to pick the restaurant. But she's dying to see you. Since she learned about your program, you're pretty much her hero."

"I heard Mace was her hero."

"Don't tell him he's been replaced." Jax grins. He's so high he's practically flying, and I can't resist smiling. "But seriously. I haven't seen you all week."

"You've seen me every day," I counter.

"Yeah. But that's you and Jerry. Team Jaley. Wait, that could be us. Team Herry." He makes a face. "And even if I get you alone for two seconds, we're surrounded by three other dudes."

"And you need to get me alone because...?"

"Isn't it obvious?" His grin melts me to my core. "I want to do wicked things to you, Wicked girl."

So truth time. Since we hooked up in my office earlier this week, I've been doing my best to act professional.

Channel the best parts of my father, the record executive, and bring them to the studio.

But Shannon Cross never had to deal with Jax Jamieson looking at him the way he's looking at me right now.

"I thought we had an ending."

"An ending has multiple parts. This entire album is an ending to my career. It has multiple tracks, multiple verses..." his mouth is hot on my ear. "We could have multiple lots of things."

Shit.

The problem isn't the physical. At least, it isn't only the physical.

It's that I've never been able to hold back with Jax. He's like a storm, tearing through me, leaving me in pieces even when he doesn't mean to.

He can't help it. It's his nature.

But we have other problems.

I shove the personal ones from my mind as we file into the conference room where Todd is already sitting, holding a copy of the file I emailed him not an hour ago.

"What the hell is this?" he asks.

"It's the track listing for the album," I reply, dropping into a seat as Jax takes the next one over.

Todd holds up the sheet. "It's four tracks."

"Right. We're making an EP called *Now*. Have you listened to the tracks? The first two are clear singles. We can release them in a matter of weeks. We've worked up a marketing plan to support this."

"Tell me you're fucking with me. This is what you've been working on for the past month?" He lifts the paper. "We're doing an LP." He turns to Jax, dismissing me as if I'm there to bring them coffee.

Jax opens his mouth to issue a stinging retort, but I lift a hand.

He drops back in his chair, folding his arms over his chest. This is my fight, and I'm grateful he's letting me take it.

"If you read his contract," I start, "it doesn't specify an LP. Now, maybe our lawyers didn't do their job. Or maybe my father, like me, thought it would make sense to make the right album at the right time. Which," I can't help adding, "is an EP."

"What are you now, his lawyer?"

"I'm an owner of this company. And someone who gives a shit how this album turns out." Todd goes red but I don't stop. "Now. Do you want me to tell Derek you're stuck on this idea of making an LP? Because you'll be making it without Jax."

Todd's gaze flicks back to Jax, who looks up from where he's inspecting his nails. He slings an arm over the back of his chair, appearing every bit the artist who'd rather be anywhere but in this meeting, though I'm sure he's smirking on the inside. "She's right. We gotta get back. My kid's got swim camp this summer."

I could hug him.

When Todd shoves out of his chair and stalks out the door, I do.

“He always have that much of a stick up his ass?” Jax asks as we walk back from the conference room side by side.

I hide a smile. “Some days it’s higher.”

“I dunno what Derek saw in him.”

“Track record. He’s conservative, has turned out a lot of big albums.”

“Least we got the go ahead on the EP.”

It’s a small win, but it doesn’t feel like it.

I wave to Derek’s admin, who’s packing up for the day. Her gaze flicks from me to Jax.

“Do you think Todd knows?” I venture as we make our way down the hall to my office.

Jax’s expression darkens. “What? That I fucked you senseless in your office Tuesday night?”

I flinch, hoping to hell no one overheard. “Yeah, that.”

“How would he? I was on my best behaviour in that meeting. Which, come to think of it, is getting old.”

He holds the door to my office for me and I duck through.

I’m barely inside when he spins me around, pressing my back against the wall. I’m breathless before his hips pin mine in place.

"Come for dinner," Jax murmurs.

The offer he's making with his body feels very different than dinner. "And then?"

"And then I'll make you come so hard your toes cramp for a week." He flashes me a boyish smile that has my knees going weak. "Unless you're busy."

"I am meeting someone shortly."

Jax's eyes flash.

The jealousy shouldn't make me happy.

But hey. No one's perfect.

I slip out from between him and the wall and circle my desk, dropping into the chair. "He's kind of amazing. He has blue eyes and blue hair—"

"Tyler." He shakes his head. "What the hell is it with that kid? He's got Annie wrapped around his finger too. I never should've let her do this after school thing… ah well. What do you say?"

My hesitation elicits a frown.

"It's not that I don't want to spend time with you," I start, "it's just… we need to focus on this album. And we said this was an ending…"

"Right."

"…And I don't want to get attached. If you're trying to sleep with me—"

"I'm totally trying to sleep with you." His bluntness doesn't make him any easier to turn down. Not when he's standing so close and wearing that T-shirt that pulls tight over his body and those jeans that fit every part of his lean legs to perfection. “But I also want to spend time with you. I’m not asking for forever. I want to show you I fucked up. That the way we ended things isn’t the way I wanted them to end. I’m not that guy, Hales.”

My heart’s issuing a warning, but he’s being so reasonable, it’s hard to argue in my head.

When the three of us go out for dinner, Annie picks some vegan place, and over cashew cream bowls, she babbles all about her time in the studio.

“The best part is that no one tells you what to do or not do,” she goes on, her eyes flicking between her food, Jax, and me like a laser pointer. “I’ve never seen so many guitars before.” She shoots me a look. “Hey, Haley. What would happen if one of them got broken? Not me,” she protests at her father’s rough intake of breath. “I’m just saying.”

“Those instruments cost thousands of dollars,” he states.

Her eyes widen. “No one’s done anything on purpose. But you might want to look at the guitars.”

I groan inwardly. If something needs repairs, it’s going to come from my pocket.

The reality is, things happen from time to time. They’re kids. Things break.

“It’s fine, Annie.”

She blows out a breath, relieved. “But it’s not Tyler,” she adds. “Tyler’s super careful. And he knows everything.”

Jax groans. "I'm sure he doesn't know everything."

"He does. He's so talented. Don't you think so, Haley?"

"He's pretty talented."

Jax shoots me a look, and when Annie goes back to her food, I can't resist winking at him. Damn, it's cute watching him dad. He was always loving with her, but now there's this extra protectiveness that he's comfortable with, like familiar clothes.

I didn't expect it to be this attractive.

When I'd learned I was pregnant, a lot of emotions had washed over me. Denial. Terror.

Eventually, possibility.

Some small part of me had hoped that it might be a reason for us to figure things out.

Which I know now was naïve.

Before the miscarriage, I'd come round to the idea of being a single mom. I had enough to provide for two between my earnings working with Carter and my inheritance.

When it happened, I hadn't expected the pang of loss, the mourning. But there it was. It took months before I got my head on straight.

Now, seeing Jax with Annie? It's like all the emotions, all the possibilities, rush back.

"You guys gang up on me," Jax murmurs when Annie goes to the bathroom, taking a long drink of water.

I find a smile. "It's girl talk."

"Girl talk. You mean about boys."

I snort. “Newsflash. Girls talk about things other than the opposite sex. We talk about dreams. Fears. Failures. The future. Things guys never talk about.”

He turns that over. “Sounds scary.”

“The alternative scares me more. That you can spend all the time without talking about it.” I take a sip of my drink. “‘You can live a hundred years without really living a minute’.”

“More Kierkegaard?”

I love that he remembers. “Close. Gilmore Girls.” He laughs. “My mom and I used to watch it. I have a feeling Annie would like it too.”

“Hales?” Jax’s expression shifts and there’s an intensity that steals my breath. “Sometimes guys think about those things.”

My hand tightens on the water glass, the icy sweat making my grip slippier, because suddenly I’m thinking about those things with him.

We have more in common now than ever, given my work at Wicked, and I love talking with him, hanging out with him.

But even though I’d probably survive having my heart broken by Jax a second time, I’m not ready to line up for it.

I finish my food and set down my fork. “You ever talk to Grace?”

“We’re on the outs since I won custody. Annie sees her on holidays. Every few weeks in between. Though my sister wasn't thrilled with the idea of us coming to Philly for a couple of months."

"She must miss Annie so much. It's too bad you guys couldn't come to an agreement."

He cuts a piece of his food, eats it. "The judge is checking in in a year. If Grace's situation has stabilized..." he trails off.

"There's still a chance the arrangement could change?"

He shifts. "There's always a chance things could change."

And there it is. No matter how much we control life, there will always be uncertainty.

Annie returns, dropping into her chair. "Are you coming over, Haley? You can. It's totally fine." Her intelligent eyes focus on me.

I glance toward Jax, but he's grabbed the bill. He's busy paying it, or acting as if he's not listening.

Annie leans in. "If it helps, my dad never has people over."

He blinks at her a moment before dissolving into a huge grin that has my chest squeezing.

"Okay," I agree. "For a little while."

We drive back to his place together and go up the elevator.

"It's after ten and a school night. Bedtime, squirt."

She salutes with an eye roll and closes her door.

"You've raised quite the kid."

"Before tonight, I can't remember her calling me her dad."

"Really?" A bubble of emotion rises up in my chest.

"Yeah." He goes to the kitchen and pours two bourbons. He passes one to me. "Remember the first time we drank this together? Because I sure do."

Jax's knowing look has me squirming. "I think I stripped in your foyer. It was mortifying."

"You had me the second I opened the door," he says, solemn.

"You still owe me. I always feel vulnerable in front of you."

Jax cocks his head, considering. Then he reaches for my phone on the counter.

My breath catches even before he hooks a finger in the waist of my skirt. "I'll make it up to you."

He tugs me into his bedroom. It's not so different from the one in Dallas, but it's more homey looking. Like someone picked out the individual elements. But the décor is the last thing on my mind when he scrolls through my phone and puts on a song.

My eyes widen.

"I was holding that for a friend," I protest as the opening chords of "I Love Rock 'n' Roll" play.

"Uh-huh." He points at the end of the bed. "Sit."

I do.

He takes two steps back, his gaze locked with mine. I

have no idea what's happening and I'm about to ask when his next movement stuns me silent.

Jax Jamieson reaches for the hem of his shirt.

And, with a wicked gleam in his eye, he strips.

I don't know if it's the sight of his abs or the bourbon coursing through me that's responsible for the wave of light-headedness.

Maybe both.

I dissolve into laughter, trying to keep my voice down since Annie's across the hall.

He peels the shirt over his head and tosses it at me. I catch it. "Pretty soon I'm going to have more of your clothes than you do," I murmur.

Jax winks at me. "I don't think so, babysitter."

I couldn't have pictured Jax from two years ago doing this. He took himself way too seriously.

I'm cracking up and so turned on at the same time, and I had no idea before this moment that was even possible.

I lean back, content to watch the show.

When his hands go to the button of his jeans, I swallow.

He works the button free. Then the zipper.

"You slowed down," I complain, breathy.

"It's called a striptease for a reason, Hales." But his warm voice is tinged with roughness too, as if he likes watching me watch him.

I try and fail to hold in the moan as he works his pants

off and steps closer to me.

"What's wrong," he prods, the smug grin never leaving his face.

My gaze tries to take all of him in. His broad chest, hard shoulders, rippling abs, muscled legs. The outline of his obvious erection through his shorts.

"How are you still so fucking hot," I mumble.

Some of the smugness fades as he bends over, pressing a scorching kiss on my startled mouth.

"You want to do the honors?" he asks when he pulls back, glancing at his shorts.

"I feel like I need dollar bills."

"Hales," Jax says evenly, "I'm a zillionaire. You're going to have to do better than that."

He's ridiculous, and I love it. Handsome and playful and totally irresistible. I love how his hair falls over his face. How he smells, tastes. The feel of his skin, smooth over muscles, under my hands.

I pull down the waistband an inch at a time.

He's hard and thick and perfect and eye level, and my mouth waters just looking at him.

"Can I tell you something?" I whisper.

"What."

"I never blew anyone before you."

The humor falls away, replaced with heat and something else. "Seriously?"

I shake my head. "I mean, I've watched people do it in porn. Even read up on how to do it, in case I wanted to someday." I flush. "But I never wanted to before."

"You're telling me you lost your oral virginity out of spite?"

"Yes. And it was totally worth it."

I reach for his cock, shifting forward because all I want is to lick him but he pushes me back on the bed.

"That's not how this works."

"No?" I prop myself up on my elbows, breathless and turned on and a little exasperated at being denied. "Fine. Go on and mansplain it to me, Jax."

But my irritation doesn't bother him a bit. He reaches for my skirt, and I'm glad it's stretchy because he manages to strip it down my hips without lifting me off the bed. My shirt comes next.

Jax's gaze darkens with appreciation as he takes in the soft pink lace-covered bra and panties.

"How this works is you lie on that bed and let me worship you."

Okay, well that doesn't sound terrible.

Even though he says it like it's way more than sex.

Especially since he does.

Jax drops to his knees, and my exhale trembles through my lips.

"The first time we did this," he says, his voice a rasp, "I told you the value of my songs." I swallow the laugh at the memory. "It's not my go-to line, but man, it got you wet."

His grin fades and I realize that even on his knees, he's

no less strong, no less compelling. I would do anything he asked.

"Should've known then you'd choose Wicked over me."

The moment of seriousness has me swallowing. "I wanted you both. I wanted it all." I reach toward him, running a hand through his hair.

His breath is warm on my stomach as he closes in. "What if you could have it all? Not for forever," he says before I can protest that it's impossible. "For now."

If there's one thing I've learned in the past two years, it's that life takes you on a ride. You need to fight for what you believe in, but you also need to be prepared to have it all ripped away at any second.

My hands fist in the comforter because I know I'm not going to stop him tonight. I want to give him everything he wants.

"Okay," I whisper, and I swear his eyes change color. "What are you waiting for, Jax Jamieson? Rock my fucking world."

He tugs my panties down and I lift my hips, his amber gaze never leaving mine.

His mouth drops. He presses a kiss to the inside of my thigh and I shiver.

Then he licks a fiery line from my core up over my clit.

I grab his hair on an ugly noise that's half moan, half protest.

Because *shit*, that's intense. It's as if he's inside me in a whole new way, and I can't hide anything from him like this.

I'm so tempted to stop him.

"Damn, you're beautiful," he murmurs against my slick skin.

I force myself to relax my hold and squeeze my eyes shut.

Every inch of me's feeling his lips, his tongue. The way he plays me as if I'm his instrument and he's the best in the world.

After a minute, it's starting to feel good.

"OhmigodJaaax..."

The comforter scratches my bare back and I arch to get away from it, closer to him.

When his fingers join in, pressing deep inside me, I think I hit the ceiling.

Jax pulls back to shift up my body. "I love how you taste," he murmurs. "I can't believe I've been without it my whole life." Then he kisses me, and I taste myself. It shouldn't be so hot, but it is.

When he drops back down my body, his lips, his tongue, his hands, work together in such beautiful concert I can't speak. Can't breathe. Can't do anything but exist in complete and utter awe of him and the way he makes me feel.

He drags me up the cliff, to the edge. When I'm hovering on it, gasping, grabbing at his hair, he waits a long moment, as if to imprint in my mind the fact that he brought me there.

Then he shoves me off it.

I bite my cheek to keep from screaming as wave after wave of pure sensation tears through me.

Jax's real magic is that he blows my mind utterly, completely, then the next second he makes me forget there's ever been any other way.

As I struggle to catch my breath, winded and wrecked and staring at the dimmed overhead light, I wonder if that was his plan all along.

15

"Is that real?" Tyler hefts the Grammy, weighing it.

"It's papier-mâché."

The door opens, and Haley sticks her head into the conference room. "You're late for your interview—whoa. What's going on?"

I glance around the room, which is lined with glass cases and awards.

"Show and tell. Light some fires under some asses. I figured there was enough memorabilia at Wicked, but Annie wanted to do it. So I had some stuff packed up and shipped here."

Haley looks around the room in amazement at the stacks of instruments, photos, and awards covering the long table and arranged around the outside of the room. "Wow. I'm surprised you wanted to dust all this off. I thought it might bring back bad memories."

I shrug. "Not a big deal. The kids are having fun."

Annie's showing some of my old costumes to the other kids.

"Can I put this on?" Tyler holds up the logo T-shirt and a pair of leather pants from my first tour.

"The jacket, sure. Not the pants. That's crossing a line." I turn back to Haley. "You gonna bust me for taking a break, boss?"

"I guess not."

I steer her to the back corner of the room. Chords start up as one of the kids grabs my guitar.

Her eyes fly wide. "Is that your—"

"It's just my old Telecaster, it's fine." I take in her expression. "But something's wrong."

"It's this interview you're doing. I didn't expect you to have to go through the media circus to make this album."

I brush a thumb over her cheek.

"You know I've been doing these since you were Annie's age."

Haley sighs out a breath. "I know."

But it's cute that she's worried about me.

A lot of things she does are cute. The ones that aren't are either frustrating—like when she argues with me over a track, or the lunch order, or whether I can touch her when we're both bent over the soundboard together—or completely intoxicating.

Three nights ago, we went for dinner with Annie. Haley came over after.

And *stayed over*.

It wasn't just sex, though holy shit was that insane. The things she let me do to her, the things she wanted to do to me… on paper I've done it all before but it's never been like that.

It's never *meant* that.

I knew it while I was getting her off with my tongue, feeling her body tight everywhere. When I was stroking inside her, our sweat mingling, telling myself to hold out for one more minute so I could see her fall apart.

Afterward, I'd held her in my arms as we stayed up all night talking and laughing and teasing.

It's getting harder to admit this is part of our ending. I want to take our three minute song and make it four, or five.

We leave the kids in the room—I'd told Annie to keep an eye on things, not that I'm worried about it really—and start down the hall toward the elevator.

"I heard you were recording with the kids yesterday," she says as I hit the button for G and the doors close.

"It was fun. Tyler's got something."

She smiles. "I know he does."

The doors open and we cross the lobby.

"Cross started this program. In the past two years, I've taken it up a notch. Now they get experience mixing, producing. I borrow time from the marketing team to talk about how to sell the music. From anyone who'll help."

Haley follows me out into the sunlight, slipping on

sunglasses, and to the Acura. I hit the locks and grab the passenger door so she can shift inside.

I round to the driver's side, then I take my seat and turn on the engine.

"I'll help."

Her eyes widen. "Really?"

"Any way I can. In the past month, it feels like you helped me get my kid back, Hales. And my music." I swallow the emotion rising up. "I know I wasn't the easiest to convince, but I'm stubborn like that."

"Sometimes we both are," she says softly.

I force my attention to the road as we navigate the heavy traffic to the studio.

For the past two weeks, we've been busy with the album.

I've also sat in on two sessions with the kids.

They're talented, and I know Haley's really into it.

What I didn't expect was for me to be into it. I like watching them mess around and screw up and try new things. I learn from them, too. It's a different way to do music than I ever thought of.

Given what I've been through, the ups and downs, I can mentor them, be with them, see the world through their eyes. It makes me feel like maybe I didn't screw everything up. Like maybe the unpredictable roller coaster I lived can help *them* live.

We get there, park, and go inside.

The interview I'm about to do is for national television, but they'll record here and broadcast across a bunch of networks.

Serena's waiting to greet us at the soundstage... with Todd.

"Run out of real work to do?" I drawl as he looks between us.

"Just came to supervise the company's investment." He turns away, getting on his phone, and I watch him wander the edge of the studio like a dark shadow.

Serena introduces me to the host while I get mic'd up. I take a seat on the stool—why these places have dumb little stools, I have no idea—and we get a countdown.

When it reaches zero, the female host with the big TV smile accosts me. "Jax Jamieson is back, world. And he and Riot Act are doing a new album. Why now?"

It's best to stick close to the truth with media. "I wasn't sure I had something left to give. Someone convinced me I was wrong."

"Aren't we glad they did? You retired for two years and did cologne commercials."

"I did *one* cologne commercial," I correct, raising a brow.

"It's good to have you back. When's the tour?"

I swallow my surprise. I know better than to outright deny something, just as I know better than to prop it up. I keep my voice level as I say, "I'm focusing on my family right now. My daughter."

"Her mother's not in the picture?"

"No."

"I think I heard a thousand ovaries break across America. You heard it here first, ladies. Jax Jamieson is unattached."

"Actually," I say, not sure why it bothers me to hear her say that, "that's not true. Outside of my family, there's only one girl who's ever had my heart."

Her eyes gleam like she's just spotted a hundred dollar bill stuck to her designer shoe. "Who's the lucky woman and what did she do to land you?"

I search for Haley across the room, find her gaze.

"She yelled at me, and hit me, and then followed me around for months."

Her jaw drops, and she's shaking her head, tightly.

"She sang my songs even when I told her not to. She kept all my secrets and pretty much showed me how to live again."

The head shaking stops as Haley's eyes glass over. My chest tightens as I swallow the grin.

"So the way to your heart is through stalking?" the host asks, bringing me back.

"Nah, so please don't try it. This particular version of stalking can't be replicated. It was a onetime deal. I read it as charming. It should've been weird as fuck."

"Wow. Okay then. We're playing the first official clip of a song from Riot Act."

I take off my mic and feel eyes on me. Not Haley's—

she's pulled into a conversation with Serena. The head of production.

This is not the kind of inconspicuous I promised to be.

Todd shoves his hands in his pockets, spanning the distance between us in a few strides. "Are you trying to start a rumor? Or you just know how to leave them wanting more?"

"That's my job."

The album's nearly done. Working these crazy long days has been good for me, done something for me, being back in the studio feels like it's changing me in other ways. Besides that I wear more jeans—which delights Annie to no end—it feels like my brain's getting back on some track I didn't know I'd jumped.

"It's interesting." Todd's gaze lands on Haley as she exchanges a few words with the host, and I wonder how long I've been staring.

"What is."

"Wicked tried to contact you for months. Then she calls and you come running."

He's trying to bait me, and I force myself to stay easy-going. "Apparently she asked the right question."

I turn away from him and Serena catches my eye. "Jax, can I talk to you about promotion?"

She walks me to one end of the stage while Todd stalks toward the door. She sighs when he leaves. "There's something you need to know. If the album's not a success, Haley's program will get cut. I'm telling you because she won't put that pressure on you, but I want you to know that what you're doing here matters."

As Serena goes to meet her friend, a stone settles in my stomach.

When Haley called me back here, she made a play for my soul. For the man she knows I can be.

She took that chance on me.

Not in the past.

Right now. Despite how things ended last time. Despite how I treated her, and everything she's been through.

Which makes it that much harder to remind myself this is all part of our ending.

16

HALEY

Two months ago I wouldn't have believed it was possible.

That Jax would come back. That he'd record the kind of songs that leave me breathless. That we'd save the program.

But when the album drops, it drops with a bang.

"No matter what Kyle says, the cake is not that bad," Serena prods. "It's a party. Look happier. The critics giving early reviews have said it's good, but we both know it anyway. The first single's getting airplay. This is what people want."

"I know."

This party has an entirely different vibe than Jerry's retirement party. This one's small. Private. Personal.

It's not five hundred people.

It's not even fifty.

It includes the band. A few other artists. The staff at the studio. The kids, at Jax's suggestion.

My gaze lands on Tyler, who's laughing with Annie and some of the others.

Serena and the entire PR team have been promoting their asses off. I hope it's enough.

"You in a sugar coma?"

I turn to find Jax behind me, looking gorgeous in faded jeans, white sneakers and a Pink Floyd T-shirt. "There you are. I'm surprised you made it with all the interviews you're doing."

He shrugs. "Might as well get as much publicity as we can."

"Jax, no matter what happens? This album is amazing."

A grin takes over his handsome face. "It's not bad."

Over the past two weeks, he's been working his ass off to get this album finished and mixed. The whole band has.

I don't know why he's started doubling down, but I appreciate it.

The first track was a love song that went down easy.

The second, about growing pains, stuck a little.

The third was about taking your time.

The fourth...

The fourth, called "Line of Sight," was about changing perspectives. Seeing things in new ways.

I never expected to like another song more than the

one Jax wrote two years ago and left on the floor of a diner, but I love this one.

Recording it was bittersweet, because I didn't want it to be over.

And maybe he didn't either.

I've gotten used to working next to him again in the studio during the day. It's amazing how fast the old pattern came back, even though we were only on tour for a month. Sometimes I think it was the best month of my life.

Todd's been lurking over us the whole time, so we've been keeping it strictly professional.

But Jax would text me, tease me. We'd exchange secret smiles and laughter.

I don't want anyone getting the wrong idea about why he's here.

Because why we're here is to make this album. Not to see if there's some kind of second chance for us.

Jax and I haven't talked about what would happen when the album is finished because we both know there's an expiration date on this.

We each have responsibilities. You could say we didn't choose them, but we did. Jax found Annie, and he decided to be there for her. I chose this program, these kids, even when it was hard.

The door opens, and we all turn toward it.

Derek's there, with Todd in tow. "We have the

numbers. The album's gone gold. At this rate, it should hit platinum by next weekend."

The room erupt with cheers.

I throw my arms around Jax's neck, burying my face in his shoulder in delight. "Oh my God. Jax...you have no idea how much this means."

"I think I do." He pulls back. His face isn't quite a reflection of the ecstasy in mine, but it's close. "Serena told me you bet the program on this."

Apprehension starts up in my gut as I scan his expression. "Are you mad?"

"No. It means a lot that you have that kind of faith in me. I'm glad you dragged me back here. I needed this."

"Me too."

Something deeper in his gaze makes my heart kick in my chest. Because he's right.

Derek interrupts my daydream. "Haley. A word."

I tear my gaze from Jax and follow Derek out to the hall, shutting the door after us.

The sounds of the party all but disappear.

Thank you, soundproofing.

"So I guess the program is saved."

His mouth is a stern line. "About that. Something went missing from a rehearsal room a few weeks back. The one where your kids practice."

My smile fades a little. "A lot of people practice there."

"A lot of people are professional musicians," Todd

states. "And the rest are children who wouldn't think twice about selling a guitar."

My minds works to connect the dots.

"In light of this violation," Derek interjects, "I can't in good conscience recommend we pursue your program."

I hold up a hand. "It's a misunderstanding. None of my kids would do that. If you don't believe their reputation, believe mine. I have never done anything to compromise my personal integrity or this company's."

Todd lets out a skeptical sound. "Your reputation is worth less than it used to be."

I fold my arms over my chest, not bothering for once to hide my resentment. This guy has taken enough of my time and patience and for a second I wish I still had control of the company so I could fire his arrogant ass. "What the hell is that supposed to mean?"

But instead of rising to the bait, he smirks. "As you know, there's a security camera in each studio. We were searching the footage. The angle doesn't show the instrument that went missing, but we did find something very interesting."

The tone of his voice has alarm bells going off in my head. I have no idea what he might have found, so why the hell is he being—

My eyes fall shut.

Me blowing Jax.

He doesn't have to say it.

Every part of me's boiling with humiliation and indignation. But I force my chin up.

"Derek, I swear to God—"

His face lines with regret. "I understand you're upset, and I assure you, we will destroy the footage. But we also need to make a decision about the program."

"You can't force me out of the company."

"No. But the majority shareholders have been onside with the idea of cutting the program for two months, even before this latest incident." The conflicted expression on his face doesn't make his words easier to digest. "It's done, Haley. We can give you two weeks to wrap things up."

It's done. The phrase echoes in my brain as he leaves.

It takes me a moment to realize Todd's lingered behind.

"I'll go somewhere else to run the program," I state. "We'll take what we've started and find a new home."

He smirks. "You really will be starting over. The recordings are company property. Every song those kids have laid down since this program started. It's all in the legal agreement they sign when they walk in the door."

I feel myself go pale.

How I find my way to my office, I have no idea. But I'm sitting on my desk, swiping at angry tears when Jax's voice interrupts me.

"Hales." I look up to meet his concerned gaze. "What happened?"

"They're cutting the program. The album's a huge

success, and they're cutting it anyway." I hate how my voice sounds. I hate feeling weak.

Jax's body stiffens, his gaze jerking toward the hallway. "Was this Derek or that prick Todd?"

"I'll figure it out. You've done more than enough." I manage a watery smile. "I dragged you and your daughter across the country on a week's notice to write and record all new original material. Your work here is done. You paid me back by delivering a platinum album."

"I hope that's not all I delivered." The warmth in his tone has me thinking about everything that's happened between us.

He drops onto the desk next to me, toeing the carpet as he shoves his hands in his pockets.

If someone told me we'd have another shot at an ending, I'd have called them crazy. But we have had, and it's been beautiful.

Jax's album is complete. In some ways, this is the culmination of what I wanted when I took over Wicked from Cross.

I wanted to find another Jax.

I did. I found it in him, when he didn't think it was there.

I swallow the lump in my throat. "Three years ago, all I wanted was to matter. I wanted you to teach me how, and you did." I rest a hand on the denim covering his thigh as emotions roll over me in waves. "You did, and I'm so grateful."

My gaze lifts to his. He turns my words over in his mind. "That's nothing, Hales. You helped me get my kid back in a way the lawyers couldn't. And my music."

It takes everything in me just to breathe right now. To tell my body that everything's the way it's supposed to be.

Because I just lost my program, and it feels as if I'm about to lose something that matters even more.

I squeeze his hand, looking past him to the Ireland picture.

"I always liked that one," he says, as if he can read my mind.

"Me too. Do you ever miss him?"

"Cross?" I expect him to laugh, but he just looks around the office. "Sometimes. He gave me someone to blame, and blaming is easier. You can't push against the world when there's no one to resist."

"The first time I came to this office after learning Cross was my father, he gave me shit for asking bad questions. Said there was one question I should be asking, and if I knew what it was, I'd know him better."

"And?"

"The question is why he sent me on tour with you."

Jax's gaze scans mine. "You wish he was still here so you could ask him?"

I shake my head. "I don't need to ask him. I know."

Somehow a piece of hair slipped into my face, and I tuck it back before turning toward him.

"I was the daughter he didn't know what to do with.

You were the son he could never ask for. And as much as he fucked up… I think he knew we'd be good for each other, Jax."

Jax shifts off the desk and steps between my legs, tilting his face toward mine. His touch is comforting on my thighs.

I was holding it together until this moment, but when his mouth grazes mine once, twice, my arms wrap around him and hold him against me. Every ounce of emotion and need pouring out of him is destroying me, and I lose myself in the kiss.

I hate the idea of not having him next to me in the morning, not being around him, not sharing his smiles and his moods.

We break apart, breathing heavily.

"When are you going back to Dallas?"

"This weekend."

I nod, but it's mechanical.

"It doesn't mean we can't be friends, Hales," he murmurs, the words spilling into one another in a very un-Jax-like way. "I want you to call me. I swear to God I'll answer. Not just if you're pregnant. But of course then too." I hiccup a laugh. "If you have a bad day. Hell, a good one. I want to know. Promise me."

Nodding is easier than speaking, but Jax waits until I find my voice. "I promise," I whisper.

I wait until he's retreated to the hall before I close the door quietly and let the tears stream down my face.

17

The next few days feel like I'm going through the motions. Finishing media that suddenly feels pointless. Fending off offers from my agent, which are exploding now that I have a new album. Calling my housekeeper to make sure everything's set for when I get back. Packing up my clothes, both the T-shirts and the preppy ones.

Endings always suck, and I can't decide which are worse. The kind where you're ripped apart, where nothing but evil forces could keep you separated?

Or the kind that happens when you're an adult and you have to walk away on your own steam.

Definitely that one.

"I'm sad you're leaving." The boy's murmured voice has me glancing in the rearview mirror.

"Me too," Annie says back.

I clear my throat. "We're almost at Tyler's house."

"Can we drive around a little more?" Annie pleads.

Two pairs of eyes find mine in the mirror.

They're kids. It shouldn't get to me.

Except it's like stomping on my soul that's already beaten and bloody.

"Ten more minutes," I say.

They continue to talk in the back, quietly with little bursts of laughter thrown in. Like they'll never get to talk again, even though something tells me they'll be texting every night for weeks.

If someone had told me three months ago we'd get this comfortable in Philly, I'd have called them out on it.

But I like seeing my old band mates. Driving around town in my rental that's almost as familiar as my Bentley.

Annie's even settled in at school.

I slow the car when I realize whose neighborhood we're in. Big houses watch over the street, tucked behind trees older than me and the kids put together.

I notice the sign before the house, and I hit the brakes. "What the fuck..."

"What's wrong?" Annie chirps from the back seat, suddenly alert.

I pull over and start to dial her number, then I change my mind and hit another.

"Hello, this is Serena."

"Her house is for sale. Why."

Annie and Tyler are looking on now.

"Jax." She blows out a breath. "We really have to stop meeting like this."

"Tell me."

"She's been thinking about it for awhile. I guess she decided it was time to make a change."

Time to make a change.

The sign seems to taunt me, which is fucking weird, because I'm not in the habit of hearing voices from dead guy's Victorian mansions.

I've been thinking about what she said about Cross bringing us together.

Now, she's leaving the company. Selling the house.

It's like she's shedding the last part of him, which shouldn't bug me because God knows I wasn't the guy's biggest fan.

But it feels more final than our ending, like she's erasing the past somehow. I'm not just losing her, I'm losing what brought us together. Our common ground, and I'm just sitting here staring at the damned sign like a moron.

I need to be back in Dallas. Not just because of Annie. Because that's what I chose. It's my life.

But I've spent a lot of time beating myself up for what I should do.

Resolve sets in. "Get her to take the house off the market. Say whatever you have to. That your rat infested the attic with rabies. I don't care. And I want a meeting. Now. The band. Lita. You. No Haley."

I hang up.

"What's going on?" Annie asks.

"Change of plans." I wheel the car around.

18

HALEY

When I enter Carter's office, it's the same as I remember it, plus a few new awards. The walls are covered in obscure-looking equations and comic book covers. It's perfect for him. He's a genius who refuses to grow up.

"I have an idea for a new project," I say.

I explain it to him. He listens, raising a brow on his unusually tan face.

When I finish, my former professor's eyes sparkle. "What happened to Mr. Teenager-bait Musician?"

I shouldn't be surprised he knows about Jax. "He was here to cut an album. It's over."

Jax left two weeks ago.

Fifteen days if you're counting.

We've texted a bit but he's been especially vague about his activities since returning to Dallas. And neither of us has suggested talking on the phone.

Probably because he gets, like I do, that we can't continue the way we were here. There's a new normal and we need to respect that if we're going to move forward with our lives.

I keep telling myself it's going to be fine, but I miss having him here, smelling him, laughing with him, lying next to him.

"Carter, if you're gunning to be my rebound, I'm flattered. But it's not going to happen. Business only."

He shrugs. "Fine. I've been in Costa Rica for the last six weeks. Might go back. I don't need some kid hanging all over me."

I know he's joking about the last part. "You've been there six weeks?"

"Never even noticed, did you?" He smirks. "The beauty of the internet. School semester wrapped in April, which means if I'm not teaching, I can work anywhere. Should've tried it ages ago."

We hash out a plan for the app on his whiteboard, and I confirm when I can code the first part by.

"Huh. You really are done with your other life."

The words hit me. My other life.

Is that what it'll feel like in a few months? That it was another lifetime? The thought makes my chest ache.

I leave Carter's office and walk around. Campus is quiet, but a few students are chatting along the paths, on the benches. I could've been one of them.

I still can. I can do anything I want.

I'm keeping my shares in the company. But I'm done working at Wicked.

On the way home, I call Serena. "Hey. Do you want to hang out tonight?"

"I'd love to, but I need to work late." My friend sounds strange, as if maybe she feels badly that she's still all-in at Wicked when I'm trying to move on.

"Sure, no problem." I swing in the doors of the house.

"I do need a coffee break though. So talk to me. Any offers on the house?"

I hear her chair creak in the background and picture her going to the kitchen for java.

"Yes, finally." I think of the FOR SALE sign in the driveway. I don't need five thousand square feet of Century-home luxury and I've been meaning to list the house for months. It finally feels like the right time. "We wondered why it was taking so long but my realtor found this blog post about the house being haunted. Apparently that sparked interest like crazy."

"Huh." She sounds far away. "Perfect. Listen. How are you doing with the whole Jax leaving thing?"

I blow out a breath. "It sucks," I say honestly. "I'm trying to focus on a new program with Carter, then I pull out my phone and start typing some emotional text to Jax. I can't send them because we agreed we'd be grownups about this." I sigh out a breath. "Just tell me one thing. Are we still getting messages about the album?"

"It's insane," she replies immediately. "Everyone's

connecting to it, feeling it. I mean, come on. It went platinum."

I feel the weight on my shoulders lift a little. "I don't care about that part, Serena. I'm just so glad he made it. That it matters to people."

I don't know if it's my words or the wistfulness in my voice that has her concerned. "Haley, maybe we should talk. I can duck out of work in an hour or so—"

"No, it's fine. Seriously. But can I borrow Scrunchie tonight?"

"Of course. And we're on for lunch tomorrow."

"Wouldn't miss it."

I pick up Scrunchie using my spare key for Serena's apartment and take him home.

Then I curl up on the couch, stick in my earbuds and hit Play on the album I've been waiting to listen to like this.

To feel.

To remember.

I've listened to these tracks hundreds of times. Spent hours tweaking them. Now, Jax's voice seducing me through the headphones is pure catharsis.

"The ground under your feet shifts with everyone you meet

You have a choice, a chance

To keep it all and curse your fate

Tell yourself it's all too late

Keep counting wrongs until they're right or find a new line of sight."

Tears roll down my cheeks through my eyelids. Not because I'm sad.

Because I'm happy.

I'm so fucking happy he made this for the world.

Made it for *me*.

For all of us.

Scrunchie sniffs my neck in support.

After awhile, I force myself to open my notebook computer and go through emails.

Tomorrow's my last official day at Wicked. I need to turn in my pass, and clean out my office.

I scroll through the emails, Scrunchie shifting under my hand as I stroke his soft back.

Maybe I need a skunk.

An email comes in from Tyler asking about our last day in studio. I think of his bright future, snuffed out by Wicked's failing.

I had to tell the kids this week that the program's cut. I didn't tell them that the recordings are Wicked's property.

Now, hearing Jax's album, that seems like the bigger crime.

An idea comes to me.

You can't make him Jax, a voice says. *But you can protect his work. His voice.*

Shifting upright so fast I almost dump Scrunchie from

my lap, I dig out the contact list from our board of directors materials.

Then I reach for my phone.

19

HALEY

Last night I slept with Scrunchie in my bed. I like to think it fortified me for the day ahead.

I get up and shower, then I pull on my battle gear.

Jeff gives me a double take as I sweep in the front doors. "Morning, Miss Telfer."

"Morning, Jeff." I hitch the empty box on my hip, my Converse sneakers silent on the carpet.

Upstairs, I clean out the office, giving instructions to a man from a moving company on how to care for my father's art.

"You can't take that."

A cold voice has me looking toward the door. "Excuse me?"

Todd sneers. "That's company property."

"It's my father's."

"Shannon Cross would've driven this company into

the ground if he'd been here longer. His death—and you selling out—were the best things to happen to Wicked in its history."

I lift the picture and hold it against my chest like a shield. "I didn't realize you knew him."

"He had a chance to hire me. He didn't."

I lower the picture as understanding dawns. "Can I give you some advice, Todd?" I don't wait for him to respond. "Getting revenge on a dead man is hard. Getting anything from a dead man is hard. Respect. Love. Attention. If that's all you want out of life, you'll be waiting a long time."

His gaze narrows, and I lay the frame carefully on the desk.

I lift the file I brought then nestle it under my arm.

I feel Todd on my heels as I pass through the familiar halls down to Derek's office, where I knock before opening the door.

He's on a call and stares at me as I grab the handset from him. "Sorry. This will only take a second, Derek will call you right back." I hang up.

"Haley. What the hell?"

He shifts back in his chair.

"I have something for you to sign. My lawyer drew these up." I set the file in front of him. "The rights to the recordings and files from the after-school program."

His brows rise. "I didn't realize this was on your mind."

He flips through the pages. "We need to put this by the board."

"I already did. I circulated the proposal by email yesterday and got sign-offs from the other major shareholders."

His confusion grows. "So if they've signed off, this is a formality?"

"It's done, Derek," I say, relishing the words a bit too much. "But I thought I'd give you the respect of asking for your signature as CEO."

Todd grunts. "You can't take those. That's years worth of recordings. Terabytes of data."

I glance over my shoulder, acknowledging him for the first time. "What I'm paying for the rights to those recordings is more than fair. Especially considering you called them worthless."

And it is. In fact, it'll be the proceeds from the sale of my house.

Derek signs and I close the folder with a smile. "Gentlemen. I'll see you in the next board meeting."

I stride back down the hall to my office. At the computer I'm about to leave, I double-check that all the relevant files have been uploaded, as I requested from IT, and removed from Wicked's file system.

A feeling of satisfaction works through me. Everything the kids created in that studio since the program's inception is mine.

In legal terms only.

Really, it's theirs.

"Haley!" Serena calls from a window as I take my boxes out to my car. I load my car and wait until she comes down, out of breath. "Damn, running isn't as good for me as it's supposed to be."

"Am I late for lunch?"

"No. You're right on time."

"Good. Because after, I'm going on a little trip."

"Where?"

"Dallas." I grin. "I need to tell Jax something, and it's better in person."

A strange look crosses her face. "Fine. But after lunch." She trots in front of me, and I follow her around the building.

"Where are we going?" I call after her.

Serena stops in front of a massive bus that has me freezing in my tracks.

"Why is Jax's bus here." The doors are open, and my friend's acting like I didn't just ask a question. "Serena..."

Before I can find words, a form appears in the doorway.

Jeans.

A tight T-shirt.

Messy hair.

Amber eyes that stop my heart when they find me. "Hi, Hales."

Jax.

I try to say the word, but all I can manage is to keep breathing.

Being around him has that effect on me, whether I haven't seen him in days or years.

Finally, enough synapses fire to create language.

"What are you doing here?"

"Apparently I bought this years ago. It's how I kept other people off it."

"Don't tell me you blew through your money already and have to tour again."

"Not quite. I did have some ideas for how to spend my retirement, though."

He invites me onto the bus, and with only a moment's hesitation, I follow him up the stairs. My jaw drops.

The living room has been redone. Instead of dark maroon, it's white with bright colors. He leads me through where the curtain used to be. Now, it's a clear door.

"What the..." His couch and other furniture is gone. In its place, equipment. Instruments. "It's a studio?"

"Yup. On wheels."

"But how did you—"

"Acoustics? Jerry helped spec it out. We redid the interior." He pats the inside wall. "Put on a few layers of absorption materials. Keeps outside noise out and all the good stuff in. I finally got to put those home reno skills to good use."

I can barely take it all in. "It's amazing, don't get me wrong, but why did you do this?"

He grabs my hand. I try to ignore the tingling as I wrap my fingers tighter in his. He pulls me back to the front of the bus, where Serena's leaning against the wall with a dopey expression on her face.

"You didn't notice the pictures?" he asks.

Now I do.

They're the ones from the studio, of the kids. Intermingled with ones from Jax's tours. On stage, and on the road. Images of Jerry, Lita, Mace, Kyle, Brick, Nina, me. Even one of Cross.

My gaze catches on a plaque at the front, and I run a hand over it. "'Big Leap Studio,'" I read under my breath.

"Now we can take it to kids at any school."

"Wait—what do you mean we?"

His eyes gleam. "Come on. You didn't think I'd let you produce without me? Jerry wants a proper retirement, and you can't supervise a dozen junior high students alone."

"You're staying?"

Jax nods, and my breath sticks in my throat. "Here, Dallas, it doesn't matter anymore. I'm tired of doing what I decided I wanted years ago. Because I don't need to lock myself away. Everything we've done here has made me realize I have choices. I always have, even if it didn't feel that way." Tingles run up my arm and I glance down to see him rubbing a circle in my palm. "Annie's on board, and Grace has agreed to a schedule of sharing time. Because I need my kid, but I also need you, Hales. I love the shit out of you. I think it started the night you got my phone back. Or maybe when you told me I was second best to Leonard Cohen." His dry comment has me grinning. "The point is... If you're my cliff, I'll take you every time without looking back."

My chest is so tight I think I'm suffocating. But it can't be, because I'm expanding from the inside out. It's as if I'm going to burst from all of it, and rationally I know it's impossible, but I can't come up with another explanation for the fluttering of my heart, the shivers across my skin.

"But... I was going to come to you," I say when I can manage it. Words are hard when he's looking at me like I'm the answer to everything, but I try. "I needed to do something that mattered, and I thought that's what I was doing by taking over Wicked. I wanted something bigger than me." I think of the kids' music. Music that's now theirs. "But I realized that I don't want to do something bigger than *us*, Jax. I don't want to believe there's *anything* bigger than us. And we can't have an ending, because I'm not done loving you yet." His amber gaze works over mine, his jaw tight with emotion. "I love you more than I thought I could love someone. It's then and it's now and I don't know what will happen tomorrow. But I want to find out with you."

Jax's mouth comes down on mine, and I grip his arms to stay upright.

His kiss is hungry, but more than that, it's home. Not the kind of home that promises safety or security, because nothing can promise that.

The kind that promises compassion, and love, and kindness, and support. I know he's the man I want to have it all with, the ups and the downs.

When he finally pulls back, he nods to Serena. "I want you to hear something."

She pulls out her phone and hits Play on a song that's familiar and new at once.

"That's Tyler's song." I keep listening. It's different than the version he sent me, because Jax comes in on a verse. Amazement bubbles through me.

"Posted it this morning, with a little Riot Act bump. It's had three million streams since we put it up."

"You recorded this at Wicked?"

"Yup. Wicked's going to have a hard time arguing with the program's success now. It's pulling in ad revenues already."

My head starts to spin and I reach for the wall to steady me.

"You okay?"

"I just signed a deal. Anything recorded by my kids in that studio until eight a.m. today is mine. Exclusively."

His face splits into a grin. "Even better."

"Todd's going to freak," Serena comments. "I don't want to miss this."

With a wink, she disappears down the stairs.

"Who's Todd?" Jax mutters.

My mouth twitches. "No idea. I'm kind of preoccupied."

Jax's eyes darken, and I know what's going through his mind when he says, "me too."

20

"Hales? You here?" I call from the front hall.

I make my way to the master bedroom to find her rummaging in the closet.

I sneak a look at her cute ass in those jeans as she arranges clothes on hangers. Her hair's up on her head in a bun, and I'm wondering if I can tug it out with one hand or if it'll take two.

"I'm not sure about this 'living in a hotel' thing," she tosses over her shoulder, oblivious to my thoughts.

"You were the one who wanted to sell your house. If you want to buy something new, we can swing it. Unless you'd rather sleep on the bus."

"Definitely not. And since you're keeping your house in Dallas, it seems crazy to have two."

I grin. "Hales? I know people with ten."

She shudders.

"Where's Annie?"

"Out getting ready for dinner. With Tyler."

My interest is officially piqued. Anytime my kid is safe and out of the house and Haley is here, I start to think of some really great ideas.

My gaze drops to the computer on the bed. "You were coding late last night. And again today."

"Mhmm." She turns back to me, lips curved in a knowing smile. "We have this new app—"

I cut her off with a kiss. "You can talk nerdy to me when my tongue's inside you." Without letting her go, I grab her computer and set it on the bedside table none too gently.

Her mouth falls open and I know she's going to protest before she says a word. "Jax, we have an hour before the dinner meeting to talk about growing Big Leap Studio. Serena set it up, and the kids will be there, and—"

"And I'm not spending the hour between now and then hearing you talk about whatever you're working on with Carter."

I topple her onto the bed and she gasps, laughing. "I do not talk about Carter."

"You're not going to. That's why we're going to have this conversation when my tongue is inside you."

"Good luck with that," she says, but it's breathy. "It's going to take more than your sweet talk, Jax."

"I know."

I strip her shirt over her head, take a second to appreciate the satin of her bra underneath, then reach for my guitar case next to the bed. With a few quick moves, I unhitch the strap from the guitar and hold it out.

Her mouth forms an O. "What are you doing?"

"Wrists out."

"Tell me this isn't ending in a dungeon."

"No dungeons. Just you and me."

She complies, and that alone has me hard. I wrap the soft, wide strap around her wrists and pin them over her head. "Better."

"If you say so." The edge in her voice tells me she's nervous. And excited.

I fucking love making her that way.

There's nothing to prove with this woman, but I've got two years to make up for.

I take my time, skimming my hands over her curves. Unbuttoning her jeans and tugging them down so she's in her underwear. Haley squirms but doesn't move her hands. I hold her hips down on the bed.

Shit, I want to eat her alive.

"What are you doing?" she asks breathlessly.

I strip my shirt over my head, her dark eyes watching every move. "What does it look like?"

My jeans next. And my shorts.

She wets her lips. "I want to touch you."

"No."

Surprise has her blinking. "Jax?"

"Hales. Don't make me tie you to the bed." I shift over her, avoiding touching her flushed skin except where my lips meet her ear. "Because then we definitely won't make dinner."

I couldn't care less about dinner. She's a fucking buffet, and I want to savor every bite. So I do, starting with her lips.

I kiss her, my fingers threading in her hair. Her arms reach up, but I push them back down so all she can do is writhe against me.

Damn, I like that. My cock twitches against her thigh.

"Tell me how good it feels." I move down to her neck, her shoulders. Light kisses punctuated with the scrape of teeth that make her shiver.

"It would be better if you were inside me," she murmurs.

I suck her hard nipple through the thin lace of her bra, and she jerks against me. "That's the point," I groan.

"Of what?"

"You. Like this."

"That you have to tie me up so we don't both get what we want?"

I grin, because I love how smart and direct she is. Hell, I love everything about her as she lies on my bed, flushed and wanting and so damned real it makes me ache to think of her as mine. "Exactly."

My hands move down, my mouth too, covering every inch of her. Memorizing her body. Until I'm between her thighs, and she moans when my tongue swipes over her clit.

"Jax."

"Uh-huh."

"Some people say don't meet your heroes." She pants the words. "I respectfully disagree."

I chuckle as I move up her body, my gaze moving from her chest to her flushed face to the binding on her hands. I stroke a finger up her arm, and she shivers. I press the strap into the mattress over her head, and her chest rises.

"Me too. I love you, Hales."

"I love you, Jax."

I plunge into her and I'm lost. I pour everything I have, everything I am into her.

Because the thing is, she's already all of it.

EPILOGUE

Haley

Three months later

"I can't get it right," I murmur to no one.

My fingers fly over the keyboard, making adjustments. I play the chorus again, closing my eyes and focusing on what's streaming from the headphones.

Nope. DRE had it right the first time. I change it back.

Jax was right. Big Leap is a self-contained studio, and it took me two months to realize it. What's amazing is that starting this fall, we can take it to a school or a library—anywhere really. But it's still a tour bus. Which means spending too long on it can drive you crazy.

The tapping on my shoulder makes me jump.

"Sorry to scare you," Annie says, her golden eyes lightening in surprise. "My dad's looking for you."

"Oh." I set the headphones around my neck. "And he didn't come himself?"

She has a strange expression on her face. "He's on his way. Just... be nice, okay?"

I'm completely confused as she wanders toward the front of the bus and drops into a seat with her cell phone in her hands. She sneaks a covert look at me.

I shake my head. I love working with kids, but they still stump me sometimes. "Hey, your mom's coming up tomorrow, right?"

She nods. "For the weekend."

Annie still calls Grace her mom and now calls Jax her dad. Is it weird? Sure. Aren't all families?

Grace's been visiting. She and Jax have issues, but they're working through them.

We've been running a test of a summer program here. Forty kids get time each week in the bus.

The plan is to go back to Dallas in the fall and spend the school year there. We can take the bus to schools across the region, and I can continue to work on projects with Carter, remotely.

Annie's made Jax swear to come back to Philly next summer.

Because in Annie's words: Tyler.

In the past two months, Big Leap's benefited from some news coverage after the single Jax helped produce went gold. That hit is paying for the costs of running the bus, and we worked with the legal team to make sure the kids get compensated through an education fund they can cash in at eighteen if they decide not to pursue school.

It helps that we've put out two more singles, both based on recordings I bought from Wicked, that have been remixed and mastered with the help of my program and Jax's ear. One of them Lita even came in on.

When I told her what happened at Wicked, she dropped an interesting tidbit.

Apparently Todd hit on her when she recorded her last album.

And texted her constantly with some seriously inappropriate propositions after she told him to stop.

Now Wicked's looking for a new head of production.

Motion in the corner of my eye snags my attention and has my stomach flipping as the sexiest guy on the planet climbs the steps.

"You texting Tyler again, squirt?" Jax murmurs to his kid.

"No."

Which means yes.

In two weeks, Annie will be back to school. At least Jax's concern about her finding friends in Philly seems to be ill-founded. Most nights he has to drag her home from hanging out with kids from school and from the studio. Like Tyler.

For all my insistence that he's completely well-intentioned, I see how he looks at her when he's teaching her to play guitar.

Jax thinks Annie will forget him three months after we're back in Dallas.

I say we'll be paying for him to fly in and visit by then.

"Hales?"

I set the headphones on the desk in front of me, leaning back to take him in. I don't even notice what's tucked under his arm, because he's as beautiful as the first time I saw him. His body's hard, lean. Amber eyes that convey way more than they should. A face sculpted from marble, with a mouth made for whispering secrets that make you wet.

He pulls the plexiglass door closed so it's just us here in the studio. "How's the track?"

"It's driving me crazy," I confess. "But I almost have it."

He holds out the hoodie and the frustration melts away.

"You found it!" I gush. "I thought it got lost in the move."

We've been back together for three months, and it's better than I could've imagined. I love working with him. Even if he makes me want to tear my hair out sometimes. He's beyond talented, and any arguments we have are always compensated for by the making up that happens after.

Jax drops onto an amp across from me, shoving the hair back from his face. "Maybe you should put it on."

I take the hoodie, blinking at him.

That's when I realize something's tucked in the front pocket.

I go to pull it out when I notice Jax isn't over me.

He's at eye level.

On one knee.

My throat dries as I pull the box out of the pocket. "Jax..."

He takes it from me, holding it between us. "I never thought I'd find someone who makes me feel like you do. Someone who helped me believe I had a choice again. It doesn't take a crowd to make me feel like a king. All it takes is you."

"*Jax...*"

He shakes his head, but it's the emotion on his face, the conviction on it, that shuts me up. "I don't know what I did to deserve you. But I'm not questioning it anymore."

His gaze drops to the sweatshirt but I can't tear mine from him.

"Hales?"

"Yeah."

"Read the sweatshirt."

"It's been three years," I manage. "I think we've established I have no idea what you put on the damned sweatshirt." But I force my gaze down to it and realize it's embroidered. Black-on-black, nearly invisible, in script that matches his handwriting.

Marry me, Hales.

A gasp from behind me makes us both turn. The plexiglass door is wide open, and two sets of eyes are on us.

Tyler's are amused, poking out from under his hair—which today is green.

Annie's amber eyes are horrified. "You weren't supposed to propose on the bus!"

"Why not?" Jax demands.

"It's not every girl's dream!"

"You have dreams of getting proposed to?" Tyler asks. Annie flushes, but Jax misses it. His attention is back on me.

"Hales, I'll ask you anywhere you want. Every day for the rest of our lives. We need to have more kids. Cuz Annie's old enough to babysit, so it's cheap from here on in."

"I heard that!" Annie gushes, then gasps. "Dad, she *still* didn't answer."

"Good point." Jax shifts back on his heels, eyes intent on mine. He opens the box and lifts the ring.

It's simple. One diamond in the center, blinking in the light from the window.

"Your move, Hales."

I bite the side of my cheek as emotions rush through me.

Annie sighs. "Come on, Haley, don't do this to him."

"What am I supposed to say?"

He's starting to look uncomfortable. "Yes would be a start."

I pretend to consider it. "Well. I guess I'd better." I lower my voice so only he can hear. "I mean, you're Jax fucking Jamieson."

Jax's grin splits his face, and even before he slips the ring on my finger, I know I've done something right.

JAX

"I'm not sure why you wanted to drop me off. I have a car."

I follow Haley through the carpeted halls of the campus building. "I felt like it."

She peers through a doorway. "Hey, Carter."

"Haley." He comes into view.

Surrounded by books and computers and awards, Dr. Christopher Carter is shorter than I expected.

Which makes me inordinately happy.

His gaze drops, and he makes a noise in his throat. "You got engaged?"

"Last week. We're moving to Dallas in the fall. Carter, this is Jax."

I step up next to her, and he raises a brow.

"Jax. As in Jax Jamieson," he says.

I grin. "Yeah. You've heard of me, Connor?"

"Carter."

"Right." I wrap my arm around her waist.

She checks her phone. "So I sent you the latest for our meeting today. Did you get the code?"

"Yeah." But that blue gaze is squarely on me, as though he's sizing me up.

Bring it.

"Does your boyfriend want to stay?"

"Fiancé. But he's right, I gotta go, Hales. Shooting a clothing ad spot." I pat my rock-hard abs through my shirt. "It's hard to keep in shape after thirty, right? But they keep calling."

"Uh-huh." The other man shoves his hands in the pockets of his douchey trousers.

"See you tonight." I turn to Haley, tugging on her waist to bring her lips up to mine.

Her eyebrows shoot up, but she lets me kiss her.

At first.

Then she's totally into it. She knows it's bullshit, but she can't stop her fingers from digging into my biceps. Just like I can't stop the way holding her has blood rushing to my cock.

Before the situation can get too far out of control, I pull back.

She's blinking and I'm a little dizzy too, but I keep it together.

Haley's lips curve like she's onto me, but she stifles a snort. "See you, Jax."

"Later, Hales." I turn for the door.

"Yeah. See you, Jax."

I lift a hand over my head. “See ya, Connor.”

I shove my hands in my pockets and whistle as I start down the hallway.

Thank you for reading the Wicked trilogy! I hope you loved reading Jax and Haley’s story as much as I loved writing it.

Dying to know what’ll happen with Jax, Haley, Annie, Tyler, and more?

They make appearances in Serena and Wes’ story, Easy Love...but there’s even more to come! Wicked was conceived as a trilogy, but everyone’s been asking what’s next for Jax and Haley.

If you’re not ready to give them up, you can **pre-order Forever Wicked, Jax and Haley’s wedding story** - with more from Annie and Tyler, Serena, the band, and more!

Also, stay tuned for Annie and Tyler’s trilogy - coming early 2020.

Finally, subscribe to my Insiders List to hear about new books, sales, and more first: http://www.piperlawsonbooks.com/subscribe

Enjoy this book?

Here's how you can help (in two minutes or less)

I'm going to share something kind of personal. Something I haven't shared with that many people in my life...

I want to write full-time. There it is.

It always seemed crazy, but guess what. After three years of writing on midnight caffeine trips after long days at the office, I'm so close I can taste it.

You can help me make the final push. (Yes, YOU!)

I don't have the advertising budget of a big publisher. But I do have something that's worth way more.

The most amazing readers in the world.

Honest reviews are the best way to get the word out about my books. If you loved this (or one of my other books!), I'd be beyond grateful if you could take two minutes to leave a quick review.

Thanks for being awesome, for inspiring me every day, and for helping make it possible for me to do something I love.

xx

Piper

WHY I WROTE "WICKED"

Confession: I've always wanted to write a rock star romance.

But I knew if I did it (1) it probably wouldn't feel like any other rock star romance out there, (2) it couldn't be about the bougie lifestyle, it had to be about basic human crap we all deal with, (3) it needed a quirky heroine who was, in the words of one of my readers, 'flawed but not broken'.

I planned it out in 3 parts over more than 2 years because I didn't want to focus only on the music, or the family drama, or the tour. I wanted to show the ups and downs of Haley and Jax's life. I wanted this book to be about how at the end of the day, we get to make our own choices, even when it feels like we don't.

That beautiful truth is something I can write books about all day long.

We get to decide how we think, how we feel, how we

act. And we can't control the universe, but we control who our friends are, how we spend our time, whether we make ourselves vulnerable, and the stories we tell about our lives. The parts we've lived, and the parts yet to come.

It also means we don't have to have a 'perfect' past, we don't need to be famous, or rich, we just need to decide how we want to show up every moment of every day.

Thank you for spending part of your day with Jax and Haley.

XX,

Piper

P.S. Think other romance readers might enjoy Wicked? Please consider leaving a review for Wicked Girl (or the Wicked series)! Reviews help readers find books, and you could help someone you've never met find their next read. Which is kind of awesome, if you think about it.

ALSO BY PIPER LAWSON

~ WICKED SERIES ~

(Jax + Haley)

Good Girl

Bad Girl

Wicked Girl

Forever Wicked

~ PLAY SERIES ~

PLAY

(Max + Payton)

NSFW

(Avery + Charlie)

RISE

(Riley + Sam)

~ MODERN ROMANCE SERIES ~

Easy Love

(Wes + Rena)

Bad Love

(Logan + Kendall)

Twisted Love (coming soon!)

(Ben + Daisy)

~ TRAVESTY SERIES ~

Schooled

(Dylan + Lex)

Stripped

(Nate + Ava)

Sealed

(Dylan + Lex novella)

Styled

(Ethan + Jordan)

Satisfaction

(Kent + Dahlia novella)

ABOUT THE AUTHOR

I read and write stories where the girls aren't doormats, the guys aren't asshats, and secondary characters aren't second-class citizens. A card-carrying millennial, I have two business degrees and zero hope of starting a fashion label (unlike my Travesty characters). I crave quirk the way some people crave kink, and believe life is too short not to do what—and who—you love.

My home base near Toronto, Canada is shared with my wonderful sig other. I know he's the perfect man because not only is he TDH (tall dark & handsome), but he will beta read for me under duress. And really, that's what love is. Beta reading under duress.

To my readers: I'm beyond grateful to you guys who make it possible for me to write. Thank you for buying my books. And inspiring me. And sending me wacky ideas. You're the reason I keep doing this.

I love hearing from you! Stalk me on:

The Interwebs➔www.piperlawsonbooks.com

Facebook➔www.facebook.com/piperlawsonbooks

Twitter➔www.twitter.com/piperjlawson

Goodreads➔www.goodreads.com/author/show/13680088

THANK YOUS

This book wouldn't have happened without the support of my awesome advance team and reader group (ladies - thank you for the support, nail biting, and patiently rocking in the corner while I finished part 3). Pam and Renate, thank you for your eagle eyes! Nothing gets by you. Mandee, thank you for creating Jax's rock star-worthy signature, Jax is at least 20% more badass now. Natasha, you are the most amazing designer, thank you for letting me tweak this until we got it just right. Lindee, I couldn't imagine better photography to inspire my books. Cassie and Devon, thank you for questioning, polishing, and pointing out I meant to say IV chord, not iV chord. Danielle, thank you for the amazing promo graphics, and generally helping me stay organized and making sure I don't release new books in a vacuum. Plus of course Mr. L, the world's best beta reader and the guy who makes sure my world doesn't break while I'm sequestered in my writing cave. Thank you all from the bottom of my heart.

Line and copy editing by Cassie Roberston
Cover by Natasha Snow
Cover photography by Lindee Robinson

Made in the USA
Middletown, DE
13 March 2020

86335508R00357